Praise for the other Howard M[...]r mysteries

"This one is surefire. I [...] read the next one."
—Jack A[...] [...]nalist

"Terrific. . . . I couldn't [...] [...]garet Truman, author of
Murder at the Watergate

"An awesome debut. . . . This one is great, a joy to read, a book I not only couldn't put down, but didn't want to put down." —Eleanor Taylor Bland, author of *See No Evil*

"Far and away the most engaging mystery story I've read in a long while . . . I sense a big success here."
—Thomas Fleming, author of
Liberty! The American Revolution

"A superb debut novel."
—Carolyn Hart, author of *Death on Demand*

"Mystery readers rejoice! . . . This gripping tale has an authentic Southwest flavor—don't miss it!"
—Francis Roe, author of *Under the Knife*

And for Robert Westbrook:

"Westbrook knows how to mix satire with action."
—*New York Times Book Review*

"What a marvelous novel—and a pleasure to read a mystery that is both suspenseful and funny." —Margaret Truman

"Westbrook delivers . . . mercilessly witty social satire."
—*Publishers Weekly*

"Exciting, funny, and entertaining." —*USA Today*

RED MOON

———∞∞∞———

A Howard Moon Deer Mystery

Robert Westbrook

A SIGNET BOOK

SIGNET
Published by New American Library, a division of
Penguin Putnam Inc., 375 Hudson Street,
New York, New York 10014, U.S.A.
Penguin Books Ltd, 27 Wrights Lane,
London W8 5TZ, England
Penguin Books Australia Ltd, Ringwood,
Victoria, Australia
Penguin Books Canada Ltd, 10 Alcorn Avenue,
Toronto, Ontario, Canada M4V 3B2
Penguin Books (N.Z.) Ltd, 182–190 Wairau Road,
Auckland 10, New Zealand

Penguin Books Ltd, Registered Offices:
Harmondsworth, Middlesex, England

First published by Signet, an imprint of New American Library,
a division of Penguin Putnam Inc.

First Printing, June 2000
10 9 8 7 6 5 4 3 2 1

For Gail,
my traveling star

My thanks to Dan Slater, my editor, and to Ted Chichak, Gail Westbrook, and Deputy Marshal/Medical Investigator Bill Hubbard of Red River, NM. This is a work of fiction. The town and county of San Geronimo do not exist, except in my imagination; nor is there a San Geronimo Art Association or a missing Georgia O'Keeffe painting such as I have described in this story. All names, characters, places, and incidents are products of the author's imagination or are used fictitiously. Any resemblance to actual events or locales or persons, living or dead, is entirely coincidental.

The Rainbow Man and the Angel of Mercy

The Rainbow Man arrived in San Geronimo one day in mid-October, pushing a supermarket shopping cart down the highway.

As shopping carts go, his was a Cadillac: shiny chrome with red plastic trim and rubber wheels that didn't squeak. *Lucky's* was written in bold letters on a plastic strip along the front, and the Rainbow Man believed that it was a very lucky cart indeed. He had pushed it across the desert all the way from California to New Mexico, a perfect mobile home for any spiritual journey. There was plenty of room in the basket for his meager belongings, all neatly protected from the weather in individual black plastic trash bags. There was even a child's seat, a convenient spot for his water bottle, Bible, sketchbook, and his Beretta 9mm semi-automatic pistol.

He arrived during the best time of year in northern New Mexico, on an autumn day when the cottonwoods were sparkling gold, the sky a deep violet-blue, and the high meadows of the nearby mountains already touched with snow. This was tourist season in San Geronimo, the time of the annual Fall Arts Fest—a two-week municipal orgy of arts and crafts, painting, sculpture, jewelry, ceramics, weavings, and food.

Good luck to all! I'm the Rainbow Man! he wrote with chalk on the small blackboard that dangled on a leather cord around his neck. He flashed his blackboard at people he passed on the road; even though he refused to speak with his mouth, a person who had taken a vow of silence did not need to be rude. He found San Geronimo a pretty town. There were quaint streets of adobe buildings and an old Spanish plaza surrounded by shops that sold lovely, useless little things. The Arts Fest had drawn quite a crowd. Busloads of overweight people from Texas and Oklahoma drove through the plaza pointing their camcorders out the windows at the lean arty types who lived here: men with ponytails and self-involved mouths, women with short hair and strange piercings. The lean arty types, of course, believed themselves vastly superior to the fat tourists with the camcorders, and they kept their noses (metaphorically speaking) high in the air. The Rainbow Man, who had been very avant-garde himself once, got a kick out of this. Personally, he made it a point to be strictly democratic, flashing his blackboard at hipsters and gawky outsiders alike. *Good luck to all! I'm the Rainbow Man!* Few dared to look back at him in return except very briefly and from the corners of their wary eyes. The Rainbow Man was accustomed to this. He really didn't mind.

He was oddly dressed in patches of fur and leather, and rainbow pants with stripes of blue, green, red, orange, and yellow running down his legs. He was tall and bony with an angular face and wide cheekbones. He was worn by the weather, blistered by the sun. His age and ethnic origins were unclear. He might have been thirty or fifty, Native American, Hispanic, perhaps even Arabic. It was hard to say; nothing about him related in a normal way to the workaday world. He smiled nearly all the time, a huge toothy grin.

The Rainbow Man had come to town on a divine mission. When you worked for God, there was always much to do, and so little time! He found a place to sleep in the trash-filled woods behind McDonald's, and he came and went on his important errands. The days passed. He spoke frequently with God, and also the lesser angels who were assigned to his case; he went about his business, ignored and studiously unseen by the busy little town.

One day, while standing on a sidewalk not far from the town plaza, the Rainbow Man chanced to see a beautiful young woman through a restaurant window. She was seated at a small table covered by a white linen cloth.

Oh, she was lovely! She had long blond hair and a radiant, medieval kind of face, not at all the usual sort of beauty you see in magazines or movies. She wasn't fashionable, and she wore no makeup. She was too tall, gawky even, and objectively speaking, her nose was probably too large. But there was a great haunting sweetness about her. The Rainbow Man really couldn't take his eyes off her. They were only separated by a pane of glass. But for a homeless person on the sidewalk, she sat across an unbridgeable divide.

The beautiful lady was not alone. She shared her table with a young Indian man who had a round moonlike face and long, shiny black hair. The restaurant was crowded and noisy, the small tables jammed closely together, the waitresses moving back and forth at such a frantic speed they occasionally knocked against someone's elbow or chair. But the blond woman and the Indian man talked with their heads close together, oblivious to the busy room, an island to themselves. Neither of them noticed the homeless man on the sidewalk outside the restaurant who was staring at them with longing and wonderment.

They ate funny little pastries with spinach and cheese inside, and some things that the Rainbow Man didn't even recognize. Cuisine had certainly changed during the twenty years he had been "away," as he liked to put it—in a maximum security prison in California. He watched intently as the couple in the restaurant window finished their lunch and then lingered over coffee and dessert, laughing often, entirely absorbed in their conversation. Ah, to be young and in love! He watched as the man paid the bill, then they both rose from the table and came out the front door onto the sidewalk. They kissed briefly, mouth to mouth, then parted. The Indian walked off quickly up the street, and the young woman headed thoughtfully, at a slower pace, in the opposite direction.

Dear Lord in heaven! She was coming his way! The Rainbow Man felt suddenly, horribly, shy. For the first time in years, he imagined what he looked like, dirty and dressed in ragged clothes. Such a pretty woman shouldn't have to look at someone like himself. He wanted desperately to turn away and hide. But he couldn't move. He just stood there paralyzed, stuck to the sidewalk, staring at her.

She came closer. She was smiling to herself, absorbed in her private thoughts. Then her step faltered, her eyes focused, and she saw the homeless man standing in front of her. Her smile froze, but only for an instant. After the first shock, the warmth of her smile returned. This was astonishing: she actually, truly *looked* at him! Her eyes were pale blue, almost gray, the color of early dawn; they seemed to deepen as she took in his ragged clothes and his appearance. *Oh, lovely lady! Don't fret!* He only wished he could tell her half of what was in his heart. But then, with a friendly little scrunch of her nose, she continued on her way. Their brief moment was over. She was gone.

But, wait! What was she doing now?

The lovely lady had taken only a few steps down the sidewalk when she stopped, turned, and faced him again. The Rainbow Man's heart began beating so violently he was afraid he might faint. This was incredible! She walked back to where he was standing, she reached into her handbag and found a five-dollar bill.

"Here, this is for you," she said. She gave him the money and for an instant, her hand touched his. Her touch was warm and fragile and sent an electric shiver up his spine.

Her pale dawn-blue eyes filled with kindness. "You know, there's a shelter at the Methodist church," she said. "They'll feed you there, and you can spend the night."

The Rainbow Man was nearly delirious with joy. He wanted to kneel on the sidewalk and kiss her feet, but he knew this would frighten her, so he restrained himself. Oh, she was an angel! No human being, certainly, had showed him such kindness in many, many years. Tears of gratitude came to his eyes. Perhaps this worried her, for she turned away and quickly walked down the sidewalk.

Here, this is for you! Imagine that! She had spoken to him. She had shown him mercy. The Rainbow Man was stunned; like a schoolboy, he was overwhelmed with love. He stood on the sidewalk sniffing the five-dollar bill she had given him, trying to inhale the scent of her, but it only smelled like green money. He couldn't let it end like this. He gave her a short head start, then he took hold of his Lucky shopping cart and followed her down the busy street.

*   *   *

He followed at a distance, careful not to alarm her. She turned along a narrow alleyway, passing trendy shops and art galleries, until she came to an old adobe building set in a small park of old trees and gravel paths. There were autumn leaves spread out upon the ground—like a carpet of gold, thought the Rainbow Man, in a poetic mood. The property looked as if it had once been someone's private house and garden, but it was obvious that it now served as a public space. A large sign above the door said that this was the San Geronimo Art Association. The Rainbow Man watched from behind the concealment of a stubby fir tree as the lovely lady walked up the front steps and disappeared inside.

He felt so full, he hardly knew what to do with himself. He waited with his heart nearly bursting, keeping watch on the door that she had entered, hoping he might see her again. Hours passed as he continued his vigil. Then late in the afternoon, the beautiful lady appeared again. She stepped from the building, walked along a winding path to the parking lot, unlocked a dusty white Subaru station wagon, started up the engine, and drove away. When she was gone, the Rainbow Man came out from behind his fir tree and went to stand in her vacant parking space, simply to be in a place where she had been. He breathed the air deeply, thinking to himself that this was her air, where she had stood.

There was a sign at the head of the parking place she had left. The sign said: RESERVED FOR CLAIRE KNIGHTS-BRIDGE, DIRECTOR.

He knew her name now. And where she worked.

Stalking was not a word that the Rainbow Man would have dreamed of using. Instead, he kept watch over her; that's how he saw it. For several days he watched Claire Knightsbridge when she arrived at work, he followed her when she went to lunch, and saw her each evening as she drove away in her dusty Subaru. He kept his distance. He was clever at these things; he made certain she did not spot him.

He began to know her better. She seemed a modest person, self-deprecating. She had two young children whom he saw once briefly, from a distance. She had a shy laugh. Her taste in clothes ran to comfortable corduroy pants—beige mostly, though sometimes forest-green—and baggy sweaters. Still, she looked very good in baggy clothes, and the Rainbow Man loved her with every ounce of his being. He went to sleep hungry at night rather than spend the five-dollar bill she had given him.

Of course, she was not his only preoccupation. When he thought of God and the important task entrusted in his care, he sometimes felt guilty giving Claire Knightsbridge so much of his time. But it filled him with joy simply to be near her. On the third day, Claire had lunch once again with the moonfaced Indian. After lunch, the Rainbow Man followed the Indian back to his place of employment, curious what sort of person Claire was involved with, hoping that he was worthy of her. Frankly, he was surprised by the young man's profession and wondered briefly whether he needed to purify this individual from Claire's life; in the end he decided that he must not, for this would make Claire sad. And in fact, as he considered his larger goals, it occurred to him that Claire's friend might prove to be useful. Oh, there were no accidents in life! The vague formation of a plan floated through the Rainbow Man's mind.

He became convinced that he had met Claire Knightsbridge for a divine purpose. There was evidence of God's hand in all this. He continued to keep a close watch on her, and on the fourth day his vigil was well rewarded. Late in the afternoon, Claire walked out from her building with a towel draped over her shoulders. She went along a gravel path to the far side of the parking lot and kept on going through the small park of trees toward another building nearby, a gymnasiumlike structure. A sign near the front door said PERFORMING ARTS CENTER. Once Claire was inside, the Rainbow Man pushed his shopping cart from his usual tree to get a closer look.

The building she had entered appeared to be empty—there were no classes in progress, no rehearsals, and nobody around at all. After a while, the Rainbow Man pushed his cart around the side until he came to a frosted window at the very back of the building. The window had been cracked open an inch at the bottom, and he could hear

someone singing inside. He knew the voice: it was Claire.
He edged forward to peek through the crack at the bottom
of the window, then jumped back as though he had been
burned, his heart beating wildly. Very cautiously, he moved
forward for another look.

Claire stood in a tiled bathroom singing to herself and
taking off her clothes. As he watched, she removed her
sweater, her jeans, her bra, her underpants . . . until she
was completely naked, the most lovely sight the Rainbow
Man had ever seen. She stood in a three-quarters profile
to him, her arms raised to arrange her towel like a turban
around her head. She was long of limb, pure as a figure in
a painting, sublime and wonderful. At last she stepped into
a shower stall and turned on the water. In her innocence,
unaware that someone was watching, she did not close the
shower curtain completely.

Such beauty! Her pale skin, her breasts, her thighs, the
blond fluff of a triangle between her legs. The Rainbow
Man could hardly contain his excitement. With a shaking
hand, he reached into his shopping cart and found the materials he required: a pad of paper and a pen with a very
fine point. He took a deep breath to calm himself and purge
his mind. Then, finally—his hand steady—the Rainbow
Man began to draw the Angel of Mercy, as revealed to him
fully in all her radiance, head to toe.

The Rainbow Man was a skillful artist and he used every
bit of his talent now to worship Claire Knightsbridge. He
drew her quickly as he saw her in his mind—not a pretty
woman in a shower, but as the angelic being who had
shown him kindness. He was nearly finished with his pre-
liminary sketch, when Claire Knightsbridge stepped from
the shower and saw that there was a man watching her
through the open window. She grabbed for her towel and
screamed as loud as she could.

The Rainbow Man ran from the window terrified, pushing his shopping cart bumpily along the path. He hid for
the rest of the afternoon in the bushes at the farthest end
of the small park, breathing hard, clutching his 9mm semi-
automatic in case she had called the police.

Later in the afternoon, a siren came rushing along the
main street toward the Art Association. The Rainbow Man
slipped off the safety of the gun and readied himself. But

the siren kept on wailing, fading into the distance. He stayed hidden in the bushes until night fell and a blood-red harvest moon rose above the mountains. For Claire's sake, he was glad he didn't have to kill anyone today.

PART ONE

Rainbow's End

One

Howard Moon Deer stood gazing out the window, watching the first snow of the year fall on the old adobe wall, when their client appeared in the Spanish courtyard below.

As clients go, this one appeared top-of-the-food-chain: young, tall, handsome, and finely tuned. His blond hair was pulled back tightly from an aristocratic face in a clean, polite ponytail. Everything about him suggested privilege and progressive sensibilities, except for his clothes. He was dressed oddly in black leather boots, jeans, a black turtleneck sweater, and a long black cape. The cape was trying hard to be very Toulouse-Lautrec, but the effect, as far as Howie was concerned, was more Bela Lugosi.

"Offhand, I'd say our new client is either a vampire or an artist," Howie said to Jack Wilder, who was sitting in a rocking chair across the room. "Let's hope it's the former. After a week of Arts Fest, I'd rather have my blood sucked dry than listen to another misunderstood New Mexican genius tell me how great he is."

"He's early," Jack observed, feeling beneath the crystal of his braille wristwatch.

"The snow's early too," Howie replied, apropos of nothing. It was still October, a stormy Wednesday morning four days before Halloween, and already three or four inches of virgin white fluff had floated gently down from the sky. Meanwhile, their client in the courtyard below seemed lost. His eyes traveled questioningly across the nameplates on the ground floor of the small office complex. Eventually he noticed the brand-new sign pointing upstairs to Wilder & Associate, Private Investigations. Jack and Howie had recently moved their business from Jack's kitchen into what passed in the small town of San Geronimo for a professional building—a refurbished old adobe home in the historic district downtown. Unfortunately, it just about took a detective to find the office.

Howie stepped back from where he was spying at the window. He didn't want it to appear that clients were such a rare event at Wilder & Associate that one gaped at them idiotically. He listened as heavy boots thumped up the outside stairs. A moment later there was a knock.

"Glad you found us," Howie said, opening the door with an efficient smile. "Come in. I'm Howard Moon Deer, Jack's assistant."

"I'm Robin Vandenberg," the man said, stamping his feet to shake the snow from his boots. His voice was gentle and airy. He studied Howie with a quick but intense flash of his eyes, absorbing the fact that Howie was a Native American, and probably not his idea of a private eye.

"Let me take your things . . . hey, nice cape!" Howie said, managing to keep a straight face.

"Well, it's very theatrical, of course—wearing a cape," Robin replied modestly. "But I found it at a flea market in London last year, and it's strange how it changes the way I feel about myself. I put it on, and it's like suddenly I'm a swashbuckler in an old movie. Like I can do anything. It's my magic cape, I suppose. So I wear it at difficult moments, when I need just that small extra hit of courage. Like today."

"Is that so?" Howie didn't know quite how to respond. Indians were generally more circumspect about blurting out casual self-revelations, even Indians, like Howard Moon Deer, who were a long way from the rez. He took the cape, shook the snow off on the landing outside, and hung it up on a pair of antlers mounted on the wall by the door— no relative of mine, Howie liked to say. Up close, Robin Vandenberg had a poetic face. Dreamy blue-green eyes. A finely sculptured nose. There was something elfin about his ears, which were just a wee bit pointed. He was much older than he had appeared from a distance—perhaps forty, Howie imagined—but it was a boyish face nevertheless. Like a Peter Pan that refused to grow up. He wore a small gold ring in his left earlobe, but nothing too flashy, with just the right amount of hipitude. All in all, such a pleasantly nice, upbeat sort of person—it was difficult to imagine why he was here.

Jack, meanwhile, had moved from the rocking chair to stand behind his antique wooden desk, an impractical piece of furniture with too many drawers and cubbyholes. The twin lenses of Jack's dark glasses turned in the direction of their client.

"I can't tell you how grateful I am that you found time to see me, Commander," Robin said politely to Jack, peering about the office. "A friend of mine in the state police recommended you. Captain Ed Gomez. He told me you were a very big deal in California law enforcement."

"Ah, well, that was a while ago. I've been retired for years. And please, just call me Jack. Won't you have a seat?"

Robin debated between a big wooden platform rocker and a smaller spindly rocker. One of Jack's interior design eccentricities was that every chair in the room was required to rock. The office was very homey for a detective agency; a snug, low-ceilinged room with adobe walls, a kiva fireplace at one end, and a clutter of comfortable country furniture. Katya, Jack's German shepherd guide dog, had been sleeping on the Navajo rug in front of the fire; now she stretched, wagged her tail, and came over to sniff their new client's crotch.

"Don't!" Howie told her in a firm undertone. He supposed crotch sniffing was actually an efficient way to get to know a person quickly, but one had to adhere to certain social norms. With a guilty expression, Katya slunk back to her warm place in front of the crackling logs.

As Robin settled into the platform rocker, his expression became very solemn.

"I've always been fascinated by blind people," he said unexpectedly. "But how do you manage being a blind detective? Aren't there difficulties?"

Jack smiled thinly. "There are always difficulties, even if you can see. I have Howie's help, of course, but nevertheless, I only accept certain cases where I feel I can be of use. So perhaps you should get to the point and tell us why you're here."

"It's my stepfather, Sherman Stone," Robin began. His voice had become unexpectedly hard. "Do you know him?"

"The artist? I know *of* him, but we've never met."

"Artist!" Robin snorted with derision. "Well, I suppose

he had talent at one time. He wasted it, of course, just like he's wasted everything. Sherman's like some dangerous child who breaks all his toys and then throws a temper tantrum. Oh, he can be charming and original. I was charmed myself at first—for about five minutes. But it gets old fast, believe me. His latest outrage is that he's begun stealing my mother's jewelry. This is supposed to be funny, I suppose. But the situation is intolerable."

Robin Vandenberg paused for dramatic effect. Jack remained silent, waiting for more information, his dark glasses aimed at Robin like twin barrels of a gun. This was one of Jack's favorite tricks. He knew very well how uncomfortable it made most people to be stared at by a blind man.

Robin took a deep breath and continued. "I want you to expose him, frankly. I need hard facts. Something I can take to my mother to open her eyes before it's too late."

"I see," Jack said vaguely. "Well, perhaps you should tell us more about his stealing."

As Robin spoke, Jack cocked his head slightly to one side and listened intently. Jack Wilder was a big man with a slow, melancholy manner. Comfortably stout, in his mid-fifties, with curly gray hair and a well-trimmed gray beard— Howie liked to joke that if Jack let his beard grow, he could always get a job as a department store Santa. He was dressed today in a light brown tweed sports jacket, a dark blue Brooks Brothers dress shirt, designer jeans, and soft leather Timberlane shoes. All in all, quite the spiffy country gentleman, except for the wraparound dark glasses, and the maroon necktie that had a childish pattern (if you looked closely) of striped Dr. Seuss cats with top hats.

"My mother owns some really wonderful Navajo jewelry," Robin was explaining. "My father gave it to her years ago—my *real* father, that is. There's a matching necklace, a bracelet, a ring, a watch, and a pair of earrings. It's all heavy silver set with quite extraordinarily beautiful turquoise stones—I suppose you'd call it the usual Southwestern stuff, only it's much better quality than you're likely to find today. Forty thousand dollars, I'd say, is a conservative estimate of what the entire set would be worth if it went on the market today. But it's not the money I care about as much as the idea, you know, of that man simply helping himself to our family heirlooms. Frankly, this really gets to me on an emotional level."

"How do you know the jewelry is missing? Did your mother report the loss?"

Robin laughed bitterly. "Oh, no, she's in denial about the whole thing! God forbid she should look in the mirror and see what a foolish old woman she is, married to a younger man who's robbing her blind . . . oh, I'm sorry."

"Don't worry, I'm not so sensitive. About the jewelry . . ."

"I started becoming suspicious about a month ago when it occurred to me that I hadn't seen my mother wearing her turquoise for some time. In general, those pieces come out for just about any dressy occasion. Maybe not the necklace—the necklace is fairly ostentatious—but the rest, especially the watch, she'll put that on simply to go out to a casual dinner."

"Perhaps the watch is being repaired?"

"No. I finally got up the nerve to ask her, and she said it was *not* being repaired. She was vague about it, though, and her eyes sort of glassed over. Then the other day I was up in my mother's bedroom, and she had to go downstairs for a moment to sign for a package. I took a peek in her jewelry box, and all the pieces were gone . . . simply gone! It's like I'd been kicked in the gut. I suppose it's not entirely rational. It's more than the jewelry itself. I feel like that man has violated my mother, my entire family."

Jack nodded in a kind, understanding manner that was totally contrived. It was his psychiatrist tell-me-all-your-deepest-secrets mode.

"Why don't you tell me a bit more about your family situation," he suggested gently. "Your mother, your real father, when your stepfather came along—frankly, Robin, I'm not sure this is our sort of case. But I might be able to advise you better if I can visualize this all a bit more clearly."

"Well, you know my mother, I presume? Barbara Vandenberg? Barbara Vandenberg Stone is how she likes to be known these days."

"I know the name, of course."

The name Barbara Vandenberg was literally everywhere in San Geronimo. Babs, as people called her, was the richest woman in the county, an oil heiress, a collector, and a patroness of the arts. There was a Barbara Vandenberg Scholarship Fund, which sent the best graduating student from the public high school to the college of his or her choice each year, and even a Barbara Vandenberg wing of the local Native American Arts and Crafts Museum.

"My mother's from Texas originally," Robin explained. "She met my father, Richard Vandenberg, when she was at Vassar and he was finishing up at Harvard Business School. They married a few years later, after Dad got his seat on the New York Stock Exchange. He invested a lot of my mother's inheritance in the market, and it made Mom . . . well, very wealthy. They lived in New York primarily, but they summered out here in New Mexico. They loved San Geronimo. The light, you know. Dad was something of a painter . . . he was also an expert on Native American mythology," Robin added, turning toward Howie with a hopeful smile.

Howie smiled back. His best go-ahead-and-study-me, see-if-I-care smile. Howie was taking notes, seated in the early American walnut rocking chair, a chair that was puritanical in design, and fiendishly uncomfortable. It rocked, but it did not roll.

Robin cleared his throat, and his brief smile faded. "Of course, neither of my parents had much time for children. They were so busy being rich and cultured and wonderful—know what I mean?"

"I'm not sure," Jack said delicately.

"Well, it doesn't matter now. In some ways, it's extremely liberating to have parents who barely know you're alive. As long as we were decorative at parties, Mom and Dad left Pooh and I pretty much alone."

"Pooh?"

"That's my older sister. Her real name's Penelope, but everyone's always called her Pooh. So that made us Pooh and Robin, you see. Which is fairly pukey, I admit, but there it is. I changed my name to Nick in college for a while. I thought it sounded sexy and ironic. Nick Vandenberg. Nicholas to my friends. But when I came home, everybody kept calling me Robin, and after a while I just gave up."

Jack smiled faintly with encouragement. "So you and Pooh are the only children?"

"That's right. I'm forty-one, and she's two years older. I tried to persuade her to come with me today, but she's busy. She has an art reception this afternoon."

"She's an artist?"

Robin smiled. "No, she runs a gallery. The Spirit Dreamer over on the south side of town. Her husband, Lionel Cordova—he's the artist. He's a *santero,* actually— he does traditional religious folk art, *retablos* and *bultos,* paintings and statues of saints. They sell like crazy. The reception's for him."

"All right. Now, about your father and mother, did they divorce?"

"No. Dad died. About twelve years ago he had a heart attack . . . frankly, it came as a surprise to everybody that he even *had* a heart. My mother sold the Manhattan apartment and moved into the San Geronimo house permanently. And here she remains, a big fish in a small pond."

"Where did you grow up, Robin? New Mexico?"

"No. I went to boarding school for a while in Santa Fe. But mostly I lived in New York, spending my summers in San Geronimo. Then a few years ago, I had a loft in SoHo, and I just got sick of city life. All that traffic and pollution. I had a sort of meltdown."

Jack raised an eyebrow. "A meltdown?"

"Well, a spiritual collapse, I guess you could call it. Nothing *too* serious," Robin said with a self-conscious laugh. "Anyway, whatever it was, it all got cured when I moved back to New Mexico. I own a bit of land up on Wind Horse Mountain near the Zen retreat. It's really very lovely there. I built a tree house there, actually. My studio's thirty feet up in the air."

"Really? A tree house? That must be something. So I assume you're an artist too?"

"There *are* a lot of us in this town, aren't there?" he laughed. "I paint fantasy scenes mostly. I haven't tried very hard to sell them—they're mostly for my own amusement. I also teach at the Life Circle School, an alternative K-through-eight parent cooperative near where I live."

"Tell me about Sherman and your mother. What kind of relationship do they have?"

"The first thing you have to understand is that my mother is sixty-seven years old. Sherman is much younger, he's just turned fifty-two. The age difference in itself doesn't bother me—after all, men often marry women who are much younger, so why shouldn't a woman do the same? But Sherman is the wrong man to be married to anyone, no matter what the age."

"When did they get married?"

"Five years ago. They met in Greece, on Mykonos. Mom was on a yacht with some of her French friends, and Sherman was a guest on another boat—they were anchored side by side in a cove on the back side of the island where the nude beach is. Very romantic, I'm sure. Believe it or not, Sherman rowed aboard my mom's yacht to borrow a bottle of *retsina* . . . and that was the start of it."

"You obviously believe he married her for her money?"

"Well, of course. He jokes about it, even. How every artist should get himself a rich wife. He's very open about it."

"And your mother puts up with this sort of joking?"

"She adores him. It's strange, really. The man's a total hedonist. He starts off in the morning by rolling a joint the size of a cigar, and by noon he's drinking red wine—extremely *good* red wine from my mother's cellar I should add. And he's not exactly what you'd call faithful. Frankly, when it comes to sex, Sherman seems to believe it's still the 1960s. But he has a weird charisma, and he's very handsome, I suppose. He's beguiled her, he truly has."

"Does she know he's unfaithful?"

"Yes. I think so, at least. She would have to be blind not to know . . . oh, I'm sorry, I did it again!"

Jack smiled tolerantly. "So she doesn't care that he sleeps with other women?"

"Oh, I think she cares. But it's the deal they have. It's the price she pays for being married to a very charismatic man who's fifteen years her junior. She hates boring people, you know, and you can't accuse Sherman of being *that*. She says he makes her feel totally alive."

"Okay, she adores him, she's rich—so let's get back to this question of stealing. If Sherman needs money, why doesn't he simply ask his wife?"

Robin laughed unpleasantly. "Because my mother is very tight about money, like a lot of rich people are. Oh, she'll spend it under the right circumstances, but only on her own terms. Secondly, she's no fool—she keeps Sherman on a short leash financially so he doesn't stray too far. He has a strict allowance every month. Look, something happened a few days ago that brought this all to a head—my brother-in-law overheard a disturbing conversation at a bar called Pinky's Hacienda. It's a biker dive on the south end of town. A big drug scene. There are some pool tables, and they have awful live music on the weekends. It used to be mostly an Hispanic hangout, but recently some counterculture types have started going there. The tattooed and pierced set. Pooh's husband, Lionel, likes to go there."

"This is the husband who does the religious painting?"

Robin laughed. "That's only a gig, Jack. Lionel's an atheist, as a matter of fact, but religious folk art sells, so he does it. Anyway, he was at Pinky's one night last week when Sherman staggered in and sat down near him at the bar. Sherman was so out of it, he didn't even notice Lionel was there. God knows what he was on that night. He started putting the make on some young woman who came in. He was giving her quite a line, I gather. Let's go to Mexico, we'll buy a sailboat, make love on the beach, eat fresh prawns all day and never wear clothes—that sort of bullshit. But it didn't seem to be working, so he pulled out a huge turquoise ring and tried to slip it on her finger—he was so drunk, he had trouble getting it anywhere near her hand. Thank God the girl refused to take it! Lionel only saw the ring for a second, but he was certain it was one of Mom's from the set. That ring alone is worth maybe five thousand dollars, which is a hell of a lot of jewelry to be flashing around in a place like Pinky's. Lionel was concerned, so he told Pooh, and Pooh phoned me. And we've been trying to figure out what we should do about it ever since. Finally, I went to Captain Gomez for advice since he's a friend of the family. He said that as long as my mother hasn't reported her jewelry stolen, there isn't anything the police can do. That's when he recommended you, Jack."

Jack smiled graciously, but Howie could tell he was far from pleased by the recommendation.

"There's something else I need to tell you," Robin went on. "An incident that happened a few weeks back in early October. Someone took a shot at Mom as she and Pooh were walking in the woods. The bullet missed Mom by a few inches—it broke off a branch not far from her head. She was furious. She assumed it was a hunter, of course."

"That seems a reasonable assumption, walking in the woods in the fall," Jack agreed. "Did either she or your sister see anyone?"

"No, and I agree it doesn't mean much by itself. But with Sherman trying to get his hands on my mother's money, *anything* is possible," he said darkly. "Frankly, I'm worried as hell."

"Let me get this straight. You want Howie and me to dig up some dirt on your stepfather, is that it?" Jack asked.

Robin considered this. "What I want is for you to *vet* him for me—maybe that's a better way to put it. But if there *is* dirt to find, I want my mother to know about it. You bet I do!"

Jack frowned, and for a few moments there was no sound in the room except for the logs crackling in the fireplace. Howie paused with his pen raised above the notebook. Katya, stretched out in front of the fire, let out a small snore.

"Look, I sense your hesitation to get involved in murky family matters," Robin said, jumping into the silence. "How about just giving me a week of your time? Go see Lionel—you can catch him at the reception this afternoon, and he'll tell you about that incident with the ring. Talk with Sherman, make up your own mind. My feeling is that the jewelry Sherman's been taking is only the tip of the iceberg. He's up to all sorts of mischief, and I need to know exactly what, and have some proof of it to be able to show my mother. After the incident in the woods, I need to be absolutely certain that my mother is . . . well, safe."

"Are you seriously suggesting that Sherman might attempt to kill her?"

"Like I told you, with Sherman *anything* is possible," Robin repeated stubbornly.

Jack leaned back speculatively in his rocking chair. From the semi-sour expression on his face, Howie was almost certain that he was about to decline the case.

"Let me write you a check for a thousand dollars," Robin said quickly, feeling a *no* in the air. "All I want at

the end of the week is your opinion on whether the case
is worth pursuing or not. If at that time you're convinced
my stepfather doesn't pose a danger to my mother, I'll let
the matter drop."

Jack turned his dark glasses to Howie, raising his left
eyebrow in a question mark. Howie understood the unspo-
ken question: *So what do we do with this guy?* Howie
cleared his throat and did his best to send back his own
telepathic reply: *Not every case can be the bank robbery at
Monte Carlo, Jack. Meanwhile, a thousand bucks is pretty
good money for something we can probably wrap up in a
couple of days.* Howie was a family man these days.
Frankly, he needed the money.

Jack turned his dark glasses back toward their client. He
nodded slowly. "All right, Robin. One week. Please write
your check to Wilder & Associate."

At the door, Howie took the cape from the antlers and
held it for their client to enwrap himself.

"Thanks," said Robin, flashing a pearly smile. He was all
boyishness again. "So, Howie, you're not from our Pueblo
here, are you? You're what . . . Cheyenne?"

"Lakota," Howie told him.

"No kidding? So what's a Sioux doing all the way down
here in New Mexico working as an assistant to a private
eye?"

Howie smiled. "Sometimes I wonder myself."

He watched from the window as Robin Vandenberg
walked down the outside stairs into the snowy courtyard
below. In a moment he passed through the gate and disappeared into the wintry morning.

"So what do you think of our new client?" he asked
Jack, facing back into the room.

"I'm not sure. What do *you* think?" This was a typical
Jack maneuver, turning a question around on the asker.

"I haven't really got a fix on him yet," Howie admitted.
"He worries me a little. The tree house. His magic cape.
He seems a little old to be playing king of the fairies."

"Well, if you have a bad feeling about this. . . ."

"No, the money's good. And as it happens, I'm broke."

"You sure? Family melodramas can get nasty."

"Not as nasty as the credit card statement I'm expecting in the mail. I'm onboard, Jack. Where do we start?"

"With the check, of course," Jack said with a smile. "Deposit it into our account. We'll hope it doesn't bounce."

Two

Howie arranged for Jack and himself to have a twelve-thirty lunch at The Caravan Café with Claire Knightsbridge, the acting director of the San Geronimo Art Association. Because of her job, Claire heard all the gossip in the art community and would be able to give them an overview of Barbara Vandenberg, Sherman Stone, and family. Howie also wanted to give The Caravan a try—it was the newest restaurant in town, and you had to catch new restaurants fast in San Geronimo, because they were apt to go belly-up in the wink of an eye.

Despite these two very good reasons for suggesting lunch with Claire, Jack was skeptical. "Hmm," he said. "Are we mixing business and pleasure?"

"This is strictly business," Howie insisted. "Believe me, when it comes to art in this town, Claire is completely abreast of what's afoot."

"It's your fascination with her body parts that concerns me," Jack observed. In fact, Claire Knightsbridge was the reason that Howie was currently an ex-bachelor, no longer a carefree member of Generation X, but a man with responsibilities and credit card bills to pay. Nevertheless, Jack allowed himself to be convinced that this was a legitimate business occasion—research, and all that—mostly (Howie suspected) because he too wanted to try the Middle Eastern food at The Caravan. In New Mexico, one generally had a fine selection of burritos, enchiladas, tacos, and enough green chile to kiss your digestive tract good-bye. The local cuisine was excellent, though not for sissies, but there were times a person was willing nearly to kill for a decent falafel or curry.

At twelve-fifteen sharp, Jack and Howie bundled up—Jack in his bulky Eddie Bauer goose-down jacket with hood, Howie in an absurdly noir belted trench coat (which Claire had given to him last Christmas as a joke), and they walked together through the narrow lanes of the historic district, bypassing the town plaza, toward Cervantes Lane, where the restaurant was located. In San Geronimo, it was better to brave a few inches of new snow on foot than hazard the usual snarl of traffic in a car. The old part of the town had been designed for donkey carts and horses, not automobiles.

Jack had left Katya behind in the office, despite the fact that guide dogs were generally allowed in restaurants. Katya's tail had been known to knock over glasses of wine and small children, and if you didn't watch constantly, she could inhale a plate of hors d'oeuvres with one quick slurp of her long tongue. She was a sweet dog—a $25,000 dog, as it happened, but not the first student to flunk an expensive education. So Howie took Katya's place this afternoon as a guide Indian. Jack held onto Howie's arm tightly as they walked together through the falling snow.

"Careful of the curb, Jack," Howie warned from time to time. "Hold on, there's a car coming!" Jack slipped on an icy patch in front of The Laughing Buddha Bookstore, doing a little dance in an effort to retain his balance. Fortunately, Howie managed to get a good grip on his elbow and kept him from falling.

"You okay, Jack?"

"I'm great, just *great*," Jack answered impatiently. He was a proud man, once a very important man in California law enforcement before he lost his eyesight during a police action that went tragically wrong; he did not like to be helplessly dependent on anybody. The walk took longer than usual with the snow swirling around them. The plows had already made several passes up and down the streets, creating deep drifts along the sidewalks, which made foot travel treacherous. With his hood up and beard full of snow, Jack was starting to look like Nanook of the North.

Howie was about to lead Jack across Ortega Street when he noticed a homeless man standing in a narrow alley be-

tween Thom's T-Shirts and the Silver Bear Pottery Store.
The homeless man was eccentrically dressed with a dirty
olive-green blanket over his head, Indian style, to protect
himself from the weather. Beneath the blanket, Howie
glimpsed a pair of pants with rainbow stripes running down
the legs. There was a supermarket shopping cart nearby
stuffed full of black trash bags, his sad portable home. It
was obvious why the man had gone into the alley; the virgin
snow near his feet was quickly becoming yellow, not so
virgin anymore. Howie was sympathetic. Unfortunately,
when Ronald Reagan invented homelessness in America,
he forgot to provide public bathrooms.

"What is it?" Jack asked, puzzled by the delay.

"It's nothing. Just a homeless person."

"Well? Do you want to give him a few bucks?"

"Maybe not," Howie decided. "He looks sort of crazy,
to tell the truth."

"Then, let's keep moving, please. It's goddamn freezing
out here."

The homeless man adjusted his zipper and looked up just
as Howie was about to continue with Jack across the street.
He gave Howie an odd look. A strangely *knowing* look,
Howie thought. Like they had something in common, the
two of them. Howie didn't like it much. The man disturbed
him, though he couldn't say precisely how.

"Poor guy," Howie muttered, turning his back and leading Jack across Ortega Street. They continued for half a
block, but Howie found himself still thinking of the homeless man in the snow with his pathetic shopping cart. Howard Moon Deer knew all about poverty, growing up on
a shit-poor South Dakota reservation with eighty percent
unemployment, and three times the national rate of suicide,
not to mention the assorted ills of diabetes, alcoholism,
domestic abuse, and despair. So he was acutely aware of
his great good fortune to be on his way to lunch with
Claire, rather than to be standing homeless and hungry on
the street. People had certainly helped Howie; in particularly, two do-gooder Anglo teachers on the rez who had
tutored him privately and had gotten him started on the
scholarship trail—first to a fancy prep school in Vermont,
then to Dartmouth for his undergraduate work, and on to
Princeton for his masters and his still unfinished Ph.D. It

was the rich Ivy League schools who were most generous, if you were a fashionable minority and you knew how to milk the system. But Howie had an uneasy feeling about his good fortune, and passing the homeless poor always gave him a feeling that there, but for the grace of God, went he.

The farther Howie walked from the alley, the more he regretted not giving the homeless man a few dollars. Claire would have done so, certainly.

"Jack, wait for me a second. I'm going to run back and give that guy in the alley a few bucks."

Jack was flabbergasted. "*Now* you're going to do it? Howie, for chrissake—why didn't you do this earlier? You can't just *leave* me on the goddamn sidewalk."

"I know. But look, here's a parking meter you can hold onto. Just for a second, Jack. I'll be right back."

"A parking meter?" Jack cried in outrage. "You're going to *park* me like I'm a car?"

"You'll hardly even know I'm gone," Howie assured him. He guided Jack's hand onto a metal pole and meter sticking up from the sidewalk, something for Jack to hang onto so he wouldn't become disorientated.

"Howie!"

But Howie was gone, running back down the icy sidewalk to the alley. He ran so fast that his feet slipped out from under him just as he was crossing Ortega Street.

"Yee-ow!" he cried, sailing through the air. Luckily, he came to a soft landing on a snowdrift. He picked himself up and kept going. But the alley was empty when he arrived. The homeless man was gone, leaving behind only a patch of yellow that was becoming quickly buried in the new snow floating down from the sky.

Howie walked back hurriedly to where he had left Jack, unhappy with himself and feeling like a fool.

Three

"One hump or two?" asked the waitress, when Howie ordered the Camel Driver's Special. Falafel, humus, tabouli salad, and a cup of lentil soup.

"Two," said Howie, opting for the extra falafel, two dollars more.

"One for me," said Claire with her shy laugh.

The Caravan was in an L-shaped room that was reached by descending a short flight of steps from street level. In good weather, there would be a fine view of people's feet scurrying by on the sidewalk; today there was only snow. Three other restaurants had tried to make a go of it in this same location during Howie's time in San Geronimo: Giorgio's, an Italian place that was far too expensive; The Maharajah, an East Indian restaurant that quickly got a bad reputation because everything was filthy; and David's, pronounced with a pretentious French accent—*Da-veed*—which served nouvelle New Mexican cuisine with a serious case of the blahs. Howie sensed The Caravan would soon be joining its predecessors to that great restaurant in the sky. Jack ordered a chicken gyro and a Greek salad, which seemed geographically far from any route a camel was likely to take, one hump or two.

"Anyway, the decoration committee has finally stopped quarreling long enough to get to work," Claire said, resuming the conversation that had been interrupted by the waitress taking their order. "It's an unbelievable battle of giant egos! Everyone has a different idea of how the room should look, and with all the disagreement, I'll be amazed if the auditorium is ready by Saturday night."

Claire was recounting her many woes as chief organizer of the annual San Geronimo Art Association Halloween Ball that was coming up this Saturday night in the Performing Arts Center, the PAC. This was more than a casual party: it was a benefit, the most important SGAA fund-raising event of the year, and Claire had been stressed to the max for the past several months getting it off the ground. The decoration committee was supposed to turn the PAC into a spooky enchanted forest at night, complete with papier-mâché trees, clever lighting, and murals on huge rolls of paper encircling all four walls of the auditorium. Only it was already Wednesday, there were three and a half days left until the party, and the work was way behind schedule due to petty arguments of every kind.

Tickets for the Halloween Ball had been on sale for several weeks now, $30 per person, $50 for a couple—expensive for San Geronimo, but this included a gourmet buffet dinner donated by several of the best restaurants in town, dancing until dawn with a live band, and prizes for the best costumes. There was also going to be an art sale and a silent auction, with items ranging from a season ski pass at San Geronimo Peak to a full body massage with a lady who called herself Aurora. In all, Claire had bullied nearly fifty businesses in town into donating items to the silent auction. All this had taken time and cunning. There was also going to be a land raffle, twenty-five acres in the nearby mountains that had been given by a wealthy local family; chances to win the land were $50 a shot, with the lucky ticket drawn at midnight.

In short, the Halloween ball was a huge event, and Claire was counting on it to get the Art Association out of serious debt. Her idea had been to involve the entire community in a "Save the SGAA" campaign. Unfortunately, people in San Geronimo tended to be very opinionated, and it wasn't easy to coordinate so many colorful personalities.

Howie found himself studying Claire as she recounted her Art Association woes. She was a recent arrival from Iowa, where people were more modest. In New Mexico, the land itself was dramatic, like a stage set, and those who did well here tended to be dramatic as well—big, bold, egotistical types who refused to be dwarfed by the vastness of the desert and the sky. But this wasn't Claire—fortunately, as Howie thought of it.

Claire Knightsbridge was tall and lanky, twenty-nine years old—an inch taller than Howie and six months older, a Midwestern farm girl of Scandinavian stock who had earned scholarships to college just like Howie had. She had wide cheekbones and blue-gray eyes and long, straight corn-husk-colored hair that fell down her back clear to her waist. It wasn't that she was entirely beautiful. In fact, she had slightly buck teeth and lightly freckled skin. Sometimes she looked downright funny, and made Howie laugh; other times she smiled in a certain way and looked so beautiful that he could hardly stand it. Howie had never known anyone else who could change so instantly from plain to beautiful and back again—depending on the weather, her mood, and sudden bursts of laughter. The result was strange: not certain if she was beautiful or homely, Howie couldn't take his eyes off her, trying to decide.

"Tell me, Claire, do you have much contact with Barbara Vandenberg Stone and her husband?" Jack was asking as the food arrived.

"More than I'd like, frankly. Babs is one of our big donors, of course. She gave the Art Association ten thousand dollars last summer to help repair the roof of the old building—that's where the gallery and my office are located. I appreciated the gift, naturally. The building was leaking, and I was starting to wonder how we would pay for everything. But Babs expects a lot in return for her money. I hate to say it, but she's a real bitch."

"Give me an example," Jack urged. "I'm trying to visualize her."

"Okay. A few days after I received her check for the roof, she phoned to discuss an art show we had scheduled later in the summer, something I was calling 'New Visions.' The idea I had was to give some new younger artists a chance for an exhibition, rather than the little clique of the same dozen or so people we do over and over again." Claire leaned closer to Jack so she could speak more discreetly. "Unfortunately, there were two artists I accepted into the show that Babs didn't like. One was Johnson Stadler, a newcomer to San Geronimo who I think has real talent—but apparently he was rude to Babs at some gallery opening, not knowing who she was. The other was a woman named Darlene Grayson, and I never was quite sure *why* Babs didn't approve of her. Anyway, she wanted me to kick these two people out of the show and replace them with two friends of hers. I did my best to be polite, of course—God knows, I didn't want to alienate our most important donor! But I told her that the Art Association had to have an independent position when it came to arranging shows or we would lose our credibility."

"So you told her no. How did she take it?"

"Not very well. She hung up on me, actually. Not only that, but originally the land that we're raffling off on Saturday night was supposed to have come from Babs—nearly forty acres close to the Colorado border that she's owned for years. After our phone conversation, she simply pulled out of her offer. I guess she wanted to show me who was boss. The board of directors were furious—half of them were angry at me, the other half at Babs. Fortunately, I was able to convince the Whitmans, an old ranching family, to donate twenty-five acres from a huge spread they own up in the mountains. So it worked out in the end. But I thought what Babs did was extraordinarily petty and mean-spirited."

"Just because she didn't get her way," Howie remarked, shaking his head.

"Before this incident, I got to go to her house once and see her art collection," Claire continued, taking a big bite of her falafel, speaking with her mouth full. "You probably know, she has the largest private Georgia O'Keeffe collection in New Mexico, two whole rooms of watercolors and oils. Someone told me it's the fifth largest private collection of O'Keeffe in the entire country. But I don't think it's art so much that interests her—it's more just an homage to her self-importance. I walked through her collection feeling sort of sick to my stomach, frankly. It seems all wrong to me that a rich old lady should have all those wonderful works for herself alone. They should be in a museum, where the public can view them."

"What about her husband Sherman?" Jack asked. "What do you think of him?"

Claire made a face. "He's even worse! Personally, I'd nominate Sherman Stone as the most arrogant, unattractive human being I've ever met!"

"Really?" Jack seemed interested in this. "I've heard him described as charismatic and charming."

"You're kidding!" Claire seemed dumbfounded. "Well,

I suppose everyone's entitled to their own opinion. He sculpts, I understand—I've never seen his serious work, but he's been making the papier-mâché trees for our enchanted forest this Saturday. I haven't seen them yet, but he acts like he's Michelangelo condescending to do us all a favor. Every now and then he'll strut into the PAC like he's the greatest, hippest stud on Planet Earth. All the women are supposed to faint with admiration."

"And do they?"

"Well, some of them do, I guess. *I* don't, I can tell you that! He came up to me once and said . . . well, he said some pretty crude things."

"Like what?" Howie asked casually, almost like he didn't want to bash the man's face in.

Claire sighed. "He said, quote, you've got a great ass, babe. Why don't you come over and sit on my face sometime . . . I couldn't believe it!"

"What a charmer," Howie growled, tearing into a falafel. Claire had never told him this anecdote. Probably she wanted a third person present to defuse its impact, knowing he would be upset.

"I reminded him that he was married," Claire went on, "but Sherman laughed like I was being very square and old-fashioned. He drinks a lot, and I think he takes drugs, too. I heard later that he beat up some woman badly, but I don't know the details."

"The guy just gets better and better!" Howie said. He was sitting straight up in his chair, nearly rigid. "One of his girlfriends?"

"Apparently. It's amazing to me that any woman would fall for his lines, but I suppose they do."

"Have you ever heard any stories about him stealing?" Jack asked.

"No. What kind of stealing?"

"His wife's jewelry, for instance. There's some Navajo turquoise and silver jewelry of hers that he may have taken and tried to sell."

Claire shook her head. "I wouldn't put it past Sherman. But I don't know anything about it."

"How about the children? Robin and Penelope?—Pooh, I guess, is what she's called."

Claire had met Robin once and Pooh several times, but

had no strong impression of either of them. She was astonished they both seemed so normal given their family background, but she didn't have much more than that to say about them.

"Oh, God, I've got to get back to the PAC!" Claire cried, looking at her watch anxiously. "I'm sorry I haven't been more helpful."

"No, you've been very helpful," Jack assured her.

Howie waved down the waitress and handed her his Wilder & Associate credit card. Claire turned to him while he was waiting for the card back.

"Howie, you'll never guess who I got a letter from today. Erin Yeager, my old friend from music school." Claire turned to Jack to explain: "Erin plays violin, she's really terrifically talented. She's starting up an all-female string quartet in Chicago. Everyone needs a gimmick, I suppose, to make it in show business, even classical musicians. The group's going to be called the Chicago Chick Quartet—that seems a little over the top to me, but apparently she's got serious financial backing and some dates lined up for next summer. The hope is that an all-girl ensemble with a jivey name will bring in a younger audience—the problem with classical music these days is that nearly everybody who goes to concerts is over fifty."

Claire turned back to Howie with the punch line of her story: "And Erin has asked me to be their cellist."

"In Chicago?" he asked numbly. Howie's heart felt like it was on an elevator and someone had just pressed the down button. "She wants you to join the Chicago Chick Quartet?"

"Well, it would be *based* in Chicago, of course. But there would be a lot of touring involved."

Howie didn't know what to say. Claire was watching him with her big blue-gray eyes, trying to judge his reaction. Fortunately, one of the nifty things about being a Native American, culturally speaking, was that you got plenty of practice hiding your true feelings. Howie signed the credit card slip, wearing his best wooden Indian expression on his face like a mask. The fact of the matter was that Claire Knightsbridge was an awesome cello player. She had studied cello since she was five years old and had been a member of the prestigious Iowa String Quartet before the end

of a terrible marriage the year before had sent her to New
Mexico in search of a new life. Of course, there was no
way that a classical cello player could support herself in a
small town like San Geronimo, so she had accepted the job
of acting director of the Art Association when the old
woman who had held the position for the past twenty years
suffered a small stroke and couldn't continue. Even now,
working at her stressful SGAA job, Claire woke up at four-
thirty every morning to fit in several hours of practice, usually playing through the Bach cello suites ecstatically as the
sun rose. Music was Claire's life, and Howie had always
known it would take her away from him eventually; he
simply hadn't known how soon.

"So when do you have to decide about joining this
group?" he asked just as they were leaving the restaurant.

"Not until after Christmas. We'll talk about it tonight,
okay?"

She kissed him briefly. "I love you," she whispered. Then
she disappeared out into the snowy street to make her way
back to the decoration committee and the problems that
awaited her at the Art Association.

Howie led Jack along the narrow back streets to their
office. The snow was coming down faster now in small pel-
letlike flakes, not as pretty as before, a cold shower from
heaven. *I love you,* Claire had told him, and he believed
her. But would that make it easier or only more difficult
when he lost her to the cello and the all-female string
quartet?

Four

Claire Knightsbridge returned to her office, walking a zigzag journey of three and a half blocks down the chaotic
downtown San Geronimo streets. Cervantes Lane curved
to the north, then Friar Morales Road cut south, and finally

Dolores Street pointed her east in the direction she wished to go. A snowplow had come through recently, pushing more snow onto the sidewalk and leaving red gravel behind on the roads. It made walking difficult, and the afternoon not so soft and beautiful as it had been before.

Claire was confused and upset. It would have been much better, she thought, if her friend Erin had *not* written with the offer to join a quartet in far-off Chicago. The offer was tempting, of course, and she was tremendously flattered. But did she really want to leave New Mexico and Howie for city life and the unknown? It was a difficult choice. She had brought up the subject casually over lunch to sound out the waters. *Oh, guess who I heard from today?* But it was not a casual matter. She had seen the brief, sharp, wounded look in Howie's eyes that he had tried his best to hide. The solution was simple: she simply needed to convince Howie to come with her to Chicago. But in her heart, she knew that Howie wouldn't come, that he would be out of place in her world of classical music—the endless rehearsals, the travel, and the often snooty people you were required to befriend. And that furthermore, for reasons she could not entirely understand, Howie would not abandon Jack.

Claire had been in San Geronimo for a little over a year. She had come here running for her very soul, leaving behind a life in Iowa City that had threatened to suffocate her. On the surface, her marriage had seemed ideal. Jim was fifteen years older than Claire, a full professor of English literature at the University of Iowa. They had two lovely children and had owned a pretty two-story Victorian house with a reasonable mortgage. Claire even had interesting work: a position on the Iowa String Quartet along with a number of private cello students to keep her busy. She should have been happy; but she wasn't. And the worst part of it was that she never knew precisely *why* she was unhappy. There just seemed to be a dull, aching grayness that enveloped every aspect of her life.

Then one afternoon she had come home unexpectedly after a student had canceled a lesson at the last minute. She walked into the house to find Jim on the living room floor with one of his graduate students, *in flagrante delicto*—stark naked and screwing, pumping away so violently that they did not even see her for several moments as she stood in the doorway, her cello case in hand, her mouth hanging wide open. The incident was a shock, certainly, but secretly Claire was glad to finally have an excuse to do what she had been longing to do for years: to leave, to breathe free air, to shout and dance and pull her hair, to find herself a wild Lakota lover if she wished. Without a backward glance, she had taken the children, loaded up her car, and headed off for a brand-new life in New Mexico.

And she had been happy in San Geronimo—except occasionally for her job and some problems with the children. But now the world was calling her again, forcing her to make a new decision. She didn't know what to do. Without a doubt, part of her wanted to go to Chicago and join the quartet; but another part, equally strong, wanted to remain forever in San Geronimo with Howie and let the world go to hell.

Walking back to her office in the snow, Claire wished that the sky would clear so that she might see the great mountain, San Geronimo Peak, against which the town was nestled. In clear weather, the mountain dominated the town, and Claire had come to think of it as a wise towering presence. She was certain the mountain would advise her, help her decide which path to take. But it was invisible now, shrouded in clouds.

Claire was so engrossed in her thoughts that she was nearly run over by a car as she was about to cross Dolores Street. There was a loud abrasive honk, and she jumped back just in time. She scolded herself to pay more attention. She was looking back and forth for a break in the traffic when she glimpsed a pair of rainbow pants and a supermarket shopping cart about a hundred feet behind her on the street she had just come down. It was the homeless man. As soon as he saw that she had spotted him, he pushed his cart from the plowed street over a mound of snow and disappeared in the narrow space between two buildings. This was very worrisome. Clearly he had been following her again.

Claire sighed. It was her own fault, she supposed, for giving him those five dollars last week. When would she learn to be more cautious with strangers? She had just finished a wonderfully romantic lunch with Howie, and the homeless man had looked so sad and hungry on the sidewalk. Unfortunately, her charity had apparently encouraged the man in some way, and now Claire had a problem. Several days ago, she had been using the shower at the Performing Arts Center, as she occasionally did, only to step naked from the stall and find the man peeping in at her through a crack in the window. She had screamed, terrified and angry, and for several hours she debated phoning the police. In the end she had decided to let the matter drop. The man was clearly not in his right mind, but she didn't think he was actually dangerous. She wanted him out of her life, certainly, but she didn't particularly want him thrown in jail.

Claire had not told Howie about the incident. For one, she knew he would be upset; and secondly, she was afraid he would convince her to call the authorities. In doubt, alternating between pity and worry, Claire had done nothing. She had hoped that the homeless man would simply wander off and leave her alone. But here he was following her again.

Lord! This was just what she needed with everything else going on in her life—a deranged person who had some odd sort of crush on her!

Claire turned and walked quickly through the snow back to the safety of her office.

Late in the afternoon, close to four o'clock, Claire sat at her desk in her cramped office at the Art Association talking on the telephone to Maria Salazar, the personal secretary to Jimmy Juarez, the mayor of San Geronimo. Claire had a new problem: she had not yet received the necessary permit she needed for Saturday night to sell alcohol at the Halloween benefit. This permit had been promised to her weeks ago, so it was all very frustrating. The mayor, at least, understood that art was economically important to San Geronimo, so she was hoping he would step in and facilitate the matter with the town council.

Maria was telling her not to worry when Claire looked up from her desk and nearly swallowed her tongue. The homeless man had just stepped into her office, closing the door behind him. She could only stare at him in bewilderment. Up close, he was the oddest figure she had ever seen.

His face was strangely elongated—wide in the middle, with big cheekbones, a huge mouth, and a narrow chin and forehead. To go with his rainbow pants, he wore a jacket that was sewn together with patches of fur and leather, along with a shapeless hat of dirty maroon velvet. On his feet, he wore old knee-high black leather boots that had a military appearance but looked as if they had been found in a town dump. There were all sorts of things dangling around his neck—a necklace with the teeth of some animal, a crucifix, a key, a pair of sunglasses on a string, and a small blackboard dangling on a leather thong. All in all, he looked to Claire like a cross between a mad medieval wanderer and some postapocalyptic survivor of nuclear war. Yet for all that, his smile was gentle and reassuring.

"Are you all right?" Maria was asking on the phone.

The homeless man raised his small blackboard at her. He had written: "Please, do not worry! I am your friend the Rainbow Man!"

"I'm okay," Claire said tentatively into the receiver. "I'll talk to you later, Maria."

She put down the phone and tried to look stern. "You're very lucky I didn't call the police the other day," she told him. "That was a bad thing you did, looking at me through the window when I was taking a shower. Do you understand that? It was very wrong, and you can't do it anymore. I want you to stop following me, or I *will* call the police and they'll put you in jail."

The man's face was full of concern. He erased the blackboard with the sleeve of his jacket and wrote quickly with a small piece of chalk: "The Rainbow Man is very sorry. I have brought you three gifts."

He had a colorful Guatemalan bag slung across his shoulder, and from it he pulled out a drawing pad of thick expensive paper. He handed it to her with a small bow. Claire opened the pad to the first page, and her cheeks filled with a slow blush. The drawing was of her, naked, standing on a cloud in a kind of classic, Botticelli pose. After the initial shock of seeing a depiction of herself in the nude, Claire could not help but notice that the craftsmanship was astonishingly good, both delicate and expressive, drawn with a fine-tipped pen. Anatomically speaking, the figure was correct in every detail except for a pair of angel wings sprouting from her back. It was herself to a tee, an idealized self, but clearly identifiable.

She began turning the pages of the pad. Every page was a drawing of her, always nude, always shown with angel wings. Sometimes she was standing in a virgin meadow, other times floating in mist. The more she studied the work, the more Claire understood that, objectively speaking, these drawings were superb. It wasn't only the extremely controlled craftsmanship of his pen; there was an indescribable ethereal quality to the work. Even the wings were wonderful, sweeping and grand, wings that longed to fly. The drawings reminded Claire of the mysticism of William Blake. As director of the Art Association, people brought her paintings, drawings, lithographs, woodcuts, and every other form of artistic endeavor every day. But it was rarely anything as good as this.

Claire turned page after page, utterly absorbed. She knew very well that the woman in the drawings was only superficially her. The figure had her face and form, but a great deal more as well—a heavenly being who was the sum total of all love, all mercy, all kindness. As she studied the work, she wondered what she was going to say to the self-styled Rainbow Man who was obviously crazy but had so much talent. She wanted to encourage him to keep drawing, but discourage him completely from any more peeping through windows.

At last she looked up.

The Rainbow Man was standing before her with a gun in one hand and a key in the other. The gun was big and black and terrifying, the barrel pointed directly at her breast. For a moment, Claire couldn't breathe. Then she opened her mouth and screamed.

The Rainbow Man shook his head. His eyes were full of something he was trying to say to her, but Claire only understood the gun in his hand. She screamed again, louder than before, and this time the homeless man was so startled that he dropped the gun. It bounced against her desk and fell onto the floor with a clatter. She was terrified that the gun would explode with a shower of bullets as it hit the floor. It didn't, but it was hard to know which of them was more frightened, the homeless man or herself. He turned with a stricken expression on his face, opened the door, and ran from the office. She heard him collide with someone in the hall and then keep going, fleeing awkwardly from the building.

A gallery volunteer, a retired woman in her sixties named Nancy, appeared in the office doorway. She looked pale and shaken.

"Are you okay, Claire? I tried to stop him, but he just pushed me aside."

"I'm all right," Claire said, catching her breath. Her heart was pounding, and she felt dizzy. "I'm all right," she said again.

"I'll call the police."

"No, you'd better let me do that. Let me just catch my breath first. I think it was mostly some kind of misunderstanding."

Claire picked up the big blue-black pistol from the floor, handling it carefully. What was it he had written on his blackboard? *I have brought you three gifts.* The drawings were certainly a gift—but the gun? She hoped not, for Claire disliked firearms. As for the third gift, she thought there had been a key in the man's other hand, but she didn't see that anywhere on the floor. He probably took it with him.

"I'll call the police," Claire told the volunteer. "You'd better go back to the gallery in case someone comes."

Alone in her office, Claire sat at her desk and picked up her phone to call the police. But her eyes fell on the drawing pad that lay open near her telephone, and her finger hesitated before pressing 911. She turned a few more pages. The drawings were truly wonderful. *She* certainly wasn't an angel—Claire knew that very well! But she wasn't so sure about the homeless man. There was an unearthly beauty in his work.

She put the phone down without dialing. Claire didn't know what to do. The police in San Geronimo were not known for their delicacy. They would certainly miss the subtlety of this particular situation, that, yes—it was worrisome for someone who was obviously insane to be going around with a gun peeping at women through windows. But at the same time, the odd homeless person who called himself the Rainbow Man seemed to have a gentle side to

him and an extraordinary amount of talent, and Claire
wasn't certain he meant anyone harm.

Claire Knightsbridge believed in talent; it was part of her
personal semi-pagan religion.

She decided not to call the police but to bring the whole
matter to Howie tonight, along with the drawings and the
gun.

Five

Howie spent the first part of Wednesday afternoon setting
up a new client file for Robin Vandenberg on the office
computer, typing in the notes he had taken in the morning
during Robin's visit and starting a spreadsheet on money
so far received ($1000) as well as current expenses: *$29.00
incl. tip, lunch with Dir. SGAA, research.* As an ex-bureaucrat, Jack was a stickler about paperwork. He often told
Howie that seventy percent of being a cop was knowing
how to fill out forms correctly. "That certainly makes police
work sound like a fascinating career choice," was Howie's
response. But this afternoon he was glad to have something
to do. Concentrating on work, no matter how petty, was
better than thinking about Claire.

While Howie was on the computer, Jack spoke on the
telephone to Santa Fe, nudging a police buddy to run a few
names through the Department of Public Safety's database:
Barbara Vandenberg Stone, Sherman Stone, and just for
the hell of it, Robin Vandenberg. The cop in Santa Fe,
Detective James Hastings, was the nephew of a retired lieutenant in California who had once owed Jack some favors.
Howie was always amazed at how Jack was able to milk
an elaborate network of retired cops to gain access to re-
stricted databases and other favors.

Within half an hour, Detective Hastings called back with
his results. There was no sheet at all on Robin Vandenberg.

Mrs. Barbara Vandenberg Stone had several outstanding parking tickets, but was otherwise a blameless citizen in the eyes of the law. Sherman Stone was another story. There was an old drug arrest from 1974, listing Sherman's address at that time as 1341 Agua Fria Road, Santa Fe. He had tried to sell an ounce of marijuana to an undercover cop in the Santa Fe Plaza; not the crime of the century, but he had done a little time over it, six weeks in jail plus one year's probation. In 1986, living at a different address in Santa Fe, Sherman had been charged with passing a bad check at a restaurant, but had paid back the money to avoid jail time. The next official mark against Sherman came in 1998, an arrest for drunk driving in San Geronimo. Sherman had spent the night in jail, received a $500 fine, and had his license suspended for six months: he had been clocked doing 97 mph in a 55 mph zone.

This was the extent of the Vandenberg Stone clan's known illegal activity, and Howie made a note of the various crimes in his newly created client file. After a while his busy fingers came to a stop on the computer keys as more urgent thoughts of Claire flooded his soul. Howie knew suddenly, with sadness, that he must encourage Claire to go to Chicago to fulfill her talent. It would be inexcusably selfish to keep her in San Geronimo just because he needed love and companionship and a beautiful woman next to him in bed.

"You've got to go for it, Claire!" Howie muttered.

"What's that?" Jack asked from behind his big desk on the other side of the room.

"I said we'd better get going, Jack—to Pooh's reception for her husband over at the Spirit Dreamer."

They took Jack's Toyota, a fire-engine-red four-wheel drive pickup truck. The truck was on semipermanent loan to Howie, since Jack couldn't drive, and because Jack stoutly refused to drive in Howie's ancient two-seater MGB convertible, a car he dubbed "the deathtrap." Jack was a nervous passenger, and Howie didn't much like being his chauffeur. In Jack's blindness, he was free to imagine the worst. Reckless drunks careening down the road. Big shots on cell phones yapping away so furiously, they missed stoplights. A world of darkness in which the wind raged against the truck windows with hurricane force. Before leaving the parking space behind the office, Jack insisted that Howie put the Toyota into four-wheel drive. It wasn't necessary—the snowplows had cleared the roads very well by now. But Howie did it anyway, just so Jack would feel more secure.

Katya rode inside the cab because of the weather, her hind legs on the floorboards, the top half of her body mostly in Jack's lap. Katya loved riding in cars. Every now and then, her enthusiasm got the better of her and she gave Jack a big wet kiss with her tongue.

"Stop that!" Jack barked. "My God, what I put up with!"

Jack was a self-described "cat person." A German shepherd would never have come into his life except for the accident of blindness, so he and Katya had a tempestuous relationship. Howie drove south out of the historic district onto the main thoroughfare, a four-lane road that moved quickly from the quaint and the old to the new and the ugly: strip malls, supermarkets, car dealerships, motels, and every fast-food franchise known to mankind. Twenty years ago, San Geronimo had been a town of four thousand souls; today the population was close to eleven thousand. The growth was a case study of unplanned sprawl.

The Spirit Dreamer was located in one of the few remaining adobe buildings in a block that began with Arby's and ended with Wal-Mart. This was not a picturesque part of town, but the "serious" art galleries tended to favor such locations, anything to separate themselves from the touristy plaza, where art concerned itself exclusively with scenic Southwest sunsets and pretty hollyhocks growing against adobe walls. Howie parked and came around to let Jack out from the passenger side. With some difficulty, he managed to keep Katya inside the cab, leaving the window cracked open an inch for her nose.

He led Jack inside a single long, narrow room that was full of art but empty of humans; probably the snow was keeping people away. The exhibit consisted entirely of traditional northern New Mexican religious art. There were *retablos,* pictures of saints painted on wood, and many *bultos,* carved wooden statues of saints. The work was primitive but colorful, part of a native folk art that was unique to this corner of New Mexico. In 1680, the Pueblo Indians revolted against Spanish rule, killing the Catholic priests and driving out the soldiers. Without priests to keep them in line, the illiterate Spanish farmers who remained during this time invented their own version of Christianity, the Penitente Brotherhood, a mystical folk sect that practiced self-flagellation; they also created religious folk art to decorate their primitive churches, or *moradas*. But this was a while ago. Today, *santos* (the generic term for both *retablos* and *bultos*) were more apt to decorate restaurant walls and the homes of newcomers to the area than to be found in churches. They were a popular item, like strings of dried chile, a way to supply some instant New Mexican atmosphere to any room.

Howie was standing with Jack, looking at a folksy painting of the Virgin Mary complete with obligatory halo, when a blond woman in her mid-forties came out of a back office and approached them with a gallery smile, entirely false.

"Aren't they wonderful?" she cooed.

"Great," Howie agreed. In fact, Lionel Cordova's work seemed very generic to him. In the *retablo* he was studying, the Virgin Mary stood in a field at night with a crescent moon over her left shoulder. Her hands were raised in prayer and two goats had gathered at her feet, to gaze at Mary in adoration. Everything was suitably stylized, imitating the primitive work of peasant farmers. It was pretty, but in San Geronimo you saw work like this by the factory load.

"The one you're looking at is only eighty-five dollars. Lionel insists that his work remains affordable. It's part of the folk tradition, he says. He wants to make sure that ordinary people, not only collectors, can own them."

"How nice," Howie murmured. He was always concerned not to hurt an artist's feelings, even the wife of an artist's feelings, because these people, he understood, were extremely sensitive. Howie turned his attention from the painting to the woman. There was no doubt that she was Pooh Vandenberg. She bore a startling resemblance to her brother. The same pixie face, even the slightly pointed elfin ears. Her hair was pulled back tightly from her face into a ponytail, just like her brother. She wore no makeup. She reminded Howie of a flower child who had not aged so much as wilted with time. She should have been pretty—

everything about her was delicate, almost exquisitely formed. But she looked unhappy and tense.

"Let me show you my personal favorite of Lionel's, his Santa Maria of Guadalupe," she said to Jack with a hopeful smile, sensing correctly that he was the one with the money.

"Frankly, my dear, it would be entirely wasted on me. I'm blind."

"Oh!" she said, staring into his opaque glasses. She was momentarily speechless. A blind man at an art opening was a real showstopper.

"Would you, uh, like a glass of champagne?" she managed heroically. "You're, uh, a little early, but we're just getting under way."

"Actually, we're here to talk with Lionel," Jack said. "You must be Penelope. I'm Jack Wilder, and this is my assistant, Howard Moon Deer. We spoke with your brother, Robin, this morning."

"Oh," she said. Then more dramatically: "*Oh!* Well, this isn't a very good time for *that*. What with the reception and all."

"It's why we got here before the crowd," Jack remarked. "Please, I'd appreciate having a word with you both."

They spoke in a tiny office at the rear of the gallery with the door open so that Pooh could keep an eye peeled for the hordes of eager gallerygoers who were certain to arrive at any moment. Lionel Cordova was a slight, middle-aged Hispanic man with a nervous mustache, limpid brown eyes, and wavy brown hair. He was smaller and more delicate than his wife. His hands were fluttery and well-manicured. He sat at a cluttered desk with a bemused smile on his face. Pooh remained standing so that she could quickly leap upon anyone who wandered into the gallery, and because there were only three chairs in the office.

"I should warn you, I was absolutely opposed to Robin going to a private detective," Pooh told Jack. Her sales-pitch smile was gone, adding several years to her face and a mean downward turn to her mouth.

"Why's that?" Jack asked.

Lionel laughed. "It's because Pooh's afraid the old lady will write us out of her will if we cross her!"

"It's not that at all, Lionel!" Pooh said sharply. "You

know perfectly well that I've never cared at all about the money. It's just that I believe my mother should be left her privacy. I think it's dreadful, the idea of hiring a stranger to snoop out our family secrets."

"Then, you don't believe that your stepfather presents any . . . problems?" Jack paused, deliberating over the right word. "I understand a bullet came very close to killing your mother earlier in the fall while you were both out walking?"

"Oh, we just heard a shot nearby, that's all—Robin always exaggerates when he tells the story. Frankly, autumn is a good time to stay indoors. As for Sherman, he's a jerk. He's a *terrible* man," Pooh declared. "But it's my mother's life, and she insists on living it exactly as she pleases. Believe me, she's extremely competent, and she won't appreciate this meddling into her marriage."

Howie found himself looking back and forth from Pooh to Lionel. They were a fascinating couple, both of them so small and neat and nasty. Howie had a terrible habit of imagining people in bed together. Between Pooh and Lionel, sex would be quick and rabbitlike, he decided. They probably had a few pornographic videos and were into love oils and edible underwear. With an effort, he forced his attention back to the conversation. He had missed part of an exchange; that's what happened when you were thinking about sex rather than the situation at hand.

". . . the jewelry's not the question," Pooh was telling Jack. "Of *course* Sherman took it—there's no question about that in my mind. But it belongs to my mother, the whole kit and caboodle. So if she doesn't mind . . . oh, here are some people! And thank God, they're *not* smiling!"

Two people, an elderly man and woman, had come into the gallery. Pooh donned her own smile like a mask and joined them, closing the office door on Lionel, Jack, and Howie.

"Why is it good that they're not smiling?" Howie asked Lionel.

He laughed, a high-pitched sound. "Because people who come into an art gallery with a smile on their face hardly ever buy anything. The reason they're smiling, you see, is that they *know* they're not going to buy anything, so they feel like intruders—their smile is a little make-nice apology.

Believe me, serious art buyers *don't* act apologetic when they come into a gallery."

"Interesting," said Jack. "Yes, I can imagine that. Tell me, how well do you know Sherman Stone?"

"Ah, my father-in-law!" Lionel said with a mocking smile. "Oh, well enough. I predate him, of course. I was in this family years before Sherman arrived. Sometimes he can be quite funny. Other times, like that night at Pinky's, he gets so blotto that he's a real pain in the ass."

"What night exactly are we talking about?"

Lionel counted backward on his delicate fingers. "Today's Wednesday. So Tuesday, Monday, Sunday, Saturday, Friday . . . it was last Thursday night."

"Do you go to Pinky's often? I understand it's a tough sort of bar."

"It's not that tough. A lot of the artists in town go there. It's the only place in San Geronimo where you never see a tourist, and that in itself is blissful."

"I understand on Thursday night, Sherman was trying to pick up a woman?"

"Yes. Sometimes Sherman just goes up to a girl and says, 'Hey, honey, I want to screw you so bad I got a hard-on just thinking about it'—or something to that effect. You'd be surprised how often it works. But that night in Pinky's, he was in a romantic mood, offering her a trip to Mexico, the works. Finally he brought out the ring. I recognized it right away as the obscenely large turquoise stone that Babs generally wears on her right hand. It's an ugly thing, really. I was sitting halfway across the room, actually, but it's a ring with a lot of flash and glitter."

"Tell me, knowing Mrs. Stone, do you think she would be angry if she knew what her husband was up to that night?"

"Oh, you bet! She'd have Sherman's balls on a silver platter if she thought he was giving away her favorite ring to a twentysomething pickup in a bar! Fortunately for Sherman, the girl wouldn't accept the ring. She forced him to take it back."

"Well, the jewelry's still missing, I understand. She must suspect her husband."

Lionel shook his head. "Yes and no. She suspects but

doesn't want to know the worst. A woman like Babs spends a lot of her life avoiding reality."

"Sherman must be out of touch with reality as well, risking a cushy marriage by stealing her jewelry."

"Well, he was drunk and stoned that night. And when Sherman the Stoner is drunk and high, he doesn't consider the consequences."

"High on what? Marijuana?"

"Harder than that."

"Cocaine?"

"Smack. That's Sherman's latest kick. Heroin's made quite the comeback as the drug of choice here in New Mexico. You'd be surprised how many of our local avant-garde do lines. They snort it, of course—it's just not chic to shoot up."

Jack pursed his lips and seemed momentarily at a loss as to how he wished to conduct this interview. "I'm trying to determine whether Sherman is actually dangerous," he said finally. "Do you have any ideas about that?"

"I think he's dangerous to himself."

"But not to his wife?"

"Well, perhaps. A person like that who's totally self-destructive . . . they can pull down the people closest to them when they drown. Very often the people who are trying to save them."

"Do you know anything about Sherman's background?"

"He comes from old Santa Fe money—at least, they had money once. Unfortunately, they lost it pretty much around the time that Sherman was a teenager. The father, I understand, was an impractical man—he put all the family resources into some real estate scam that went belly-up. I'm sure it was difficult for Sherman to grow up believing he was a prince, only to find out that he was a pauper."

"Are any of his family still in Santa Fe?"

"His brother, I believe. But, of course, Sherman doesn't tell me all that much about himself. He thinks I'm a boring old in-law, and generally does his best to avoid me. If you're interested, the person you should talk to is Gilmer Good Day. That's Sherman's best buddy. Do you know him?"

"He's a Native American artist, isn't he?"

"Not *a* Native American—he's *the* Native American artist in these parts. The man has done very, very well." Lionel turned his gaze on Howie. "Gilmer's a Cheyenne, of course, not one of our local Indians. He moved here. Like you, I bet."

Howie nodded. "Yep," he agreed.

Lionel shrugged. "Well, everybody who's anybody ends up in San Geronimo eventually. This is the new scene, the cutting edge. The Paris of the Southwest."

Howie wasn't certain if Lionel Cordova was being sarcastic or serious. Before he could decide, Pooh came bursting into the office.

"Fantastic! I've just made a sale," she said in a low voice. "So get your ass out there and mingle, Lionel. They want to meet you."

"Ah, the muse calls!" Lionel said grandly, standing up from his desk. He turned to Jack just as he was leaving the room. "Anyway, I wouldn't worry about Sherman too much, if I were you."

"No? Why's that?"

"Because if all his bad habits don't kill him, I imagine someone else will."

Jack raised an eyebrow. "Like who, for example?" he asked.

"Like maybe even me," Lionel whispered playfully. "If Babs doesn't leave her fortune to Sherman, some of that lovely money could come my way. And, man, I'd give up this crappy artist life in an instant!"

Six

When Howard Moon Deer was a child on the reservation, his great-uncle, Horace Two Arrows, often tried to explain the ways of the world to him.

One day when Howie was eight or nine, he asked his great-uncle a question. *"Tunkasila,"* he said, using the respectful Lakota word for grandfather, "What's the difference between white people and Indians?"

Two Arrows did not answer for a very long time. He was a leathery old man, born in the days of Crazy Horse—God only knew how old he really was. He and Howie were sitting parked in Two Arrows' broken-down '52 Ford pickup truck, going nowhere, their usual spot for long summer afternoon conversations. The old man held a can of beer in his lap from which he took an occasional sip. For a wise man, he had a few bad habits, though Howie had never seen him drunk; the beer simply made him more meditative as the afternoon progressed.

"Well, *takos*," he said finally, using the affectionate word for grandchild. "Think of it this way. The Indian, when he makes a camp circle, builds a small fire and then sits close to it to stay warm. But the *wasicu*—(white man: literally, He-Who-Takes-The-Fat)—when the *wasicu* makes a fire, he builds a very large bonfire, and then must stand back at some distance so he will not be burned. That is the difference, *takos*, between the white man and the Indian."

Howie remembered these words all his life. He was astonished the first time he ever went camping with white people to see how they indeed put huge logs on their campfires, sending enormous flames shooting ten feet into the air, endangering the forest, making it necessary for them to stand well back from the fire in order not to be roasted like human marshmallows. Two Arrows' words were literally true, but of course the real meaning was metaphorical. The white man wasted energy prodigiously, using up the bounty of the earth in an orgiastic spending spree that was completely divorced from real need. They watered their lawns on rainy days, they kept electric lights burning in homes when they were gone, they drove flat suburban streets in huge tanklike four-wheel drive SUVs that wasted colossal amounts of fossil fuel. It was hard to figure out. But a wise native took advantage of the *wasicu's* wastefulness to save a bundle.

Jack's wife, Emma, worked at the San Geronimo public library, and she had arranged for Howie to pick up a used computer today that he was buying as a surprise for Claire's children, Jonathan and Heidi. Three years ago, the library had paid nearly two thousand dollars for the computer, but now they were thrilled to sell it to Howie for $150. The PC was still in perfect running order, and it had a very nice color monitor, but it simply wasn't the latest thing anymore.

Late Wednesday afternoon, Howie drove Jack and Katya to the library. He left Jack seated at a table in the main reading area while he followed Emma to a storeroom where she had the computer waiting for him in a big cardboard box. Howie liked Emma Wilder. She was Jack's age, a little stout from Jack's cooking, a gray-haired woman with bright, kind eyes and a natural way about her. She was dressed casually in jeans and a beige sweater and comfortable shoes. Emma never bothered much about makeup or her hair. She always said that the best thing about being married to a blind man was that she didn't need to fuss much about her appearance.

Emma turned to Howie when they were alone in the storeroom. "I want you to tell me something, Howie. Has Jack been target shooting behind our house?"

"Why, no, Emma. I don't think so," Howie lied. "That would be quite a feat for him in his condition."

"And dangerous too," Emma said darkly. "He wouldn't know if there was an animal or a person nearby. He could even hit a passing car."

Howie nodded in agreement. "Yes, I can see that," he said.

"But Jack *can't* see it. That's the problem. Look, Howie, I hope you don't encourage him in any foolishness. I'm awfully glad to see him doing so much—there was a time a year or two after he lost his sight when I was deeply worried about him. He seemed to just give up for a while. But now . . . well, you know what I mean. He's blind. He's never going to be able to see again. Whether he likes it or not, he has to accept certain limitations."

Oh, boy, certain limitations! Tell that to Jack! Howie thought with a grim smile. As it happened, he knew for certain what Emma only suspected: that Jack had a whole arsenal of handguns hidden in strategic places around their house, and for several months he had been involved in a crazy plan to teach himself to shoot again.

"Howie, if you see Jack with a gun, I want you to let me know," she said. "It's not safe for a blind person to be shooting at things. Will you promise me?"

"Well, sure," he said. He gave Emma a kiss on both cheeks, European-style, then picked up the big cardboard box before she could wring any more promises from him.

The box wasn't heavy, but it was awkward to carry. "See you, Jack," he said in motion as he staggered through the reading room. Jack would get a ride home with Emma today.

"Call me first thing in the morning," Jack ordered. He was grouchy because Emma had plans to stop off at a cocktail party on the way home, an event for Friends of the Library that Jack would have done just about anything short of divorce to avoid. "I'll want a full report on Gilmer Good Day!"

"You bet."

Howie steered the Toyota pickup northward on the two-lane highway out of town with the big cardboard box riding next to him on the passenger seat. The sky was in motion, fantastical, as fast-moving clouds alternated with bright shafts of late afternoon sun. The first winter storm of the year was starting to break up and blow off to the east. One moment the sky began to clear, revealing a small patch of blue and a hint of San Geronimo Peak, the great brooding presence that guarded the town; then with a rush, a new flurry blew in, turning the world once again into a tempest of swirling white.

After leaving the Spirit Dreamer earlier in the afternoon, Howie had phoned to make an appointment with Gilmer Good Day, currently the most successful artist in San Geronimo—in all of New Mexico, for that matter. Gilmer traveled in the Vandenberg Stone crowd, a pivotal member of the local art scene, and Howie had thought of trying to see him even before Lionel Cordova had suggested it. He had met Gilmer a few times at local gallery openings and had found the man interesting. They had something in common: they were both natives from distant places, outsiders to the xenophobically closed Pueblo Indian culture of San Geronimo. Gilmer was a Cheyenne, as Lionel had said, and the Cheyenne had close historical ties to the Sioux—though Howie had heard somewhere that Gilmer had grown up in southern California, not exactly Indian country. Howie didn't know the whole story of Gilmer's origins, but what he did know gave them a slight bond. Beyond that, of course, the famous Cheyenne artist had nothing in common with an obscure, semi-impoverished Lakota Sioux graduate student who was twenty years his junior. Still, he had remembered Howie on the telephone and had said it was fine for him to drop by.

Eight miles north of town, Howie took a right turn off the main highway onto the narrow road that climbed eastward to the tiny old village of Valverde in the foothills about a mile away. The town of San Geronimo stood at seven thousand feet in the high desert, but the altitude of Valverde was higher still at nearly eight thousand feet, high enough to find itself in a greenbelt of piñon, cottonwoods, and even some aspen. Green was a color that attracted wealthy Anglos; the village itself was still poor and Hispanic, but just beyond the village, a switchback road led higher to a flat mesa top, the Valverde Mesa, which in recent years had become the most expensive part of San Geronimo County. It was a small community of about a dozen houses where rich people lived or had second homes they visited two weeks out of the year. On a clear day, there was a million-dollar view from the Valverde Mesa to the mountains to the east, and the vast expanse of desert to the west. Rich people in New Mexico were big on views.

Howie drove up the switchback road, treacherous today because of the snow, glad for the truck's four-wheel drive. At the top of the mesa, the road passed along a lane of expensive houses that stood discreetly hidden behind thick adobe walls on four- or five-acre parcels. One of the houses was the Vandenberg Stone estate, where Babs and Sherman lived. Howie slowed down, curious to get a glimpse of the place, but he could only see the blue roof of the house in the fading afternoon light above the high wall. He continued another quarter mile along the narrow road until coming to a dead end. Gilmer Good Day's house was a huge, futuristic pseudo-adobe, the last house on the road, standing magnificently poised at the edge of the mesa, peering off across a steep valley to the mountains beyond. There were several boxlike sections of the house stacked upon each other, entire walls of tinted glass, and large sundecks. An impressive place, though it reminded Howie too much of the sort of impersonal Southwest architecture you were apt to find in Santa Fe.

A red Jaguar convertible stood parked near the front door, half buried in the early snow. Gilmer had certainly done very well for himself. He had made his fortune with stylized paintings of Native American life: hunting scenes, sacred dances, old women and men with faces half-shrouded in hooded blankets. Personally, Howie found the paintings too decorative and posterlike for his taste, but this was a minority point of view. You were apt to find a Gilmer *Good Day* in every dentist's waiting room in New Mexico, as well as in banks and hotel lobbies.

Howie rang a buzzer by the front door. Gilmer answered through a speaker, telling him to walk around to the back of the house and follow the path to his studio. The path passed along the side of a large corral where four Appaloosa horses stood in the snow, pretty as a picture postcard. Howie smiled, remembering something his great-uncle Two Arrows had told him once, that in traditional Lakota society a man, however poor, was considered to have tribal standing when he had acquired four horses. Howie wondered if you got extra points for having a Jaguar as well. He kept moving along the path, not certain why he was thinking so much about Two Arrows recently. The old man had died when Howie was thirteen; years had passed when he rarely thought about his great-uncle, involved as he had been in more modern preoccupations—college and distant places and a life that was greatly different from that on the rez.

Howie knocked on the studio door. "Just come in!" a voice called from inside. Howie stomped snow from his Sorel boots and found himself in a large brightly lit workroom.

"Hey, welcome," said Gilmer. "Be with you in just a minute."

"Oh, I, uh . . . I, uh, didn't know you were working."

To Howie's embarrassment, there was a naked young Indian woman standing on a slightly raised wooden platform in the middle of the room. He didn't know quite where to put his eyes.

Gilmer was amused. "Relax, Moon Deer—I'm sure

you've seen a woman before. I'm just finishing up. Is it still snowing outside?"

"Sort of sputtering," Howie sputtered.

Gilmer Good Day was a tall, handsome man in his mid-forties, very distinguished-looking. Even if you didn't know he was a famous artist, you would know just by looking at him that he must be somebody. He carried himself with a cinematic bearing, bigger than life. His hair was long and black and wild, touched with gray, hanging loose to his waist, kept from his eyes by a dramatic red headband around his forehead. The hair danced when Gilmer moved; it shimmied and flowed like some living creature. His face was strong, big-boned with a prominent nose. There were dark semicircle shadows beneath his piercing brown eyes, but Howie thought the shadows only made him look more artistic, more intense. Gilmer was dressed in jeans splattered with multicolored patches of paint and a likewise splattered once-white T-shirt that said MONTREAUX JAZZ FESTIVAL on the back. That was a nice touch, a European jazz festival, very hip; Howie wondered if you could send away for the T-shirts, or if you actually had to attend the event. The room was warm, probably for the comfort of the model. Gilmer stood in front of an easel with a palette in one hand, a brush in the other, his painting hand working quickly and surely on a large canvas.

"Come take a look at it if you want," Gilmer offered.

Howie stepped up to the easel, feeling honored to see a work-in-progress by such a famous man. The painting was barely started, hardly more than a rough impression of a young native woman standing in a village plaza next to a well with her arms raised to carry a clay pot on one shoulder. Howie couldn't tell if the painting had artistic merit, but it was not a realistic scene; in his experience, young Indian women didn't lounge around naked in public squares.

"It's a study for a mural I'm doing for the Albuquerque airport," Gilmer explained while he worked. "The thing's going to be thirty feet wide and ten feet high. It'll take me nearly a year to do, a pictorial history of New Mexico—lots of Indians and conquistadors, even a few New Age hippies searching for the meaning of life." Gilmer chuckled. "To tell the truth, I was planning a big mushroom cloud at the center of the thing to celebrate the birth of the atomic bomb at Los Alamos, but the airport commission vetoed that idea in a hurry."

Howie was feeling a little dull, finding himself in the presence of such a vivid, artistic personality. "Really" he managed.

"You bet. Art's not an easy game, Moon Deer. They're paying me a million bucks for this, but I gotta toe the line. After we argued about the mushroom cloud, we had our next fight over tits."

"Tits?"

"Oh, absolutely! They said I could have breasts but no nipples. What sort of woman is that, for chrissake? They're worried, you see, about tourists flying in from Kansas and fainting at the sight of a human body."

To prove he wasn't from Kansas, Howie hazarded a more direct look at the model on the dais. She was a dark, earthy woman in her early twenties with heavy breasts, long black hair sweeping down her bare shoulders, and a thick bushy triangle of pubic hair. She stood with her arms raised, holding an imaginary clay pot. Howie presumed she was from the San Geronimo Pueblo, but she could have been Navajo or Hopi, he wasn't sure. Her eyes were very dark, and there was a small mole, a beauty mark, on her left cheek. All in all, she was striking and voluptuous.

"Gilmer, I gotta pee," she said, speaking for the first time. *Pee-ee-ee,* she said, stretching out the word into an onomatopoeia. Her voice was a disappointment, just a modern girl with a modern whine, not the timeless native creature she appeared to be. "I've been standing here for two hours. And you know I don't like strange guys wandering in here gawking at me."

Howie was probably more embarrassed than she was. With a blush, he turned away. "I, uh . . . honestly, I, uh. . . ."

"Well, let's stop for the day," Gilmer told her. "I believe you're scaring the shit out of my Lakota brother here."

"So, a private detective, huh?" Gilmer asked. His voice was ironic and mischievous.

"I don't actually have a P.I. license myself," Howie admitted, feeling a need for strict honesty. "I'm Jack Wilder's assistant."

"I've heard of Jack Wilder. He's blind, isn't he? This is astonishing—a blind detective and an Indian sidekick. I'm not trying to be rude, Moon Deer, but someone actually hired you guys?"

"Well, yes. I can't say who, naturally. But I'm hoping you can give me some general background on Barbara Vandenberg and Sherman Stone. At this point I'm fishing, really—I don't know precisely what I'm looking for. Mostly I'm just trying to understand the family."

Howie and Gilmer were seated facing each other in two low-slung modern armchairs with a coffee table between them in a corner of the studio. Howie was grateful when the model put on her clothes and left the room.

"Hey, I'm glad to help if I can," Gilmer told him. "Frankly, I think a boy like you could use a crash course on the Vandenberg Stones. You have to watch out for these rich white people, believe me, or they'll eat you up alive. Turn you into Man Corn, my friend."

"Will they?" Man Corn was an old Navajo expression referring to the cannibalism that was said to have been practiced by the Anasazi. Howie certainly didn't want to end up on the wrong end of the food chain.

"Well, Sherman and Babs—they're the king and queen of our little art world here, I guess you could say. Babs believes she's a great collector, and Sherman thinks he's some sort of genius outlaw artist. It's wonderful how if you have enough money, you can believe whatever you want."

"But you think they're fooling themselves?"

"Look, Moon Deer. These people are my friends. I enjoy their company. But art is something else. For art, you've got to have self-discipline. What Sherman and Babs have is self-indulgence."

"I've always heard Babs has quite a collection," Howie mentioned. "Doesn't she have two rooms full of Georgia O'Keeffes?"

"Yes, but her collection is very mixed," Gilmer said dismissively. "There's some good stuff, sure—the way she throws her money around, she was bound to pick up a few good pieces. But mostly it's very minor stuff. The thing with Babs is she has no real taste. She buys by volume and by name, but she can't tell the difference between good and bad."

Howie shifted to a different topic. "Are Sherman and Babs"—he tried to think of a clever way to put it, but it came out very banal—"happy together?"

Gilmer laughed raucously at the question. "Why, sure they're happy! Why shouldn't they be? They each have everything they want from one another. Sherman's got himself a rich wife, and Babs has a presentable escort. At least Sherman's presentable when he can stay on his feet."

"I understand Sherman has affairs."

Another laugh. "Hey, you bet he has affairs! You would too if you were married to Babs Vandenberg. You've seen her, haven't you? The lady has a face like a bulldog."

Gilmer seemed to enjoy talking about the Vandenberg Stones. The conversation went on like this for nearly half an hour. But it was mostly what Howie had already heard. Babs Vandenberg had tons of money, and an ego to match. Sherman was an alcoholic, a self-destructive artist who could be rude and impossible, but also charming, original, and childishly full of fun, depending on his mood. As for the rest of the family, Gilmer admitted he couldn't much stand Robin or Pooh, or Pooh's husband, Lionel.

"These children of wealthy people—they're tragic, Moon Deer. They're crippled souls," Gilmer told him. "They never amount to anything."

"But Pooh runs a gallery, that's something," Howie objected. "And Robin's an artist, isn't he? I understand he's built himself a tree house up on Wind Horse Mountain. Maybe that's a little flaky, but he's doing what he wants."

"Listen to me, Moon Deer. Pooh runs her gallery at a loss. Mommy has to bail her out every six months or so. As for Robin, have you *seen* his art? My God, the kid paints elves and fairies! He has some serious problems. He's a pedophile, you know."

Howie tried not to show his surprise. "For real?"

"You bet, for real. Don't spread this around, but Robin was arrested in New York for molesting some eleven-year-old girl. Babs got him out of it by paying off the parents. It's the reason he had to come home to New Mexico. I know about this from Sherman, who got it from Babs."

Howie wondered if this was the full story of Robin's so-called New York meltdown. "That doesn't sound good," he sighed.

"No, it's lousy. Emotionally speaking, Robin is eleven years old himself—he probably thought the girl was his own age. I'll bet he's your client, isn't he?" Gilmer flashed a wicked smile. "The kid's terrified his mother is going to leave the family fortune to Sherman. So he's trying to get the goods on his stepfather, right?"

"I can't say who our client is, Gilmer," Howie repeated unhappily. "Back to Sherman, I understand that Babs keeps him on a short leash financially?"

"Yeah, that's Sherman's great tragedy. Here he's married himself a rich wife, but when it comes to money, she's tight as a clam. It's not that she's a miser, Moon Deer, it's a little more complicated than that. Babs uses money to control people. She spends freely on herself, what *she* wants, and she'll bail her children out of trouble from time to time because that makes them dependent on her, you see. With Sherman, the way she controls him is by keeping him chronically semi-broke."

"But Sherman has his sculpture. Doesn't he sell them and make money on his own?"

Gilmer shook his head. "No. It's not that he doesn't have talent, he's just totally impractical. He makes these huge strange pieces of junk sculpture, all sorts of things welded together—they're big enough so that only museums or office buildings would have the space to show them, but they're not what those kind of people want. The work is too disturbing for office buildings, and not quite slick enough for museums. As a result, he hasn't connected with the public. When he does sell something, all the money goes back into the materials he needs. Making sculpture can be an expensive hobby, Moon Deer. At least the way Sherman goes about it. Basically, like Pooh with her gallery, he operates in the red."

"So how does he get by?"

Again, the wicked smile. "Well, Babs helps out, of course. She'll give him money to buy most of the raw materials, the metal and stone he needs for his work, as long as he gives her the receipts. But that doesn't give Sherman any room for his flamboyant lifestyle—and his many bad habits, of course."

"He's a junkie, I understand," Howie mentioned, "as well as a womanizer and an alcoholic."

"Exactly. And smack is how he makes ends meet."

Howie had to think about this for a moment. "He deals heroin?"

"Right again," Gilmer agreed. "I'm not sure how much you know about the local drug scene, Moon Deer. Española is the heroin capital of northern New Mexico, supplying Santa Fe, Los Alamos, and all the outlying areas. That's where Sherman scores—he'll go down there every week or so and come back with enough shit to keep himself high and make some spending money. Don't get me wrong, he's not a big-time dealer. He only sells to a dozen or so friends in San Geronimo, mostly art people. But it's enough to keep him going."

"Tell me something, Gilmer. Do you think Sherman would steal things of value from his wife, jewelry, for instance, if he needed extra cash? Perhaps to buy heroin?"

"Of course. He wouldn't think twice."

Howie shook his head. The Vandenberg Stone family was starting to discourage him. Fortunately, this promised to be a brief case.

Gilmer smiled at Howie's dismay. "Let me give you some advice, Moon Deer. Mingle with these people, but don't get too close. Keep a certain distance. I tell you this as an elder brother. Keep yourself safe."

Gilmer walked Howie to the door and stood by while he got into his boots and coat.

"So, Moon Deer. You grew up on the rez in South Dakota, I hear. Pine Ridge?"

"Rosebud," Howie corrected him.

"And then what? You got yourself educated at the white man's schools, didn't you? Where'd you go?"

"Dartmouth, then Princeton."

Gilmer laughed. "That makes you one hell of a fancy Sioux, I guess! How'd you manage it?"

"Oh, I did the whole scholarship thing," Howie said vaguely. As it happened, New Englanders were a particularly guilt-ridden lot, and part of Dartmouth's original charter was to educate Indians; a lot of Indians passed through the Native American Department—NAD, as it was known—

so it wasn't really such a big deal. And once he did well at Dartmouth, of course, Princeton wasn't such a big leap. Frankly, Howie didn't want to go into all this, but Gilmer was curious and wouldn't leave it alone.

"So you got your B.A. at Dartmouth and went on to Princeton for what—your master's degree?"

"Right. In cultural anthropology. I finished that a few years ago, and now I'm working on my Ph.D."

"No kidding? Then, what the hell are you doing as an assistant to a private eye?"

Howie shrugged. "Well, it's supposed to be a part-time job. I came out here to New Mexico to visit some friends, and I ended up staying longer than I planned. Anyway, I was burned out on academia. I'd been in school all my life, and I was looking for a break. Then I met Jack one day, and he offered me a job—an opportunity to do a different kind of research, was the way he presented it to me. I thought it would be interesting, and it has been, mostly. I'll get back to my dissertation eventually. I'm still enrolled in the graduate program—Princeton's pretty decent about giving people like me a lot of time."

"Then, don't be an idiot. Finish up your Ph.D.," Gilmer told him.

Howie smiled faintly. Recently, both Claire and Emma had been giving him the same advice. Even Jack brought it up occasionally. Personally, Howie was uncertain whether it had been a great fortune to receive such a fine education, or if a terrible harm had been done to him, to be removed so completely from his native roots. Like every Indian ever shipped off to a white man's school, he had discovered that he could never go home again. By the time he had passed through college and spent a year in Europe on a fellowship, he was no longer accepted as a Lakota by his people; and indeed, he truly did not have much in common with old friends and family to whom even the closest town, Rapid City, South Dakota, was a distant place they would probably never visit in their lives.

"How about you, Gilmer?" Howie asked, hoping to avoid more questions about his past. "What kind of reservation did you grow up on in southern California?"

Gilmer grinned. "The Malibu reservation. Then I went to UCLA. So, you see, though I'm not an Ivy League Indian like you, I've been around too. I went to the Sorbonne for a while. The French are really nuts about American Indians. I got laid all the time over there. *Parlez-vous français, Moon Deer?*"

"*Oui, bien sûr. J'habitais Paris pendant presqu'un an.*"

Gilmer clapped his hands together delightedly. "Oh, this is really good! We got ourselves a lot in common! We're both goddamn exiles, aren't we?"

"Are we?" Howie asked, throwing the question back.

"You bet. I grew up in a trailer. Did you grow up in a trailer, Moon Deer?"

"A beat-up old Airstream," Howie admitted. "But I didn't think there were trailers in Malibu."

"Oh, there are. A real trailer park, even. A place called Paradise Cove. Did you ever see the old TV show *The Rockford Files*? James Garner played a P.I. who lived in a trailer—Paradise Cove was where it was filmed. A lot of movie people lived there. Not the big stars, of course. More the actors like my father who were on the fringes of the industry."

"Your father was an actor?"

"Sure. Don't you think a Cheyenne can make it in Hollywood? My dad was in a ton of Westerns. He was the sort of Indian who used to circle wagon trains whooping and hollering and looking like a crazed savage. He got shot by John Wayne in three separate movies. That's something, don't you think?"

It was something, all right, Howie thought, walking out into the night. Something pretty damn depressing. He turned up his trench coat collar against the hard chill, thinking about his great-uncle Two Arrows as he walked along the path to the pickup truck. He wondered what Two Arrows, born in the time of Crazy Horse, would think of this nouveau native life that Howie had found for himself where Indians spoke French together and talked about getting laid in Paris. Unfortunately, Howie's French was better than his Lakota; like many of his generation, he knew little of his native language, and he doubted if Gilmer Good Day spoke a word of Cheyenne.

For the moment, nothing seemed to feel in its right place. Not himself, not the millionaire Native American artist he had just left. Not even the cold stars overhead that were winking at him slyly through a break in the clouds.

Seven

Howie lived in the far northern end of San Geronimo County, six miles north from· the Valverde turnoff, only twenty minutes from the Colorado border. He drove home deep in thought, pondering the odd fate of being a postmodern Indian.

Traditionalists back on the rez were always talking about rediscovering one's roots as a Native American, but as far as Howie could see, it was impossible to turn the clock backward in time. People who tried just became very angry—like fundamentalist Christians. Anyway, this was a new chop suey planet, electronically connected, where you could go from enchiladas to falafels in a blink of an eye, and learn as much from Zen Buddhism as a Sioux Sun Dance. So why limit yourself to fry bread?

"Sure, I'm Lakota," Howie said aloud as he drove. "But above all, I'm a citizen of the world!"

Deep in such weighty thoughts, Howie almost did not see the figure at the side of the road. He had just rejoined the main highway from the Valverde turnoff and was heading north, climbing up a long grade. It had stopped snowing, and the moon suddenly burst free of the clouds, nearly full, lighting up the white fields and San Geronimo Peak with an eerie phosphorescence. Just as he reached the top of the long grade, the beams of his headlights illuminated the back of a man in strange clothing pushing a supermarket shopping cart along the highway. With the brilliant moon and the sparkling new snow, the figure made for such an odd sight that Howie wasn't sure if he was hallucinating.

As he drew closer, he saw it was the homeless man he had seen early in the day in town. Howie downshifted, slowing to a crawl. There was no traffic, no houses nearby, not another car anywhere in sight. It was unusual to find anyone walking on such a cold night on this lonely stretch of road. The homeless man was trudging up the edge of the pavement where the road had been plowed, moving with grim purpose, his body bent forward, refusing to acknowledge Howie's headlights behind him, pushing his shopping cart up the steep hill like Sisyphus with his famous rolling stone. The effort seemed heroic but vaguely doomed.

Howie didn't want to make the homeless man's life more difficult with his intrusive headlights so he pulled to the center of the road and drove on by. As he went past, he saw that the man still had his blanket wrapped around him, Indian-style, but this did not seem like very substantial protection on a night like this. There was something almost Biblical about the poor guy and his effort to push the shopping cart up the highway. Everything about him looked mad. Howie sighed, once again finding the homeless person a disturbing sight. But he was eager to get home to Claire and his warm house. He reached the top of the hill, shifted into a higher gear, and sped away down the road.

Damn it! This isn't any of your business! He tried to reassure his conscience, but still, he felt guilty doing nothing for the man, just driving by. He continued for another quarter mile, gradually allowing his right foot to ease from the gas. He told himself the usual excuses; that he was tired, that the highways of America were full of weird broken people and you couldn't stop and help them all. Yet he had heard a weather forecast earlier in the afternoon—the temperature was expected to dip to 8 degrees Fahrenheit tonight, the coldest night of the year so far. A person could die out here. Howie made a U-turn and drove back to where the homeless man had just reached the top of the grade and was stopping to rest. Howie did another U-turn, came up behind him, and stopped.

"Hey!" Howie called, rolling down his window. "Listen, you're going to freeze out here with only that blanket around you. You'd better let me run you back into town."

The man turned to face Howie. In the moonlight Howie watched as a strange, merry smile spread across the man's face. He was tall and angular, and he carried himself with an odd dignity. Howie could see that beneath his blanket, he wore all kinds of dangling things around his neck. The homeless man's smile grew merrier and merrier, but he did not speak.

"Look, it's going to go down to eight degrees tonight, so you've got to find some shelter," Howie told him, setting the emergency brake and stepping from the cab. But this made the man nervous. His smile faltered, and he clutched the handle of his shopping cart possessively, as if Howie meant to steal it from him.

"I'm only trying to help you," Howie explained. "I know a church in town where they'll feed you and give you a bed. You can put your cart in the back of the truck, and I'll drive you there. Do you understand what I'm saying? *I'd . . . like . . . to . . . help . . . you,*" he repeated, saying the words slowly, the way you speak English to a foreigner who isn't likely to understand a single word anyway.

The man smiled his crazy, merry smile again. He seemed to decide that Howie wasn't a thief who meant him harm. While Howie waited, he brought out a small blackboard that was hanging on a leather cord around his neck and started writing on it with a piece of chalk from his pocket. He wrote without hurry and then turned the board toward the Toyota's headlights. Howie read two brief sentences, both written in capital letters:

THE RAINBOW MAN DOES NOT RIDE IN CARS
THE RAINBOW MAN WALKS TO GOD

Howie nodded. Experience had taught him to be wary of palefaces who claimed to be on a religious mission. They were a materialistic race, these people who had arrived after Columbus, but once they got religion, they could really go off the deep end, particularly in a place like New Mexico where Jesus sometimes landed in flying saucers.

"I see," Howie said judiciously. "But, look, if you let me give you a ride into town, I'll take you to the nice church. A very good place for any Rainbow Man, I'm sure. And it will be warm. They'll feed you. Unless you have some really good winter camping gear in that shopping cart of yours, you'll die if you try to stay out here tonight."

The homeless man wiped the blackboard with a corner of his blanket, and then he wrote again. He held the blackboard steady for Howie to read in the headlights. This message wasn't so nice:

THE RAINBOW MAN GIVES YOU WARNING
LEAVE THIS PLACE OF SIN WHILE YOU CAN

He wasn't smiling anymore. He looked grim and angry. "Well, okay," Howie told him. He had done his best. What more could he do? He stepped back into the truck and released the emergency brake. But the Rainbow Man gestured for him to wait while he wrote another message on his board. This one was in script, small letters written in a remarkably neat and flowing hand:

go home
take care of your angel
you have been blessed, howard moon deer
sin no more

Howie was stunned. "How do you know my name?" he demanded.

But the Rainbow Man only shook his head and would not answer. He raised the blackboard above his head like a mad prophet, like Moses with his tablet of stone. Howie was starting to feel spooked.

"How do you know me?" Howie asked again. But he was thinking maybe he didn't really want to know.

The Rainbow Man advanced his way with a menacing expression on his face and the blackboard held high, like a weapon that he meant to bash down on the truck.

"Okay!" Howie agreed, putting the truck into gear. "I'm outta here, man."

Howie was shaken. He put his foot to the accelerator, eager to get away, racing through the gears until the speedometer told him he was traveling 65 mph.

"That," Howie declared aloud, "was definitely a weird encounter!"

But how in the world did that crazy man know my name?

This was a serious matter for an Indian, and Howie, despite his posh East Coast education, wasn't entirely beyond old superstitions. When an enemy knew your name, he had your number.

Howie was driving up the dirt road to his cabin when another more worrisome thought occurred to him:

How did the Rainbow Man know there was an angel waiting for him at home?

Eight

Howie rented a one-room cabin on the open sagebrush not far from the mountains, a guest house that was part of a large estate owned by his trust fund friends, Bob and Nova Davidson. The cabin was modest, but it was snug, it was cheap, and it was home. There was smoke pluming from the chimney and a warm yellow glow spilled from the windows to greet him.

When Claire and her two children moved in a year ago, some creative additions had been necessary. As Howie pulled into the driveway, the truck headlights swept past Claire's tipi in the backyard. It was a pretty tipi with colored ribbons flying from the tops of the poles and a red buffalo painted on the canvas. Howie always smiled when he saw it, for it had taken a blond lady from Iowa to make a real Indian out of him. Claire had bought the thing in Oklahoma. For her, the tipi symbolized liberation: a new life, no bullshit, no mortgage, no commitment except to live for the moment—just the thing for a romantic paleface who had grown up on the edge of the prairie with a vivid imagination and probably (like Howie) too many books. Howie had helped her put the tipi up last fall; he had needed to consult some of his hippie neighbors as to the proper method of placing the poles, which was embarrassing. *Tipi* was even a Lakota word—the word for "dwelling"—which made Howie's ignorance particularly mortifying.

On the other side of the yard from the tipi stood a small house trailer, which Howie had borrowed last spring from his landlords, Bob and Nova. The trailer made a convenient bedroom for Jonathan and Heidi. Howie and Claire slept in the tipi, and they used Howie's ex-bachelor cabin for a kitchen, bathroom, and common living space. Cables zigzagged across the sagebrush from the cabin to the tipi and trailer so that everyone could have electric blankets, reading lamps, and CD players—the basic necessities of life. It was an impromptu situation, a temporary solution to their housing needs while Howie and Claire did their best to put off, month by month, the consideration of long-term plans.

Should they rent a bigger house together? Should they try to make a real go of it as a family? It was Claire, more than Howie, who wasn't ready to consider such questions, even before the Chicago offer had come into the mix. *I just came out of a horrible ten-year marriage, Howie!* was her constant refrain. *So let's live day by day for a while.* Which seemed reasonable, except the time was adding up.

Howie lifted the large cardboard box from the passenger seat and staggered up the path with it to the cabin. He juggled the box onto one hip to open the door, stomping snow from his boots. The cabin was warm and full of cooking smells from the kitchen. Claire's two children were sprawled across the floor working on their Halloween costumes for the weekend. Jonathan was nearly nine, a serious, handsome boy with dark hair. Heidi was seven and blond, like her mother, almost dangerously cute. Claire was by the stove with an apron over the all-purpose blue jogging suit she generally wore at home. She stopped cooking long enough to give him a quick kiss on the lips.

"Mmm, you're cold," she said. "What's in the box?"

"A surprise for the kids," he told her in his most mysterious voice. He brushed aside a box of Legos from the kitchen table and set down the heavy cardboard box. There were children's toys and clothes everywhere in the small room. Howie sighed just a little, lamenting the lost orderliness of his bachelor days.

It was only after setting down the box that he saw the worry in Claire's gray-blue eyes, tension creeping around the corners of her mouth and eyes. She didn't look quite right somehow.

"Have a good afternoon?" she asked, trying hard to be bright and cheery.

"A very arty afternoon. I went to a gallery opening, and then I stopped off to visit Gilmer Good Day. I'm starting to feel like a regular culture vulture. How was the rest of your day?"

She looked away. "I'll tell you about it later," she said, shooting a quick glance at the children engrossed in their costumes on the floor. Howie studied her, wondering what was wrong.

"Mom, is dinner ready yet?" Jonathan asked.

"Dinner!" cried Claire, rushing for the oven door. "Oh, my God!"

Dinner was macaroni and cheese, slightly burned. Frankly, Claire wasn't the greatest cook in the world. Her recipes came straight from the side of the Kraft's box, with some sliced-up hot dogs mixed in with the noodles as tonight's gourmet addition. Ethnically speaking, Claire's cuisine was classic Iowa. At least he was starting to wean her from Jello casseroles. One of the first dinners she had ever made for Howie was Ring-Around-the-Tuna: pieces of tuna, cucumber, and olives embalmed in a shivering mold of bright green Jello. It was enough to give a person lime day-glo nightmares. Naturally, Howie never said anything about it, not wishing to hurt her feelings. But he had subtly given her the *New Basics Cookbook* for Christmas last year.

Howie was kicking off his boots when the kids started shouting at each other, arguing over a piece of elastic they both wanted for their Halloween costumes. He sat down on the floor where they were working.

"Hey," he said, "I can get you another piece of elastic, if that's what you need."

"He won't let me use the scissors either!" Heidi said hotly, glaring at her older brother.

"That's a lie! I let you use them, then you wouldn't give them back to me!"

"I bet I can find another pair of scissors," Howie said sagely. Stepfatherhood was a constant challenge. He knew very well that the children were not happy that their mother had taken them away from a nice, middle-class two-story house in Iowa City to live in the wilds of New Mexico. They thought their mother was nuts. And they missed their real father, especially Jonathan.

"So what are you going to be on Halloween?" Howie asked.

"*I'm* going to be a princess!" Heidi declared, forgetting for a moment her fight with her brother. Generally, Howie had a much easier time with her than the boy.

"Wow! A princess!" he said. "How about you, Jon?"

Jonathan's dark eyes were full of antagonism. But he spoke politely: "A ghost."

"A ghost! Cool!" But Howie's voice sounded false in his own ears. He was always trying too hard with the boy.

Claire had finished scraping off the charred parts of the macaroni and cheese. Now she tried to pick up the big cardboard box to clear the table for dinner.

"Good Lord, this is heavy! What's in this thing, Howie? A bomb?"

"You're warm. But not *quite* that high-tech."

"Hey, look, Jonathan! Howie got you and Heidi a surprise," Claire said. She too, often tried too hard with the boy it seemed.

Howie stood up from the floor, took the box from Claire, and set it down on the couch. Heidi, who was very big on surprises, gathered excitedly by Howie's legs to examine the present.

"What's inside?" she demanded.

"Take a guess," Howie suggested.

"A dollhouse?"

"No-o . . . what do you think, Jon?"

He shook his head. "I dunno. A TV set?"

"No-o," Howie told him. This was a contentious issue; Claire refused to allow a TV into the home while her children were young, and Howie had not owned one for years. Then quickly, before Jonathan's face could register further disappointment, he spilled the beans. "It's a computer. I got it for you guys."

Heidi jumped up and down. But Jonathan was more cautious. He seemed to believe that nothing really good would ever happen to him in New Mexico.

"A computer, Jon!" Claire echoed encouragingly. But the boy waited, unconvinced.

"Well, it's a used computer," Howie admitted, opening the box, starting to pull it out. "But it has a good fast modem and tons of gigabytes and whosey-a-thingers and more chips off the old block than you'll probably need for a while. Emma helped me get it from the library—they're putting in a new system."

Howie pulled it out piece by piece: the monitor, the keyboard, the boxful of enigmatic computer innards. Jonathan's face darkened. "It's a PC," he pronounced finally, almost devastated, his voice full of disgust. "Macs are so much better."

"Jonathan!" Claire scolded. "Look, an IBM is a really good computer. I bet it cost a fortune new."

"Dad has a Mac. And he says IBMs suck."

Claire's face flushed red with anger. "Believe me, your father isn't always Mr. Right," she said, her voice rising. "Listen to me carefully, young man. Howie went out of is way to do something nice, so don't act like such a brat!"

This situation was spinning out of control. "Claire, it's okay," Howie told her, trying to calm things down.

"No, it is *not* okay. This is a *wonderful* present," she insisted tightly. "I bet it has Windows 98 and everything."

"Well, Windows 95," Howie admitted.

That was the last straw: prehistoric software from the dawn of time. Jonathan spun free of his mother, ran into the bathroom, and locked the door behind him. Meanwhile, little Heidi, hating the tension, buried her face in the bed and started to cry. Howie put his hands gently on Claire's shoulders. She was rigid.

"It's okay, Claire," he said again, soothingly. "Maybe the kids will like the computer once they try it out. If not, I'll use it in the office with Jack. I only paid $150 for it, so it's no big deal. I guess a lot of people prefer Macs—I should have thought of it."

Claire turned suddenly and was in his arms, hugging him fiercely.

"Oh, Howie! I don't know why this all has to be so hard!"

"Hey, coming here to New Mexico is a big change for all of you. But we'll make it work. I know we will."

If only you don't go to Chicago, he added in his mind. Between job offers and tears, it certainly wasn't easy to be a family man these days. Claire held him closely and cried, Heidi was sobbing facedown on the bed, while Jonathan was crying bitterly in the bathroom.

"It's all going to work out," he said again in a soothing voice. But sometimes he wasn't so sure.

Eventually, Claire pulled away and wiped her eyes with a tissue. "Well, let's get dinner on," she said with a sigh. "IBM or Mac, the kids have to eat. Would you set the table?"

"Of course."

Howie picked up Claire's day pack from one of the kitchen chairs. To his astonishment, a gun tumbled out from the unfastened top and hit against his knee. It was a big, nasty-looking automatic. Howie tried to catch the pistol before it hit the floor, but it bounced off his knee, fortunately not firing as it clattered against the floor.

Claire laughed hysterically. "My God! That's the second time that's happened today! My nerves can't stand this anymore!"

Howie stared at the weapon in disbelief. Claire was a pacifist and didn't believe in guns. It wasn't at all like her to be packing a pistol.

"Claire! What are you doing with this thing?"

Claire kept laughing uncontrollably. It was from the tension, not a real laugh, but it took her a moment to catch her breath and answer.

"This is what I was going to tell you about later."

Howie picked the gun up carefully from the floor. "I think you'd better tell me about it now."

Nine

Just after ten o'clock that night, Jack Wilder lay in bed propped up with several pillows listening to Emma read aloud to him from their current novel-in-progress, Edith Wharton's *The Age of Innocence*. Jack made a grand emperorlike figure in the bed. Emma generally read him a chapter of a book every evening, though they missed an occasional night when their lives became too busy. The Wharton novel had been in progress now for nearly a month, and they were about halfway through the story. Jack enjoyed their end-of-the-day ritual, though sometimes his mind wandered.

The wind rattled the windows of the big old house. The Wilders lived in a carefully restored two-story adobe farmhouse with several acres of land on Calle Santa Margarita, a residential neighborhood on the northeast edge of town. Emma had inherited the property years ago from an aunt when she and Jack were still living in San Francisco. In those years, Jack had been a busy police official, climbing quickly up the bureaucratic ladder to the rank of commander, while Emma managed and eventually owned a small bookstore in Northbeach. But each summer they made the trek to San Geronimo for two or three weeks of vacation to busy themselves with the house that Emma had inherited. Summer after summer they knocked down walls to create larger rooms, enlarged the windows, put in modern plumbing, and planted flower beds and a lawn, making the sorts of changes that people from California were apt to do with old New Mexican homes. The idea had always been that they would retire here eventually; they just had not known how soon that retirement would come.

Their bedroom was on the second floor, a snug room with a kiva fireplace in one corner, a low *latilla* ceiling of branches stripped of their bark and set in a herringbone pattern, and true adobe walls of mud and straw. (Unlike many ex-Californians, Jack and Emma had resisted the urge for cement that was plastered to resemble adobe, even though this would have been a good deal easier, avoiding the constant care that real mud required.) As the wind howled outside, the Wilder's two tiger-striped cats, Sushi and Sashimi, snuggled up with them on the bed—Sashimi generally making herself comfortable on Jack's stomach, the softest place in the house. Katya, who was not allowed on the bed, was stretched out on a scatter rug by their feet.

The bedside phone interrupted Emma in the middle of a sentence.

"Let's let the machine get it, Jack. It's after ten," Emma suggested. After ten was late in rural New Mexico.

Jack debated while the phone rang a second time. It was

the lateness of the hour that worried him; the call might be important. He reached for his bedside extension.

"Yes?"

"Hello, Jack? This is Robin Vandenberg. I hope I didn't wake you."

"No, that's okay. What's wrong?" Jack's hearing, which had become very sharp since losing his eyesight, had detected a nuance of anxiety in Robin's voice.

"Well, nothing's wrong exactly. Look, you're going to think I'm a real flake, but I've decided not to go ahead with the investigation we were discussing this morning. I'd like to cancel the whole thing, if you don't mind."

Jack was silent. The investigation, as Robin called it, had not interested Jack even slightly until this moment; he would have turned it down altogether if he hadn't sensed that Howie was in real need of the money. But now that the case was being pulled out from under him, his curiosity was at last aroused.

"I see," he said cautiously. "What made you change your mind, Robin?"

"Oh, nothing specific. I've just been thinking about it. Whatever my mom has done with her jewelry, it's between her and Sherman. He's her husband, after all, and it's wrong for me to interfere. Not only that, but frankly if you *did* find something . . . well, it could make waves. A scandal, you know. This is such a small town. So the more I thought it over . . . it just seemed best to let the whole thing be."

What Robin was saying was reasonable, but Jack didn't believe a word of it.

"Has someone gotten to you, Robin?"

"What do you mean?" Robin asked sharply.

"Has someone been bending your arm, warning you that you'd better not investigate your stepfather?"

Robin gave a nervous little laugh of denial that was not the least bit convincing. "Oh, no. Not at all. I assure you, this is my decision alone. Honestly."

The more "honestlys" and "I assure yous" that Robin added to his denial, the less believable it was. Strange. Robin Vandenberg was obviously lying, but why?

"Are you still there, Jack?"

"Mmm-hmm," said Jack.

"Look, I know this is an inconvenience for you. And it's all my fault for being so wishy-washy, so I'd like you to keep the thousand dollars I gave you. As long as we understand that your investigation is absolutely to end. I've thought this over very carefully. And . . . well, that's it, I'm afraid."

"All right, Robin," Jack said placidly. "But Howie and I don't accept payment for what we haven't done. I'll deduct one day's work and expenses and send you the balance."

Robin seemed relieved to get out from his arrangement with Wilder & Associate so easily. His tone was suddenly lighter, almost carefree. "Hey, that's really very nice of you. Look, once more, I'm sorry about wasting your time."

"That's all right. Good night, Robin . . . son of a bitch!" Jack swore angrily the moment he set down the receiver.

"What happened?" Emma asked.

"I don't know. We just lost our client. But he's lying to me about something. The whole thing's strange as hell. I hate to get cut off just when an investigation's starting to roll!"

"But, Jack, over dinner you told me that your new case was totally boring and you were only doing it for Howie's sake."

"That was then," Jack said grouchily. "And this is now."

"Do you want to hear more Edith Wharton?"

"Not tonight, Emma. If it's all right, I'll take a rain check. I need to think a bit."

"Well, happy thinking, darling," Emma told him, picking up her own novel-in-progress, a feminist story by a young woman writer that she knew Jack wouldn't like.

Jack sat in bed thinking, hardly moving a muscle. He was so still, he might have been asleep except for an occasional long *hmm* that escaped his lips, almost a meditative growl. Ten minutes passed, and then he reached abruptly for the bedside telephone. He punched in Howie's number, his fingers moving swiftly over the plastic squares. He was not surprised this time of night when Howie and Claire's machine took the call. He spent the next few minutes barking out instructions of what he wanted Howie to do tomorrow.

When the phone rang in the cabin, Howie was involved in serious connubial pursuits inside the tipi with Claire, deep in bed beneath a pile of blankets, with a bearskin rug thrown on top. The skin was synthetic, a make-believe bear, since Claire liked animals and was philosophically opposed to hunting for sport. Even so, it had a fierce head, glass eyes, and huge claws. At the moment its brown body rolled in tsunami waves of passion, riding the seismic storm coming from beneath the covers. A bear, a blonde, and a tipi—as far as Howie was concerned, this was a fine way for any postmodern Indian to get in touch with his roots.

Claire fell asleep almost immediately after sex, curled close, her long hair spilling over his shoulder. But Howie could not sleep. He lay on his back and listened to her rhythmic breathing and the crackle of the fire. There was a Schubert string quartet, *Death and the Maiden,* playing softly on the CD player. Gusts of wind howled through the poles, shaking the canvas walls around them. The tipi was cozy, adapted for modern life as much as a tipi could be. Howie's ancestors had put up with smoky fires on dirt floors that turned everything a yucky black. But last summer Howie had installed a small cast-iron woodstove with a pipe passing up through the smoke flap, cleverly sealed against rain and snow with a metal cap that only leaked a little.

They had talked for nearly an hour before sex, after Claire had put the children to bed in their trailer, with many hugs and promises that they would all try harder in the future for better communication. When Claire was able to turn her attention to Howie, she told him about the crazy homeless man with the rainbow pants, and how she had made the mistake of giving him five dollars on the street one day last week, causing him to develop some odd kind of crush on her. She told him the whole story: how he had peeked in through a window when she was taking a shower, and how he had shown up at her office this afternoon with a gun and a sketchbook full of naked drawings of her.

Howie wasn't certain which he found the most disturbing, the gun, the sketchbook, or the homeless man peeping in at Claire. He had turned through the sketchbook, page by page, full of conflicting emotions. As Claire had warned him, the drawings were astonishingly good. The technique was masterful, but the genius of them was more profound:

they revealed the inner Claire, the radiance beneath her gawky Iowa-ness—in a sense, the very reasons Howie loved her. Certainly, the drawings were idealized; it was a bit silly to see someone you knew depicted with angel wings. And yet, the Rainbow Man had captured something of Claire's basic goodness. He had somehow caught the mysterious thing in her that just about knocked Howie's socks off whenever he heard her play passionate music on the cello. The wings, though perhaps silly, were not cute wings. They had a great dramatic sweep to them, a kind of upward surge. These were wings that desperately *wanted* to fly. And fly in the exact same way that Claire flew, metaphorically speaking, when she played a few special pieces of music, particularly Beethoven.

And then there was the matter of the gun. Claire was still uncertain about involving the police. Despite the gun, she did not believe the homeless man meant her harm. "In an odd way, I feel like he's *my* guardian angel," she told Howie. "He does frighten me, of course . . . it's just all so unsettling! I wish I could do something for him, but I don't know what."

Howie didn't know what either. Guardian angel or not, the homeless man was mentally unbalanced—maybe stark raving mad! It was an unpredictable situation, and they couldn't allow him to keep on stalking Claire as he had done. Meanwhile, Howie had not mentioned his own strange meeting with the Rainbow Man tonight on the highway, only a few miles away. He had not wanted to worry her further, at least not tonight; he would tell her in the morning, however, because Claire needed to take this more seriously. Personally, he was not convinced that the Rainbow Man was as benign as she imagined; on the side of the road tonight, he had sensed something frightening about the man. Howie had briefly feared for his life when the homeless man had started walking toward him.

Tomorrow he would bring the gun and the sketchbook to Jack and get some professional advice. Meanwhile, sex had been Dr. Moon Deer's prescription for putting scary things out of mind. But it seemed to work better for Claire than for Howie, who lay awake long after she had fallen asleep, his mind swirling with worry. Between the homeless man and the drama earlier with Jonathan, they had not touched on the other troubling matter: the offer Claire had received to join the Chicago string quartet.

The CD player switched off. It was getting late. Howie disengaged from Claire gently, blew out the candle next to the bed, turned down his side of the electric blanket, and tried to sleep. But sleep wouldn't come. He shifted from one side to the other. Outside, it had begun to snow again, the flakes performing a little tap dance against the canvas tipi. Howie was starting to drift off when he heard a car door shut somewhere nearby. It was a subtle sound. With the wind, the falling snow, and Claire's breathing, he wasn't entirely certain he had heard it. The closest house was Bob and Nova's, a ten-minute walk. No one would drive up their private road this time of night. As he listened, he thought he heard footsteps crunching in the snow.

Howie sat up in bed, fully awake. Inside the tipi the darkness was broken only by the glowing embers of a dying log in the woodstove. Careful not to wake Claire, he slipped out of bed and searched for his clothes. A tipi did not retain heat, and with the fire almost out, the air outside of bed was bracingly cold.

Claire stirred. He had woken her after all. "Mmm, where you going, honey?" she asked sleepily.

"Gotta pee."

"You're my knight in shining armor," she said for some reason, turning over and falling asleep again. Probably she had been having a dream. At the moment Howie felt more like a knight in fuzzy Polartec. He stepped into his boots, leaving his laces untied, and slipped out the front flap with a flashlight in hand. To his surprise, the wind was much warmer than it had been earlier in the evening, almost tropical, if you could say that during a snowstorm. Instead of clear and cold, a new system had moved into the San Geronimo valley. Big wet flakes came slashing down sideways at him. Howie played the flashlight beam around the backyard, but he could see nothing beyond a three-dimensional chaos of falling snow. He could just make out the shape of the kids' trailer, but the windows were dark and quiet.

He moved toward the cabin thinking that perhaps he was wrong about the sound he thought he'd heard. In a storm things shook and moved and made ghostly noises. Once inside the cabin, he stood with the lights off, listening.

There was nothing. His hair was wet from the snow. He reached for the kitchen towel hanging on the refrigerator door, then changed his mind. If the kid had tried to dry their hair with the kitchen towel, he would have given them a lecture; a stepdad had to set a good example, and practice what he preached.

Howie walked toward the bathroom to get a proper towel. He had his hand on the doorknob when the bathroom door burst open. It seemed to explode in his face, sending him staggering backward half a dozen feet against the kitchen table. Howie was totally unprepared as a dark figure leapt at him out of the bathroom. A fist beat repeatedly against the side of his head. Howie raised his arms to protect himself, but the next blow came to his stomach. The pain took his breath away, making him double over in agony.

The darkness of the cabin, the surprise, the speed in which it all had happened left Howie helpless. He felt his legs pulled out from under him. A boot kicked out against him as he lay on the floor, catching him in the ribs. The pain was excruciating. Worse, he could only lie waiting for more pain to come. But now he heard the figure escaping toward the front door, crashing over furniture as he went. Then his attacker was gone, leaving the front door open behind him, his boots crunching through the snow. Howie struggled slowly to his feet. He was out of breath but not hurt badly. By the time he staggered to the open door, he saw red taillights speeding away from his driveway. In the falling snow he wasn't certain if it was a car or a van. He thought briefly of giving chase, but knew that by the time he found his car key and started up the Toyota engine, the intruder would have reached the highway and be long gone.

His lip was bleeding. Howie turned on the lights and picked up a kitchen chair that had fallen over. He poured himself a shot of cognac from a bottle on an upper kitchen shelf and then sat down wearily. All in all, he couldn't imagine who had attacked him or why. He didn't think it was the Rainbow Man because the figure in the dark had come in a car, and the Rainbow Man had said he didn't ride in cars. But it was hard to say. Maybe the Rainbow Man was a liar.

Howie was trying to decide what this was all about when

he noticed the red light on his telephone answering machine blinking. He stared at it for a few minutes, wondering if he was ready for more interaction with the world. Finally, braver with some cognac in his stomach, he punched the play message button.

It was Jack's voice:

"Howie, I just got a call from our client. Our ex-client, I should say. He's fired us. Said he changed his mind and we should keep the thousand bucks, that he didn't want to create a family scandal, and a few other things as well. But it all sounded like bullshit to me. I think someone got to him. Maybe his mother, maybe his stepfather, maybe it was his sister, Pooh. I don't know, but I want to find out. If Robin really has changed his mind, that's up to him. But if he's acting under duress, I feel a responsibility to help get him un-duressed so he can make a free decision. What I want you to do, Howie, is drive out to his house tomorrow and give him his money back, minus our expenses and one day's salary. I'll let you figure out the bookkeeping. But while you're there, see if you can prod him gently and get him to tell you what happened to make him change his mind. I think you might have a better chance on your own. Be his friend, Howie. Play nice New Age Indian and see what you can suck out of him. Give me a call afterward. Other than that, it looks like we're unemployed, bubba."

The machine clicked off. Getting beat up and unemployed on the same evening was not Howie's idea of a perfect day. He poured himself another shot of cognac and hoped that it was only an illusion that his life seemed to be falling apart.

Ten

Howie woke in the tipi on Thursday morning, as he did almost every morning, to the sounds of Claire's cello coming from the cabin. It was nearly seven o'clock, so she had been up for several hours by now, practicing intensely. Howie was in awe of her discipline. He lay in bed listening to the cello's deep rumbles and high wildly frolicking melodies, only half-awake, unwilling to move.

By the time he dressed and walked across the yard to the cabin, Claire had put away her cello and the children were up and busy fixing themselves bowls of cereal. With a bleary eye, Howie poured himself a cup of coffee from the automatic maker.

"Guess what? There's no school today!" Heidi cried happily.

"Classes have been canceled because of the snow," Claire explained. "We just heard it on the radio."

"I'm sorry, Howie," Jonathan told him with downcast eyes. "For the way I acted last night. About the computer, I mean."

"Hey, don't worry about it. It's fine," he said.

Claire came over and kissed him on the lips. Then she backed away and looked at him with concern. "What happened to your face, Howie? You've cut yourself."

"I slipped in the snow on the back steps last night coming into the house to pee," he lied. He had meant to tell her the truth, but not with the children nearby. Claire's eyes filled with skepticism. "I'll tell you about it later," he promised.

After breakfast, Howie took Jonathan cross-country skiing out on the desert, transformed over the past twenty-four hours into an unfamiliar world of strange white shapes.

Child-care arrangements, always complicated at the best of times, were even more complicated today because of the school closure. Claire couldn't afford to take a day off work, not with the Halloween benefit coming up on Saturday. Fortunately, she had a four-wheel drive station wagon that would get her safely into town, as long as she drove slowly. It was decided that Claire would drop Heidi off in town to spend the day with her best friend, Tyler Jessup. As for Jonathan, Howie and the boy would spend the morning together, then Howie would drop Jonathan off at his friend Ryan Grubach's house. This meant that Howie wouldn't get to talk to Robin Vandenberg until the afternoon, but what the hell. Jonathan was only going to be nine years old once in his life, and the boy was in serious need of some male bonding.

Howie led the way on his narrow cross-country Rossignols, cutting a track through the dense wet snow. In long strides they glided across the high desert on an old trail that skirted close to the base of the mountains and then headed south toward town. The morning was misty white, ghostly, and still, much warmer than it had been yesterday. The sky was heavy with threatening clouds. It looked like it might snow again at any moment, or perhaps even rain.

"How you doing?" Howie called out behind him.

"Okay!" Jonathan called back. There was a new energy in his voice. Jonathan was a determinedly athletic boy. Last year Howie had begun teaching him to downhill ski, and would do so again this season when the San Geronimo Peak ski area opened on Thanksgiving Day. It was something they could share; Jonathan would be more confident this year, and Howie would be able to take him down more difficult slopes. Meanwhile, cross-country did not have quite the same thrills as alpine skiing, but it was good to be outside on any boards at all this early in the season.

They skied in silence in single file alongside the fence of a large ranch, past horses and cows and a farmhouse with smoke coming from the chimney. To the west, the white desert stretched seemingly forever beneath the low sky. To the east, the mountains formed an abrupt wall, their tops cut off by the clouds. From a distance the desert looked flat, but in fact it was a sea full of waves: on skis you discovered the endless small hills and arroyos that undulated across the land.

Every now and then, Howie looked back to make sure that Jonathan was following behind in his tracks.

"Am I going too fast?"

"I can keep up," Jonathan called back with a beaming face.

Howie remembered something his great-uncle Two Arrows had told him when Howie was about the age that Jonathan was now. "You are a small piece of the sun, *takos,*" Two Arrows had said. "That is the thing that is alive inside of you."

Howie, who was very literal in those days, studied his arms and legs with great interest. "But if I am the sun, grandfather, why aren't I shining?"

"Ah! This is a very good question! You *are* shining, but you cannot see it. It is the belief of our people that no one is able to see his own piece of sunlight except as it is reflected in the faces of those around you, particularly your children—when you have children one day, *takos,* you will see how this is so."

As a child, Howie had more or less understood what Two Arrows meant. But he had not understood fully, in his heart, until just this moment, watching Jonathan ski toward him, the boy's face full of light.

"This is great!" Jonathan said, skiing closer. "Thank you for taking me, Howie."

"Hey, did I ever tell you about my great-uncle Two Arrows? He was a wise old man who used to take care of me when I was a kid. Well, he used to drink too much, but he knew a lot of things anyway. . . ."

Howie told Jonathan some of Two Arrows' stories as they skied side by side for several miles, teaching stories about Iktomi, the Trickster, and how the old man had shown him the Lakota way to walk quietly in the woods and catch fish from a stream with his bare hands. As he talked, a fine mist began to fall, closer to rain than snow. The temperature was well above freezing now, probably almost forty. Sweat trickled down Howie's forehead, and his undershirt was sticking to his chest. After an hour the mist had definitely turned to rain, and they were back in single file, sometimes separated by as much as a hundred feet. Up ahead, Howie could see the small village of Valverde and the road that cut east to the San Geronimo Peak ski area. Beyond the village he could spot the expensive houses on top of the Valverde Mesa with their arrogant windows surveying the valley below. About a mile away he could just make out the big Vandenberg Stone house as well as a corner of Gilmer Good Day's fancy mansion.

The rain was starting to come down harder, washing the snow from the sagebrush. Howie decided it was time to head back, cutting west alongside a sagging barbed-wire fence toward the main highway and then making a gradual loop across the desert toward home. He had just started skiing in the new direction when he heard the obnoxious mosquito-whine of a snowmobile climbing to the top of a hill just to his south. Like every cross-country skier, Howie disliked snowmobiles—they were noisy, gas-fuming monsters that had all the delicacy of a chain saw. The engine grew louder, and soon Howie saw the machine and rider about a hundred yards away at the summit of the hill. The snowmobile was black, its rider dressed in black as well—an ebony helmet with a plastic shield and a black snowsuit. As Howie watched, the figure stood up from the saddle of the machine to survey the snowy desert below. Then he, or she—Howie couldn't tell at this distance—settled back into the saddle, revved the machine, and disappeared with a nasty growl behind the far side of the hill. The engine's whine gradually faded, then ceased entirely.

Howie continued skiing. He came around the corner of the barbed-wire fence and then broke a trail in a northwest direction that would take them almost directly home. He had an open field on his right and a line of trees to his left—piñon mostly, but also some towering old cottonwoods and Chinese elms. The trees bordered the Rio San Geronimo, more a fast-moving stream than an actual river. Meanwhile Jonathan had fallen quite far behind, so Howie stopped to take a drink of water from the plastic jug in his day pack, allowing the boy a chance to catch up. He had the jug to his lips when he heard a gunshot reverberate in the heavy silence of the morning. It was not a loud shot, probably only someone hunting rabbits with a .22. Howie looked around, but saw no one. Of course, sound was tricky

to judge on a day like this beneath a looming sky; perhaps
the shot had come from far away. Nevertheless, Howie was
glad to see Jonathan closing up behind him, skiing hard.

A growl of thunder rolled across the valley. The morning
wasn't quite as idyllic as it had been before. First a snowmobile, then somebody shooting a gun, and now apparently
they were about to have a thunderstorm. Howie was putting his water jug back in his day pack when a movement
near the line of trees caught his eye. He was surprised to
see a person hobbling on foot through the snow several
hundred feet away, coming from the direction of Valverde
and moving in a lopsided gait toward the river. Howie
frowned. It was the homeless man with the rainbow pants,
who had a way of showing up in some very odd places. As
Howie looked around, he realized that they were less than
half a mile from the grade on the highway where he had
seen the homeless man last night.

"Hey, Rainbow Man, hold on a minute!" Howie shouted.
"I want to talk with you!"

The man glanced his way but kept on hobbling toward
the trees that bordered the river. There was something
wrong with the way he was moving, clutching his side and
limping through the snow at a frantic and uneven pace. The
scene was unsettling, though Howie couldn't say exactly
why. Suddenly, the homeless man fell on the snow just before he reached the line of trees. He picked himself up with
some difficulty and staggered onward.

"Hey!" Howie called again. "Are you okay?"

The Rainbow Man made no answer. He wobbled un-
steadily into a stand of evergreens and disappeared from
view. Just then, with the suddenness of weather in New
Mexico, there was a flash of lightning, a great boom of
thunder, and the rain turned into a downpour. Jonathan
was still about fifty feet behind him on the trail. Howie
gestured to him to stay where he was and then skied quickly to the
edge of the trees where the man had disappeared. There
was blood on the snow. Dark red droplets against the frosty
white, the color running in the rain.

Howie continued skiing into the trees, pushing past the
scratchy limb of a piñon toward the river. There was thick
underbrush alongside the water, a snarl of growth. Howie
rounded a huge juniper bush and saw the homeless man

lying on his back in the snow, his rainbow pants and the entire lower part of his body submerged in the icy stream. He was breathing hard, grunting in pain like a woman in labor. Howie stepped out of his ski bindings and ran over to him.

"What happened?" Howie asked, kneeling next to him. "Come on, I bet you can talk. Tell me."

The Rainbow Man opened his mouth, trying to speak, but no words came out. His eyes were yellow with fear, and there was a small trickle of dark blood coming from his nose, washed down his cheek by the hard falling rain.

"Ruh," said the Rainbow Man, making no sense at all.

"I'll get help," Howie told him. He turned, hearing a commotion in the nearby brush. It was Jonathan coming into the undergrowth on his skis, following Howie's tracks. Howie stood up to intercept the boy.

"Look, Jon, there's been an accident," he said carefully. "So I'm going to need your help. Okay?"

"An accident?" the boy repeated, gazing at Howie with his serious dark eyes. Then he glanced over at the figure lying halfway in the stream. "Oh!"

"I want you to ski as quickly as you can to the first house you find where there's someone at home. You tell them it's an emergency, okay? And you ask to use the phone to call the police. Just say there's a man badly hurt, and we need an ambulance. Wait for them to arrive, then bring them here as fast as you can. Can you do all that?"

The boy nodded vigorously. "I'll call 911," he said.

"That's great, Jonno! Now, go!"

Howie had never called him Jonno before, a nickname born in an emergency. The boy flashed Howie an oddly grateful look, then he did a kick turn on his skis, dug his poles into the snow, and hurried away. Howie turned back to the wounded man. The rain was coming down so hard now that Howie was afraid the man might drown as he lay faceup to the sky. He knelt on the ground and tried to shield the man's head from the torrent by leaning forward with his own upper body. It was an intimate gesture, bringing Howie's face inches from the homeless man's lips.

"You've been shot," Howie said with certainty. "Who shot you?"

The man tried again to speak. *"Ruh . . . ruh,"* he said. It was the same incomprehensible sound he had made earlier.

"I don't understand," Howie told him. "You've got to try to tell me again. Who shot you?"

Howie lowered his left ear closer to the man's lips.

"Red," he managed. It came out in a hoarse whisper, almost a sigh.

"Red? Red what?"

With a torturous effort a new word came: *"Moon!"*

The man stared upward into Howie's eyes, pleading to be understood.

"Red moon? Is that what you're trying to say?"

He nodded, very slightly.

"Red moon," Howie repeated, not understanding. "Is that an Indian? Is that the person who shot you?"

Rainbow Man's yellow eyes opened wider, and a gagging sound came from the back of his throat. He looked to Howie like a fish gasping out its life.

"Just hang in there," Howie told him anxiously. "An ambulance is on the way."

But the man was dying. Howie knew this without the need of any doctor to tell him. The dying man stared upward at Howie with his eyes full of incomprehensible terror. Howie stared back, unable to look away. The eyes of the dying man seemed to be trying to tell him something of vast importance. Something so final, so large, so boundlessly beyond time and measure that no words would ever do.

"What?" Howie whispered. "Tell me."

But with a small exhaled sigh, the man's eyes went blank. Just like that. One moment there was someone there, the next moment the eyes were empty and Howie was alone. He had never seen anyone die before. Not up close, inches away.

Howie was spooked. This was scary stuff, watching a person die; it made you wonder about the fragility of life, how easy it was for the whole show to end without much warning. Meanwhile, the rain had penetrated his ski clothes, he was wet and cold and shivering. But he couldn't tear himself away.

Howie was still kneeling on the ground, staring with fascination at the dead lump of nothingness, when he sensed someone coming up behind him. He was starting to rise when it felt like an entire tree came crashing down on his head. There was a bright dry flash of pain. The pain expanded in a circle until it engulfed him.

Howard Moon Deer fell forward, dizzy and nauseous, into the icy stream. An angry red moon glared down at him inside his skull. *What a mystery!* he thought. *Red moon, red moon, so deep and bright!* He tried to get up from the water, but he couldn't. It was just too hard.

From far, far away he listened in dreamy contentment as a distant siren came rushing his way.

PART TWO

―∞∞∞―

Day of the Dead

One

On Thursday morning after Emma left for her job at the library, Jack Wilder started a big pot of chicken soup. This required blind navigation and some tricky work with knives, but Jack had his kitchen well under control.

He found some chicken in the refrigerator, leftovers from dinner earlier in the week, and put it in the pot along with a chopped onion, a green pepper, minced garlic, ginger, a jalapeño, parsley, a bay leaf, chicken bouillon, salt, pepper, thyme, water, and a good stiff shot of Kentucky whiskey. It was astonishing what whiskey could do for a soup; it got rid of the culinary blahs in a hurry. This would do to get things started; later in the day, he would remove the bones and add potatoes, carrots, and whatever stray vegetables he could find in the fridge.

Jack had mastered the art of blind cooking after many early disasters of blood, bruises, and meals burned to a crisp. Once the soup was simmering, Jack made his way to the back porch to pursue his latest attempt to expand the limits of his handicap. He felt about with his hands until he located one of three fifty-gallon plastic food bins that stood to the right of the back door. The bin was three-quarters full of pinto beans, and he reached down until he felt a plastic Ziploc bag that was buried nearly a foot beneath the surface. The bag contained a .22 automatic Ruger Mark II pistol with a bullet in the chamber and a fully loaded magazine. In the next bin over, buried deep in the brown rice, Jack found a box of ammunition. The third fifty-gallon bin—Katya's dry Science Diet dog food—contained a more serious gun, a Smith & Wesson Chief's Special .38 revolver, but he wouldn't need that today. The hidden weapons were a subterfuge, since Emma had never liked guns much, even in Jack's police days, and she liked them less now that he was blind. It seemed best in this instance to leave her in the dark.

There was a loud clap of thunder as Jack stood on the back porch. A moment later he heard the patter of rain on the roof. This was unusual weather for autumn in New Mexico, but Jack was undeterred. He found his raincoat and his cell phone, closed up Katya and the two cats inside the house by feeding them an unexpected midmorning snack, and quickly gathered together from the back porch the remaining items he would require this morning: three cheap portable AM radios, a ball of string, and a bag of two dozen rubber baby bottle nipples.

Ready for action, Jack walked out to the backyard with his white cane tapping and sweeping in front of him.

Jack had found the perfect place for target shooting on the three acres of land they owned, a spot about a hundred feet behind the house in the trees with a hill behind it to stop any stray bullets. Jack used the string to tie one of the small radios to the branch of a Chinese elm. He turned on the radio to a scratchy AM country station that broadcast from Santa Fe. It was the cheapest radio he could find at Wal-Mart, $5.99; the reception and sound quality were terrible, but this was of no importance. When the radio was in place, he gave it a push so that it would swing back and forth on the string, a moving, talking target. Then he paced exactly twenty strides back across the snowy ground.

He set down his cane and a bag of supplies near a rock, then he took the .22 pistol from his raincoat pocket and slipped one of the rubber baby bottle nipples over the end of the barrel. The rubber nipple would act as a silencer, a trick he had learned years ago from a Mafia hitman in San Francisco—he would need to change the nipple after several shots when the rubber became ragged, but other than that it was more effective than the tubelike attachments that were mostly an invention of Hollywood. "Suppressor" was a more accurate word, because you couldn't entirely silence the explosion of a gunshot. Revolvers, of course, couldn't be silenced at all, since the sound could easily escape through the open ends of the cylinder chambers. An automatic was essential if you wished to be discreet. It was also helpful to use subsonic rounds, guns such as a .22 that fired bullets at velocities lower than eleven hundred feet per second—more powerful rounds were like tiny jet planes breaking the sound barrier, creating a secondary explosion. Jack had thought this out carefully, since he didn't want to alarm his neighbors.

Now he only had to blast the country station off the air. Jack's model was Zen archery, which he believed was a good approach for a blind marksman. The main idea in Zen archery, as he understood it, was *not* to aim. Aiming implied a goal and the illusion that there was a divide between oneself and the target. In fact, there was no divide. The target and the shooter were one, and in order to connect with the target you only needed to understand this essential oneness. What could be simpler?

Jack released the safety, raised the pistol in a casual, almost random manner, listened to the music, then pulled the trigger. The gun emitted a small *plip* and kicked back slightly in his hand. But the radio kept playing, an overheated song about a country boy falling for a big-city gal. Jack did his best to empty his mind and tried again. *Plip!* But the song kept soaring to a woeful climax. Jack had a liking for old cowboy songs and folk music, but he couldn't stand this sort of slick Nashville product. Over the past few months, he had managed to hit the radio only once, and that was standing five paces from the target. Nevertheless he was certain he could do it. He raised the barrel and fired two more rounds, thinking to himself, *I am the bullet speeding to its mark.*

Plip! Plip!

But the radio didn't quit. He paused to put a new rubber nipple on the end of the barrel and then tried again. He remembered a joke that Howie had told him. *Question: What did Buddha say to the hot dog vendor? Answer: Make me one with everything.* A silly joke, but this was precisely what Jack needed now, to be one with everything. And sweet Buddha in heaven, how he would relish knocking this horrible country station off the air! But shot after shot, he kept missing. He stopped to reload the clip several times, but the station would not quit.

It was raining harder now, and even with his raincoat, Jack was starting to get wet. But he was frustrated, and he didn't want to stop. He tried various approaches, from Zen indifference to murderous intent. He aimed, he aimed-not. But nothing worked. Finally, he paced five strides forward, but even from here he couldn't hit the damn radio.

Jack was refitting a new nipple over the end of his .22 when the cell phone in his jacket pocket gave a chirp. He raised the device to his ear.

"Jack Wilder," he said gruffly.

He had expected the caller to be Howie, but it was not. It was Captain Ed Gomez of the New Mexico State Police. Jack listened to the voice coming through the telephone, and a scowl came to his face.

"Is he all right? . . . son of a bitch!" he swore. "Yes, yes . . . you bet, Ed. Give me five minutes, and I'll be ready."

Jack sighed and shoved the cell phone back into his pocket.

He turned and began walking toward the house when he remembered that he had left the radio hanging from the tree still squawking away. The station was playing a thirty-second roundup of the news. More ethnic atrocities in the Balkans. More partisan bickering in Washington.

Jack wheeled around, raised the gun without thinking, and fired. The radio shattered in mid-sentence, its transistor guts spilling onto the ground.

Two

"Morning, Jack," said Captain Ed Gomez, helping Jack and Katya into the black New Mexico State Police cruiser in the driveway. Jack had Katya fitted up in her harness, and she was excited to be off on an adventure.

"How you doing, Ed?" Jack asked when they were settled in the car, with Katya in the backseat behind the iron mesh.

"Been better. These damn roads have turned into icy

slush, like some kind of giant slurpee. We have two accidents north of town, and a real bad one on the south end.
We were helicoptering a girl to Albuquerque when the call
came in about the shooting."

Ed Gomez had the voice of a heavy cigarette smoker,
hoarse and raspy. He smelled to Jack like a stale ashtray.

"Any more word on Howie?"

"He'll be okay. It's a concussion, but not bad. The doctor
wants to keep him in the hospital overnight for observation,
though Howie seems to be anxious to get out of there."

Jack felt a rush of acceleration as Captain Gomez headed
the police cruiser out the driveway and onto the back roads
to the hospital, skirting the crowded center of town. Jack
made certain his seat belt was fastened tightly; Ed Gomez
was the commanding officer in charge of the San Geronimo
substation of the state police, but Jack was not entirely
convinced that he was a safe driver. From Howie's description, Jack pictured Ed Gomez as a handsome man, wiry,
tall, late-fifties, with distinguished gray hair and a thin mustache. Imagine a Hispanic Clark Gable, Howie said, only
thinner and dry and leathery from a lifetime in the New
Mexico sun. Over time Ed had let out a few personal details of his life, though not many. His wife had divorced
him a few years ago. There was a child from the marriage,
a son in his early twenties. But the boy belonged to a gang
and had been arrested recently for selling cocaine. A bitter
pill for a cop.

"So what happened?" Jack asked as they were driving.

"Well, it's the damnedest thing. Howie and this boy, Jonathan—the son of the lady he's seeing—they were cross-
country skiing when they saw the victim limping through
the snow across a field toward some trees. He looked like
he was hurt, so Howie skied over to investigate and found
the guy was shot. He was still alive, but going fast. Howie
sent the boy to call 911, and while he was waiting for help
to arrive, the victim managed to say two words. Red moon.
That's all he said, red moon—whatever the hell that means.
Then he died. Howie was pretty unnerved, I guess, watching someone die up close like that. He was staring at the
body when someone managed to sneak up and hit him over
the head, apparently with a tree limb. I think we can as-

sume it was the killer, but why he attacked Howie is as much a mystery as everything else about this incident."

"And the victim—who was he?"

"A Hispanic male, approximately forty years old. A homeless person, it seems. He was dressed in rainbow pants and a peculiar jacket, a patchwork of leather and fur. We haven't ID'd him yet. He didn't have a wallet or any identification. Howie calls him the Rainbow Man."

"Because of his pants?"

"Because that's what the victim called himself. Howie had seen him last night on the side of the highway and stopped to offer him a ride. The guy didn't speak—he wrote out a message on a blackboard around his neck that the Rainbow Man didn't ride in cars, referring to himself in the third person. A religious nut, it seems, and crazy as a loon. We get exotic characters like this passing through San Geronimo from time to time."

"So you're sure he wasn't one of our local homeless?"

"Well, *I've* never seen him around, or heard any reports about him. I have one of my men checking with the town police and the sheriff's department, but so far we've got nothing."

"You said he was shot?"

"Right. We're still waiting for the medical investigator's report, but offhand it looks like a small entrance wound in the fleshy part of his right side, just above the hip. There's no exit wound, and he was able to limp for some ways, so what I'm thinking is maybe a small caliber bullet got lodged in his kidney. Howie says he heard a rifle shot a few minutes before he saw the victim. It sounded like a .22 to Howie, some sort of small rabbit gun, which would make sense. If it was a kidney shot like I suspect, the victim would have been able to run for quite a while before he died eventually from internal bleeding."

"How's Jonathan doing?" Jack asked. "Claire's going to be worried."

"Oh, the boy's fine. He's with Howie's rich hippie neighbors at the moment. Bob and Nova Davidson. I guess they're sort of family. We haven't been able to reach Claire yet, but I sent an officer over to the Art Association to find her."

Jack sat quietly in the speeding car, trying to figure out what this was all about.

"So," he said, thinking aloud, "a homeless man, not entirely in his right mind, gets shot while he's running through a field. Howie skis over in time to hear the man's last words, red moon. Up to now, this could be a stray bullet from someone hunting nearby. But then Howie gets knocked silly from behind, and suddenly this doesn't look so accidental anymore."

"Maybe whoever shot the Rainbow Man wanted to make certain he was really dead," Ed suggested.

"Or maybe the victim had something on him that the killer wanted. Did it appear as if the body had been searched?"

"Nothing obvious. By the way, we've sent our John Doe's prints to Santa Fe . . . yes, I know what you think of the DPS computer there, Jack, but I've put a rush on it and maybe we'll get lucky."

"With Santa Fe, luck is certainly needed," Jack agreed dryly. Compared to California, Jack was continually astonished by the amateurish quality of New Mexico's law enforcement. It was a poor state, of course, ranked among the poorest in the union, and this fact impacted the quality of all services, including the police. In San Geronimo, the town started their officers at $8.00 an hour, which made it difficult to find qualified people. As for the Automated Fingerprint Identification System, or AFIS, run by the Department of Public Safety in Santa Fe, it was a joke. It often took from six to eight weeks for the computer to spew forth a match. That was a lot of mañanas, as far as Jack was concerned.

"Anyway," Ed said with a sigh, "Cory should be able to give us his examination report later in the afternoon."

"I see," said Jack without enthusiasm. Cory Borstein was the part-time Deputy Medical Investigator for San Geronimo County—the rest of the time, he ran a pharmacy on Hernandez Road, dispensing pills and toothpaste and shampoo. In New Mexico, as in a number of Midwestern states, medical examiners were not required to be doctors, and many of them knew very little about forensic science. A doctor needed to sign the actual death certificate, but in San Geronimo this was generally done without an autopsy, based simply on a two-page report supplied by the field examiner.

"We're going to send the body to Albuquerque once Cory is finished," Ed added, seeing Jack's skeptical expression.

"A pity it's so late in the week!" Jack remarked. This was another peculiarity about the state. The University of New Mexico funded six pathologists who generally received the more suspicious death cases. Unfortunately, it was Thursday, and the corpse wouldn't arrive in Albuquerque until late in the afternoon, possibly not before tomorrow morning. The UNM pathology lab was closed on the weekends, so if there was a backup of corpses in Albuquerque, there was a very good chance that the autopsy on the homeless man wouldn't be performed until Monday morning at the earliest. In New Mexico, the day of the week on which a person died often had an absurdly large effect on any subsequent murder investigation, sometimes derailing an investigation before it got underway. On Monday morning, the UNM pathologists usually found themselves with a large collection of stiffs on their doorstep from the weekend slaughter, often more than six people could efficiently handle. And so—like the doctors who signed the death certificates—they were apt to simply accept the verdict of semi-trained field examiners like Cory Borstein, a pharmacist with little forensic training. The ex-bureaucrat in Jack bridled at these things. All in all, he often complained, New Mexico was a fine place to get away with murder.

"At least with the snow, there will be footprints," Jack suggested hopefully. "Have you been able to establish where the victim was coming from?"

Ed seemed embarrassed. "Well, we had a bad break with the weather. It shouldn't have rained this time of year, certainly not so hard. It's pretty much washed everything away, making a real mess of things. And there were lots of people walking around in there before we declared it a crime scene . . . yeah, I know, Jack, you don't have to say it. But you've got to remember, the boy, Jonathan, called it in as an accident. He's a pretty bright, articulate boy, by the way. But apparently Howie told him, quote, there's been an accident, unquote. So EMS came, and a sheriff's car responded as well. They walked around some, and when they saw the man was dead, they called us in. By the time we realized it was a shooting, all sorts of people had been tramping around."

Jack struggled to keep the professional disapproval from his voice. "Any houses near the crime scene?"

"Not in the immediate vicinity. There's a farm about a quarter of a mile away, but they were inside and didn't see anything—it's where Jonathan went to call 911. Valverde's about half a mile away, as the crow flies. Do you know Valverde, Jack? There are about a dozen fancy houses on the mesa there. They all have quite a view. I've sent one of my people door-to-door, but so far nada. A rainy morning—people were inside, apparently minding their own business."

"Isn't the Barbara Vandenberg Stone estate on the Valverde Mesa?"

"Right. That Indian artist lives there too. Gilmer Good Day. Do you know him?" .

"Howie does," Jack said, frowning. He wondered if it was a coincidence that they had been hired and fired yesterday by Robin Vandenberg, the same day that Howie had gone to see Gilmer Good Day in the afternoon. Coincidence worried Jack, though there was indeed a certain amount of serendipity in the world. Ed touched the siren as they made their way along a busy street.

"What I'm thinking, Jack, is that this could be a hate crime," Ed suggested. "After all, why kill some poor homeless person unless it was done as a kind of sick sport?"

"Well, that's a possibility," Jack agreed. "Of course, with those rich houses nearby, you can't entirely rule out burglary."

"Burglary? I don't quite see that."

"Well, let's say our homeless man breaks into one of those houses on Valverde Mesa and steals something valuable—jewelry, for instance. Unfortunately the owner comes home, grabs his trusty .22, and reacts perhaps a bit too vigorously. Maybe he chases after the burglar and takes a lucky shot while the man's running away across a field. Now, of course, he's afraid to report the incident because he doesn't want to be charged with murder."

Jack liked this possibility more than a hate crime scenario because it would explain why Howie was attacked from behind; the shooter would need to get his piece of jewelry back, or whatever else the burglar had taken, so that it would not tie him or her to the shooting. In New Mexico, like other places in the country, you could use a gun to protect yourself only when your life was demonstrably in danger; but shooting a burglar in the back was homicide, no matter how angry you might be.

Ed lit a cigarette and inhaled greedily. The thick smell of tobacco in a squad car reminded Jack nostalgically of the old days, of coffee in paper cups and bags of donuts.

"Was there a road nearby?" Jack asked, cracking open his window.

"Highway 270, the road up to Colorado, is only a couple of hundred yards from the crime scene. What are you thinking?"

"I'm just trying to imagine the different possibilities. Is there any sort of pull-off at the side of the highway? Someplace a person could park?"

"Sure. There's a parking area near where the highway crosses the Rio San Geronimo—fishermen use it all the time."

"And how far is that from the crime scene?"

"Maybe a five-minute walk along the river."

Jack didn't want to appear like some ex-big-city cop telling the backward rural cop what to do. Still, he was accustomed to running investigations, and it was difficult to keep quiet when something obvious is overlooked. "I'll be interested in what your crime-scene people find in that parking area," he said, hoping that Ed had thought to examine the spot.

"Well, that's where the ambulance parked," the captain admitted unhappily. "And several of the county cars. It was the easiest place to park and get to the accident quickly. It's a shame, of course. The whole area got torn up with vehicles coming and going before anyone realized the situation."

For Jack, it was a continual frustration not to be in charge. Howie liked to say that New Mexico wasn't really America, but rather a Third World country off on its own. Things were done differently here, at a much slower pace. *So relax, Jack,* Howie told him. *Inefficiency is beautiful in its own way.*

But Jack could not relax. He fell into a gloomy silence as the cruiser pulled up to the emergency entrance of Sisters of Mercy Hospital. As he grew older, it often seemed to him that he was the last competent person in a fraying world. It put a great weight of responsibility on his shoulders, forcing him to be a kind of ultimate backseat driver.

Ed slammed on the brakes just as they were about to park, sending Jack shooting forward against his shoulder harness.

"Sorry," Ed apologized. "An old lady in a wheelchair wasn't looking."

Jack sighed. See what happened when his concentration lapsed for just an instant?

Three

Howie was on an examination table in a curtained-off area of the emergency room, working hard to convince a doctor that he was all right, when he heard Jack's voice down the hall.

"I don't have a headache. I'm fine, honestly, Dr. Zinnerman," Howie insisted, reading the doctor's name tag for added sincerity and smiling to show just how fine he was. "All I need is some fresh air."

Actually, he felt awful. Like a chorus line of mules were doing high kicks inside his head. The pain left him fuzzy-minded. He had done his best to tell the police everything that had happened, but he had a vague sense that he had left out several key parts. He couldn't remember waking up this morning or having breakfast, though the memory of cross-country skiing with Jonathan was very clear. It was disturbing to feel so jumbled. Worst of all, the eyes of the dead man still seemed to be staring at him from a spot just inside the back of his head. The eyes were haunting and terrible, demanding something from Howie, though he was not certain exactly what. Meanwhile, the emergency room filled him with an unreasonable fear of death, all the beeping machines and cold stainless-steel instruments. He was certain he would feel much better if only he could get away from this claustrophobic place and take a long walk outside.

"I really do recommend that you stay overnight for observation, Mr. Moon Deer," the doctor was saying. The doctor had a resonant voice and the hairiest hands Howie had ever seen on a two-legged creature. "A concussion can be serious business."

Not as serious business as watching someone die, Howie was tempted to say. Not as serious as having a pair of eyes follow you wherever you go. But it took all his energy just to keep smiling and looking full of beans. While Howie was busy acting peppy, Jack appeared in the curtained-off area with Captain Ed Gomez next to him, holding lightly onto Jack's arm.

"Fab!" said Howie, not certain from what distant recess of his brain this slang had come. The wires were decidedly crossed. "You're here to spring me, so let's bounce."

Howie was one of the slim minority in New Mexico who had medical insurance, thanks to his job with Jack, who had old-fashioned idea of social responsibility. Howie was filling out the necessary insurance forms when Captain Gomez got a phone call from the mayor, who needed to see him right away about something—probably a favor concerning one of the mayor's many relatives, most of whom were on the town payroll. Personal favors and nepotism were the core of San Geronimo politics.

"Damn, I've got to go! Jack, tell me something—are you going to investigate this shooting, or what?" Ed asked as he was leaving.

"Well, I'm not entirely sure," Jack lied. "I may make a few inquiries."

"Just keep me up-to-date, that's all I ask."

"You bet," Jack agreed.

Ed arranged for one of his troopers to give Jack and Howie a ride home before hurrying out the emergency room exit to his parked cruiser. Howie guided Jack in the opposite direction along an antiseptic hospital corridor to where Katya had been left with an elderly candy-striper volunteer. Katya was almost unbearably happy to see Jack. Howie felt pretty much the same way a few minutes later when he saw Claire appear through the sliding automatic glass doors from the parking lot.

"Howie! My God!" she cried. "Are you all right?"

"I'm fine, honest. Just a bump on the head. Is Jonathan . . ."

"He's with Nova. Are you *sure* you're okay?"

Howie held Claire tightly in his arms. She felt good all over. There was nothing quite like holding a girlfriend in your arms to make a person understand how preferable life was to death. The two eyes hovering in the back of Howie's head seemed to blink and turn away, giving them a bit of privacy.

"This is starting to get a little crazy for me," Claire admitted with a sigh, pulling back. "First the poor homeless man leaves me with that gun and all those drawings. Then the next day he's killed, and you're attacked. . . ."

"Whoa! Hold on, what's this about a gun and drawings?" Jack demanded.

"Didn't Howie tell you?"

"Ooops," said Howie, rubbing his head. A large portion of reclaimed memory came sliding back into his scrambled head like the missing piece of a jigsaw puzzle. "I think I told the cops everything that happened today, while skiing and all. But I sort of forgot some stuff that happened yesterday," he admitted.

"Howie, are you *sure* you're all right?" Claire asked. "Your face is very pale."

"Now she's calling me a paleface!" Howie managed. But in fact he felt insubstantial, like a man dreaming on his feet.

"This gun," Jack mentioned. "Where exactly is it now?"

"Back at the cabin. It's a Beretta, an automatic of some kind—I don't know the caliber. Should we get it?"

"Let's think about this. I don't want Gomez to get a bee up his butt about withholding evidence. I tell you what. You're obviously suffering a mild case of amnesia, Howie. Very common, in fact, after getting hit on the head. . . ."

"Jack, I'm okay now, really."

"*Listen* to me. You are *not* okay. Your amnesia is going to linger a few more hours. Things are happening too fast, Howie, and I don't like that. So let's give ourselves a little

time to sort things out. Frankly, I'd like to get a head start
on our local Keystone cops before they start muddying up
the water. First, I want you both to tell me the entire story
of your dealings with this Rainbow person from start to
finish."

They dismissed the driver that Ed Gomez had left with
them and drove from the hospital in Claire's old Subaru
station wagon. Jack sat in the back with Katya, between a
soccer ball and a stack of Tin Tin books, despite Claire's
polite insistence that he be in front. The car was sticky
from children's fingers and smelled to Jack like an old sock.
He tried his best not to be a nervous passenger or embar-
rass Howie in front of his lady. One had to humor these
young people, after all, and pray that their ancient car
didn't break down. He didn't even object when Howie
wanted to stop off at the New Wave Café for a cappuccino
to go, saying he thought it would perk him up. Howie was
part of a new generation that apparently couldn't go for
more than a few hours without gourmet coffee.

Jack listened first to Claire's version of the story and
then to Howie's as they rode in the Subaru between the
hospital, the New Wave Café, and then on to Calle Santa
Margarita. When they reached Jack's house, they sat for a
few minutes in the driveway while Howie finished up his
account. Unfortunately, Claire became angry when she realized that Howie had deliberately kept from her his meeting yesterday with the Rainbow Man on the highway and
the prowler who had been in their bathroom last night.

"Howie!" she exploded. "I need to know what's going on!"

"Well, the children were there. I didn't want to worry
them. I was going to tell you, Claire, I was just waiting for
the right moment. . . ."

"Actually, I think it's *very* condescending. Do you think
I'm some sort of little woman who can't bear to hear the
bad news? That's a very chauvinist macho attitude."

"I'm *not* a chauvinist macho person, Claire. And what
about you not telling me about that homeless guy peeping
in through the window while you were taking a shower?"

"That's different. Anyway, I told you eventually."

"It's not different. And I was going to tell you eventually too."

"All right, I didn't tell you about the shower thing because you would have gone after that poor man like some crazed bull, and I wasn't certain I wanted that."

"Crazed *bull*?" Howie asked incredulously.

"Well, okay, maybe you're not that macho, Howie," Claire admitted, giving around. "But you're a soft macho, and that's even more insidious—you know you are, so admit it!"

"Maybe we should talk about this at home. . . ."

While the two young people squabbled over macho, hard and soft, Jack drifted off into his own thoughts, glad that he and Emma had different matters to fight over. He wondered if the bathroom prowler was the Rainbow Man or someone else, as Howie seemed to believe. It was an amorphous situation, ill-defined, and it worried him. One person was dead, and he felt danger in the air. The victim was more than simply an unhinged homeless person; evidently, he was an exceptionally talented artist, which made his journey to San Geronimo, a town noted as something of an art colony, more complex. Jack was certain that there was a story here that needed to be learned. Every murder was a tale of passion—greed, jealousy, fear, ambition, hatred. As an investigator, you had to involve yourself in the human story and ask yourself, what passion? What greed? In this case, Jack did not have the glimmer of a clue.

"Well, we simply need more information," Jack said aloud, feeling for the door handle. "Howie, go home and phone me with the serial number of that gun, please. Once you've done that, let your amnesia clear up. Call Ed and tell him about the gun and the drawings—he'll want them, of course, and he'll also want statements from both of you. I wouldn't be surprised if he pulls you into the substation for a few hours, so you might want to arrange some child care before you call him. Be as truthful as you can, naturally, but don't give away the name of our quasi-client— who I still want you to see, by the way."

"Howie, you should help Jack into the house," Claire said in an undertone to Howie.

"I can find my way from here," Jack assured her as he stepped from the car.

"Jack's being soft macho," Howie observed to Claire.

"Howie! Honestly, I'm going to *do* you!" she cried.

Jack left the young people, glad not to be young himself
anymore, and let Katya guide him up the path to the front
porch. The rain had stopped, though the air was gusty and
damp and smelled to Jack like the storm might continue at
any moment. He wondered if Howie and Claire would
make it as a couple. There was obviously a sexual charge
between then, a lot of hormones kicking up a fuss. Yet
other currents seemed to be pushing them apart. But what
did Jack know about young couples these days? It had been
a very different world in the sixties in San Francisco when
he met Emma: great music, no AIDS, all of them riding a
wave of sexual liberation and new thinking. Despite the
Vietnam war, it was a time of profound optimism, particularly in California, where a sense that one could make the
world a better place pervaded.

It was this optimism, most of all, that had gone missing
from youth in the postmodern time, Jack thought to himself
wearily as he walked up the steps to his front porch. Just
then, Katya growled and let loose a sharp bark.

"What, girl?" Jack stood without moving near Emma's
porch swing, but he heard nothing.

Katya barked again. Was there someone in the house?
Jack felt suddenly vulnerable. He turned toward the driveway thinking he would call Howie, but Claire's Subaru was
already pulling away, shifting gears noisily as it gathered
speed down the road. Jack turned back to the house and
stood quietly listening, taking in his surroundings. But he
sensed nothing out of the ordinary. Katya was wagging her
tail now, so perhaps it had only been a stray dog or cat
passing through the yard. Frankly, Katya was sweet, but
she was not exactly the Einstein of the doggy world.

As Jack stood on the front porch, he heard a meow, then
a moment later a cat rubbed up against his leg. He reached
down and stroked Sushi, the fattest of the two Wilder cats,
knowing her by her gorgeous bulk. Well, this explained
Katya's barking. The two cats were quick and clever, and
they liked to torment Katya in a thousand ways. And yet
Sushi should not have been outside, for he had specifically,
carefully locked the two cats inside when he had left the
house earlier for the hospital. Jack tried to think if there
was any way she might have gotten outside on her own.
An open window? He didn't think so. Could Emma have

stopped home from her job at the library and let her out?
That seemed unlikely as well. If Emma had come home,
she would have done her best to keep the cats inside, for
there was a dangerous dog next door as well as occasional
coyotes in the neighborhood.

Jack pulled the two front door keys from his pocket. The
first key opened the dead bolt, the second the door itself;
in rural New Mexico, most people paid little attention to
locking their homes, but as an ex-big-city cop, Jack was a
stickler when it came to security. He began with the top
lock, slipping the key inside the slot. But there was something wrong; the key would only turn the wrong way, closing the dead bolt rather than opening it.

The dead bolt had been left open.

There could be no mistake now. It was possible that
Sushi might have gotten outside somehow on her own, but
Jack *never* forgot to lock the dead bolt on the front door.
He was careful about these rituals. He decided not to use the
front door after all, but had Katya lead him around to the
rear. He came in through the back pantry, stopping to dip
his hand deep into the fifty-gallon bin of dog food for the
Ziploc plastic bag with his Smith & Wesson Chief's Special
.38 revolver, a more serious weapon than the .22 semiautomatic he had been using for target practice earlier in the
morning. With the revolver in his right hand, Jack walked
cautiously into the kitchen.

He was greeted by a warm cooking smell and the sound
of something bubbling on the stove. Jack was devastated
by his own carelessness. He had left the burner on beneath
the chicken soup he had started this morning! Of course,
he had been distracted by the call from Captain Gomez
that a man had been shot and Howie was in the hospital.
But this was no excuse. A blind person had to pay the
strictest attention to small details. He could have burned
the house down! Fortunately, he had left the soup on a low
simmer, and there had been plenty of liquid in the big pot.
Still, this was a frightening break of concentration, and now
Jack wasn't sure of anything.

If he had left the soup on, wasn't it also possible that he
had not locked the dead bolt? Holding the gun between his
legs, Jack found a large wooden spoon and stirred the pot.
He had been lucky this time. It was a warning, but he must

not be careless again. When he was satisfied that the soup wasn't burned on the bottom, he walked into the living room and opened the front door for Sushi, who was meowing outside. Then he spent the next half hour going through the house room by room searching for any signs of a possible intruder. It was hard to say. The downstairs bathroom window was open an inch at the bottom, but Emma might have left it this way.

He walked up the narrow creaky wooden stairs to the second floor and the small home office that Emma had created from one of the upstairs bedrooms. This was where they kept important papers, bankbooks and such. Jack sat in the rocking chair by the desk and felt with his hands for the contour of Emma's desktop computer, the tray containing household bills, the lamp, the telephone. Everything appeared to be in its proper place. But could a person who had left the stove on this morning truly be certain of anything? In his blindness Jack had learned to hold onto the reality of the world by small rituals and a very thin thread. Now it seemed to him the thread of certainty was not broken, perhaps, but he had lost hold of it briefly.

Jack was standing up from the rocking chair when the phone on the desk rang abruptly. He was so startled that he staggered comically backward against the chair, nearly firing the revolver in his hand. With an effort he steadied himself and picked up the receiver on the third ring.

"Yes?" he breathed.

"It's me. I've got the serial number for you," Howie said over the wire. "Are you ready for some memorization?"

"Hold on a second," Jack told him, sitting down again at the desk. He felt for a pad of paper and a pencil near the computer. "Okay, what is it?"

"Nine, eight, seven, three, five, seven, zero."

This was an easy number to memorize once Jack saw the pattern. The first three digits—nine, eight, seven—were simply a matter of counting backward. Then three, five, seven—the next three digits were odd numbers, each one increasing by two. And finally a zero. Still, in his new uncertainty, Jack used the pencil to scrawl the numbers as well as he could on the pad; if he forgot them, Emma would be able to read them to him.

"All right. I got it. Don't forget to call Ed Gomez."

"Are you okay, Jack? You sound funny."

"I'm fine," Jack told him, hanging up the phone. He wasn't fine—he needed to get a grip on himself. He could not afford blind panic. From the early weeks in the hospital, he had known that in order to survive his new condition, he must go about life in a careful, calm, and scientific manner, one thing after another.

"All right, I lost my head there for a bit. I just need to regroup again," Jack said aloud to the empty house. "I can do this. I am competent, I am calm, and I am very careful."

Not only that, but now he had a starting point, a serial number for a gun. It was a thread to grasp. Jack picked up the phone and dialed the unlisted number of a senior member of the San Francisco Police Department.

Four

Emma Wilder arrived home from the library at close to six-thirty on Thursday night. She found Jack in the kitchen peeling red potatoes over the sink while simultaneously talking on a telephone that was cradled between his left shoulder and ear.

"Well, that would be great, Tommy, I'd really appreciate it," he was saying into the receiver. "Yeah, New Mexico's been very good to us . . . no, we're about four or five hundred miles north of Carlsbad Caverns, actually. Almost up in Colorado . . . Tommy, for crissake, the desert here is not *anything* like Palm Springs. You should get your ass out of California occasionally and see the rest of the country. San Geronimo is up about seven thousand feet, it snows here in the winter, the works. . . ."

Jack spoke for a few more minutes and then put down the phone. Emma came over and kissed him on the cheek, her face still cold from being outside.

"That was Tommy Yang," he told her. "You remember Tommy?"

Emma had to think for a moment. "Lieutenant Yang?"

"Right. Except he's Major Yang now. He's risen in the world." *Thanks in large part to me,* Jack thought. For years he had been Tommy's rabbi in the SFPD, helping the younger cop up the bureaucratic ladder. Now Jack had just cashed in a little on Tommy's indebtedness, giving him the serial number for the Beretta 9mm pistol that the self-styled Rainbow Man had dropped in Claire's office.

"The soup smells wonderful," Emma said, stepping closer to peek inside the pot. "Did you have a good day?"

"Well, yes and no. There was a shooting this morning, Emma. A homeless man got killed. Howie was in the wrong place at the wrong time—a particular talent of Howie's, I should say—and he got himself knocked silly on the back of the head."

"Oh, no!"

"He's fine. A minor concussion. But the shooting was very odd, and Howie's upset about it, naturally. He was kneeling next to the victim when he died, which leaves an impression. The dying man said something strange before he croaked, just two words—red moon. Does that mean anything to you?"

"Jack! Don't say 'croaked'! My God, it's a horrible way to talk about someone dying, and it makes you sound like some nineteen-thirties gangster!"

"I was trying to be droll, dear. So what about red moon?"

"It doesn't mean a thing to me. Could it be an Indian name?"

"Possibly. Though Howie says it doesn't mean a thing to him either. Of course, a modern sort of Indian like Howie—I often suspect that kid knows a good deal more about Paris bistros and who won last year's Princeton–Harvard game than Native American customs."

"Jack, you really aren't being very nice tonight. I've had long talks with Howie about his Lakota childhood. He's just very multicultural. Now, tell me about this shooting. Is it something to do with one of your cases?"

"Well, I don't know. Perhaps in a tangential way. It really is the damnedest thing."

Emma took off her coat and sat at the kitchen table while Jack spent the next ten minutes giving her a rough summary of events, from Claire's five-dollar generosity to the shooting that morning. Jack often used Emma as a sounding board; she was practical and very clear about life, and sometimes she was able to see things from a fresh perspective that suddenly made sense of the nonsensical. But in this case, she remained as puzzled as he was.

"There's something particularly ugly about killing a homeless person," she said angrily.

"Why do you say that?"

"Because the homeless are so vulnerable. They've lost so much already. And from what you told me, this man had mental problems as well. It just seems terribly unfair to injure someone who's helpless like that."

"Ed Gomez thinks it may be a hate crime."

"Does he? There certainly is enough hate in the world these days. What do you think?"

"I don't know. There are a lot of complicating factors. The one that interests me the most at the moment is that our crazy man was also a first-rate artist—according to Howie and Claire, anyway."

"Well, why not, Jack? Maybe you need to be a little crazy to *be* first-rate. Think of van Gogh."

"Emma, van Gogh didn't go around with a Beretta and a blackboard around his neck pushing a shopping cart down the highway."

"Yes, but he could have, don't you think? . . . you know, I think I like this Rainbow Man, Jack. I hope you find whoever shot him."

Jack smiled at Emma's leap of faith, turning the dead man into a mad but likeable genius.

"There's one more thing," Jack mentioned. He was hesitant to bring this up because he didn't want Emma to worry. But he needed her seeing-eye assistance. "When Howie and Claire dropped me off this afternoon from the hospital, I could have sworn someone had been in our house. Do me a favor, Emma—look around a bit and see if anything's missing or been moved. Particularly in the upstairs office."

Without a word, Emma sighed and left the kitchen to investigate. Jack busied himself straining the chicken bones from the soup while Emma wandered through the house. She was gone for nearly fifteen minutes. When she came back to the kitchen, she was upset.

"Damn it, Jack! Someone's gone through my desk. And our filing cabinet. Even our clothes drawers!"

"Is anything missing?"

"Nothing's missing that I can tell. But things have been moved around. It's not just one thing, it's a lot of things. Do you know who it was and what they were looking for?"

Jack shook his head. "I don't have a clue. Tell me, did you leave the downstairs bathroom window open this morning?"

"Let me think . . . no, I don't think so. But there's a chance I left it unlatched."

"Well, that's probably how they got in." He could visualize how it would be: Someone walking around the outside of the house checking all the windows, finding a bathroom window that opened, then climbing through. The intruder almost certainly left by the front door, which explained why the dead bolt was open and Sushi outside. It wasn't a casual burglar, or their TV set and CD player would be gone.

Jack stood with a tomato in his hand, lost in thought. Why break into Howie's cabin last night and then his house today? What did Wilder & Associate have that someone wanted? He couldn't imagine. Jack was mulling over the possibilities when the kitchen telephone rang. It was San Francisco getting back to him about the Beretta 9mm semiautomatic. Emma took the tomato from his hand, sensing that dinner could be a long time coming to the table tonight unless she pitched in.

"Commander Wilder? This is Sergeant Henderson of the SFPD. Major Yang asked me to call you, sir."

"Yes?" purred Jack. Sergeant Henderson had an unusual voice, swallowing his words and speaking from the back of his throat. Jack often tried to imagine people from their voices. Sergeant Henderson, he sensed, was a shy and gangly man making an effort to survive in a garrulous profession. Most likely it was an annoying task for him to make nice to retired brass in faraway New Mexico, but if so, he was hiding his annoyance very well.

"I'm sorry this has taken so long to get back to you,

Commander. I ran the serial number of the gun you were interested in through the NCIC computer, but I got a flag telling me that all inquiries about that particular weapon needed to be directed to a Bureau number in Washington. Then it took me a while to find someone who knew anything about your Beretta."

Long time? Jack thought with amusement. It had been less than an hour since he had spoken with Tommy Yang, setting this inquiry in motion. *You should live in Mexico, Sergeant!*

But Jack only said: "It seems this gun has a history, huh?"

"Yes. The Beretta is connected to an old murder investigation—it was stolen from an art collector by the name of Juan Antonio Mendez, who was found dead in his home in Santa Fe in a 1974 murder/burglary case that's still unsolved. Mendez was an Argentinean—he happened to be the nephew of the president of Argentina, which is why the FBI got involved. The file is still open, though there hasn't been any activity in the case for over twenty years."

"An art collector? Well, that's very interesting. Was he shot?"

"No, his head was bashed in with the base of a floor lamp. If you're interested, I can give you the names of the Santa Fe detective and the special agent from the Bureau who led the investigation back then. Hard to say if they're still around, of course."

"Well, I'll see if I can chase them down," Jack said. "I'd like to see the file, if that's possible."

"You'll need to ask the FBI for that, I'm afraid."

The sergeant gave Jack two names. Lieutenant Ernesto Flores of the Santa Fe Police Department was the man who caught the case originally in August 1974. Then three months later, when the investigation appeared stalled, Special Agent William S. Katz of the FBI took over. Jack hoped he could locate them.

"Let me know if I can help you with anything else," the sergeant said politely, clearly eager to get back to more important matters than an unsolved murder/burglary from a quarter of a century ago.

The moment he hung up, Jack repeated the important names to himself. Just to be safe, he also spoke the infor-

mation into a tiny cassette recorder he kept on a shelf near
the kitchen telephone. First he needed to find the end of
the last message. It was a shopping list he had made for
himself a week ago: ". . . garlic, one can tomato paste,
one pound prawns, tequila . . ." A very good meal, Jack
remembered fondly, rewinding to the head of the tape. He
pressed the record button and said distinctly: "Lieutenant
Ernesto Flores, Santa Fe, 1974 . . . S. A. William S. Katz . . .
Juan Antonio Mendez, Argentina."

On Friday morning, after Emma left for work, Jack sat
at his kitchen table with the telephone, gaining leads, reaching dead ends, patiently speaking with one person after
another. He enjoyed this sort of work. It was slow but
satisfying to follow an old trail in a methodical manner,
retrieving seemingly lost information from the past.

He discovered that FBI Special Agent William S. Katz
had died of natural causes in 1987, and that no new mate-
rial had been added to the file of the unsolved murder of
Juan Antonio Mendez since 1979, five years after the crime,
when for all practical purposes, the case had been left to
dangle forever. Of course, there were thousands of unsolved cases such as this in police files, cases never officially
closed but left forgotten. In the late morning, Jack managed
to reach an old FBI friend in Denver, Special Agent Kevin
Neimeyer, who promised to fax him a copy of the Bureau's
file on the case.

Jack had luck in Santa Fe. He spoke to a Lieutenant
Jimmy Martinez, who did some checking and called him
back with the name of an old police buddy of Lieutenant
Flores, a Sergeant Chris Pachecho—evidently Lieutenant
Pachecho now. Flores had retired from the Santa Fe police
in 1982, but Pachecho was a younger man and had only
retired himself in 1996. Jack was able to get a phone number for the retired lieutenant in the southern New Mexico
town of Truth or Consequences, surely the only place in
the world ever named after a television game show. Pachecho was helpful on the phone, but unfortunately he had
lost touch with Ernesto Flores many years ago. He really
didn't know if Flores was still alive, but he had a number
for Ernesto's niece, Nancy, who might know where Ernesto was.

Working the telephone in this way, Jack made his way slowly into the past. It was time-consuming work. Some people that Jack called were not in their offices or at their homes, and he had to wait for them to call him back. Around noon, his left arm was starting to cramp from holding the telephone to his ear, and he took a short break to throw a stick outside for Katya. Close to one o'clock he began to wonder why Howie had not reported in. He tried Howie's cell phone, but there was no answer. This was annoying. Jack had bought Howie a cell phone and paid the exorbitant monthly charges so that he could be reached when he was in the field. But Howie was not the cell phone type; half the time, he simply forgot the thing at home.

"To be honest, I feel embarrassed going around with a cell phone," Howie complained. "Like I'm some big-shot Hollywood phony."

"Tough!" Jack told him in return. "Use the damn thing anyway, please. There are times when I must be able to reach you."

Times such as now, for instance. Despite the annoyance of an assistant who had gone missing, Jack kept on with his telephone canvassing, and close to four in the afternoon, he finally reached Ernesto Flores, the Santa Fe lieutenant who had long ago headed the investigation into the death of Juan Antonio Mendez. The ex-cop lived today in Tempe, Arizona, with his son and daughter-in-law, a spry old man of eighty-nine who was glad to talk about an old murder case while a TV game show played somewhere in the room.

"Well, yes, I *do* remember that one," he said wistfully. There was a faraway quality in his voice that worried Jack just a little. "I always thought some kids did it—we never found them, though."

"Kids?" Jack prodded.

"The way the crime scene was set up, it looked like the victim came home unexpectedly and surprised a burglary in progress. The gun you mentioned, the nine-millimeter Beretta, was registered to Juan Antonio Mendez—we knew from his housekeeper that he kept it in a drawer in his downstairs den. The crime happened at night, by the way, about ten or eleven o'clock, I remember. Mendez came back early from a party because he wasn't feeling well. He must have come into his house, sensed something was wrong, picked up the Beretta, and then gone into his living room to look around. You know how these things go—Mendez was inexperienced with firearms and probably would have been safer without a gun. Somehow the burglars got the jump on him. There was a fight, some furniture got knocked over in the scuffle, and a few shots were fired into the ceiling and walls. By the time it was over, the burglars had bashed the guy's head in with the base of a floor lamp, and they kept the Beretta for a souvenir. The gun never turned up, anyway . . . where did you say you found it, Commander?"

Jack simplified the story, saying only that the Beretta had been found in the possession of a homeless person who had himself become a murder victim.

"Well, isn't that the darnedest thing?" said the retired lieutenant. "I can't tell you how much time I spent trying to find that gun!"

"You keep saying *they*," Jack mentioned. "What makes you think there was more than one burglar?"

"Just from the way the crime scene was arranged. The victim was strong—a homosexual, by the way—a big man who worked out in a gym and took care of himself. It looked to me like at least two kids were involved. One must have held Mendez and tried to get the gun from his hands, while the other worked him over and struck him with the lamp, which was the fatal blow."

"And what made you conclude the burglars were kids?"

"Because of the nature of what was stolen—booze, stereo equipment, stuff like that. There were bearer bonds in the house and some other things that more experienced burglars would have taken. Of course, we investigated the victim's personal life as well to see if someone had a motive to kill him and had maybe arranged a make-believe burglary to throw us off. But that didn't lead anywhere. Mendez was a lonely man with few friends, and those few friends all had very good alibis for the night of the killing. The way I always imagined it, some local teenagers were bored and decided to have themselves a little fun, and then the whole thing turned sour and got out of hand when the owner of the house appeared with a gun."

"You said that Mendez was an art collector. Was his collection in the house?"

"Oh, sure. But it was mostly undisturbed."

"*Mostly* undisturbed?" Jack pressed.

"Well, this is the strange part about the case. Like I told you, most of the stuff that was taken was the kind of things kids would go after—booze and electronics. But there was one painting that was snatched. Just one, but it happened to be the most valuable piece in the collection. To tell you the truth, I was never able to figure out why the kids took it, or even how they knew it was so valuable. For a while I had a theory that maybe someone else came by that night after the kids had left. Someone more experienced who saw the body on the floor and the way the house was trashed and took advantage of the situation to get a little something for himself. But this idea went nowhere. You know how it is. Maybe I would have gotten somewhere eventually, but the FBI took over the case."

"They didn't get anywhere either," Jack assured the old cop. "Tell me about the painting that was stolen."

"Well, it was a landscape. A desert scene at night with a moon in the sky. Hard to believe, but the thing was worth a hundred grand back in seventy-four, so it must be worth a fortune today. It never turned up anywhere, as far as I know."

"Do you remember the artist?"

The old man sighed. "It was that old woman. The one with the craggy face who lived by herself up there in northern New Mexico in the middle of nowhere . . . Christ, my memory's gone for names!"

"Georgia O'Keeffe?" Jack asked with a surge of interest.

"Yeah, that's the lady."

"I see. And the painting never turned up?" Jack said mildly. "You're right, of course. A Georgia O'Keeffe would be worth a good deal more than a hundred thousand dollars today. Tell me . . ."

Jack paused. He almost didn't want to ask the question. He had a sweet and palpable sense of connection, of knowing the answer in advance.

". . . tell me, Lieutenant. What was the name of this painting?"

"The name of the painting? Wait a minute . . . 'Blue Moon,' " said the old cop. "No, '*Red* Moon'—that's it. The moon in the painting was blood red—not very realistic, if you ask me. But what do I know?"

"Bull's-eye!" said Jack, finishing the conversation and putting down the receiver.

Red Moon! And wasn't it interesting, Jack thought gleefully, that the homeless Rainbow Man had died with the name of this stolen Georgia O'Keeffe painting on his lips less than a mile from the home of Barbara Vandenberg Stone, who happened to own the largest private O'Keeffe collection in New Mexico?

The trail was suddenly hot, and Jack was eager to get going. But he needed his assistant and wheels to get around. He tried Howie's cell phone number again, but there was still no answer.

"Damn it, Howie!" Jack cried in frustration, slamming down the phone. "Where the hell are you?"

Five

Howard Moon Deer began Friday morning in a fine mood. He drove by himself, enjoying the solitude in the red Toyota pickup on the two-lane highway that cut northwest across the open desert to Wind Horse Mountain, where Robin Vandenberg had his tree house.

The weather had cleared overnight, leaving a fresh blue autumn morning. The full extent of the San Geronimo valley was visible for the first time in several days: a great high desert bowl nearly fifty miles across, surrounded by a ring of solemn mountains. Seen in its totality, it was a forlorn landscape, wide and empty, like being on the roof of the world. Some of the local New Agers liked to compare San Geronimo to Tibet, but Howie always thought more of cheesy old science fiction movies—a lost valley in which you could almost imagine flying saucers landing on the sagebrush. The tallest mountain was San Geronimo

Peak to the east, slightly over thirteen thousand feet, white and sparkling this morning in its new coat of snow, with the town of San Geronimo sprawled out at its feet. Wind Horse Mountain, where Howie was headed, was only eleven thousand feet, just a hill as things went in this part of the Southern Rockies.

Howie had phoned Robin earlier in the morning to say he would stop by with a refund check. "Can't you just put the check in the mail?" Robin had asked over the phone in a dead monotone, his voice empty of life. "Honestly, I'm not in the mood for company right now."

"Look, I'm going to be in your neighborhood anyway, and I'll need you to sign a receipt for our bookkeeping," Howie lied. "I'll only stop by for a minute. Besides, I'm curious to see your tree house."

In the end, Howie had more energy to insist than Robin Vandenberg did to object. Something had certainly happened to Robin since their office meeting on Wednesday morning, and Howie was determined to find out what it was. After a forty-five-minute drive, the highway left the desert and became a dirt road as it climbed steeply into the trees. Howie passed geodesic domes and school buses with metal chimneys sticking out their tops and strangely shaped free-form adobe homes. There were even a few tipis.

The local name for Wind Horse Mountain was Hippie Hill, because the land was remote and cheap and you could live here pretty much as you pleased, unfettered by county building codes. Most of the original 1960s hippies were gone by now, replaced by a younger retro generation that had grown up on old Grateful Dead albums and liked to pretend they were flower children spawned from the Summer of Love. Recently there had been a new migration of the Y2K crowd here as well, people who were fleeing the cities and suburbs, determined to grow their own food and live off the land. Howie sometimes imagined that this was the way the world would end, not with a bang, but with a bunch of crazy paleface Americans playing Indians in the woods.

The snow, which was almost completely melted down in the desert, became deeper as Howie climbed in altitude. The road had been plowed, but it was treacherously clogged with mud and ice. Howie put the Toyota into four-wheel drive around nine thousand feet, just as he was passing the turnoff to the Wind Horse Mountain Zen Institute. There were no signs to the institute, for it was said that true seekers would find the way, and all others need not apply. Howie knew the way because he had briefly dated a young woman named Shanti, who had spent a summer here "trying to find herself." She had taught Howie Tantric yoga, some intriguing positions designed to achieve enlightenment through sex, and for a few months he had been very enlightened indeed.

Howie continued past the unmarked road to the Zen Institute through woods that were lovely, dark, and deep. At last, almost at the top of the mountain, he came to the driveway to Robin's property. The driveway was only partially plowed by some four-wheel drive SUV megamonster that obviously had more clearance and power than the Toyota. Howie parked along the side of the main road, not wanting to get stuck. He slung his green day pack on his back and walked up the driveway into a forest of old evergreens whose branches were heavy with snow.

After a five-minute walk, he turned a corner of the road and saw a green Land Rover with a sticker on the rear bumper that read I BRAKE FOR ELVES. It took Howie a moment to see the tree house itself, since it was covered with roughly cut wooden shingles that almost succeeded in camouflaging the structure into the forest. The main part of the house was a rustic two-story hexagon that rested on the ground, encircling the biggest, oldest mother of all fir trees in the forest. It looked like a place where an elf or a friendly hobbit might be happy. There were oddly shaped round windows and a peaked roof—just a little too cute for Howie's taste. He gradually let his eyes climb up the trunk of the huge tree. About twenty feet above the roof of the lower cabin, there was another structure, the tree house proper, which hung suspended above the forest floor, supported by cables attached to the limbs. Another ten or fifteen feet above this, there was an open platform high in the upper branches, probably used more in the summer months than the winter. The three levels—the cabin on the ground, the tree house proper, and the open platform—were connected by an ingenious highway of rope ladders and suspended walkways. The whole thing was a boy's ultimate fantasy, very Swiss Family Robinson.

Howie approached the lower cabin. There was smoke rising from an elaborately long and meandering stovepipe that worked its way through the branches of the tree. The front door was handmade like everything else here—a Dutch door, with a lower and upper half that opened separately. The doorbell was a string of sleigh bells attached to a leather strap. Howie gave the strap a jingle.

"You found me," Robin said without enthusiasm, opening both doors.

"Hey, this is an amazing place you've got here!" Howie told him.

"Well, I like trees," Robin said with a shrug. "In the eighties, I spent four months living up a tree in the north of England, as part of a protest. It was a forest that lumber interests wanted to cut down. We stopped them."

"I remember hearing about that," Howie agreed. "There are still some protesters living in trees in northern California, doing the same thing."

Again, the same lifeless shrug. "For some people it was a hardship I guess, living in a tree for months at a time. But I loved it. I found I could think very clearly up there. I didn't want to come down."

"Maybe you were a squirrel in a previous lifetime?" Howie suggested.

Robin only sighed. He didn't invite Howie inside. His face looked sallow and pinched. He was dressed in jeans and a thick black turtleneck sweater, his blond ponytail pulled back tightly from his face. On Wednesday morning he had looked so boyishly bright that Howie found it hard to believe he was in his early forties. But today that boyishness was gone, and Robin appeared shriveled and older than his age.

"So you have the check?" Robin asked.

"I just have to make it out," Howie told him, taking the green day pack from his back. "May I come in? It would be easier to write the check if I have a table."

Reluctantly, Robin stepped aside to let Howie into a sitting room that was dark with polished wood, as neat and small as a ship's cabin.

"Wow!" said Howie, The room wrapped around the

trunk of the tree. There were small tables and chairs, and candles in pewter holders on the tidy shelves. At the far side of the room, a cozy fire burned in a small cast-iron stove. Howie had to bend over to keep from hitting his head on the low ceiling.

"I feel like I've just stepped into a children's book," Howie admitted. *"Wind in the Willows,* maybe."

"Arthur Rackham," Robin agreed. "That's who illustrated *Wind in the Willows.* He's my favorite artist."

Robin seemed to perk up slightly, talking about art. Howie had heard people describe everyone from Brueghel to Jackson Pollock as their favorite artist. But never Arthur Rackham.

"Will you show me around? I'd really love to see the tree house itself," Howie asked.

"Frankly, I'm not up to it. I didn't sleep well last night."

"I'd really enjoy seeing what you've done," Howie pressed. "You know what they say about us Indians—we were the first environmentalists. I'm big on trees myself."

"Well, maybe just a quick tour. . . ."

Robin led the way through a trapdoor from the sitting room upstairs to a tidy little bedroom above. The second level was smaller and even more spartan than down below. There was a single bed at one end and a bookshelf of polished mahogany. Howie was not surprised to see that Robin's choice of literature ran to fantasy: *The Lord of the Rings, Treasure Island, Robinson Crusoe,* and a scattering of Jules Verne, Robert Heinlein, and stories of dragons and princesses and knights in shining armor. It would have been a very nice bedroom for any ten-year-old. But Robin Vandenberg was not ten, and Howie felt a vague undercurrent of wrongness. As he continued to scan the bedroom, his eye fell upon a series of framed photographs hanging on the wall just to the side of the bed, and everything that seemed wrong coalesced. Howie walked closer to see the photographs properly. They were old black-and-white prints of prepubescent girls, either entirely undressed or wearing very little. There were six photographs in all.

"They're Lewis Carroll's," Robin told him defensively.

As it happened, Howie knew that, though he wasn't certain that this made their presence in Robin's bedroom any better. Howie had seen some of these photographs before in the Metropolitan Museum in New York, and even a few in *The New Yorker.* The great Victorian mathematician and author of *Alice in Wonderland* had enjoyed photographing unclothed little girls. Two of the pictures above Robin's bed were of Alice herself, dark-haired and innocently sexual, gazing into the camera lens with all the uncensored libido of childhood glittering mischievously in her eyes. It was hard to call the photographs pornography; frankly, Howie wasn't certain *what* to call them. They were the work, after all, of one of the great figures of the nineteenth century and had been displayed in museums around the world. But they worried Howie nevertheless.

He turned back to Robin, who was watching him intently.

"I know what you're thinking," he said in a sullen voice. "But it's not like that. Dirty minds make innocent things seem unnatural. It's not my fault that the world's gone hysterical about sex."

Howie thought this was as good a moment as any to bring up what Gilmer Good Day had told him. Frankly, it was a subject Howie found embarrassing and would rather have left alone.

"Look, I know all about your meltdown in New York," he said.

Robin stiffened. "What do you mean?"

"I know that you were arrested for molesting a young girl and that your mother had to pay the parents a lot of money to get you off."

"Who told you that?" he cried angrily, his face flushing red. "It's a lie! It's a goddamn lie!"

"It doesn't matter who told me. I'm a private investigator, and I find things out that I need to know."

"It was Sherman, wasn't it? Oh, that shit! My God, that asshole, that goddamn sucking shit hole. . . ."

Robin went on for some time in this manner, unleashing a string of obscenities unlike anything Howie had ever heard. Robin was so angry that the obscenities came tripping out of his mouth as jumbled malapropisms, some very original, with phrases like sucking shit hole that Howie found highly evocative. He had never seen anyone get so red-faced angry quite so fast. "Shit balls screw!" Robin cried, slamming a fist down on one of his tiny elfish tables. "Tell me! It was Sherman, wasn't it?"

"Well, suppose it was?" Howie countered. It wasn't Sherman Stone, of course, who had told Howie about the New York meltdown, but he was interested in gleaning more from Robin's rage.

"I'm going to kill him, I really truly deeply am," Robin said more calmly. The English language was almost starting to return to him. "That man is evil. I just wish I could erase him from the universe, Moon Deer."

"Then, why did you call Jack and me off the investigation?"

"*Why*?" Robin shouted. "For God's sake, I should think that's pretty goddamn obvious! *This* is the reason. He blackmailed me. And then he went and told you about it anyway! That shit, that goddamn. . . ."

"About what happened in New York?"

"Of *course* about what happened in New York! What the hell else are we talking about? He came over here on Wednesday night and laid it out for me, all the filth—how it would be for me in San Geronimo if a rumor got out that I was some kind of monstrous sex offender who had been arrested in New York for molesting a little girl. What gets me is that it's so unfair. So goddamn unfair! It's not even true, for chrissake—I wasn't charged with anything. It was all a mistake. But who would believe me? There's no defense against a rumor like that. For chrissake, I *work* with children—I told you, I'm teaching art at this alternative school. I'd lose my job, people would never let me near their kids again!"

"So you did what Sherman told you?"

"Wouldn't you? That bastard was holding a gun against my head. He threatened to destroy my life. My God, a thing like that—I'd have to leave here and go somewhere else."

Robin Vandenberg was close to tears, emotionally devastated. Howie proceeded cautiously, in the most gentle voice he could summon. "So he blackmailed you. What did he want?"

"He wanted me to fire you and Jack. He didn't want there to be any kind of investigation. So I did it. I did what he said. And then he went and told you anyway!"

"But how did he find out that you had hired me and Jack?"

"I don't know. I assumed maybe Lionel told him, or Pooh, They're all against me. They really are."

"How about your troubles in New York? Did Sherman say how he learned about that?"

"Oh, well, *yeah*! I mean, *this* part is no mystery! My wonderful mother told him. Who else? She tells Sherman everything. Just like she's going to leave that bastard all her money. Why should she worry about her children?"

"Yet she paid to get you out of your New York jam," Howie mentioned. "That shows some concern for you, doesn't it?"

Robin laughed bitterly. "She did that for herself, not for me. So there wouldn't be a scandal, you see. She courts a certain level of notoriety, you understand—she's such an egomaniac, she likes to flaunt convention, knowing it will get her noticed. But my New York thing promised to be too sleazy even for her. I think she was afraid respectable art dealers wouldn't take her seriously anymore."

"What exactly happened in New York, Robin?"

Robin Vandenberg sighed and shook his head. "You want to know? All right, I'll show you. Come with me."

"Where are we going?"

"Upstairs."

Howie followed Robin Vandenberg up a rope ladder that was dangling from the tree's upper branches. The ladder was made of wooden steps with holes drilled out at each end and a knotted rope passing through. Clever, but Howie was not prepared for the way the ladder twisted and swayed as he climbed. He had a queasy feeling in his stomach, brushing sometimes against the boughs of the tree. He concentrated on looking upward to where he was going, rather than downward at the dwindling ground. Robin climbed like a monkey, completely at home, disappearing quickly through a hole in the floor of the next level up. Howie followed more slowly, but at last he came out through the trapdoor that led into a low-ceilinged room. Robin stood waiting.

"Amazing!" said Howie, looking about him.

"It took me nearly five years to build this," Robin said proudly.

This mid-level of the tree was Robin Vandenberg's art studio. Like everything else he made, the carpentry work was exquisite and detailed and small—everything crafted, it seemed, for tiny folk. Much smaller folk, certainly, than Howard Moon Deer, who felt large and clumsy in the space, unable to stand fully upright. There was an easel, a tiny chair, and a small workbench on one side of the room near a window. The rest of the space was taken up with cleverly built cabinets and wooden drawers that were full of drawings, canvases, and art supplies. A door led to the platform deck outside in the branches, where Robin said he worked in the summer. Outside the window Howie could see a wicker hot-air balloon basket on a pulley and rope in which Robin might raise and lower various art supplies to this level of the tree.

As for the art, it was all fantasy—pictures of elves, fairies, wizards, gnomes, and monsters—mostly watercolors, but also a few oils. There were princesses in high towers, and elfin warriors with swords drawn to meet their doom. Oddly, the work wasn't very good. At least, it seemed odd to Howie because Robin Vandenberg was clearly a master carpenter, very good with his hands. But when it came to art, his technique was not particularly skillful. The colors were often muddy, and the compositions seemed lopsided and unpleasing to the eye. At best they had a kind of comic-book look to them. With all the New Agers in town, there would be a market for this sort of fantasy art, but Robin had not quite pulled it off. Howie could see why he would need to hold down a straight job teaching school.

"Okay, look at these," Robin said, pulling out a group of unmatted watercolors from a sliding wooden drawer. "This is Sun Fei. I wasn't *molesting* her. My God, I was only *drawing* her! It was art. But everyone just went off the deep end about it."

Sun Fei was a Chinese girl, eleven or twelve, exotically beautiful. Robin had done more than a dozen watercolors of her as a little naked fairy, often in a diaphanous robe, but mostly wearing nothing at all. Sometimes she hovered in the forest air, her delicate wings beating like a dragonfly. In other scenes, she knelt by small forest ponds, or rode on the back of friendly animals. All in all it was a pretty world she inhabited in Robin's imagination, and he had managed to draw her with more skill than he had accomplished with his other work. The drawings were pure fantasy, but not a particularly dark fantasy, as far as Howie could judge.

"She was the ultimate fairy," Robin said with a small sigh of regret. "I just had to draw her."

"Then, you didn't . . . well, you know."

"No, I did not touch her. I am *not* a pedophile," Robin said with a clenched jaw. "I am an artist, and she was my model."

"And this is the whole story?"

"All there is to it. Sun Fei's parents ran a small Chinese lunch counter on the ground floor of my building on Prince Street. We became friends after I started going there for takeout. She was such a sweet little girl, entirely natural. Eventually I asked her to pose for me, and it was no big deal, it was totally innocent. But then her parents found out, and they took it the wrong way. They really flipped out. It was nuts how the whole thing got misinterpreted by people. My mother had to give the family twenty thousand dollars to take care of their shocked sensibilities. Frankly, I think Mom got taken for a ride—you should have seen this family. They would have *sold* me that child for about a quarter of that!"

Howie was having trouble making up his mind if Robin Vandenberg was an innocent artist or a dirty old man, or some combination of both.

"Were you arrested?" he asked.

"Well, the cops hauled me in one afternoon. It was a gruesome experience, but I was never actually charged. Then after Mom paid off the father, the police didn't really have any evidence, so they never pursued the matter. Sun Fei, bless her, stuck to her story—she told them that all I did was draw her."

"Her story?"

"The truth," Robin insisted. "It's not my fault we live in an age of sexual hysteria. But you can see how this would look if it got around town. My God, I'd have to move to South America . . . you know, what really gets me is that

Sherman went ahead and told you about this after I kept
my part of the bargain! I detest that man, I really do."

"Did he say why he wanted you to call off Jack and me?"

"He didn't need to. I understood perfectly well. There
are a lot of things you could uncover that Sherman
wouldn't want my mother to know. Like I told you
Wednesday morning, my mother indulges him, but even
she has her limits." A cold smile came to Robin's lips.
"You know what? I just thought of something. Now that
Sherman's not keeping his side of his little blackmail, I'm
free to do what I like. I don't want your refund after all—
I want you and Jack to keep on digging and find out whatever you can about the bastard."

"You want us to stay on the case?"

"You bet."

Howie felt uneasy at being part of anyone's revenge. "I'll
need to consult Jack about this," he said. "We'll get back
to you."

"I'll give you more money," Robin promised. "I'll give
you anything you want. Just get the dirt on my goddamn
stepfather!"

Howie climbed down the unsteady ladder to the ground.
It appeared they had a client again after all. If they could
stomach the job.

Six

Driving down from Wind Horse Mountain, Howie remembered his cell phone. Frankly, he did not remember his cell
phone very often. As far as Howie was concerned, cell
phones were a kind of electronic mosquito. They disturbed
his serenity, his sense that one should not have to be at
the beck and call of the hysterical world.

Nevertheless, he knew that Jack would be wanting to
hear from him. While negotiating the muddy road, he

picked up the phone from where he had thrown it this morning onto the passenger seat. He pressed Jack's preset number, but the call didn't go through. The small display screen read NO SERVICE. Cell phone service in northern New Mexico was spotty at best, and apparently he was in one of San Geronimo's many black holes. Secretly, Howie rejoiced.

"I tried, Jack!"

The road from Wind Horse Mountain joined Highway 270 just above the long grade where Howie had spoken to the Rainbow Man in the snow on Wednesday night. From this intersection Howie could choose to go north to his cabin or south into town. He turned south, slowing down as he approached the spot at the top of the hill where he had seen the homeless man with his shopping cart.

The shopping cart!

"Sucking shit hole!" Howie said aloud, letting his foot off the gas. Unfortunately, he had forgotten all about the shopping cart, and both Jack and Ed Gomez were going to be annoyed with him. As far as Howie could remember— and he had come to doubt his memory—the Rainbow Man had his supermarket cart at this spot on Wednesday night, but he didn't have it on Thursday morning when Howie had been skiing with Jonathan. So where was the Rainbow Man's portable home?

Howie did a U-turn and came around to park on the shoulder of the road at the top of the hill. He turned off the engine and stepped from the cab with a pair of Jack's old field binoculars that were kept in the glove compartment. The hill stood at an altitude of nearly 8,300 feet, offering a perfect view of the desert and mountains in all directions. Howie raised the binoculars to his eyes and began to scan methodically from south to east, past houses, sagebrush, and higher areas of piñon and juniper. A mile or so almost due east of where he was standing, Howie found the small village of Valverde, and—higher in altitude—the expensive houses perched on the top of the Valverde Mesa with their grand view of everything. He could just make out a corner of the Vandenberg Stone estate.

He kept scanning gradually northward with the binoculars, over the fields and houses and double-wide trailers.

About a half mile from Valverde Mesa, he spotted the trail where he had skied with Jonathan yesterday morning. He found the Rio San Geronimo, the field where he had seen the wounded man limping, and the stand of trees by the river where he had died. As he continued to scan, his binoculars found the highway and two black New Mexico State Police cars parked at a pull-off alongside the river, not far from where Howie had been attacked.

Howie lowered the binoculars and studied the landscape with his naked eye. The way the roads were laid out, he hadn't realized how close together everything was. By automobile Valverde Mesa, the place by the river where the homeless man had died, and the hill where Howie stood now were quite distant from each other. But as the crow flew, it was a different matter. Howie imagined someone could walk from Valverde Mesa overland to where the Rainbow Man had died in less than fifteen minutes. And, of course, it would be much faster still if you had a four-wheel ATV or maybe. . . .

A snowmobile!

Howie felt like kicking himself! He had completely forgotten about the snowmobile and the figure in black with the helmet he had seen yesterday morning only minutes before he heard the rifle shot. Sadly, his memory was a piece of Swiss cheese with many holes. But it was all coming back to him at last, unless he had forgotten something else.

He stood with the binoculars lowered by his side, taking in the larger picture: the place by the river where a mad but unusually talented homeless artist had died, and the big Vandenberg Stone estate on the mesa, where the matriarch of the San Geronimo art scene lived with her heroin-snorting, jewel-thieving, blackmailing husband. Howie could feel the palpable sense of connection between the two locales.

He returned to the cab of the truck and tried Jack again on the cell phone. This time, nothing happened at all, not even a NO SERVICE announcement. On closer examination, Howie saw that he had let the battery run down—another annoying part of being a cell phone owner, of course, was that you had to take time off from thinking about more important matters (sex, food, and the meaning of life), to remember to recharge boring little batteries.

"Hell, I'm just not a cell phone type, Jack!" Howie said aloud to his absent boss. In disgust, he threw down the useless device onto the passenger seat. He put the binoculars in his day pack, locked up the truck, and headed off on foot in search of a missing supermarket shopping cart.

The ground was wet and often muddy, but Howie had his fur-lined Sorel boots, which helped in this terrain. He walked down a sloping hillside of piñon toward the river where the homeless man had died. The distance was farther than it appeared from the road, in part because the trees made it impossible to walk in a straight line. He passed signs that animals had come and gone. Elk poop. Owl droppings. Some very large holes whose occupants Howie could only guess at.

Howie climbed down into the thick undergrowth alongside the Rio San Geronimo. He imagined that the two state police cars he had seen with his binoculars had something to do with a continuing investigation of the crime scene, so he stayed well east of that area, wishing to avoid any more official conversations. He crossed the river on a fallen tree, feeling lucky to have gotten to the far side in a dry condition. Once on the north bank, he climbed out of the trees and quickly found the fence in the field where he had skied yesterday with Jonathan. The snow was completely melted, so there were no ski tracks, but Howie was able to walk along the side of the fence and retrace their route.

After walking for ten minutes, he came to the place where he had looked up from the trail and seen the snowmobile and rider above him on a hill. He trudged up the hill, stopping every now and then to catch his breath—it was steeper and higher than it appeared from the bottom. There was another good view from the top when he got there. To the southeast he could see the Vandenberg Stone house very clearly now from where it stood behind a high adobe wall on Valverde Mesa. This hill would have made a good place for someone who needed a lookout to spot something, or somebody. But there was no sign that a snowmobile had been here yesterday. Howie was starting to think that perhaps his memory was still playing tricks on him when he spotted a small patch of snow on the north side of a clump of piñon. On the snow were the unmistakable tread marks of a snowmobile.

Howie kept searching for more tracks, walking in a wide circle. The sun was high in the sky, and the temperature was nearly sixty, not good weather for snow to survive. Still, there were a few remaining patches of Wednesday's storm here and there in shaded places, and Howie found more tread marks about fifty feet to the southeast of the first patch. The snowmobile had compressed the snow so that it melted more slowly than on the rest of the ground. Five minutes later he found a third track. Together, the three tracks formed an arrow that pointed in a straight line to the Vandenberg Stone estate to the top of the mesa.

Howie needed no more encouragement. He followed the arrow to Barbara Vandenberg and her husband Sherman Stone.

Seven

The Vandenberg Stone house was a sprawling adobe hacienda, salmon-pink in color, beautifully aged, surrounded by big old trees and several acres of grounds that were overgrown in a willful neglect. The place had a kind of 1920s silent movie star grandeur to it, a sleepy sense of decay. A meandering old adobe wall, crumbling in places, enclosed the entire estate, the same salmon-pink color as the house.

Approaching the house overland from the north, Howie encountered a heavy iron gate set into the wall. The gate was hanging open, partially off its hinges, which Howie took as an invitation to walk inside. A path took him through the bare late October branches of an apple orchard and then past a circular stone fountain that was empty of water. It was probably very pretty here in the summer, but at this time of year, the grounds seemed desolate and sad.

The path led him around the side of a three-car garage

that stood across a gravel driveway from the main house. The garage was big and old-fashioned with a room on top, perhaps used for servants' quarters. The garage doors were closed, but Howie circled the building and found a dusty window on one side. He peered through the glass into the gloomy interior and was not surprised to see a shiny black snowmobile sitting in the half-light.

There was a side door near the window, and Howie was tempted to get a closer look at the snowmobile. The silence of the big house nearby was thick and profound; there appeared to be no one around. He opened the side door into a dark, cool garage interior, smelling of oil and dust. He decided to chance a quick exploration. He walked inside, leaving the door open behind him to allow as much light in as possible. There was an old Bentley sitting in one of the carports; a classy car, but it looked as if it hadn't been driven in years. In the middle port stood a more practical automobile for New Mexico, a recent model Land Rover. The snowmobile was parked in the third port, the one closest to the side door. It was a fancy new Yamaha.

Howie walked in a slow circle around the snowmobile wishing he had a flashlight so he could see better. He wasn't certain what he was looking for. Blood? A stray bullet shell? Some announcement that this was the snowmobile he had seen on Thursday morning? But there was nothing. Or if there was, Howie did not have the forensic skill to spot it.

Since there was no one around, he climbed onto the saddle of the snowmobile and took hold of the two handlebars. *"Vroom! Vroom!"* he said.

"What are you doing in there?" a voice asked sharply.

Howie was so startled he bit his tongue. There was a figure standing in the door where he had entered. It was a woman, though he couldn't see her face properly with the light behind her. He sensed that she was young by the way she was standing, so he knew it couldn't be the owner of the house, Barbara Vandenberg Stone.

"I, uh . . . well, I was just admiring the snowmobile," Howie stammered nonsensically.

"You're trespassing," she told him.

Howie climbed off the saddle apologetically. "Look, I'm

sorry. I was hoping to speak with Mrs. Stone, and I got a little carried away, I guess."

"If you wanted to see Mrs. Stone, you should have come to the house."

"Are you, uh, one of the family?"

"I work here," the woman told him. "I'm the *maid*," she added, emphasizing the last word in a voice that carried the slightest hint of sarcasm.

Howie hoisted his day pack over his shoulder and followed the woman out of the garage door into the sunlight. To his surprise, he saw that she was Indian. She had smooth olive skin, black hair, dark eyes, and a small mole on the corner of her mouth. Sarcasm or not, she was indeed dressed in a black maid's outfit, complete with white apron. Howie had the odd sense that he had seen her before, though he couldn't place her. Her voice was familiar as well, though for the life of him, he couldn't imagine from where.

"Does the snowmobile belong to Mrs. Stone?" he asked.

"What do you think? Everything here belongs to Mrs. Stone."

"She goes riding on it?"

The maid laughed. "You think Mrs. Stone rides around on snowmobiles?"

"Well, no. From what I've heard, I imagine it's her husband who uses it. I saw snowmobile tracks on the way over here. I was wondering if Sherman went out riding yesterday morning."

"I'm not supposed to talk about what goes on around here," the maid said sullenly. She turned abruptly and began walking toward the main house. Howie followed after her. She was an attractive woman, twenty-three or twenty-four. Voluptuous, he thought, probably with some Spanish blood. She was nice to look at, all in all. He wished he could remember where he had seen her before.

"Is Mrs. Stone at home?" he asked, addressing her back. "I really do want to speak with her."

"Whom should I say is calling?" she asked in a mocking voice.

"Howard Moon Deer. You can tell her it's about the homeless person who was shot near here yesterday morning."

The maid kept moving toward the house, not stopping to comment or look his way. Howie followed her doggedly. "So, you're from the Pueblo, I guess?" he asked, attempting to get through to her native to native, trying to receive any kind of smoke signal at all.

She turned just before she reached the front door and glared at him. The San Geronimo Pueblo Indians were a conservative people, closed to outsiders. They had lived in their well-photographed adobe condos with ladders going up and down the roofs since the thirteenth century. With such long roots, they tended to feel superior to less settled folk, like the nomadic Sioux. Howie tried smiling at her, but it did nothing to alter the unfriendly expression on her face.

"I'll ask Mrs. Stone if she'll see you. You can wait in the living room," she said finally. "Take off your boots. I vacuumed this morning."

Dutifully, Howie took off his Sorels and left them near the front door. He followed the maid in his socks through the foyer into an enormous gloomy living room. There was a dark ceiling of great wooden beams and rafters overhead and a clutter of artwork on the walls. The decor was a cross between Old New Mexico and a Wyoming hunting lodge: hardwood floors covered with navajo rugs, leather armchairs, heavy wooden tables, wrought-iron lamps with leather shades. The artwork on the walls was disappointing, not the Georgia O'Keeffe collection he had been expecting. The paintings were all of cowboys and Indians, kitschy images from the frontier, the sort commissioned by the railroads around the turn of the century to promote tourism to the West. At the far end of the room, there was a massive stone fireplace built from smooth river rock. An elk head was mounted above the hearth. The elk's glassy eyes seemed to give Howie a warning: *you too could get stuffed and mounted if you don't watch out.*

"Wait there," she said, indicating an antique bench at a far side of the room. The bench looked like it might have come from the Spanish Inquisition and was surely the least comfortable piece of furniture in the entire gloomy room.

Howie sat down obediently and watched the Indian woman walk from the room. Just before she reached the foyer, she stopped to pick up a plastic bucket from the floor and a few synapses fired a tentative connection in Howie's brain.

Could it be?

"Excuse me, but what's your name?" he asked, determined to get one more look at her.

"Anna," she said reluctantly, turning for a moment. Then she disappeared.

He was certain now. The small mole on the side of her mouth gave her away. It was no wonder he hadn't recognized her. The last time he had seen Anna was in a wildly different context, standing naked on a dais in Gilmer Good Day's art studio. She had been Gilmer's model for the mural he was doing for the Albuquerque airport. Howie shook his head in amazement, sensing that life in the Vandenberg Stone mansion among the decadent rich might hold some more surprises for a modest country boy such as himself.

Howie waited on the hard bench, convinced he'd been forgotten. He glanced at his watch from time to time. It was 3:23. The next time he looked, it was a quarter to four. There were no lights on in the room, and outside the windows the autumn afternoon was already starting to dim into a gray-blue twilight. The Vandenberg Stone house was starting to make him feel edgy.

Howie was wondering if he should go off in search of Anna, the art model maid, when he heard a woman's voice rise unexpectedly from a different part of the house:

"Sherman! You lousy son of a bitch! I will *not* be treated like this, by you or anybody else—do you understand me?"

The woman's voice was deep, almost masculine, full of moneyed authority. A man answered, more softly. His words did not cut with the same weight, and Howie could hear only a vague mumble.

Then the woman spoke again: ". . . no, that's not good enough, not by a long shot. So listen up, my darling. I fished you out of the sea, and I can throw you right back if I choose. Oh, yes, my charming man, I can, indeed! You'll be a starving artist again so fast you won't know what hit you!"

Howie decided that an assistant private detective did not need to feel embarrassed to eavesdrop. He leaned forward in concentration, hoping to hear the rest of the conversation. But now both voices dropped in volume, turning into an indistinct murmur of male/female discord. Howie was settling back on the bench when a gunshot shook the house. It was thunderous, a concussive impact against his eardrums.

Howie jerked to his feet and stood motionless, listening for danger. When he was able to breathe again, he ran from the living room, up the hallway to where he thought the shot might have come from. He threw open the first door he came to—it was an empty bathroom. He tried the next door—this one opened onto a wood-paneled billiard room. There was a smell of gunpowder in the air. A stout, older woman stood with a huge, long-barreled revolver in her right hand, a gun with a pearl handle that looked like something Wyatt Earp might have used. Across from her, on the far side of the billiard table, a lanky younger man stood clutching his stomach in pain and astonishment, his face drained of blood, staring at the woman in dismay. Neither the man nor the woman paid any notice to Howie in the doorway.

"You idiot!" the woman said scornfully.

The man staggered and did a strange little dance. Still clutching his stomach, he tottered back two steps and almost fell. But then he seemed to catch his balance; he swayed drunkenly and staggered forward several feet toward the billiard table. Somehow he managed to stay on his feet, defying gravity. Howie bounded forward and took hold of Sherman Stone's arm just as he started sinking slowly to his knees.

"Babs!" Sherman cried in a strangled voice. "I'm done for! Kiss the children for me!"

"We don't *have* any children, you asshole!" she replied severely. "At least, not together, I'm happy to say."

Sherman was on his knees now. A horrible death rattle came from his throat, and his face twisted in pain. Then at last he fell forward and lay still upon a dark red Navajo rug. Howie moved around the billiard table to the woman and took the huge revolver from her hand, unwrapping her fingers from the trigger guard. She glanced at Howie in surprise, as though she were just now noticing him. Her mouth opened, but before she could speak, Pooh Vandenberg burst into the room. Howie had no idea where she had come from.

"My God!" Pooh cried out, taking in the scene. She was out of breath, panting hard. Her voice became very thoughtful, almost cunning. "Mother, look what you've done . . . you've killed Sherman!"

Babs gazed at her daughter contemptuously. "For chrissake, don't be an idiot."

"But. . . ."

"Sherman's only having his little game."

And in fact, at this very moment, the body on the floor sat up with a mischievous grin on his face. Sherman Stone rose to his feet, unbloody, not even slightly dead. Howie had seen Sherman from a distance at art openings, but this was the first close-up look he'd had of the man. He was handsome in a peculiarly East Coast Yankee way, long arms and legs, an aging preppie WASP, the sort who had the knack of wearing clothes well. He looked positively elegant in jeans and a faded blue workshirt and loafers. His face was weathered and gaunt, deeply lined; his curly brown hair was just starting to gray. Robin had said that Sherman was fifty-two, but despite his lined face and graying hair, the sum effect was more youthful, almost adolescent. His eyes were a remarkable faded blue, a shade that was light and quizzical, full of ironic laughter.

"But I heard a shot!" Pooh was saying, gazing at her stepfather resentfully.

Sherman pointed at the ceiling, grinning naughtily. A bullet had splintered the wooden viga overhead.

"I only shot the gun to get Sherman's attention," Babs said with a shrug. "He wasn't listening to me. And you know how I hate that."

"Don't look so disappointed that I'm alive, Old Pooh," Sherman said with a wry smile on his face.

Pooh's eyes darted unhappily from her stepfather to her mother. Everything about her seemed wound tight to Howie. Her mouth, was screwed up in a grimace, her body was tense as a board. Her blond ponytail was pulled back so tightly from her face, it looked like torture. "This is absolutely insane! People in normal families *don't* shoot off guns to get other people's attention."

"Oh, darling, don't be so uptight," her mother told her.

"You should relax and have more fun, Old Pooh," Sherman added in a kindly tone.

Blood rushed into the daughter's face as she turned on her stepfather. Her lips snarled with rage.

"You bastard!" she cried. "And don't you dare call me Old Pooh! I won't stand for your insults!"

"He's only joking, sweets," Babs said to her daughter. "You mustn't take him so seriously. It's best to think of Sherman as a slightly absurd performance piece. He's been placed among us to keep us from getting stodgy."

Apparently, whatever argument Babs had been having with her husband was now cheerfully over, relieved by firing a bullet into the ceiling and having a new victim, her daughter, to torment.

"What if you had put a bullet hole in one of your precious Georgia O'Keeffes, Mother?" Pooh spat out. "Would that have been quite so funny?"

For the first time, Howie noticed that the walls were covered with dozens of mystical paintings of huge flowers as seen from a bumblebee's perspective. They were Georgia O'Keeffes, without any doubt, so many in one small room that Howie nearly felt dizzy looking at them.

"Oh, they're only canvas and oil, snooks," Babs said casually. "Anyway, *you* certainly won't be getting your hands on any of these after I'm gone, so I shouldn't worry about them if I were you."

"Pooh, my pet, do you think you could bob into the kitchen and fetch us a bottle of tequila and a few limes?" Sherman asked his stepdaughter agreeably. "Make-believe death has made me thirsty."

Pooh turned back and forth from her mother to her stepfather. But when she spoke, she directed all her venom at Sherman. "You think you're funny, don't you? You know what you are, Sherman? You're a gigolo. You're a third-rate con artist. You're nothing but a pathetic old drunk!" she paused briefly, nodding to herself. But she wasn't finished: "Maybe the next time someone shoots you, it'll be for real. And won't that be a hoot!"

With that pronouncement, Pooh Vandenberg turned and walked with regal disdain from the room.

"Well, well," Sherman said, shaking his head with amusement.

"Darling, you really must be nicer to that girl. Her life hasn't been easy," Babs chided.

Howie cleared his throat, feeling more than a little awkward to witness such an odd domestic drama. But the egotism of these people was sublime and absolute, a profound indifference to anything beyond themselves. They hardly seemed to notice that Howie was still in the room. Sherman put an arm around his wife's waist.

"Come on, Babs—let's get ourselves a quickie cocktail. Then I gotta split. There's a buyer coming to my studio."

"I'm in no mood for a drink—alcohol has started to bore me, if you want to know the truth. You *are* going to behave yourself from now on?" she purred. "I won't have you acting so badly, I really won't."

"Of course, I'll behave," he said contritely. Then he flashed his impish, boyish grin. "Just like I always behave—atrociously!"

Sherman kissed his wife on the lips. At the moment they seemed quite the happy couple. Then he turned, winked at Howie, and walked from the room.

Babs at last turned to Howie and regarded him shrewdly. "So," she said, "who the hell are you?"

Eight

"Heaven help the homeless in America—no one else will, that's for certain!" Barbara Vandenberg Stone was saying to Howie half an hour later. "My God, it's disgraceful to see entire families begging on the streets! And here we are, the richest nation on earth. I'm sure you know that I've been trying to open a homeless shelter in San Geronimo for years, but I haven't received a shred of support from the county. Not one scrap . . ."

The old woman had long gray-white hair tied back simply with a gold clasp at her neck; she wore a loose white robe of handspun cotton, a kind of muumuu whose primary purpose was comfort, with a secondary mission to camouflage the bulge underneath. Gilmer Good Day had said that Barbara Vandenberg Stone resembled a bulldog, but Howie found this inaccurate, not to mention unkind. She had a heart-shaped face, heavy and wide, pulled downward by the gravity of years; yet it was an attractive face in its own way, constantly animated, dominated by intense brown-gold eyes. She wore a greater clutter of jewelry, though not her missing turquoise and silver, Howie noticed. A huge Egyptian scarab ring perched on one hand, a number of gold bracelets jangled on her wrists, a string of carved ebony figures hung around her neck—little bears, skillfully done— and she wore ebony earrings to match. The effect was bohemian: a rich, arty old woman who dressed as eccentrically as she pleased.

Howie and Mrs. Stone were seated in a corner of the billiard room with the long-barreled revolver lying on a side table between them. For Howie, the conversation was heavy going. He had been trying his best to discover if she had noticed a homeless man in the neighborhood at any time in the past week or so, but Babs had a way of turning every conversation around to herself. She was impossibly self-absorbed, the ultimate small-town dowager. Along with the money, she had the arrogance, the sheer physical bulk, even the proper growly voice for the role.

"This particular homeless person who was shot, Mrs. Stone—he would be hard to miss. He was dressed in rainbow-striped pants and an odd jacket of leather and fur," Howie told her. "You didn't happen to look out your window anytime yesterday morning. . . ."

"I don't just *happen* to look out windows. When *I* was young, we learned discipline. How to concentrate on the matter at hand without letting our minds wander."

"Yes, I can imagine. But did you. . . ."

"Who did you say you are again? You're obviously not with the police."

"I'm Howard Moon Deer. I'm an assistant to Jack Wilder, a private detective here in town."

"Oh, yes. I've heard of him. Wasn't he the police chief in Seattle, or some place like that?"

"He was a commander in the San Francisco Police Department, not the chief. But back to the person who was shot—he called himself the Rainbow Man. Does that ring any sort of bell?"

"You're not a Pueblo Indian, are you?" she said studying Howie intently, as though she had just made a shrewd discovery.

"I'm Lakota, ma'am."

"Are you? I've always felt a very strong bond with Native Americans. I'm part Cherokee, actually, on my grandmother's side. It's the reason, I think, that I care so much about spiritual and artistic matters. Money has never interested me, not in the least."

"I understand you own a snowmobile?" Howie tried.

"Well, it's Sherman's toy, really. Frankly, I can't stand snowmobiles myself—they're such nasty little machines. But what does that have to do with a homeless man?"

"Someone was out on a snowmobile yesterday morning, Mrs. Stone. I'm wondering if perhaps they saw anything."

She shrugged. "I'd like to see snowmobiles outlawed. It's positively disgraceful how they pollute the woods with all their noise. But Sherman will not be dissuaded. I've tried, believe me. He's such an overgrown child, really—it drives me to distraction, but what can I do?"

"Did he go out yesterday morning on the snowmobile?"

"I don't have the proverbial foggiest. I was working in my office all morning and not paying any attention. But was there really enough snow for one of those horrible little machines to function properly?"

"Just barely enough," Howie told her. "Before it melted so quickly in the rain."

"Well, you should ask Sherman," she suggested with indifference, already bored by the subject. "I suppose it's possible he went out, but I really don't keep track of such things."

"I'm sure the police have already asked you this, but did you hear a rifle shot, by any chance? Around ten o'clock?"

"Yes, they *did* ask me, and I told them that I did *not* hear a shot—and a very good thing too, or I would have been extremely upset. As you may know, I've been trying for years to outlaw hunting in San Geronimo County, to create a special 'Life Zone,' as I like to call it. A place where all beings will be treated as sacred. . . ."

It was impossible to keep her to the subject at hand. She was off again, describing her role in what seemed to Howie an exceptionally hare-brained scheme. Apparently she had given money to several county commissioners when they were running for office in the expectation that they would instigate a county-wide ban on hunting when they were elected. But did they fulfill their promise? Of course not! Rabbits were still shot right and left by barbarous morons who sometimes even ate the cuddly little things. Poor Babs. She let Howie know that it was not at all easy to be someone like herself with a frustrated vision of peace and beauty on earth.

Howie's mind and eyes roamed to the Georgia O'Keeffes on the walls. He was a big fan of O'Keeffe, but it seemed almost obscene that one person should own quite so many.

"Please look at me when I'm speaking, young man," she ordered. "I simply hate it when people don't listen to what I'm saying."

"Well, I was—"

"You were admiring my O'Keeffe collection. Georgia was a great friend of mine, of course. We used to have lovely dinners together. I was the only collector she could tolerate, you know. She used to say what a marvelous thing it was that there was someone like me who was truly able to understand her work. And, now, my young friend . . . what did you say your name was?"

"Howard Moon Deer," he repeated for the third time.

"Well, Howard Moon Deer, I've enjoyed our chat. But I really have a great deal of work to do today."

"Just one more question. Red moon," Howie said quickly. "Does that phrase mean anything to you?"

"Red moon?" She scowled and shook her head. "No, it doesn't mean a thing. Why should it?"

"It's what the homeless man said before he died. Just those two words. Red moon. He was very weak, and he made a real effort to say this, so it seems to have been important to him."

"How curious. Was he entirely in his right mind, do you suppose?"

"Right mind isn't exactly the expression I'd use to describe him," Howie admitted.

"Red moon," she said again. "I wonder if he was talking about a painting?"

"Painting?"

"This *does* stir a memory, but it's all very long ago. . . . Be quiet for a moment and let me think. I detest people who talk and talk, and won't let a person remember anything!"

Howie waited dutifully as the old woman closed her eyes and made a dramatic show of trying to remember. Meanwhile, a small dog trotted into the room. It was a nasty little thing, a cross between a large rat and a small fox. Howie watched in astonishment as the dog lifted its leg and peed against a corner of the billiard table.

"Uh, Mrs. Stone. . . ."

"*Please* do not speak to me!" Babs said imperiously. She opened her eyes. "Red moon . . . red moon . . . yes, there's definitely something about that name . . . but how annoying to not quite be able to remember!"

Without warning, the old woman rose decisively from her chair. "Come with me, Howard Moon Deer. We'll have to investigate this further."

Howie followed Mrs. Stone down a corridor and up a flight of stairs to her "art library," as she called it—a room lined with floor-to-ceiling bookshelves in a far wing of the mansion on the second floor. The shelves were stuffed with art books and brochures from old auctions. Howie remained standing while Babs searched the shelves, pulling out books and pamphlets, then stuffing them back impatiently. This was a distinctly different side to Barbara Vandenberg Stone than he had seen before. She worked with concentrated, obsessive energy, oblivious to Howie, sometimes getting on her hands and knees as she examined the lower shelves. Her library was chaotic, overflowing with papers and books and occasional loose prints that fell out from between the pages.

The old woman continued searching for nearly forty-five minutes, her mouth set with determination. Howie eventually sat down cross-legged on the floor to wait. At last Babs stood up from where she had been kneeling by the lowest shelf and put a glossy brochure onto the table.

"Yes, this is what I was looking for," she said.

Howie stood up creakily from the floor and peered at the brochure. The cover said Seret & McPhearson, Auctioneers, and announced an estate sale in Santa Fe on November 10, 1965, consisting of the collection of a Dr. Jonas Rudman.

"Jonas Rudman was a well-known doctor in Santa Fe," Babs said. "I saw him myself once or twice for various things, because in those days in San Geronimo, believe me, it was best to avoid the medical profession here in town. Rudman was an interesting man, independently wealthy, a collector mostly of Western art—the majority of it was pure rubbish, but occasionally, he picked up something first-rate . . . ah, here's what I was looking for."

Babs opened the brochure to the fourth page, which showed a single color reproduction.

"Tell me, what do think of *this*?" she asked, obviously pleased with herself.

Howie studied the print. The subject itself was simple: a landscape of the desert at night, a twisted old piñon in the foreground, and a glowing red-orange harvest moon overhead. Howie thought it was a remarkable work. The landscape was naturalistic, just the way a desert would be, yet at the same time mystical, implying something more than what was there. The colors themselves were fascinating, capturing a childlike sense of awe: the hugeness of night engulfing a dreaming land. Everything about the painting was electric and alive. At the bottom of the page, he read the words:

Red Moon
36" x 24"
1929

"Cool," Howie said after a while.

"*Cool*?" Mrs. Stone chided. "You must learn to speak the English language more precisely, my young friend."

Howie smiled apologetically. "I've never been much good at describing art. So this painting was auctioned off in 1965—do you have any idea who bought it?"

"None at all. I believe I was in Europe at the time of the auction—these brochures just come to me in the mail, you know. Strange, I haven't thought about 'Red Moon' for years and years. I wonder what happened to it?"

"It disappeared?"

"From public view, anyway. Some collector probably has it locked away in a vault."

"Is it okay if I borrow this brochure?"

"You know, I'm really very proud of myself that I remembered. I sometimes suspect that I was a detective in a previous life!"

"Yes, I'm sure you were, Mrs. Stone," Howie assured her. "But the brochure. . . ."

"Oh, take it!" she said with irritation. "But bring it back, or I will absolutely have your scalp. Once I've collected something, I absolutely never, *ever* let it get away!"

Nine

Howie was headed out the front door of the Vandenberg Stone house when he saw the maid, Anna, kneeling by the huge stone fireplace in the living room. She had just added a log to the fire and was pausing to stare dreamily into the flames. Howie wondered what she was thinking about. He changed course and walked from the foyer into the living room to have another try with her.

"This is a big house for you to clean all by yourself," he said pleasantly. "Don't you have any help?"

"I manage okay," she told him, standing up from the hearth. She seemed embarrassed that Howie had caught her in a dreamy moment.

"You know, I didn't recognize you at first from Gilmer's studio. Do you model for him often?"

"What's it to you?" she demanded, her dark eyes smoldering.

Howie didn't expect them to have an instant powwow

just because they were both Indians, but he still wasn't certain why he kept striking out with her.

"I was only curious. I mean, you're going to be immortalized by a famous artist in a big mural at the Albuquerque airport—that's sort of incredible."

He thought she was going to say something cutting, but instead she sighed and shook her head. "I just hope nobody recognizes me when they see that thing! Do you think they will?"

"No, probably not. People walk through airports quickly, focused on getting to their planes. Anyway, you know how it is with white people—all Indians look pretty much the same to them."

"It's not the white people who worry me. It's my family—they'd really freak. A good thing no one I know from the Pueblo ever goes anywhere—much less anywhere in an airplane!"

"Well, it's art," Howie told her.

"It's *money*!" Anna told him sharply. "And Gilmer happens to pay very well. He says I'm a perfect type, whatever that means."

"How much do they pay you here?"

"Not much," she answered with a casual bitterness. "But to hell with them! I'm saving up to open a shop in town. I'm not going to always be a maid."

"What kind of shop?"

"I thought of an art gallery at first. Indian art. But I'm sick of art and even sicker of artists. So maybe I'll sell clothes. I don't know."

"Well, you're ambitious—good for you," Howie said encouragingly.

"I'm *not* going to end up like my mother," Anna declared. "She has five kids, and my dad beats her up when he's had too much to drink. I'm *not* going to live like that. There's too much alcohol and abuse on the reservation. It's time that Indian women stood up for themselves."

"I agree with you there," Howie told her. "Speaking of alcohol and abuse, it seems to get pretty wild around *here*. Do these people act like this all the time?"

She laughed sharply. "This family is crazy! But I don't care. I get what I want from them. One day I'm going to travel. I'm going to visit California. I'm going to do all kinds of things."

Howie believed her. Most native women he knew on reservations were content to live the old traditional life, but more and more of them were like Anna, looking for ways to bust loose. Anna looked like she could bust loose any moment.

"Look," he said, "I really need to know if Sherman went out on his snowmobile yesterday morning. The man I work for, Jack Wilder, will give you a reward for any information you can give us. Maybe two hundred dollars."

But Howie had apparently moved too fast. Just when he thought he was making some progress with Anna, she stiffened and turned away.

"I don't know anything about Sherman's stupid snowmobile. Why don't you ask him yourself?"

Howie sensed she knew something she was keeping back. But he wasn't sure how to get her to talk.

"I wish you would tell me what you know." Bribery hadn't worked, maybe sincerity would. "The man who was killed . . . well, I saw him up close just as he was dying. It's really spooked me. I need to find out what happened to him."

"I can't talk to you anymore. I've got work to do," Anna said briskly, moving from the hearth across the huge living room.

Howie followed after her. "Well, I'll ask Sherman then. He's in his studio?"

She paused at the foot of the stairs and turned to Howie. "If you're going to talk to Sherman, maybe you can give him a message for me."

"Sure," said Howie obligingly.

Anna was about to say something. But then, to Howie's disappointment, she changed her mind. "No, forget it. It wouldn't do any good. Sherman never listens anyway."

"That's pretty much what Mrs. Stone said when she shot up the ceiling just now," Howie mentioned.

"Did she?" Anna gave him a searching look, then she turned and began walking quickly upstairs. Howie couldn't help but notice that the back hem of her uniform came down a good six inches above the bend of her knee, showing a lot of leg.

"Wait a second," he called after her. "Where's Sherman's studio?"

"Out back," she said, not stopping in her flight to the upper reaches of the mansion. "The Quonset hut. Now, leave me alone!"

Architecturally speaking, a Quonset hut did not fit in any way with a classy old New Mexican mansion, but the Vandenberg Stones apparently did whatever they pleased without regard to convention or style. Howie found Sherman's art studio at the end of a path in the rear of the estate. It was not yet six o'clock, but the autumn night was already dark as midnight, the stars twinkling in the icy sky overhead.

Walking up the path, Howie began to hear rock music. At first there was only a deep rhythmic thud, but soon a soaring guitar joined in. It was vintage Jimi Hendrix played at top volume, growing ever louder as he approached the door of the metal building. Howie tried knocking, but he wasn't surprised when there was no answer; it was impossible to compete with the music inside. Finally he tried the door, found it wasn't locked, and stepped inside a dark, cavernous space that was more like a factory warehouse than an art studio. There were chains and hoists dangling from the high ceiling and junk metal everywhere: pieces of wrecked cars, old engines, even a pile of broken typewriters. A few of the pieces of junk had been welded together into odd shapes that might conceivably be called sculpture, Howie supposed, though everything he saw seemed haphazard and unfinished.

Sherman sat on a disembodied car seat in a pool of light at the far end of the studio, near a large wood-burning stove. Howie had heard Sherman tell his wife that he was meeting an art dealer here, but if that was true, the meeting was clearly over. Sherman was alone, hunched over a small mirror in his lap, using a razor to arrange two lines of white powder. Heroin, Howie guessed from what he had heard of Sherman's habits. But then again, this white powder could be a different thrill—methamphetamine or cocaine, the other two drugs that were chic at the moment with the local fast set.

Something made Sherman look up. He saw Howie,

scowled, then returned to his preparations, tapping and scraping the mirror.

"Hey!" Howie shouted. "Can I turn down Jimi? I'd like to talk."

"Whatever," Sherman mouthed.

The stereo was stacked on a bookshelf not far from where Sherman was sitting. Howie turned the music down to a murmur. Sherman, meanwhile, had put a rolled twenty-dollar bill to his left nostril and was busy snorting up one of the lines. It struck Howie as an ugly gesture, crude and desperate.

"Ah!" Sherman sighed. "Where would we be without drugs? Wanna line?"

"No thanks."

"What? Are you philosophically opposed? Or just an uptight asshole?"

"Neither, really," Howie told him. "I have my own mind-altering substances, they just don't happen to be white powder."

"Really? Like what?"

"Books, Italian opera, good red wine."

"*Books*!" he mocked. "What ripe bullshit! You gotta get with it, kid. The old shit just doesn't make it anymore."

Howie shrugged and sat on a second disembodied car seat that faced Sherman. He watched the artist snort the remaining line with his other nostril. It *was* heroin, Howie decided from the laid-back expression that came over Sherman's face. His whole being seemed to go slack. He crossed his legs and regarded Howie from a cosmic distance.

"Well, well, another goddamn Indian—just what I need!" Sherman said sarcastically, wiping his nose with the back of his hand. In this harsh space surrounded by junk and drugs, Sherman didn't look as elegantly handsome to Howie as he had in the house. "So okay, tell me," he said, "what do you want?"

"I'm Howard Moon Deer. . . ."

"I know who you are. My stepson hired you to investigate me and my wicked ways. That little poof has always been eager to bust up my marriage. He'd like his mommy all to himself, I'm sure. And all of Mommy's money too."

"So you blackmailed him," Howie mentioned. "You

threatened to expose his New York past if he didn't fire us."

Sherman grinned. "Did he tell you that? The kid has more balls than I thought!"

"Why did you do it, Sherman? What were you afraid that Jack and I would find?"

"Hey, in this family you gotta fight fire with fire, that's all. You lay down for a single second, someone will roll right over you. Believe me, Robin only got what was coming to him."

"From what I understand, what happened to Robin in New York was a misunderstanding. He was only drawing that little girl, not. . . ."

"Oh, for chrissake, I couldn't care less if Robin screws little girls or elephants in the zoo!" Sherman said with a sigh. "I hope you didn't come over here just to spoil my high, Moon Deer. Frankly, I crave occasional relief from my wife and her family—fun as they all undoubtedly are."

"Who told you that Robin had hired me and Jack?"

Sherman smiled. "Babs told me, naturally. There are no secrets, you know, between a loving husband and wife. And who told Babs, you're wondering? Well, it was darling Pooh, my stepdaughter."

"Why would she do that?"

"To suck up to momsy, of course. To show what a devoted daughter she is so that momsy will continue to fund her silly-ass gallery and her pathetic loser of a husband who keeps trying to peddle his fake religious art . . . Are you sure you don't want to snort a line, Moon Deer? It's a lot more fun than Italian opera or talking about my in-laws, believe me."

"Did you take out your snowmobile yesterday morning?" Howie asked, ignoring the offer.

"Why are you interested?"

"You probably heard about the homeless man who was shot. There were tread marks from a snowmobile on a hill near where he died. I was wondering if you saw anything."

Sherman seemed interested. "Really? You sure it was a snowmobile?"

"I saw it," Howie told him. "I was out cross-country skiing yesterday, and I saw a black snowmobile and someone riding it, wearing a black ski suit and a helmet."

"Well, it wasn't me."

"Did you see the homeless guy hanging around Valverde the last couple of days?"

"I see a lot of homeless guys," Sherman said vaguely. "This is America, land of the haves and the have-nots—and, oh, what a gulf between them!"

"You would have remembered this particular homeless person," Howie assured him. "He wore pants with rainbow stripes down the legs."

"Doesn't really ring a bell," he said. "But then I meet so many colorful people here in glamorous New Mexico. Hard to keep them all straight."

"Have you ever heard of a Georgia O'Keeffe painting called 'Red Moon'?"

He shook his head. "Nope. But I'm not much of a fan of Georgia O'Keeffe. My opinion is that she's highly overrated. All those feminists, you know—they just had to find themselves a lady artist of their own to get gaga over. Now, if you don't mind, I have some work I need to do, Moon Deer—the muse calls, and I don't particularly remember inviting you into my studio."

Sherman stood up from the car seat and crossed the floor of his studio. He switched on an overhead spotlight, illuminating a garish piece of junk sculpture that Howie had not noticed earlier. The sculpture was huge, made from parts of a motorcycle, an old refrigerator, and several computer screens welded together to form a chaotic heap of dysfunctional modernity.

"This is art that has relevance to today, Moon Deer," Sherman lectured, picking up an acetylene torch. "Not pretty flowers and bullshit cow skulls on the desert."

For all Howie knew, Sherman was right. But he still preferred Georgia O'Keeffe, relevant or not. Howie paused. He had come to Sherman's studio on impulse, but he was starting to think he should have waited for Jack. Sherman had told him nothing. He was certain that Jack would have done much better.

Just as he was leaving, he tried one of Jack's tricks.

"By the way, Sherman, I know Babs keeps you on a tight rein when it comes to money. So I'm curious how you can afford to feed your habit—were you able to sell that turquoise jewelry you stole from her?"

With a pop, Sherman lit the acetylene torch in his hand. Howie had to jump back to keep from being scorched.

"You know, Moon Deer, I have to tell you something about artists. We really hate people who disturb us when we're working. I mean, we *seriously* hate it." Sherman turned up the blue flame on the torch and pointed the nozzle directly at Howie, who had to jump back a second time.

"Are you getting the picture, Moon Deer?"

Moon Deer got the picture.

Ten

Howie and Claire quarreled Friday night over dinner at the Holy Mountain Pizza Company. It was one of those nights when everybody seemed to be at odds. They couldn't even agree on pizza toppings. Howie wanted prawns, spinach, Greek olives, caramelized onions, and roast red peppers. Claire's choice was the free-range chicken, pineapple, and enoki mushrooms. And the kids wanted pepperoni, period. Howie's solution was to get three pizza so everybody would be happy, and this was what they ended up doing. But Claire thought it an undue extravagance, more food than they needed, particularly since the Holy Mountain Pizza Company was far from cheap.

Looking back, Howie could point to a number of reasons that the evening turned out so badly. Claire was stressed: she had been working like a maniac all day, the Art Association benefit was tomorrow night, and she couldn't imagine how it was all going to come together in time. Child-care arrangements had been especially difficult this afternoon, demanding part of her frantic attention: an after-school piano lesson for Jonathan, and a play rehearsal for Heidi, who was in a children's theater group. Dinner was late, as well, which didn't help matters—Howie had met Claire and the kids at the restaurant at seven o'clock, so everybody was tired and hungry.

As for Howie, he was upset that Jack had upstaged him, discovering the meaning of the victim's last words, Red Moon, on his own, and doing so at home with just a few phone calls. Howie felt that all his running around today had been a colossal waste of time. He had reached Jack finally on a pay phone at a gas station across the street from the restaurant, after ordering dinner. Standing in the cold, he spoke with Jack for nearly half an hour, recounting the progress of his day as well as the various items he had forgotten and then remembered: the missing shopping cart and the black snowmobile on the hill. Jack was particularly interested in the snowmobile, as well as the fact that Howie had traced the machine almost conclusively to Sherman Stone. Jack seemed to think they were making definite progress.

As for whether or not they would accept Robin back as a client, Jack said they had better think about it first. The case had become much more complicated since Robin had come to them on Wednesday morning, and Jack wanted a better idea of how the pieces of the drama fit together before committing Wilder & Associate to any one player. In short, they did not at present have a client. This was all very well for Jack, who could afford to have scruples—Jack had a generous pension package and a house that he and Emma owned free and clear. But it was not so great for Howie, who had just ordered a dinner that would come to at least sixty bucks.

Discouraged, Howie walked back across the street to the restaurant to discover that his pizza had arrived at the table five minutes ago and was cold. He sat down with a sigh and ordered a five-dollar glass of house wine. (Now the meal was sixty-five dollars, warned the adding machine in his mind, even more with tip.)

Then the real trouble began. Jonathan was gobbling up the pepperoni pizza so fast that Heidi got tearful and accused her brother of eating more than his share. In the squabble that followed, it came out that the reason Jonathan was so hungry tonight was that a group of Hispanic boys in his class had stolen his lunch. This was a loaded issue, and very sad. Over the past year, Jonathan had often come home from school with a bloody nose and stories of how his Hispanic classmates had been terrorizing him. When Claire phoned the school to complain, the principal was mildly sympathetic but had done nothing. The fact was that Hispanics were the majority in this part of the world, they greatly resented the wealthy Anglo newcomers, and as a result, gringo children in northern New Mexico often had a terrible time in the public schools. Many of the Anglo parents who could afford it sent their kids to private schools, furthering the cultural divide.

Claire exploded at this latest assault, the theft of a turkey sandwich she had made with loving care. "I've had it! I'm sick of talking to the principal and having him not do a damn thing! I'm going to sue the school district, I swear to God. I'm going to call the ACLU tomorrow and get some-one to represent us. It's intolerable that they allow this kind of blatant racism against Anglo children!"

"Claire, you have to try to see it from their point of view," Howie said unwisely. "The last thirty years, a lot of Anglos have been buying up the land here, raising property values and taxes, looking down their noses at the local peo-ple. The Spanish people have been in this valley for four hundred years, and they see their entire way of life threatened. . . ."

As an Indian, Howie knew very well what it was like to be on the wrong end of discrimination. Secretly, he be-lieved that Jonathan could benefit from the experience, as long as it didn't go too far: to understand firsthand what it was like in America for all those who were not members of the white dominant race. But Claire was outrage. Jona-than was her baby, of course, and she was incensed that people were treating him badly simply because of the color of his skin.

"So what are you saying, Howie? You're telling me that racism is *okay*? My God, I don't believe this!"

"Of course, racism is not okay, Claire. I'm only trying to tell you that it's the Spanish who believe *they're* the victims, and in a way they have a point. . . ."

It was a hopeless conversation. They were all tired, hun-gry, grouchy, and stressed-out. Howie should have left it alone, but instead he tried to tell Claire that as a blond, protestant person of northern European ancestry she really didn't know diddly about racism in America. Simply put, she had never experienced it happening to her—except here in New Mexico, where for the first time in her life, she found herself in the minority. Well, welcome to the club! The point Howie wished to make was that she should examine her own attitudes and perhaps be more tolerant. Contacting the ACLU, Howie believed, would only put Jonathan in serious danger at school.

Howie and Claire kept their voices down because they were in a restaurant and the children were present, but by the time Howie paid the bill (it came to an even seventy dollars) the air between them was glacial. Howie walked from the pizzeria with Heidi, while Claire followed a dozen paces back with Jonathan. Howie felt hollow with depression. He certainly hadn't meant to fight with Claire tonight. Somehow it just seemed to happen. He led the way across the street and down the block to the SGAA parking lot, where Claire had left her Subaru. He was passing by the Hopewell Gallery, holding onto Heidi's hand, when a drawing in the window caught his eye.

"Let's stop to look at the picture, sweetie," Howie told her.

"I'm *cold,* Howie!" Heidi said.

"Yes, but just for a minute."

The drawing that interested Howie was a portrait of a man, delicately done with a fine-tipped pen. The craftsmanship was familiar, as was the subject of the drawing: Sherman Stone. The artist had perfectly depicted the gaunt, deeply lined Yankee face, the ironic eyes, the self-indulgent mouth, the arrogance of his chin. It was an extremely perceptive psychological portrait, capturing Sherman's charm, but also his monstrous, infantile ego. The eyes seemed to say: "I'm the center of the universe, so the rest of you can go to hell!"

"Look at this, Claire," Howie said as Claire reluctantly joined them at the window with Jonathan.

"Oh, great, this *really* makes my evening!" she said sarcastically. "You know I can't stand Sherman Stone!"

"Yes, but look at the drawing itself."

Claire studied the drawing, and her expression changed. "It's the Rainbow Man, isn't it? It's his work—it has to be."

"That's what I was thinking too."

Claire kept staring at the drawing until Heidi and Jonathan cried out that they were tired and cold and wanted to go home.

"That's really an awfully good portrait," she said thoughtfully as the children dragged her away. "It captures something about Sherman that's . . . disturbing."

Howie was more interested in crime than art at the moment.

"Yes," he said. "It's good. It's so good it makes me wonder how exactly Sherman got himself drawn by a homeless artist he told me he had never met!"

Eleven

Early Saturday morning, haggard from lack of sleep, Howie drove to Calle Santa Margarita to pick up Jack. Howie's sleepless condition was due to the fact that he and Claire had not made up. Every time he had tried, the fight only seemed to erupt anew, like smoldering hot spots from a forest fire that you can't quite get under control.

"So I bet you're going to Chicago now, where all the different ethnic groups just love each other like crazy," he had taunted.

"Yes, maybe I *will* go," she had taunted back. "At least my children won't be terrified to go to school!"

It was an ugly fight, the worst he and Claire had ever had. They tried to make up before blowing out the candle in the tipi: a brief kiss, a promise to talk more calmly tomorrow. But the rift between them was far from healed. Howie hated fighting with Claire. All night long, he had tossed and turned, unable to sleep, listening to Claire beside him sleeping like a baby. Close to dawn, he had dozed fitfully for about an hour, but that was it. Now he was a wreck, it was Halloween, and he would need to struggle through what promised to be an especially busy day.

Not only was Claire's big party tonight, but he had agreed to take the kids trick-or-treating earlier in the evening. He had his costume in a duffel bag thrown into the back of the cab, for he doubted there would be time to return home and change. The stress of all these things, combined with lack of sleep, left him with a burpy acidic feeling in his stomach. It happened to be a picture perfect autumn day, but the beauty of the day only accented Howie's gloom: a crisp blue sky, dark and translucent, the mountains so finely etched against the clear air that they seemed to have tiptoed closer to town overnight. Howie pulled into the Wilders' driveway and found Jack in a mood as fine as the weather, obnoxiously well rested and upbeat. Even Katya was wagging her tail. Howie wanted to spit at them all.

"Great day!" Jack exhaled as Howie helped him into the cab. "What's that marvelous smell in the air?"

"Cow shit," Howie informed him.

"Tell me again about this drawing of Sherman Stone you found. How certain are you that it was done by our Rainbow Man?"

"Well, I thought so last night. But what the hell do I know?"

"Correct me if I'm wrong, Howie, but you seem slightly off-key this morning, mood-wise."

"Hey, I'm fine," Howie insisted. "Just fine."

Jack rode in silence for several minutes. "You had a fight with Claire?"

"You got it, Sherlock."

Howie felt slightly more human twenty minutes later after a brief pit stop at the New Wave Café for his favorite power breakfast: a double cappuccino with bear claw. Sarah, the pretty English waitress, even flirted with him, and this was as good as a caffeine hit for a guy in need.

"A lot to do today!" Jack was saying energetically as they walked up the steps from the courtyard to the second-floor office of Wilder & Associate. "First, I want to stop by the Hopewell Gallery. Then I'm thinking we'll pop down to Santa Fe."

"Okay, but I have to be back by five," Howie warned him. "I'm taking the kids trick-or-treating."

"Good God, it's Halloween already?"

"It sure is."

Jack tended to live in his own special time zone, particularly when he was preoccupied with an investigation.

"I'd better call Emma, tell her to get some candy for the neighborhood kids."

"Jack, Emma knows it's Halloween," Howie explained patiently. "She's looking after Jonathan and Heidi tonight for a few hours while Claire and I are at the Art Association party."

"No kidding?"

"We arranged this a week ago. You know, sometimes I think you live on the dark side of the moon . . . hey, I'm sorry. I didn't mean for that to come out like it did."

"Quite all right. I used to be a big fan of Pink Floyd," Jack replied obscurely. Howie got the reference. But honestly, sometimes Jack was too much. A genius, in his way, but also a space cadet of the first degree.

When they reached the second-floor landing, Katya began pawing at the office door and making little worried sounds, high-pitched and agitated.

"Hold on," Jack cautioned, speaking softly.

"What for?"

"Just stop a second and listen. The last time I heard Katya whine like that, someone had just broken into my house . . . *quiet,* Katya!" he ordered.

Jack and Howie stood on either side of the office door, waiting, listening. But all they could hear was Katya, who continued her high-pitched whine despite Jack's command for quiet.

"Stand back," Jack whispered, "and open the door slowly."

"Look, Jack, Katya's a sweet dog," Howie whispered back, "but I wouldn't bet the farm on her deductive instincts."

"Yeah," Jack agreed. "But open it slowly anyway."

Howie turned both keys, top and bottom, and carefully swung open the office door to Wilder & Associate. For a moment he found it difficult to breathe. "Shit!" he said, surveying the damage inside.

"What's wrong?"

"We've had a visitor, I'm afraid. The office has been trashed, Jack. All the drawers have been pulled out. There are papers all over the floor. Your desk is over on its side. Jesus, what a mess!''

Howie led Jack into the office, avoiding the chairs and lamps that had been knocked over. His heart was beating rapidly in his ears, sending out a little morse code of panic. He was spooked and it took him a second to figure out why. It was his body remembering the last time he had been attacked, the shadowy figure that had rushed him so unexpectedly from his bathroom. Katya's tail, always active, slapped against a rocking chair and the sound made Howie spin around in a martial stance ready to take on any danger.

"Relax," Jack told him. "Whatever visitors we've had, there's no one here now but the three of us."

"*Three* of us?"

"You and me and Katya," Jack told him dryly. "What the hell's wrong with you?"

"Hey, I'm cool," Howie managed. He took a deep breath to steady his nerves. "It's just that this is starting to get me psyched-out. First that guy in my bathroom, then someone breaks into your house, and now this. I wish I knew what they're looking for."

"I should think that's obvious. The painting, of course. *Red Moon*."

Howie was stunned. "You're kidding? Why should anybody think that *we* have *Red Moon*?"

"I'm not sure. But I'm willing to bet that the painting is what this whole thing is about."

"But a painting, Jack!—that's kind of big and bulky, not something you'd look for in a drawer."

"Hmm . . . well, yes and no," he said mysteriously.

Howie was not happy, thinking of all the work he was going to need to do in order to get the place cleaned up again.

"What I'd like to know is how the hell they got in?" Howie asked, outraged.

"Oh, it wouldn't be difficult, not for an experienced burglar. . . . What are you doing?"

Howie had just picked up the receiver of one of their two telephones. "I'm calling the police, of course."

"No, you're not. Put the phone down, Howie."

"But, Jack, we've got to report this for our insurance."

"It doesn't matter. We have too much to do today without getting embroiled for hours with our local all-star amateurs. Please call the Hopewell Gallery instead. Right now I'm more interested in finding out how Sherman Stone happened to know the homeless man."

Arthur Hopewell, the owner of the Hopewell Gallery, was a pale middle-aged man with black shoulder-length hair and a New York accent. When Jack explained that they were private investigators looking into the death of a homeless artist whose picture was displayed in the gallery's window, Hopewell quickly agreed to meet them at his store at nine-thirty, a full hour and a half before the gallery usually opened.

"To tell you the truth, I've been worried about that drawing," Hopewell said as he let Jack and Howie and Katya in the gallery door. "It seemed almost too good for some crazy guy."

According to Arthur Hopewell, the Rainbow Man had drifted into his gallery on Monday afternoon with a drawing he hoped to trade for a sleeping bag. The man was obviously "mondo bizarro," as Hopewell put it, communicating by writing messages on a blackboard dangling around his neck. But the drawing he wanted to trade, simply put, was terrific. Not only that, but since it was an extremely clever study of Sherman Stone, a well-known personality in town, Hopewell was certain he could turn a profit.

"Did the homeless man say how he had come to draw Sherman?" Jack inquired.

"No. To be honest, he came during Arts Fest. There were a lot of other people browsing in the gallery, and I wanted to get the guy out of here fast. Maybe he was talented, but frankly he stank up the place. He needed a shower, bad. I told him I didn't have a sleeping bag to trade—Christ, I'm an art gallery, not an army surplus store! But I offered him a hundred bucks for the drawing, which I thought was fair. With a hundred bucks, hell, he could buy his own sleeping bag."

"And he accepted your offer?"

"Not exactly. He wrote on his blackboard that he had priced a sleeping bag at Wal-Mart, and it came to $63.95

with tax. And that's what he wanted for the drawing if I couldn't trade directly for what he wanted: $63.95. Not a penny more, not a penny less. I asked him why, for chrissake? He wrote, quote, the Rainbow Man does not profit from art, unquote. Like I said, the guy was mondo, man. Totally out there."

If turning down money was a sign of a mentally unbalanced American, Arthur Hopewell was not so afflicted himself. Howie noticed a price tag of $425 on the drawing of Sherman Stone, which was a substantial profit on his $63.95 investment. The price was presently beyond the expense account budget of Wilder & Associate, but Mr. Hopewell agreed to run off a photocopy of the drawing on the machine in his back room for a mere $20. To cover expenses, he said.

Santa Fe, ninety miles to the south, was everything that people in San Geronimo feared might happen to themselves one day if they didn't watch out—and some said it had already happened. To them, Santa Fe was an object lesson of what can happen to a quaint and lovely place that is despoiled by too much development and tourism run amuck.

Howie made the drive in an hour and a half by letting the speedometer drift to 75 mph. Luckily Jack spent a good deal of the drive talking on his cell phone to his various police connections and didn't appear to notice the speed. Howie came into town on St. Francis Drive, then took a left on Cerrilos Road into the heart of the Southwest theme park that had once been a city. Jack had arranged an early noon lunch at the St. Francis Hotel with Detective James Hastings, with whom he had spoken several times this morning. Detective Hastings of the Santa Fe Police Department was the nephew of a retired lieutenant in California, part of Jack's incestuous network of aging cops who all seemed to owe each other favors from twenty years back.

Howie stopped at a patch of lawn near the state capitol to allow Katya to become acquainted with several bushes. The next stop was the parking lot of the St. Francis. Howie left Katya in the cab with the window cracked open an inch, then he guided Jack into the stately, old-fashioned hotel. Lunch here was nothing special, but Jack had chosen it for the meeting today because it would be uncrowded and convenient.

Detective Hastings was waiting for them at a corner table in the restaurant, a large airy room with French doors overlooking the street. "Good to meet you, Commander," the detective said, standing up as they arrived. Like a lot of people, he did a double take when he realized that Jack was blind. But he covered himself quickly.

Hastings was a big baby-faced man with a floppy dark mustache and a potbelly protruding from his tweed sports jacket. Howie imagined he was in his early forties. His eyes were moist and sad and a little suspicious, like most of the cop's eyes that Howie had seen. The detective found Jack's hand, shook it vigorously, then did the same with Howie.

"I only have half an hour, I'm afraid, so we'd better order" he said. "So, you were friends with my Uncle Will?"

"Well, a friend of your Uncle Will's ex-partner, Doug," Jack told him. "How's Will enjoying his retirement?"

"Not too much. He died five years ago." Detective Hastings lowered his voice. "Look, Commander, I've been thinking of making a move to California before too long, either L.A. or San Francisco. I'm sort of ready for a change from New Mexico, if you can dig what I'm saying. You don't happen to know any people out there still?"

Jack indicated that, yes, he knew *lots* of people. Exactly the right people, in fact, to help the nephew of an old friend's ex-partner move up the ladder in California law enforcement. With this tit-for-tat arrangement of favors exchanged, the waitress came by and they all ordered club sandwiches and iced tea. At last the detective opened his attaché case and started pulling out papers.

"I've been making a few calls and gathering together some information you might find interesting. Let's start with Mr. Sherman Stone," he said. His voice was wheezy, a fat man's rasp, chronically out of breath; but his tone was all business. "The first thing I did was pull the file on that 1974 dope bust you told me about. Sure enough, your Mr. Stone tried to sell a lid of pot to an undercover agent in the Santa Fe Plaza. It was a first adult offense, no biggie, but we had a district attorney back then who took an ounce of marijuana more seriously than it would be taken today. Stone got a few weeks' jail time and then had to enroll in a rehab program. I have some background on your guy from the forms he had to fill out to get into the program. Date of birth, education. I haven't really had a chance to look through this myself yet . . . you want all this, Commander?"

"Since we're short on time, let's concentrate on 1974 when he entered the program. Who did he list as next of kin?"

"His mother, Mary Evans Stone, 2908 Old Santa Fe Trail. His father, Christopher, apparently died in 1971 . . . there's also an older brother, by the way, Dr. Maxwell Stone. I've met him, as a matter of fact. He's a dentist—periodontist. Has a practice over on St. Michaels Drive."

"Really? Do you know him socially or professionally?"

"Professionally. I've had to have some root planing and shit like that recently. Isn't it a bitch? Your teeth are fine, then wham—your gums go."

"Howie, write down Dr. Stone's address, please," Jack ordered. "Then give his office a call and see if he can squeeze us in for a quick meeting this afternoon."

Howie thought it in bad taste, vaguely masturbatory in appearance, to use a cell phone in a restaurant, so he took Jack's phone outside to the parking lot. Dr. Maxwell Stone's receptionist offered him an appointment for December 10, but Howie impressed upon her the fact that this was an important personal matter concerning the doctor's younger brother, Sherman. Howie was put on hold. He listened to a refrain of "Satin Doll" and almost the entirety of "Lullaby of Birdland" before the receptionist returned. Dr. Stone could fit him in briefly at two-thirty this afternoon, if that was convenient. He told her it was.

By the time Howie returned to the restaurant, the club sandwiches had arrived and the conversation had shifted to a new area.

"October fourteen," the detective was saying, looking at a sheet of paper in his hand. "That's when the robbery detail received a fax from Barbara Stone's insurance company with a description of a turquoise-and-silver set that had been reported stolen in San Geronimo—matching necklace, bracelet, ring, watch, and earrings. We were alerted to keep an eye out for the goods in the Santa Fe area. Then on October fifteen we received another fax to cancel the alert."

"So the alert was only posted for one day? Had the jewelry been recovered?"

"That I can't tell you. The insurance company only said we didn't need to look for it anymore. It's an outfit named Sangre de Christo Insurance, by the way. They're in Albuquerque."

"Write it down, Howie."

"I'm writing, Jack. We have an appointment with the peridontist at two-thirty."

"Then, I guess we'd better floss," Jack said, making one of his rare jokes. Howie tried to summon forth a laugh, but it came out more like a hacking cough.

"Okay, let's talk about heroin," Jack said to Detective Hastings.

"Right, you mentioned that on the phone. Actually, the narcotics people over at DPS couldn't tell me a thing about Sherman Stone. If he's been dealing smack, he's off their radar, I'm afraid."

"Hold on a second . . . Howie, try to get the O'Keeffe Museum for me—I left voice mail earlier for an assistant curator named Carol Wardman, but she hasn't gotten back to me. See if you can get us an appointment for later in the afternoon . . . sorry, Jim. We're juggling a busy load this afternoon. Let's say a small-time dealer like Sherman Stone wanted to buy heroin—he'd go to Española, I imagine?"

"Exactly. There are a couple of major players there."

Howie left the table again with Jack's cell phone, this time taking along several sections of his club sandwich to nibble on while he played secretary. He sat in the cab of the truck with the phone and fed Katya one of the triangles of his sandwich because she seemed so pleased to see him. He reached the Georgia O'Keeffe Museum and talked with Carol Wardman, who had just returned to her office. In a thin, nasal voice she told Howie that she could possibly make an appointment with him the week after Thanksgiving, but he would need to phone a few days in advance.

This was unacceptable, Howie replied in his best big-shot voice, telling her that he had important information about a lost Georgia O'Keeffe canvas by the name of *Red Moon*, and if she was interested in talking about it today, fine—otherwise he had a call in to the Getty in Los Angeles.

She changed her tune—and her tone—immediately.

"Would five this afternoon be convenient?" she asked.

Unfortunately, five was not convenient. Mr. Moon Deer would be trick-or-treating at that hour. "One-thirty," he told her ruthlessly.

Twelve

The Georgia O'Keeffe Museum was the newest museum in Santa Fe, opened with much expense and fanfare near the downtown plaza a few years back. Howie had come here last summer with Claire and the kids one Sunday when entrance was free to New Mexican residents. Otherwise, it cost a bundle to get in. Howie's verdict was that the paintings were okay—he especially liked the roomful of O'Keeffe watercolors. But it was a small museum, and there really wasn't that much art displayed, and both he and Claire had left with a feeling of disappointment. You probably needed to be a Picasso to merit devoting an entire building to just one artist.

After a brief skirmish at the front desk, a guard led Howie, Jack, and Katya through the public rooms back to a windowless office. The skirmish concerned Katya—apparently, the guards had not experienced a flood of blind people with guide dogs trying to get in their doors, and so a phone call had been required to consult with a higher authority. In the end, Katya won, being a puppy of a litigious age; no one dared offend a handicapped person who might hire a lawyer and sue.

Carol Wardman was a round, red-complexioned woman in her late thirties with plump cheeks and messy strawberry hair. Her windowless office was modern, but like a tomb. Like being buried alive in an Egyptian pyramid, complete with all the golden treasures, Howie thought. On Jack's instructions, he gave Ms. Wardman a Wilder & Associate business card.

"Well, well. Private detectives," she said. She giggled for no apparent reason, perhaps nervousness, then looked from Jack to Howie to Jack again with an increasing somberness. "So tell me, have you really found *Red Moon*? It's a painting a lot of people would like to get their hands on."

"Howie, please show Ms. Wardman the brochure. Let's make certain we're talking about the same work."

Howie got out the auction brochure that Barbara Vandenberg Stone had loaned him, found the page with the reproduction of *Red Moon,* and passed it to the assistant curator.

"Yes. This is it. It's considered one of the best of O'Keefe's late-twenties period, you know."

"And correct me if I'm wrong but it's been missing since August 1974."

"That's right. It was stolen from the house of a collector here in Santa Fe. I don't remember his name offhand."

"Juan Antonio Mendez," Jack told her. "A wealthy Argentinean. He was killed in the burglary, and the case was never solved."

Howie sensed a carnivorous quality in the way that Carol Wardman was regarding Jack. It would be a big coup, of course, for an assistant curator to recover such an important painting.

"Tell me more," she said, urging him to continue.

"*Red Moon* has come up in connection with a recent murder we've had in San Geronimo. We don't actually have the painting—yet," Jack told her. "It would be very helpful if you could tell us something of the painting's history."

"Well, it was done in 1929. It's generally considered the companion piece of a canvas known as *The Lawrence Tree* that was painted the same year. O'Keeffe had been spending time that year at the San Cristobal ranch of Frieda and D. H. Lawrence, where she completed both *Red Moon* and *The Lawrence Tree.* As you probably know, D. H. Lawrence lived in New Mexico for about eighteen months, but Frieda spent the rest of her life here after he died in 1930. *Red Moon* is actually a view of the desert from a meadow

on the Lawrence ranch. O'Keeffe gave it as a present to
Frieda once it was finished, and it remained hanging on a
wall in Frieda's bedroom until she died in 1956.

"Frieda Lawrence left the canvas in her will to a doctor
here in Santa Fe, Dr. Jonas Rudman, who was a close
friend. Rudman died in 1965 and his estate was auctioned
off. *Red Moon* was bought by the Argentinian collector you
mentioned, Juan Antonio Mendez. Then in 1974 Mendez
was killed, and the painting was stolen from his house. And
that's pretty much the entire saga.

"When the painting was stolen, all the major museums
and authorities around the world were notified, but of
course there's a huge black market in stolen art. And some
rich collectors, I'm afraid, who don't ask embarrassing
questions if something they want comes their way."

"How much do you think *Red Moon* would be worth
today?"

"That's hard to say. These things fluctuate a good deal,
as you can imagine, depending on what the market will
bear. Half a million dollars would be a conservative guess."

"May I speak confidentially?" Jack asked, leaning forward delicately in the black leather swivel chair. "I presume
you know Barbara Vandenberg Stone?"

"Up in San Geronimo? Yes, of course. We've been trying to get her to loan us some of her O'Keeffe collection
for years."

"Would you say that she's the sort of wealthy collector
you just mentioned? The sort who wouldn't ask embarrassing questions if something she wanted came along?"

The curator didn't answer immediately. "This will remain
only between us?"

"Absolutely."

"I wouldn't want to cross Babs, you know. We're still
hoping she'll leave us at least part of her collection one
day in her will. But, yes, my personal opinion is that Babs
Stone is an unscrupulous individual who wouldn't think
twice about getting any work of art she wanted in *any* possible way. There are people, you understand, for whom collecting becomes an obsession. You might not believe it but
the collecting of priceless works is like a drug. There was
an incident a few years ago when both this museum and
Babs were trying to get the same painting. I don't want to

go into the details because it's still a little sensitive. It turned out that the ownership of the painting was clouded in a number of ways. As soon as we learned that, we dropped out of the bidding, naturally. But not so Babs. I don't believe she ended up with the canvas, but it wasn't from lack of trying. So tell me—is that where you think *Red Moon* is? You think Babs has it?"

"We'll, I'm not sure, frankly," Jack admitted. "As it happens, she loaned us the brochure you're looking at, which would speak for her innocence. But then again, maybe her apparent helpfulness is only a way to throw us off track—the brochure's not really going to help us if she has the real painting hidden away."

"But you obviously have some reason to suspect her?"

"Well, yes. But I don't want to go into these reasons right now. And I don't want to accuse her unfairly, of course."

"I understand. Look, Mr. Wilder, if you actually do find *Red Moon,* will you contact me first? Naturally, the painting will belong to the estate of Juan Antonio Mendez. But perhaps they will make some arrangement with us. This is New Mexican art, after all, and it really should remain here—that's how I feel about it, anyway. Most of all, great art belongs to all the people of the world. It should be in museums, where the public has access to it, and *not* horded away in the mansion of some rich person like Barbara Vandenberg Stone!"

Jack smiled. "I take it you'd like to liberate Mrs. Stone's collection?"

"You bet, I would!"

"Hmm," said Jack. "I wonder if someone else had that idea as well."

From the dreamy upward tilt of his dark glasses, it appeared that Jack's thoughts were racing with speculations. But Howie's thoughts flooded to Claire, who had expressed the same disapproval of Barbara Stone's private treasure trove. The thought of Claire and their estrangement brought a small moan to his lips.

Both Jack and Carol Wardman turned his way.

"Indigestion," he told them.

*   *   *

Dr. Maxwell Stone, periodontist, had an office in a small medical complex just off St. Michaels Drive. This was the unscenic part of Santa Fe, the usual dull sprawl of gas stations, strip malls, and fast-food places that every strip in exurban America shares in common. Dr. Stone was a fatter, older version of his brother Sherman. He had the same weathered, aging prep school good looks and light blue eyes. But his features were broader, beef-fed with upper-middle-class living.

The dentist saw them in a tiny office behind the reception area. When Howie handed Dr. Stone their business card, he immediately became defensive.

"Look, if Sherman's in trouble again, I wash my hands of it from the start," he said heatedly. "I've done everything I can for that brother of mine over the years—I've given him money and a place to stay, and now he can just go to hell for all I care."

"When's the last time you saw Sherman?" Jack asked.

Dr. Stone shook his head warily; his brother was clearly not a pleasant subject for him. "It was exactly eleven years ago. He had been bumming around South America for a year—Chile, Peru, God knows where else. Naturally he arrived home broke and sick with hepatitis, and showed up on my doorstep expecting me to take care of him. Well, I did, of course. Even though I was married at the time to my second wife, Elizabeth, who couldn't stand him. We put Sherman in our spare bedroom, where he freeloaded off us for two months.

"Finally, as you can imagine, it was putting a strain on my marriage. Sherman was healthy again, so I asked him kindly to leave. And you know what that bastard did? He demanded five thousand dollars! I told him, no way, José. Then he said, if I didn't give him the money he would tell Elizabeth that I was, well . . . having an affair with my receptionist, Susan. He blackmailed me, my own damn brother! As it happened, I *was* having a relationship with my receptionist—in fact, Susan and I are married now, which is why I can talk about this freely. But at the time I was trying to save my marriage with Elizabeth, so I gave Sherman his five grand. But I told him that was it, I never wanted to see him again."

"Your own brother," Jack said sympathetically. "Was this the last contact you've had with him?"

The periodontist's anger seemed to deflate. He sighed. "Four years ago, I received a check in the mail from Sherman for six thousand dollars. Apparently he had married some rich lady, and he was in the clover, so he had decided to pay me back with interest. You see, this is the damned thing about Sherman—just when you think you hate his guts, he'll do something nice. He was always like that, even as a kid. All the girls were wild about him, of course. He'd treat 'em badly, but then he'd give them that charming smile of his, and they'd all forgive him. He could get away with murder."

"Get away with murder, huh?" Jack repeated mildly. "I'm interested in when he was young, actually. Particularly the summer of 1974. Were you in contact with your brother at that period of his life?"

"The summer of seventy-four?" Dr. Stone stared dreamily for a moment out a small window in his office at some shrubbery and the parking lot beyond. "Bell-bottoms, sideburns, everybody walking around with guitars . . . you sort of wonder sometimes, whatever happened to the Age of Aquarius! I was in dental school in Dallas, but I came back to Santa Fe that summer to live at home and work for a landscaping company."

"Sherman was in Santa Fe then?"

"Oh, yeah. That spring, he had dropped out of art school in New York. It was a typical Sherman stunt—he just couldn't finish anything."

"Which art school?"

"The Art Students League, I believe. He had been in New York for a couple of years, and I think he just got bored of it. So he showed up one day in Santa Fe with some artist buddy of his from back East, a Puerto Rican guy. They had hitchhiked west together and were having a grand old time. They stayed at my mother's for a few weeks, but then they got their own place not far from the plaza—Santa Fe was a lot cheaper back then. The Puerto Rican was actually very talented, I remember. He could do these amazing drawings of people, really capturing them, if you know what I mean. He'd go around to the bars and hang out in the plaza doing sketches of people, and I think he made a pretty good living at it. As for my brother, he was selling dope—he got busted in the plaza that summer."

"Do you remember the name of Sherman's Puerto Rican friend?"

"Manny, I think. Manny Salazar. No, that's not quite it. Manny . . . I wish I could think of his last name."

"Maybe it will come to you. That summer, in August particularly—did Sherman and his friend suddenly have a lot of spending money?"

"Well, I wasn't exactly hanging out with them, so I wouldn't know. I was the square older brother, you know, going to dental school and actually working for a living. What could be more bourgeois? So I didn't see Sherman very often, even though we were in the same town. What are you getting at?"

"Specifically, I was wondering if Sherman and Manny started burglarizing houses that summer to supplement their income."

Dr. Stone seemed to think about this. He shook his head. "I don't know. It's possible, I suppose, but they wouldn't have told me, of course. As for money, they always seemed to have plenty of it to party, but I always assumed it came from Manny's sketches and Sherman's dope dealing. I was envious, to be honest. I mean, here *I* was the serious one, working my way through dental school, totally broke—and my lazy younger brother has all the money. Manny left sometime late in that summer, I remember, hitching to California on his own. I had the impression that he and Sherman had some kind of falling out. Then Sherman got busted, and it took him a number of months to sort that out. He had to enroll in some kind of drug rehab thing, I recall. But as soon as he could, he left New Mexico and went back to New York. I didn't see him for years after that."

"All in all, it sounds like your brother had quite the wild youth," Jack remarked.

"Well, he was the artistic type," the periodontist said with sarcasm. "But you know, I always thought that it was his friend, Manny, who had the talent."

"Do you recall what Manny looked like?"

"He was tall, all arms and legs. Puerto Rican, with dark hair and complexion, of course. You could almost have taken him for one of our local Spanish, maybe with some Indian blood. Sort of strange-looking. He had these really intense staring eyes. I was a little afraid of him, actually. It wasn't any one thing, particularly. I remember he had this absolutely maniacal laugh. Personally, I thought he was crazy. I mean, *literally* crazy. Borderline psychotic."

"Was he . . . how should I put this? *Verbal*?"

"Oh, yes. He was a real talker. One of those guys who's always going off on long raps about Egyptian pyramids or flying saucers or lost cities under the ocean. Some pretty strange subjects . . . Lucero!"

"I'm sorry?"

"Manny Lucero. That was his name. I remember now." Dr. Stone smiled distantly, thinking back to that summer of '74. "You know, sometimes I've wondered whatever became of Manny Lucero. A person like that with so much talent, but not totally right in the head—it always seemed to me that either he would end up world famous, or turn up dead one day in some obscure ditch."

"The latter, I think," Jack Wilder informed him.

Thirteen

Claire Knightsbridge spent Halloween day in a flurry of activity, desperately trying to get the Performing Arts Center ready for the big benefit tonight. Theoretically, this was not her job—hanging banners and arranging tables and chairs and such—but at a time like this, everyone had to pitch in wherever needed.

At least the physical activity kept her from thinking about Howie. They had had fights before, of course, but never one in which they had gone to sleep without making up. Claire felt a little guilty. Life had been difficult recently, pulling her in opposing directions: Howie, her music, the job offer in Chicago, the kids, her worry about the San

Geronimo schools. Even her ex-husband, Jim, was causing trouble these days. She had not told Howie yet, but she had received a letter recently from a woman friend in Iowa City who wrote to say that Jim was consulting a lawyer to try to get custody of the children. Jim was telling everyone that Claire was obviously an unfit mother, going off the way she had to live in a tipi with an Indian, no less. Claire might need to hire her own lawyer to defend herself against the charges, ridiculous as they were. She was certain she would win a custody battle, but it would be a dirty fight, and at the moment it was the last thing she needed.

Meanwhile, it was hard to imagine how the Performing Arts Center would ever be ready in time for tonight's costume ball. By noon, the PAC was a carnival of activity. The decoration committee was still trying to get their mural up, a huge painted forest scene on a roll of paper big enough to encircle the auditorium. There was much shouting back and forth between people on ladders while down below, a team of carpenters was busy building a stage for the band at the far end of the room, pounding nails and making terrible screeching sounds with power saws.

At one o'clock, Sherman Stone arrived with several helpers and a small forest of papier-mâché trees to set up around the room. In Claire's opinion, the trees were ugly, and their odd angles and bulky trunks didn't at all fit with the enchanted forest theme of the mural. Then there was the band for tonight, a group of young Native American rockers from the Pueblo who called themselves The Dead Buffaloes. At two in the afternoon, the musicians began to arrive and set up their equipment for a sound check. An hour later, with drums and speakers and guitars in place, they turned up the volume to an earsplitting level and shook the building with a song whose lyrics seemed to consist of one line that was repeated over and over again: "Gonna rock the rez, rock the rez, rock the rez tonight! . . . ."

The Dead Buffaloes had been chosen by the entertainment committee, who had assured Claire that they could keep a beat—and besides, hiring Native American musicians would be the height of political correctness. But after hearing the sound check, Claire had her doubts. Among other things, the band members absolutely reeked of marijuana.

"Like the music, honey puss?" Sherman asked in passing, grinning and leering at her in a disturbing manner. His eyes were red and blurry. God, he was as stoned as the band! Not knowing how to respond, Claire pretended she had not heard him.

While The Dead Buffaloes were finishing up their sound check, Sherman and a group of noisy friends succeeded in hoisting a banner above the stage. In large letters the banner read: ART IS ANYTHING YOU CAN GET AWAY WITH! This was supposed to be very avant-guarde, Claire supposed, but she could only shake her head in amazement. She knew, of course, that she was terribly unhip and old-fashioned, but it was quite different being a classical musician. You couldn't "get away" with ad-libbing a Beethoven cello sonata, not on a professional level, unless you had worked many hours a day since the time you were five or six years old, like Claire had done. To be an artist here in San Geronimo, it wasn't discipline and work that seemed to be required any longer—just a huge ego and a flair for self-promotion.

Late in the afternoon, Claire realized she still hadn't received the special permit promised by the mayor allowing her to sell alcohol tonight. This was extremely frustrating and close to four o'clock she hurried back across the grounds to the smaller building where her office was located in order to use her phone. Claire walked through the empty gallery and down a quiet hallway muttering to herself with frustration, believing she was the only person in the building. But then, to her surprise, she found Sherman seated on the edge of her desk talking on her telephone, idly playing with a coffee mug that Jonathan had made for her in summer camp.

"Put that down!" she said icily.

Sherman only smiled and continued speaking. Claire was furious. She glared at him while he finished his phone call.

"Excuse me, but this is my private office," she said angrily, the moment he put down the receiver. "You should have asked before using my telephone."

Sherman stood up, ogling her with a pink-eyed grin. Not

only was he stoned, she could smell that he had been drinking as well.

"You know, you're a great piece of ass," he said with a wink. "You just need to loosen up a little."

"Get out of my office!" she ordered, her voice shaking.

"Ooo-oooh, I *like* it when sweet little Claire gets sassy!"

Suddenly, he was all over her. It happened so fast that Claire was taken completely aback. He tried to kiss her, sticking his tongue out while a hand went groping underneath her sweater. With a jerk of her head, she pulled her mouth away from his.

"Get away from me!" she screamed.

"Don't act so coy, honey puss. You want it, you know you do."

Claire struggled with the hand beneath her sweater. Sherman laughed at her efforts to get free of him.

"Come on, baby—you turn me on like you wouldn't believe," he whispered. He started to tell her all the X-rated things they could do together on her office desk.

Claire's fury gave her strength. With a mighty effort, she jerked her right knee upward and got him in the balls.

"Yeooww!" he screamed, stumbling back against the far wall. "You bitch!"

Claire reached wildly into her desk drawer for a letter opener she kept there, a small ornamental dagger. It wasn't very sharp, but she held it out with shaking hands in front of her, determined to stab him if he came after her again.

Sherman gradually unbent himself and stood upright. He saw the letter opener in her hand and grinned.

"Relax," he told her, breathing hard. "I'm not so desperate I need to get my jollies by force. I bet you're frigid, anyway."

"Get out!" she shouted.

"You know," he said, "Babs and I *own* the art scene here in San Geronimo. You're history, honey puss. You can kiss your job good-bye."

Claire lunged at him with her letter opener. But Sherman only laughed and dodged her thrust. He did a little dance out the door of her office and down the empty hall.

"Oh, honey puss!" she heard him say. "You're a real tiger!"

Claire was left alone, panting for breath and completely

appalled. She dropped the letter opener onto the floor, dismayed at how eagerly she would have killed Sherman Stone if he had given her half a chance.

Fourteen

Halloween was an Anglo custom with only shallow roots in New Mexico. The Spanish had a more serious tradition, *El Día de los Muertos,* the Day of the Dead, which came every year on November 2, two days after Halloween. *El Día de los Muertos* was a time of real death, not commercialized make-believe—a day to remember your personal dead, to visit their graves and sometimes leave behind a plate of favorite food by the headstone, or even a six-pack of beer for thirsty spirits.

All in all, Howie found the Hispanic tradition a good deal more mature, culturally speaking, than the Anglo Halloween. *El Día de los Muertos* had a kind of Jungian/Joseph Campbell resonance; candy corn and cheapo Star Wars costumes did not.

"You see, the Spanish believe each person dies three separate deaths," Howie explained to Jack in his best anthropologic manner while they were driving back from Santa Fe.

"That's a lot of dying," Jack observed.

"Well, yes, it is. First comes the physical death of the body. The second death is when the body is buried in the earth. But it's the third death that's considered the most tragic—that comes when a person is forgotten by his friends and family, and all the people of the earth. For only then is someone truly, finally dead."

"Well, well! Three deaths for one lousy corpse!" Jack said thoughtfully. He pondered the question for several miles, then added with a chuckle: "Christ, we'd need three times as many homicide cops to handle the flow!"

Howie sighed. It was only Jack's warped sense of humor, of course. But nevertheless, there were times when Anglos stuck Howie as awfully infantile. A people whose lives lacked meaningful ritual, who had turned Christmas and Easter and every other holiday into a great plastic Wal-Mart emptiness. As for Halloween, in San Geronimo it had become primarily an adult occasion, particularly among the arty set, a chance to dress up in increasingly elaborate costumes and go wild at the annual Art Association Ball. Locally, it was considered a good night to keep children safe at home; parents who did venture out with their kids generally kept a close eye on them and were careful to avoid houses where tricks seemed more likely than treats.

Howie was yawning ferociously by the time he arrived back in San Geronimo and dropped Jack off at home. He changed into his costume in the Wilders' downstairs bathroom, drove like crazy across town, and managed to pick up Jonathan and Heidi at their various friends' houses only half an hour late. They looked awfully cute. Heidi was dressed up as a fairy princess with a white tutu, tights, and a magic wand. Jonathan was a ghost, using an old sheet that he had cut up with holes for his eyes and arms.

"But what are *you*?" Heidi asked Howie, waving her wand at him imperiously.

"Well, take a guess."

She studied him, her blue seven-year-old eyes full of uncompromising innocence, not to be fooled. Howie's costume consisted of a black mask, a fringed cowboy shirt he had borrowed from his neighbor Bob, two toy six-guns in gaudy red plastic holsters on his hips, white jeans, a white cowboy hat, and pointed cowboy boots.

Heidi couldn't guess.

"How about you, Jonno? Do you know who I am?"

"A redneck?"

"*No*! I'm the Lone Ranger! Haven't you guys ever heard of the Lone Ranger?"

"Who's he?"

Howie was aghast. What kind of education did children get these days? He assured them that the Lone Ranger was a *very* important icon of Native American mythology. With this settled, they drove to one of the older residential neighborhoods in San Geronimo, not far from where the Wilders lived. Then Howie set off with them on the yearly sugar quest, joining a promenade of small witches, goblins, and alien creatures who were already wandering door to door.

Half asleep, walking from house to house, Howie found his mind drifting. He thought about Claire for a while, wondering if she was still angry with him. Then a little while later, his thoughts turned in a darker direction, speculating on murder, reminded of death by a passing skeleton. Earlier in the afternoon, while driving back from Santa Fe, he and Jack had spent some time tossing around various scenarios that would account for the facts they had acquired. As investigations went, this one was moving fast. The Rainbow Man had a name now: Manny Lucero. He also had a more tangible identity: a talented Puerto Rican artist Sherman Stone knew from art school in New York and had hitchhiked with to Santa Fe during the pivotal summer of 1974.

That August, a murder had been committed and an important Georgia O'Keeffe painting stolen from an art dealer's house. Twenty-five years later, Manny Lucero showed up in San Geronimo with a Beretta 9mm automatic that could be traced to that 1974 murder/burglary. The name of the painting, *Red Moon,* was on his lips as he died from a gunshot wound less than a mile from Sherman's house. Meanwhile, the San Geronimo medical investigator had confirmed his suspicion that Manny Lucero's death was due to a .22 bullet lodged in the victim's kidney; the victim had bled to death. The .22 slug had been recovered from the body, which was a piece of good luck. The Department of Public Safety lab would be able to match the slug to the correct rifle, if the murder weapon was found.

All these facts converged and floated freely in Howie's sleep-starved brain. He wished he could make better sense of them. Sherman Stone, of course, had a lot to answer for. He had lied, claiming that he did not know the homeless victim, when in fact, Manny Lucero was one of Sherman's oldest friends. Not only that, but Lucero had certainly seen Sherman in San Geronimo recently, since he made a drawing of Sherman as he appeared today. Jack was ready to assume tentatively that Sherman and Manny were the burglars who had broken into the house of Juan Antonio Mendez in August 1974. They had not been teenagers as Jack's source, Lt. Ernesto Flores, had suggested, but rather brash, counterculture artists in their mid-twenties. Still, Jack imagined that the burglary had gone down more or less as Flores had pictured it: two rebellious youths breaking into a fancy house as a lark, just for a little fun on an August night. Most likely they had believed themselves entitled to "liberate" a few goodies from a rich man who had more than he needed; they were artists after all, and the rich should support the arts, whether they wanted to or not. But then the burglary had turned tragic. Juan Antonio Mendez came home unexpectedly, got his Beretta 9mm automatic out of a drawer, and had ended up dead.

And then what? Why would Manny Lucero come to San Geronimo a quarter of a century later with the Beretta he had lifted from the murder scene? Howie theorized that Sherman had *Red Moon* and that Manny had come for his share of the loot. But Jack made him see that this didn't make sense: Why would Lucero wait twenty-five years for his share of the painting, if indeed Sherman had it? Of course, the possibilities were complicated by the fact that Sherman happened to be married to a woman who owned the largest private collection of Georgia O'Keeffes in New Mexico. So you had to ask yourself if Babs had a role in any of this. She certainly seemed to believe herself above conventional morality.

As Howie walked from house to house with the children on Halloween night, he had the frustrating feeling that he could almost visualize what had happened, but not quite clearly enough. No matter how he bent the facts around, they never seemed to fit completely in his mind. The mystery always came back to what exactly had brought Manny the Rainbow Man pushing his shopping cart to San Geronimo. It was probably not money, for money did not seem to be a motivating force for someone who had turned down $100 from Arthur Hopewell for his drawing, accepting only $63.95 instead. Meanwhile, it would help, of course, to find the murder weapon or some other physical evidence that would tie Sherman conclusively to the crime.

As Howie pondered, a crescent moon rose over the mountains. It was a clear, cold late autumn night with a spooky wind whispering through the bare branches of the trees. Howie walked with the children up and down the narrow sidewalks, avoiding the houses that were dark or unwelcoming, guiding them to the doorways of homes where there were lit pumpkins sitting in the windows, often elaborately carved, or dangling skeletons, or other merry signs of horror and death. By eight o'clock, as the candy bags were getting heavy, Howie led Jonathan and Heidi up the Wilders' driveway to leave them in Emma's care. Emma opened the door wearing mouse ears, whiskers, and a long tail dangling from her sweatpants. Jack was dressed in his usual at-home manner in baggy jeans and a flannel shirt, but then Jack didn't much need a Halloween costume to frighten children—not with his wraparound dark glasses and the hint of old scars around his eyes. The kids were frankly uneasy around Jack, not just tonight but every night; they said a shivery high-pitched hello to him, and gladly followed Emma into the kitchen for hot chocolate. This gave Howie a few minutes alone with Jack in the living room.

"So," Howie said, "I bet Captain Gomez felt properly upstaged when you told him how cleverly you ID'd the Rainbow Man."

Jack's smile was subtle. "Ed's off duty tonight. I left a message for him at the substation to call me when he gets a chance."

"But shouldn't you phone him at home? He's going to want to know about Manny Lucero."

"Well, we wouldn't deliberately withhold important information like that, of course. I *tried* to reach him, and the call was dully logged by the police operator. Meanwhile, we have a few hours to continue our own inquiries."

"Isn't this a little dodgy?"

"Strictly speaking, our asses are covered. Look, Howie, if I call Ed at home, all hell's going to break loose. Ed'll hop into his cruiser and haul Sherman off for a rather grim interview, I should imagine. And then poor Sherman would miss the costume ball tonight, and wouldn't that be a shame?"

"Jack! You can't be serious?"

"Can't I? Personally, I think our Mr. Stone will have his day of reckoning soon enough. Meanwhile, I'd rather give him one last night to party hearty. And maybe confide a thing or two to his new drinking buddy."

Howie didn't like the sound of this. "Look," he explained patiently, "the last time I saw Sherman Stone, he pointed an acetylene torch at me. We're not exactly drinking buddies."

"Think of this as theater, Howie, and you'll enjoy yourself. Get close to him. Find out what you can. I suspect that this is the last night it's going to be possible to have a casual guy-to-guy talk with Sherman. Starting tomorrow, he's likely to be surrounded by more expensive lawyers than you could shake a fist at, and they'll warn him very wisely to keep his mouth shut. The problem is we only have extremely circumstantial evidence for both murders, old and new. We need something more. Something concrete like an admission."

Howie shook his head warily. "No," he said. "I'm not good at this sort of thing."

Jack put his big paw of a hand on Howie's shoulder. "All you gotta do is make nice, buy a few rounds of drinks. He'll be curious what we know—if you play it right, he'll try to pump *you*. What you should do, Howie, is let him think you don't really give a damn about working for me. It's only a gig, you see, and a boy from the rez makes money from the white man anyway he can."

Howie was shocked. "You want him to think I can be bought?"

Jack smiled happily. "You see how quickly you're picking this up?"

Fifteen

The annual San Geronimo Art Association Halloween Ball was in full swing by the time Howie arrived in his Lone Ranger mask and ten-gallon hat, the toy six-guns jiggling on his hips. The auditorium was dim and crowded with fantastically costumed figures. There were mythical beasts and gods, aliens from other galaxies, half-naked women, and dozens of men in drag. Howie spotted a unicorn, several satyrs, a cave woman, a hula dancer in a grass skirt, and one man and woman strolling about without a stitch of clothing, he with an apple in hand and she with a live snake draped around her shoulders.

At the far end of the room, The Dead Buffaloes were jumping up and down on a stage that was lit by roving blue and red spotlights. Howie was glad to see some rockers from the rez making their way in the world, but he wasn't certain about their music. At the moment the lead singer was howling out a mantra in endless repetition: *"The buffalo's dead, we got casinos instead!"* Howie sensed it was what garage bands call "an original."

He wandered into the dense crowd in search of Claire. She had been talking about the decorations for weeks, but this was his first look at them. The mural that encircled the auditorium was a landscape of strange trees, stilted mountains, weird animals with knowing eyes, nightmarish birds, and a fat moon in a psychedelic sky—a white moon, Howie was happy to see, not red. Sheets of blue gel had been put over the lights to help create the illusion of being outside at night rather than in an auditorium. In addition to Sherman's papier-mâché trees, there were pine boughs spread around the room and even a makeshift cave you could climb inside and find spooky spiderwebs and ghostly hands that reached out for you. The decorations were hokey but effective, turning the Performing Arts Center into a veritable Halloween forest playground.

On the north side of the auditorium, several long tables had been set up, heavily laden with food. There was a roast pig, oysters, turkey, quiche, hams, dozens of salads, breads, pastries, even sushi—all of it donated by several restaurants in town. The buffet came with the entrance ticket, but you had to pay extra for drinks at the bar that had been set up in the lobby just outside the auditorium doors—Howie was relieved to see that Claire had gotten her special events liquor permit after all. The booze had been donated by a local business, and from what Howie could see, they were going to make money tonight. Which was a good thing, since the Art Association, like such organizations everywhere, was chronically in debt.

Howie was standing by himself in the crowd not far from

the food tables when a magnificently tall woman with raven black hair came up to him as though they were old friends.

"Moon Deer! Happy Halloween!" she cried. "My God, your costume is a *riot*! Absolutely a *perfect* political statement! . . . what do you think of mine?"

"Well. . . ."

The unknown lady was dressed in a purple robe with stars and planets and a headpiece that had several moons on wires orbiting around her head.

"I'm the Universe!" she cried. "You don't remember me, do you? I'm Tiara the sculptress. We were on a chairlift together last winter . . . remember that *marvelous* day?"

"Of course I do," he lied. He did not remotely remember Tiara the sculptress or that marvelous day. "So what have you been up to?"

She lowered her voice dramatically and moved closer. "I've been working with marble, these great gaudy pieces of stone. I have to find just the right stone, you know. A stone that really *speaks* to me and tells me what it wants to be. As an artist, I feel I'm only a vehicle for the stone to achieve it's true destiny. . . . do you know what I mean, Moon Deer?"

"Yeah, sure, a vehicle," he agreed politely. "I like that. But are you a Jeep or a Subaru?"

Her expression froze. In San Geronimo, you could make fun of Texans, the Christian right, just about anything, in fact—but *never* the scaredness of the creative process. Tiara the sculptress spotted a friend in the crowd and made an abrupt departure. Howie felt bad, driving away such a serious artist with his adolescent sense of humor. "Sorry! I must have been experiencing just a momentary past-life regression," he said aloud to her departing figure.

On his own once again, Howie kept looking for Claire. He spotted Robin Vandenberg standing alone near the stage. He was dressed in green tights, a green tunic, and a pointed green hat. Howie wasn't sure if he was trying to be Peter Pan or Robin Hood, but either way, he did not appear to be a happy camper. Not far away, Robin's sister, Pooh, was dancing with her husband, Lionel Cordova. Lionel and Pooh had both come as Indians, complete with feathered war bonnets and painted faces. This was a paradoxical breach of taste, for while it was considered politically correct for Howie to cross-dress as a white man, it was extremely incorrect for Pooh and Lionel to come to a Halloween party as Native Americans. It implied a lack of ethnic sensitivity. Personally, it seemed to Howie that if he could cross-dress, they should be able to do so as well. But, of course, San Geronimo's political correctness wasn't strictly rational. He saw Pooh and Lionel receive a very disapproving look from a passing floor lamp—a skinny woman with a lamp shade as a hat.

A few seconds later, Howie spotted Babs and Sherman Stone among the dancers near the stage. Babs was in an elaborate eighteenth-century French floor-length court dress complete with elaborate coiffure and jewels—Marie Antoinette?—dancing to The Dead Buffaloes' turgid beat. Sherman had come French as well, but from a more recent century: he wore a beret, paint-splattered jeans, dark glasses, dirty tennis shoes, and a black turtleneck sweater. Sherman made a convincing Parisian beatnik, circa 1955, and he seemed to be having more fun than his wife, dancing with a kind of jerky abandonment, trying not to spill a drink he held loosely in one hand.

The Dead Buffaloes began a new song about diabetes, unemployment, and the loss of cultural identity on the reservation—it was a tune that covered a lot of native issues. Howie yawned so hard his ears popped.

"Well, Moon Deer, you're not exactly the life of the party. You'd better let me buy you a drink."

It was Gilmer Good Day who had come up behind him. Gilmer was bare-chested and dressed in a miniskirt. It took Howie a moment to realize that he wasn't a Cheyenne in drag but rather an ancient Egyptian pharaoh, complete with a gold headdress—brass, actually, but cleverly made—and matching bracelets on his arms. Gilmer's long black-gray hair added to the King Tut look. Probably this wasn't a politically correct costume any more than Pooh and Lionel's—Howie was starting to see that Halloween was a dangerous holiday—but at least there were no Egyptians present to be offended.

"So how's life as a private eye?" Gilmer asked, speaking loudly in order to be heard over the band's wailing.

"Actually, there are some things I wanted to ask you."

Gilmer laughed. "I bet there are! But first you'd better

let me buy you that drink. Come on, it's impossible to talk with this damn music. Lord help me, The Dead Buffaloes— and I thought I'd seen everything! What the hell's wrong with Indians these days?"

It was a large question, but Gilmer didn't wait for an answer. He led the way through the crowd to the relative quiet of the lobby bar.

"How about a martini?" Gilmer offered.

"Uh, just a beer for me. I got a long night ahead."

"Don't be silly. Martinis are the latest retro-fad. I was in New York recently, and everybody's drinking 'em. When a culture runs out of new ideas, it has to re-mine the old."

"Well. . . ."

Gilmer had a commanding presence, and Howie didn't quite have the energy tonight to resist the siren call of retro-fashion: he soon found himself with a martini in hand.

"Here's to growing up in a trailer," Gilmer said, touching their plastic glasses. "You know, we've got a lot in common, Moon Deer."

Did they? This somehow worried Howie a little.

"Okay, tell me all the gossip," Gilmer insisted merrily. "What sort of dirt have you been finding on Sherman and Babs?"

"More dirt than I expected. They're a disturbing family."

"Yes, that's true. Actually, Sherman isn't so bad, once you get to know him. His problem is that it's hard to pose as a wild-eyed rebel when you've married somebody who's worth fifty million dollars. He had talent once, but now he doesn't know what to do with himself."

"You knew Sherman before he married Babs?"

"Oh, sure, we go back, Sherm and I. I warned him not to get married. But he wouldn't listen to me."

"Did you ever meet an artist by the name of Manny Lucero?"

Gilmer shook his head. "Manny Lucero? That doesn't ring a bell. Of course, I've met a lot of artists, and at my age they start to blur together. Except for the very special ones, the few with real talent."

"Lucero just might be in that category," Howie said. "He's the homeless person who got shot on Thursday."

"Really?" Gilmer's eyes narrowed with concern. "The cops were going around my neighborhood asking us all if we saw anything. To tell you the truth, I've been working so damn hard, the house could have just about burned down around me, and I wouldn't have noticed. But I thought the cops didn't know who this homeless guy was . . . Danny Lucero, you say?"

"*Manny,*" Howie told him. "Jack and I managed to ID him just this afternoon. We haven't even had a chance to tell Captain Gomez yet. And it gets more interesting—it turns out that Sherman Stone and Manny were friends in New York at the Art Students League in the early seventies. In seventy-four, they dropped out of school together and hitchhiked west to Santa Fe. Did you ever hear Sherman talk about him?"

Gilmer shook his head. "Never. And believe me, Sherman talks about everything and everybody. Are you sure your information's right?"

"Almost positive. Tell me, Gilmer—do you have any idea how many people own snowmobiles on Valverde Mesa?"

Gilmer seemed puzzled by this shift in the conversation. "Only Sherman, as far as I know. All the other rich Anglos on the mesa are so environmentally responsible, you know. They build themselves huge houses with enough hardwood floors to destroy half a rain forest, then they go on about how snowmobiles destroy the fragile ecosystem. What a joke."

"What about down in the village?"

"Down in the village, the people are too damn poor to have toys like that. Why do you ask?"

"Because a snowmobile was seen on Thursday a few minutes before Manny was shot," Howie said, leaving out his own part of the story. "It's another thing that ties Sherman to the murder. All in all, Sherman's going to have some explaining to do—specifically, how it was that an old friend he denies knowing shows up in town, and then gets shot near his house."

Gilmer frowned. "Offhand, I have to tell you—I don't see Sherman as someone capable of killing anybody. He's abrasive, sure. He can be a real asshole at times. But shooting some homeless guy—that seems a little farfetched, especially if it's an old friend of his. In his own crazy way,

Sherman is very loyal to his friends . . . and speak of the devil!"

Sherman Stone, dressed in his Paris beatnik garb, was making his way through the auditorium door into the lobby.

"Well, suck my brains!" he cried happily. "Who's buying the booze?"

"I am. You know my Lakota friend, don't you?—Howard Moon Deer," Gilmer said smoothly.

Sherman grunted at Howie, acknowledging his presence with a quick glance. At the moment he seemed more interested in alcohol. "What are we drinking?"

"Martinis. I'll get us another round."

"Not for me," Howie said quickly as Gilmer started toward the bar.

"Come on, Moon Deer. This is party time," Gilmer told him. "You can be your sober Sioux self tomorrow."

"Have a goddamn drink, for chrissake, Moon Deer," Sherman said disgustedly. "What a pussy!"

Howie supposed he'd better drink. Jack said to fit in, to ingratiate himself. Fortunately, as drinks went, martinis were astonishingly small, hardly more than a tiny gulp.

"I should eat something first."

"I'll get you an extra olive," Gilmer offered.

Howie was halfway through his second martini, deep in his undercover mode, when he spotted Claire through the crowd inside the auditorium door. She had come to the party as a human cello, her costume constructed from two large pieces of cardboard that she wore front and back—more a double bass, he supposed, because of its size. She was by herself, looking about, carrying a cello bow in her hand. Howie's heart did a little flip-flop just seeing her. It was like the feeling he got sometimes stepping outside to a particularly beautiful morning: she made the whole world appear good and fresh and hopeful. Then he glumly remembered that they were fighting.

"Catch you later," he said to Gilmer and Sherman. "There's someone I need to see."

He snuck up behind Claire. "You look good enough to pluck," he told her. "Your strings, that is."

She jumped, startled.

"Oh, Howie! I've been looking for you everywhere!"

Without warning, tears appeared in her eyes. "I'm so sorry we had that stupid fight last night!"

"It wasn't any huge deal," he lied. He held her in his arms as closely as it was possible for the Lone Ranger with dangling six-guns to embrace an oversize cello. "Hey, it's all right," he said when she began to cry. Gradually it occurred to him that there was more going on with Claire than their fight last night.

"What's wrong?"

"*Everything's* wrong!" she cried, pulling back from him and wiping the tears from her cheeks with the backs of her hands. "God, Howie, what a day! Sometimes I just don't think I was meant for this planet. Tell me about the kids. Are they okay?"

"They're fine, you don't have to worry. We went trick-or-treating, and they've got more candy than you'll probably let them eat in a year. I left them with Emma. . . ."

He saw that Claire wasn't really listening. She was tense. Her mouth was tight, and her eyes were far away. "Claire, what *happened*?"

"I don't want to talk about it," she told him. But then, abruptly, she changed her mind, unable to hold back her torrent of anger. "It's Sherman. He came on to me today. It was really yucky."

Howie felt himself go hot and cold, all at once.

"Came on to you?" he managed. "Like how, exactly?"

"He tried to kiss me. I suppose I shouldn't have gotten so upset about it—but God, what a creep! I despise that man, I truly do!"

Howie despised that man too. At the moment it was all he could do not to rush back to the bar and shove a plastic martini cup down that man's throat.

"You'd better tell me about this from the start."

"Okay, but let's get out of here. God, I can't stand this noise and all these puffed-up people another second more!"

Howie took her hand and led her out a side door of the auditorium to the edge of the parking lot. The night air was cool and blissful. The music of The Dead Buffaloes quieted to a low thud as the door closed behind them.

"Tell me about Sherman," he prodded.

Claire sighed. "I came back to my office, and Sherman was sitting on my desk, talking on my telephone. When I got angry at him, he tried to kiss me and feel me up. It was loathsome."

"Feel you up?"

"Well, you know. He groped with his hand. Became a real octopus."

"Above the waist? Or below?" Howie asked, almost casually, except for his clenched teeth.

"Above. It was nothing I didn't have to deal with a hundred times back in high school going to movies with boys. But it was just the last straw to a lousy day, that's all."

"When you told him no," Howie ventured, "I trust he stopped in a gentlemanly manner."

Claire smiled. It was like the sun coming out from behind a cloud. "Actually, I kicked him in the balls. That stopped him, believe me."

He smiled back at her. "You kicked him hard, I hope."

"Very."

"Awesome," he told her. "And as it happens, Jack and I need just a little more time to get a few facts straight, and then we're going to nail that scumball. We think Sherman shot Manny Lucero."

"Who's Manny Lucero?"

Howie had forgotten that Claire didn't know about this. He was about to tell her how he and Jack had discovered the identity of the Rainbow Man, when a woman he didn't recognize opened the side door and called to Claire. "Oh, *there* you are! Someone told me you'd stepped out here."

"What's the problem, Iris?"

"Bill Dorfman just told me that there's some drunk guy smoking pot in the men's room with two women. They're throwing toilet paper and yelling names at people and causing a real disturbance. I didn't know what to do."

Claire gave an exasperated laugh and turned to Howie. "What next, I wonder? Would you do me a huge favor, Howie?"

"They're busted, Claire. I'll take care of it."

She kissed him before he left. "You really are my favorite masked man ever," she whispered.

"Hi ho, Silver," he managed. But his thoughts were already grimly set on the encounter ahead. Howie walked quickly back inside the Performing Arts Center and made his way through the crowd to the men's room. There was really only one person in San Geronimo who could be counted on to be drunk and belligerent and smoking dope with two women in a public bathroom.

Sixteen

The musty odor of marijuana drifted out from the men's room. Howie charged through the door to find himself confronted by an unlikely sight: an aging beatnik with black shades and a beret standing with two gorgeously long-legged women in slinky clothes and stiletto heels. All three of them were laughing helplessly, making quite a racket. One of the women was a blonde, the other a redhead. The blonde had a cigar in her mouth that would have made Fidel Castro proud. But nothing was quite as it seemed. As Howie's eyes focused on the hilarity, he saw that the cigar was a joint, the women were men in drag, and the beatnik, as he suspected, was Sherman Stone.

"Oh, *look* what just walked in!" cried the redhead. "It's the Lone Ranger!"

"You can't smoke dope here," Howie told them calmly.

"I've always wanted to ride a big white stallion," the blonde said meditatively, looking over Howie.

"Look, why don't you put out the joint," Howie persisted. "You'll get the Art Association in a heap of trouble."

"Oh, yeah?" Sherman demanded. In a schizophrenic booze-addled instant, his mood had changed from laughter to snarling mean. "Let me tell you something, Moon Queer. My goddamn wife *built* this auditorium. So if I want to smoke dope here, no asshole Indian's gonna tell me I can't. You got that, *kimosabe*?"

Howie fixed an arctic smile on his face and clenched his fists, just in case he gave in to the temptation to bash Sherman Stone senseless. "Moon Queer," he repeated. "Hey, that's real witty."

The bathroom door opened, and Gilmer Good Day wandered in. "There you are, Sherman—I was starting to think maybe you got yourself flushed down the toilet."

Sherman began coughing. Suddenly he turned, bent over the sink behind him, and threw up with a terrible retching sound. He didn't turn fast enough, however, to avoid slobbering some yellow goo on the redhead.

"Yuck!" said the redhead.

"That's so incredibly gross," added the blonde. Sherman retched again and again, an extended symphony of vomit. It was so vile that the blonde and redhead both gagged and made a hasty retreat from the bathroom.

"Well, you feel better now, Sherm?" Gilmer asked brightly.

"Shit," said Sherman, standing up tentatively. He was deathly pale. His beatnik glasses had fallen from his head into the awful mess in the sink. Wisely, he left the glasses where they were. "Get me a beer, Gilmer. I need something to settle my stomach."

"You don't need a beer. Let's get some fresh air instead."

"I'll get my own beer, then!" he pouted. Sherman took a few steps from the sink, but his legs were unsteady. He staggered against the metal side of a toilet stall.

"Easy does it, bubba," Gilmer told him, taking hold of his arm. "Hey, Howie, why don't you give me a hand here with our paleface brother."

"Goddamn Indians everywhere!" Sherman muttered wildly. "Let me go!"

Howie was surprised at Gilmer's patience. "Come on, Sherm," Gilmer was saying in a kindly voice. "We've been a little excessive today. Made ourselves sick as a dog, haven't we? . . . some fresh air is just the thing."

Howie and Gilmer each took an arm and began leading Sherman Stone from the bathroom. Just as they were approaching the door, Howie slipped strategically, slamming Sherman's left shoulder against a paper towel dispenser.

"Goddamn, watch it, Moon Queer!" Sherman cried.

"Oops," said Howie, embarrassed to be so clumsy. And then, just for Claire, he was clumsy a second time. Passing through the lobby, Howie's left foot somehow got tangled between Sherman's wobbly legs, sending Sherman sprawling face first onto the floor, despite Gilmer's efforts to keep his friend upright.

"Oops again," said Howie.

"You having trouble with your coordination?" Gilmer asked, giving Howie an odd look.

"It's lack of sleep, I guess," Howie admitted.

"Just stay away from me!" Sherman said grumpily, picking himself up from the floor. He managed to walk on his own outside the building into the cold night air. Once outside, he staggered over to a bush, pulled down his zipper, and peed for a very long time. This seemed ass-backward to Howie, smoking in the bathroom and peeing outside. But, of course, he wasn't a free spirit artistic type who defied conventions.

"Feeling better now?" Gilmer asked.

"Yeah. Let's split and go to Pinky's. Christ, this party's boring as shit. Just a lot of faggots and phony asshole. You drive, Gilmer. We'll go in your Jewmobile."

"You just want to score dope," Gilmer observed.

"Of *course* I just want to score!" Sherman growled. "What the hell! You think I hang at Pinky's for the *atmosphere*?"

Gilmer turned to Howie. "Feel like a ride, Moon Deer?"

"You're not really going to help him buy heroin?" Howie asked, surprised.

Gilmer shrugged. "Well, if I don't help him, he'll find someone else who will and end up getting in even more trouble. I've seen him like this before. Believe me, he won't quit until he gets what he wants."

"Hey, I'm out of candy, goddamn it," Sherman whined. "I gotta score, man. I really do."

Gilmer smiled very slightly. "Someday I'm going to wash my hands of you, Sherman."

"Yeah, but just not tonight. I'm sick, man. And I really need you, okay? So come on, let's go to Pinky's."

Gilmer turned once again to Howie. "Well?"

Howie shrugged. "Why not? I'll just get my coat," he said. A stoned Sherman might be easier to wheedle information from than a merely sick Sherman. Not only that, but if he was lucky, he might even have an opportunity for more inspired clumsiness.

Howie ducked back inside to get his trench coat and tell Claire he was leaving. But he couldn't see her anywhere. He left hoping Claire would understand. He was doing this for her, and to appease the eyes of Manny Lucero, the Rainbow Man, who still seemed to be staring at them all from a fading distance.

The Jewmobile—as Sherman had called it with his usual flare for being offensive—was Gilmer Good Day's bright red Jaguar convertible. Gilmer asked Howie to drive, saying he would sit in back with Sherman in order to push Sherman's head out the window should he show signs of being sick again.

Howie arranged himself behind the wheel in a leather bucket seat so soft and comfortable it was like being held by a downy glove. The seat had electric controls that moved it up, down, forward, backward, and tilted it back and forth. Howie had never driven such an expensive car. He turned on the ignition, and the control panel glowed with space-age green and red instruments that made a guy feel very potent. The car had climate control, cruise control, an entertainment system, and a bunch of high-tech options Howie could only guess at. He felt like some combination of a movie executive and Captain Kirk about to head off to a distant galaxy.

"You like my wheels, huh?" Gilmer asked from the back.

"Hey, this is something!"

Gilmer chuckled. "You could own a car like this yourself one day. All you need to do is sell your soul."

Howie had to admit that if one *were* to sell one's soul, it wouldn't be bad getting a Jaguar convertible out of the deal. It was like driving a giant penis. The thing had a definitive masculine thrust and motion. It glided through the night with a soft purr of predatory power. He wished he could take it out on the open road, but Pinky's was only a few miles away on the south end of town, not far enough to see what the car could really do. Howie pulled into a dirt lot and parked between a motorcycle and an old pickup truck, hoping the Jag would survive such mixed company.

Pinky's was an old decrepit adobe building, a sleazy alternative for those in San Geronimo who hated bars full of Yuppie scum. Sherman led the way into the alcoholic gloom; he seemed all right now, like a horse who was nearly home. The air inside the bar was thick and dark, a blend of beer, tobacco smoke, and old perspiration, all mixed together with a subtle whiff of urine cakes from the bathroom. It was eleven o'clock, and Pinky's was three-quarters full, a crowd of people who looked as if they had been trapped here forever, neither joyful nor sad, simply paralyzed. Country music from the jukebox mixed with the click-clack of pool balls. A number of people were in costume, but Howie had left his mask and six-guns in the car, glad not to be the Lone Ranger anymore. Sherman waved at some people he knew and led the way to an imitation red leather booth near the pool table. Clouds of smoke floated like fog between the green velvet and the shaded light overhead. Howie put his elbows on the table in front of him, and found it was sticky with beer.

Sherman was restless. He sat with Gilmer and Howie in the booth for only a moment, then got up again almost immediately, his eyes darting around the room. "Get me a drink, Gilmer, tequila and grape, while I take care of a lil' business," he said tensely. He started to walk away, then returned to the table. "How about loaning me a hundred bucks?" he added.

"Anything else you need?" Gilmer asked dryly.

Sherman grinned. "No, that'll do. For now."

Gilmer had a brown leather flight jacket over his pharaoh costume. He pulled out his wallet from an inside pocket and handed Sherman a crisp new hundred-dollar bill. Sherman took the bill and walked away without a word of thanks. Howie watched him join two Hispanic men in biker clothes near the bar. After a few minutes of conversation, all three men drifted out to the parking lot. Howie turned to Gilmer.

"So why do you do it?" he asked.

"Why do I give Sherman money and take care of him when he's sick? Don't you help your friends, Moon Deer?"

"Sherman's not anybody's friend. He's a self-absorbed asshole whose only concern is finding his next high."

Gilmer was silent for a moment. He seemed to be debating what he would say.

"Try to imagine a long time ago in Rome, Moon Deer. Another lifetime entirely," he said finally. "I was a young Cheyenne in Europe out to get a heavy hit of culture—yeah, you can relate to that, I bet. I was so broke I used to walk everywhere because I was saving all my money to get into the museums. Well, one day when my feet were killing me and I hadn't eaten a real meal for forty-eight hours, I met Sherman Stone in the Sistine Chapel. We started talking under that big Michelangelo ceiling, and pretty soon I forgot I was hungry and my feet were hurting. We were young, we both wanted to be artists, and man, the Sistine Chapel was like we had died and gone to heaven. Do you know Rome?"

"I was there for a week once."

"We left the Vatican and walked along the bank of the Tiber all the way to Trastevere. We talked and talked and talked. Finally, I confessed that I couldn't walk another step, and I was goddamn starving. Well, Sherman had some money, and he took me into a little trattoria near an old church, and we drank red wine and ate spaghetti carbonara and big plates of osso buco and huge loaves of fresh bread. Then we talked some more about art and politics and getting laid. Sherman Stone was the most entertaining and original person I had ever met. He had an incredible enthusiasm for ideas, and his enthusiasm was contagious. That may be hard for you to imagine seeing him today—he's lost it all now, of course, all that youthful ardor. But I always remember the meal he bought me when I was hungry. I remember what Sherman used to be. Can you understand what I'm saying?"

"Well, sure."

"I wonder if you can. You're young, Moon Deer, so you don't realize yet that one of the interesting things about growing older is you see how people change over the years. Sometimes they change for the better, and sometimes it's for the worse. With Sherman . . . well, he's not in good shape. He's a junkie. He's become a problem for me, actually, but I do my best for him. Believe me, that's not the first bathroom I've helped him stagger out of, and it probably won't be the last."

"How did you both end up in San Geronimo?"

"That was an accident, I guess—if you believe in accidents. Call it fate, if you like. Or synchronicity. I didn't see Sherman for years. I came to San Geronimo by myself in the mid-eighties because I'd heard about it from Babs. I knew Babs from New York and Santa Fe—I met her in eighty-two at a show. She told me San Geronimo was a good place to be a painter. The light was incredible, she said. The kind of pure, intense light you used to find in Greece before the Mediterranean got all smoggy and polluted. So I came and saw for myself, and I ended up buying some land just down the road from her."

"Then, your friendship with Babs didn't have anything to do with knowing Sherman?"

"Babs isn't what I'd call a friend. We have a *relationship,* and that's a little different," Gilmer corrected. He laughed, seeing the expression on Howie's face. "No, not a *romantic* relationship, thank God! Babs was my patron. Or patroness, I suppose. Accept my word for it, it's impossible to make it in art without someone like Barbara Vandenberg to champion your cause. She likes to say that she discovered me, of course—that's what *she* gets out of it. Basically, she put my name out in the right places and helped me into the right kind of shows and galleries. So I owe Babs a lot, though I don't really take it personally—I was only a way for her to feel self-important. When she met Sherman on her own a few years later in Greece, she wrote to me asking about him. Sherman had mentioned that he knew me, so she wanted a full report. I told her that Sherman was a fun and brilliant guy, so I feel a little responsible for the marriage, which probably turned out to be a big mistake for both of them."

A waitress came by, and Gilmer ordered three tequila and grapes. Howie planned to drink his slowly.

"Come on, let's play some pool," Gilmer suggested, seeing that the table was free. "Knowing Sherman, this could take a while."

Howie snuck a glance at his watch and stifled a yawn. It was nearly midnight, past his bedtime. With only one hour of sleep last night, Pinky's was starting to spin in his vision like a sad old 45 on the jukebox.

Sherman returned, "borrowed" another twenty dollars from Gilmer for undisclosed reasons, and then came back to the table in a deeply pacified condition, his eyes pink with euphoria. Howie couldn't help but think about Claire across town at the Art Association. She would be getting ready about now to pull the winning raffle ticket for the twenty-five acres of land in the mountains, wondering where Howie was. He was starting to wonder where he was too. He wished wherever it was, it was someplace other than Pinky's. With Claire in the tipi, for instance, snuggled in each other's arms under the bear rug, his head on a nice soft pillow. . . .

"Wake up, Moon Deer," Sherman said dreamily.

"I'm totally 'wake, man."

"No, you're not. You're staring at me cross-eyed. And it's making me dizzy to look at you."

Howie sucked an ice cube in order to get a better grip on himself. Gilmer got up and went to the bathroom to pee. The call of nature was the most exciting thing that had happened at the table for the past ten minutes. Sitting in a bar with someone stoned on heroin was a slow-motion event, not exactly a thrill a minute. Howie wasn't certain how to work on Sherman. He sensed that if he moved too fast, Sherman would clam up and he wouldn't get anywhere. But slow had its own problems too. If something didn't happen soon, they would all be asleep.

When Gilmer left the table, Howie decided he had better try something. Anything at all.

"Jack Wilder and I spent the day down in Santa Fe," he mentioned.

Sherman's glance was poisonous. "Wow," he said. "Santa Fe. How did you stand the excitement?"

"Actually, it had its moments. Jack found out the name of the homeless guy who was shot on Thursday. Manny Lucero. As it happens, he got the name from your brother, Maxwell."

Sherman blinked, a flicker of interest showing in his bloodshot blue eyes.

"So how's good old Max?" he asked after a moment.

"Good old Max is fine. He's married to the receptionist that you tried to blackmail him about ten years ago."

"Blackmail? I sent him his money back. Didn't he get the goddamn money?"

"He got it. Six thousand dollars. That was pretty decent of you, Sherman. Paying him back with interest."

"He's my brother," Sherman said grandly, lighting a cigarette. He exhaled slowly, blowing a stream of smoke into the far horizon. "Well, well, well. You found out about Manny. I guess you guys are real detectives after all, Moon Deer. And all the time I thought you were just a stupid asshole."

Howie smiled coldly, showing teeth. "Hey, it doesn't mean diddly to me, Sherman. I couldn't care less if you knew Manny Lucero or Vincent van Gogh or Jack the Ripper. It's only a gig for me, you know, working for the white man, and I get sick of it sometimes. I find myself wishing I could think up a way to make some serious money."

"Do you?" Sherman stared at Howie. "So how much does Wilder pay you?"

"Not enough." Howie put a little self-pity into his voice. "I've got kids to think about. Jack always has his pension to fall back on—he doesn't know what it's like trying to make ends meet."

Sherman's stare was long and languid. "You want to make some money, huh? You know, maybe I could help you," he said.

"Could you? Like how?"

"Like for information, for example. Like telling me what the cops know about Manny Lucero, for example."

"Actually, the cops don't know anything about Manny. Jack hasn't told them yet."

"No kidding? Why's that?"

"Because Jack's such an egomaniac, that's why. He wants to solve this whole thing on his own. Outsmart Captain Gomez, you see. It's pathetic."

A cagey look came slowly into Sherman's heroin-glazed eyes. Mental agility, at this point, was probably not his strong point. "In other words, only you and Jack know about Manny?"

"At the moment, yeah," Howie said pointedly. Then in the interest of self-preservation, he added: "And your brother Maxwell knows too, of course."

"Good old Max'll shut up if I tell him to. Maybe I know a few of his secrets too."

"Do you? I bet his secrets aren't as interesting as your secrets, Sherman."

Sherman shrugged. "You don't know anything about me, Moon Deer."

"No? I know, for example, how you and Manny were in art school together and how the two of you hitched out west to Santa Fe in the summer of 1974. That must have been a good summer to be in Santa Fe, wasn't it, Sherman? A real killer, I bet."

Sherman's look deepened. "Very interesting," he said slowly. But then he spotted Gilmer coming out of the men's room and heading their way. Sherman put a finger to his lips.

"We'll talk about this later, Moon Deer. Just you and me, okay? I don't want Gilmer to know."

"Okay. But is there going to be some money in this for me?" Howie asked.

Sherman's smile became more cunning. "Possibly. I do believe we're going to be friends, Moon Deer. Friends—and partners."

Howie smiled back. Sherman Stone had taken the bait. This could be interesting, as long as Howie managed to keep from being swallowed along with the hook.

Seventeen

Gilmer drove the Jag as they left Pinky's, Sherman in the front passenger seat and Howie stretched out in the back.

Gilmer insisted he was sober as a judge—which unfortunately wasn't much of a recommendation in San Geronimo County—but at least he was able to keep the convertible on the right side of the road. It was said in rural New Mexico that after eleven o'clock at night, one out of every five cars on the road was piloted by a drunk driver, so they were only joining the liquid flow.

Two blocks later, Sherman lit up a joint with a greedy intake of breath. The man was incredible, a veritable dinosaur of bad habits. You would think that being drunk and stoned on heroin was enough for any one person on any one night, but Sherman was unstoppable. He found a rock station on the radio and began to dance in his seat, singing along.

Howie opened a back window when the air in the small car began to give him a secondhand buzz.

"Hey, it's cold. Close the window, for chrissake," Sherman complained.

"I'm just. . . ."

"Yeah, yeah. Don't be such a pussy, Moon Deer. A little smoke's not gonna hurt you."

"Close the window, and I'll turn on the air," Gilmer suggested, lighting a cigarette.

Reluctantly, Howie closed the window. He wasn't accustomed to drinking as much as he had tonight. Each round of drinks had seemed reasonable at the time, but somehow they had accumulated unfairly in his bloodstream. He wasn't drunk, certainly—his thoughts were very clear. But his lips seemed oddly numb, and he found he needed to articulate his words more clearly than usual. The thick cloud of tobacco and marijuana smoke in the enclosed space did not improve matters.

"Hey, let's go see the Mouse," Sherman said.

"It's late, Sherman," Gilmer told him, turning down the volume of the radio. "She'll be asleep."

"She'll wake up for me. Come on, Let's go party at her place. We'll get some beer, have ourselves an all-nighter."

"What about going back to the Art Association?" Howie suggested optimistically. "There might be some food left."

"Food!" Sherman mocked, peering at Howie with displeasure. "You've got to be kidding! And the *Art* Association—I mean, why don't you just *gag* me with boredom and be done with it! Did you hear that band, for chrissake?"

"Well, they could use some more practice," Howie admitted.

"What they need is for someone to break their goddamn

instruments over their heads! . . . Gilmer, make a left. Stop at the Chevron station so I can get some beer."

The Chevron station had a convenience store that sold liquor, a convenience allowing the people of San Geronimo to drink and drive more easily. Sherman stubbed out his joint, walked inside the brightly lit store, and returned a few minutes later with two twelve-packs of Tecate in cans. Howie tried to look on the bright side of the situation. Maybe if Sherman got drunk enough, his tongue would loosen. As it was, Sherman hadn't said another word about Manny Lucero and the summer of '74 since the moment in Pinky's when he had put a finger to his lips as Gilmer was returning to the table.

Howie knew he couldn't rush Sherman. The thing now was to bide his time and wait for another chance to be alone. If he could only stay awake, there would be more opportunities tonight as the Tecate made its inevitable journey through the human bloodstream.

"Catch," Sherman said, tossing a can of beer to Howie in the backseat. The can erupted with a small *psst* as Howie pulled the pop-top, slithering foam over Gilmer's expensive leather upholstery.

"Chug-a-lug!" Sherman said, raising his own can in a salute.

"Chug-a-lug," Howie groaned.

This wasn't Howie's idea of fun. Up in the front seat, Gilmer was talking about his latest nineteen-year-old hooker who came to visit him once a week from Santa Fe. Apparently, this was the extent of Gilmer's love life at present, a weekly close encounter of the paid kind.

"Hey, it works for me," said Gilmer. "No fuss, no bother, give the girl her goddamn money, and she's out the door. It's just the thing for an artist—people like us, we gotta save our intensity for our work."

"Balls!" said Sherman. "The thing for an artist, man, is to get it everywhere you can. And the world is full of free pussy. What'cha say, Moon Deer?" Sherman grinned at Howie in the backseat. "Do you have to pay for it, or do you get it free?"

Gilmer answered for Howie. "For chrissake, Sherman— the boy's in his twenties, he's not an old fart like us. Of course, he gets it free! But our Moon Deer's a romantic, so he's probably not the sort who'll kiss and tell."

Howie had no idea where they were going. Gilmer turned north onto Ortega Road, a two-lane street that bypassed the center of town through a quiet residential neighborhood. Sherman and Gilmer were still talking sex, chortling about the different female body parts they had known. Howie gritted his teeth, thinking about how Sherman had groped some of Claire's body parts. *Bide your time,* he reminded himself. Normally, Howie wasn't big on vengeance, but he couldn't help grinning at the thought of Sherman locked up in one of New Mexico's new private prisons for the rest of his miserable life. All Howie had to do was find out just a few more pieces of the puzzle. Meanwhile, the car was too warm, and his eyes stung with smoke and exhaustion. He closed them for just a second so they could have a rest. *Can't go to sleep!* he told himself urgently. But the motion of the car, the late hour, and the murmur of voices all conspired against him.

"Man, did I ever tell you about this chick Heather?" Sherman was saying. "She used to give me head in that back office in SoHo . . . shaved her . . . tits like ripe little oranges . . . but, man, her tongue . . . one time she wanted to. . . ."

Howie was grateful when the conversation in the front seat faded to an indistinct drone. He thought maybe he'd take just a small nap, after all. Conserve his energy. Tune back in when the talk was not quite so predictably the lies that lonely men told each other late at night in cars when there were no women nearby to keep them honest.

"Wake up, Moon Deer!"

Someone was shaking him awake. Howie was sprawled out in the backseat of the Jaguar, hugging himself in a fetal position because it was cold. He felt truly awful. His head ached, his mouth was an ashtray, and he was so tired that he felt sick.

"Lemme sleep s'more."

"You're going to freeze to death out here. Come on inside, Moon Deer."

It was Gilmer Good Day. Howie sat up slowly and rubbed his eyes. "How long have I been asleep?"

"Maybe half an hour. Come on upstairs. It's warm, and we'll get you a cup of coffee."

Upstairs? Howie allowed himself to be guided from the backseat. The night had become bitterly cold, and he wasn't dressed for it. His teeth began to chatter. He was surprised to see that they were parked at the side of the garage on the Vandenberg Stone estate—the same garage where he had found the snowmobile yesterday. Upstairs, lights were shining from the windows of the second-floor apartment. Howie gazed at his surroundings stupidly, trying to get the world in focus.

"So the Mouse—the lady Sherman was so hot to visit, that's Anna? The *maid*?"

"Sherman's fond of the domestic help," Gilmer observed. "Very convenient for him too, since she lives so close by."

"I thought maybe you . . . well, you know. When I saw Anna posing in your studio that day."

"No, I only paint her." Gilmer laughed. "Sherman's the one who *does* her.

Just then, a woman's voice began shouting from upstairs. "Screw you, Sherman! Goddamn you, you think you can just show up at two in the morning, and I'll give you anything you want! You got a hell of a nerve. . . ."

"You can see why I generally prefer to pay for my pleasures," Gilmer said. "They've been going on like that ever since we got here. Come on, let's get you upstairs to that coffee."

Howie made an effort to wake up, remembering that he had work to do. It had been a mistake to close his eyes; now he felt insubstantial, like a sleepwalker. From upstairs, Sherman and Anna began shouting a new stream of obscenities at each other.

"What about Babs?" Howie asked. "Does she really put up with Sherman screwing the maid?"

"Babs doesn't know about this particular liaison. And let's hope she doesn't find out either. She wouldn't like Sherman getting his jollies so close to home."

"She's going to hear them fighting, isn't she?"

"She hasn't come back from the party yet."

Howie walked with Gilmer up the outside stairs into a small living room and kitchen area. It was a shabby apartment but clean, furnished in a kind of late-sixties motel

Renaissance style. There was a lime-green sofa, a ratty stuffed armchair, an old TV, and a Formica breakfast counter separating the kitchen from the living area. The walls sported a few paintings in cheap frames, generic Southwestern scenes of the Rio Grande and romanticized desert vistas. Howie could hear Sherman and Anna quarreling more softly now from the other side of a closed door—the bedroom, he presumed. Gilmer was putting a kettle of water on the stove when Sherman came out from the bedroom, closing the door behind him.

"Hey, Gilmer, my man—you don't have a few bottles of bubbly over at your place, do you?" Sherman asked, ignoring Howie's presence. "I'm sort of in the doghouse, actually. A little champagne would go a long way toward making things right with Anna."

Gilmer was amused. "Maybe Moon Deer and I should leave you and Anna to figure this out between yourselves."

"No, no!" Sherman said quickly. "Don't leave until we've worked it out a little more, okay? Anyway, we'll party."

"Doesn't sound like much of a party to me."

"Come on, Gilmer, I know you always keep a few bottles of Dom Perignon in the fridge. Be a pal, for chrissake. Anyway, I bet Moon Deer's never sampled a hundred-dollar bottle of plonk. You'll be educating the kid—and frankly, he needs it."

Gilmer turned to Howie. "Well, what do you say, Moon Deer? Feel like coming with me on a champagne run?"

"I think I'll stay and have that coffee," Howie replied. The night was passing quickly, and with Gilmer gone, Howie would have a chance to resume the conversation with Sherman they had started at Pinky's.

"Well, I'll see you in a few," Gilmer agreed, shaking his head with an ironic smile.

"Flowers too, if you've got some," Sherman added.

"Yeah, yeah," Gilmer told him, walking outside.

Howie started in on Sherman the minute they were alone.

"Look, Sherman, you said earlier that there was a way I could get myself some quick money. As it happens, I just got this killer credit card bill in the mail, so I'm interested in what you have in mind."

Sherman glanced at Howie without interest. "Yeah, I haven't forgotten. But not now, Moon Deer. I've got more important things on my mind, you dig? So just relax, make yourself some coffee, whatever—we'll talk later."

"But, Sherman, this is important. My boss, Jack Wilder—he's going to call Captain Gomez tomorrow and tell him all about how you went to art school with Manny Lucero in the seventies, and a whole bunch of other things as well. Including a Georgia O'Keeffe painting by the name of *Red Moon* that happened to get stolen in 1974."

Sherman grinned. "You found out about *Red Moon*, huh?"

"Sherman!" came Anna's voice from the next room. "What the hell are you doing now?"

"I'm coming, honey puss!" Sherman called into the bedroom.

"We've got to talk this over tonight, Sherman, or it will be too late," Howie pressed.

"Sure. It's on my agenda, okay? But the night's young. Just stick around a while—I gotta settle some things first with Anna."

Sherman winked, then disappeared back into the bedroom, closing the door behind him. Howie sighed with frustration. He wasn't certain how he had gotten himself into such a dismal predicament, stuck in Valverde without transportation at nearly two in the morning. Hours had passed, and he hadn't learned anything much of value. Frankly, he'd had it. He decided he would make himself a cup of coffee, and then he'd simply confront Sherman, ready or not. There wasn't any more time for subtlety. He had to know why Manny Lucero had come back to San Geronimo and what had happened to *Red Moon*.

Howie searched in the freezer compartment of Anna's refrigerator for coffee beans. But there were none. Nor was there an electric coffee grinder on the kitchen counter to indicate that beans might be found in another location. This was looking bad. With reduced expectations, he searched through her cabinets until he found a jar of instant Yuban. It would do in an emergency, he supposed. But when he opened the jar, he saw that it was virtually empty, with only a few sad brown granules coating the bottom.

Howie was at the end of his rope. He turned off the water on the stove and knocked on the bedroom door.

"Sherman, come on out of there. We need to talk. Like now."

"Get lost, Moon Deer!"

Howie pushed open the bedroom door, but wished he hadn't. Sherman and Anna were on the bed doing the great Dance of Love that poets spoke of with such reverence. Frankly, it was a repulsive sight. Sherman's hairy ass was the most prominent feature of the tableaux, pumping up and down with gusto. Anna's legs were spread apart, and her feet were sticking up in the air, her soles dirty on the bottom. Somehow Anna's underpants had become caught on her left ankle, and they were waving in the air like a flag of truce. Howie jumped back out of the bedroom, slamming the door closed.

What next? he wondered. Wearily, Howie sat down on the lime-green sofa and tried not to listen to the rhythmic creaking of the springs in the next room.

"Oo-oh!" came a moan. "Aa-ah!"

Howie looked at this watch. It was ten after two. The next time he glanced at his watch, it was twenty after two and Gilmer had not yet returned. He yawned fiercely, trying to get a lungful of oxygen. In the next room the oohs and aahs had gradually increased in volume and intensity but gave no sign of coming closer to any conclusion. As far as Howie was concerned, this was the last straw. Meanwhile, he couldn't imagine what was keeping Gilmer Good Day, since he lived only five minutes away.

There was nothing to do but wait, and as he waited, Howie's eyes grew heavier and heavier. The bed in the next room began to sound like a ship at sea, rolling back and forth and up and down hypnotically. The oohs and aahs gradually faded into a vast oceanic distance. Claire's face appeared to him behind his closed eyelids. *Ooh*, he would like to be with her now. *Aah*, how he missed her!

Howie stretched out on the sofa and fell into a profound sleep.

AAAAHHHH! came a climactic scream. Howie stirred very slightly. It seemed to him that he had heard this sound track before. *AAAAHHHH!* she screamed again. Which was getting a little out of hand, he thought. Rude, really, when someone was trying to sleep.

He opened his eyes and was surprised to see the gray light of dawn in the windows. He remembered where he was, in the apartment above the Vandenberg Stone garage. There was a woman standing naked in the bedroom door looking down at him. He focused his eyes and saw that it was Anna the maid. Howie wished she would put on some clothing.

But there was something wrong with her. Her eyes were startled, wide open, like a frightened animal. She was breathing hard. As Howie watched, she bolted back into the bedroom and appeared a moment later in flight with a blanket wrapped around her, running across the living room and out the front door. He heard her bare feet slapping quickly down the outside stairs.

This was all very strange. Howie struggled to his feet and walked to the kitchen window. On the ground below, Anna was running immodestly across the gravel driveway as fast as her legs would carry her, the blanket flying up behind her, showing every now and then the crack of her bare rear end. She reached an old green pickup truck that was parked near a pine tree, fired up the engine, and drove away like a crazy woman, tires smoking, fishtailing from side to side.

Howie moved back from the window and cautiously approached the open bedroom door. It was a small bedroom, with hardly enough room for a double bed and a chair. Sherman was sleeping on his back, very peaceful, very still. His mouth was open, but other than that, his sleeping face had a kind of grave nobility in the chaste light of dawn. Howie thought he could see something of the old Sherman Stone that Gilmer had talked about last night, the young artist who had gazed up at the ceiling of the Sistine Chapel in wonder.

"Sherman, wake up," Howie told him.

But he didn't wake up, and Howie realized that there was a problem. He nudged Sherman, but the body in the bed only quivered very slightly. Howie pulled his hand back quickly.

The problem was that Sherman Stone was dead.

Eighteen

On Sunday morning, the first day of November, Captain Ed Gomez attended the eight o'clock Mass at our Lady of Guadalupe, the oldest church in San Geronimo.

Ed did not go to Mass regularly these days, though he had been coming more often since his divorce. What he was seeking was more the comfort of cultural continuity than the comfort of God. Our Lady of Guadalupe had been built by his ancestors in San Geronimo in 1763, back when the Anglo newcomers were still only dreaming of turning their thirteen colonies into a nation. As a boy, Ed had always helped out with the annual re-mudding of the old adobe walls, though he hadn't had time for this in recent years. The yearly ritual to repair the church was one of the traditions that used to bind the Hispanic community together, before Wal-Mart, before the new multiscreen cineplex, the ski resort up in the mountains, and the flood of four-wheel drive SUVs from New York and California.

The Sunday service at Our Lady of Guadalupe was still conducted in Spanish, which was becoming rare in northern New Mexico. Howie had once told Ed that many young Lakota no longer knew their own language, and this was increasingly true also among a new generation of Hispanics in San Geronimo. Ed's two boys, Dave and Jimmy, were a good example: they didn't speak Spanish, they had lost their cultural heritage, and it seemed to Ed that this might be the reason they kept getting in trouble with drugs and the law. If the Hispanic people in this ancient valley lost their roots, they had little else left except their poverty.

The church was cold and austere for the eight a.m. service, with fractured colored light streaming in through the stained-glass windows. Ed sat in an ancient wooden pew and tried his best not to look at his ex-wife, Gloria, and

her new boyfriend, Ray, who were sitting across the aisle.
Gloria and Ray were living together in sin, but apparently
this didn't stop them from coming to Mass. Ray was Ed's
first cousin, which made the whole affair incestuous as well,
but then nearly all the old families in San Geronimo were
related. Ray's wing of the family had always been landown-
ers, and recently Ray had made a killing subdividing one
of his parcels into a tract of one-acre lots of dusty sagebrush that he was calling Quail Run Manor. Now Gloria
would be able to have all the things she had never been
able to afford on his cop's salary. Good for Gloria; but once
the land was gone, it was gone forever. Ed was kneeling in
prayer, trying to push all the sour thoughts from his mind,
when the cell phone in his jacket pocket began to beep. He
stood up, slipped from the pew, and took the call outside in
the parking lot. Ed didn't mind missing the service. He
doubted if Jesus had much love to give him today anyway.

The call was from Deputy Buddy Rodriguez over at the
Sheriff's Department.

"Sorry to bother you, Ed, but there's been a traffic fatality in Valverde. I thought you'd like to know about it."

"I'm listening."

Buddy Rodriguez was Ed's nephew and also the son-
in-law of a current county commissioner. Success in San
Geronimo depended heavily on patronage and being related to the right people, so Buddy would undoubtedly go
far. The fatality he was calling to report involved a '78
Chevy pickup truck that had been coming down Valverde
Mesa Road, the steep switchback from the mesa top to the
village below. It had apparently lost control and crashed
through the guardrail, tumbling down the embankment and
bursting into flames.

Valverde Mesa Road was considered one of the most
hazardous roads in the county, particularly in the winter
months, and this was not the first fatality at the spot. In all
likelihood the driver had been going too fast and had
missed one of the hairpin turns. Normally, the Sheriff's Department would not have bothered to notify the state police
about such an accident, but the charred remains of the
driver had been tentatively identified as Anna Montoya, an
Indian girl from the Pueblo who worked as a maid in the
Barbara Vandenberg Stone household. Deputy Rodriguez

was aware that Ed had been interested in this family lately, so he had called.

"I'll be right there," Ed told him.

Ed turned toward the old mud church of his ancestors, crossed himself quickly, then hurried to the dead young woman.

The pickup had tumbled nearly to the bottom of a steep arroyo and lay upside down at a dangerous angle against a large boulder, its wheels in the air. The fire had been put out by the time Ed arrived, but a small plume of black smoke still drifted lazily upward to heaven—like incense, Ed thought. Or like some kind of offering to an angry god, in this case, a young woman's life.

Climbing down the steep embankment from the road, Ed got himself a palm full of cactus spines. It didn't improve his mood. A half-dozen law enforcement people and several firemen had gathered on the hillside near the wrecked vehicle. Ed could see a blackened arm hanging lifelessly from the driver's window. He really didn't want to see any more of the girl than this, not unless he had to. It was a gory death, no way to start a Sunday morning. Meanwhile they were waiting for a tow truck and San Geronimo Search and Rescue to arrive from town. Hoisting the remains of Anna Montoya from the twisted wreckage was going to take several hours, some ingenuity, and a lot of rope.

Ed was listening to one of the sheriffs idly tell an anecdote about a Halloween party he had busted last night when his cell phone beeped.

"What now?" he muttered.

To his surprise, Howie Moon Deer was calling to report a new misfortune: the death of Sherman Stone. It took Ed a few moments to put together a picture in his mind of what Howie was telling him. There seemed to be a lot drinking and carousing in Howie's tale, resulting in a possible drug overdose. Ed was afraid this was shaping up into quite a day.

Wearily, he got back into his cruiser and drove up the switchback to the apartment above the garage at the Vandenberg Stone estate, where Howie was waiting. Sure enough, Sherman Stone was stone-cold dead in bed. Ed made a quick examination of the scene. There were no obvious wounds or signs of foul play, but two deaths so close to one another on the same morning raised suspicions, particularly when the second victim happened to be lying dead in the bed of the first victim. Ed listened to Howie's full account, and then he made a number of phone calls, summoning the county medical investigator and a state police crime-scene unit.

Captain Gomez spent the next five hours questioning various witnesses and taking statements. After speaking with Howie, he went down the road and had a lengthy conversation with Gilmer Good Day. Then he questioned Barbara Vandenberg, Robin Vandenberg, Lionel Cordova, and Pooh—all of whom, it turned out, had spent the night at the Vandenberg Stone house. Returning to the scene of the pickup truck accident, he discovered that Deputy Rodriguez had located an eyewitness in the village, an elderly lady by the name of Elvira Romero. The old woman had just left her house on her way to church when she chanced to look up the mesa and see the pickup flying through the guardrail. Ed had an opportunity to question Mrs. Romero himself early in the afternoon. Unfortunately, the old woman had not seen the entire accident. She had heard a crash, and the sound of the truck hitting the guardrail. But by the time she looked up, the pickup was in the air tumbling down the side of the embankment. She watched as it exploded into flames when it hit the arroyo below, and then she called 911.

From Valverde, Ed Gomez drove north to speak with Claire Knightsbridge, and later he had a second conversation with Howie, to make certain he had the story entirely correct. Finally, shortly before three o'clock, Ed drove to see Jack Wilder at his house on Calle Santa Margarita. They spoke for nearly two hours.

After Captain Gomez left, Jack took his small cassette recorder upstairs to the bedroom and shut the door. He needed to make some notes before he forgot the details of what Ed had told him. The evidence so far was intricate and confusing; Jack could not yet grasp it in its entirety. Unfortunately, it was now nearly six o'clock and two friends, Art and Susan Bachrach, had just arrived for Sunday dinner, coming up the driveway just as Ed was leaving. This was inconvenient. Jack had agreed several days ago to cook his famous chicken enchiladas tonight. The Bachrachs owned a store in town, and Jack was very fond of their company. But not right now.

"Have yourself some cocktails, and I'll be right with you," Jack called brightly as he shut himself in the upstairs bedroom. But he didn't feel so bright. At least one of the deaths this morning was murder, and the second probably was as well. Jack felt professionally responsible; the case had begun slowly with a client he hadn't much wanted, and now it was running away from him, moving too fast. He hadn't taken it seriously enough, and this was the cost.

"Jack, it's Howie on the phone," Emma shouted from downstairs.

Jack had already spoken with Howie three times today. He picked up the upstairs receiver with an impatient growl: "I can only talk a second."

"Just one quick question," Howie told him. "Last night before Sherman OD'd, he admitted to me that he knew about *Red Moon*. He said he would talk to me about it later. So it must be somewhere in that house or in his studio. I was wondering if Gomez can get a search warrant even though Sherman's death was natural . . ."

"It wasn't natural," Jack interrupted.

"Well, accidental. Drug-related. Whatever. Burning the candle at both ends."

"Howie, pay attention. Sherman Stone did *not* OD, or suffer a heart attack, nor did he choke on his vomit. Drugs and alcohol might have claimed him eventually, but not last night. Someone smothered him with a pillow while he was sleeping. He was murdered."

Howie was silent while he absorbed this news. "How can they tell?" he asked finally.

"Petechiae," Jack answered simply.

"Petecky-what?"

"Listen up, Howie. This is about as simple as forensics get, even for a pharmacist in a small New Mexico town masquerading as a medical investigator. Petechiae are small capillaries that are found under the eyelids and inside the lips. When someone is struggling violently to breathe, the petechiae burst and splatter in little circles of blood. It's the first place an investigator looks if he suspects a person has been strangled or smothered."

"And these capillaries don't burst if it's a heart attack?"

"No. And in this case we're sure that Sherman was suffocated with a pillow because several goose-down feathers were found lodged in his throat. The pillows on Anna's bed were stuffed with goose down—expensive pillows originally, but they're quite old and leaking feathers from the seams. The DPS lab in Santa Fe will determine if the goose down in the pillows matches the feathers in Sherman's throat, but at the moment I think it's a safe bet to assume they do."

Howie moaned. "What about Anna?"

"In her case, the forensic evidence is confusing owing to the violence of the crash. Anna's neck was broken—that's all we really know for certain at the moment. Maybe it was an accident, maybe not. The truck was found in neutral, which argues for foul play, but of course it could have popped out of gear as it crashed down the embankment. Theoretically, I suppose, someone could have broken her neck, put her in the pickup, and given her a shove off the mesa—"

"Hold on a second," Howie interrupted heatedly. "You're forgetting that I *saw* Anna moments before she died—she was running bare-assed toward her truck like some crazy woman. I can't see how someone could engineer all this, know just when Anna was going to get hysterical, kill her, then arrange it all to look like an accident. There wasn't enough time."

"Look, Howie, I don't mean to be unkind, but you were set up big time, my friend. You were fast asleep, so you don't know what was possible and what was not. For all you know, the killer phoned just before you woke up, told her something that scared the shit out of her, then was waiting down the road a little ways to carry out his plan. Or maybe he had already cut her brake lines—there are lots of possibilities here. Ed's sending the truck down to Santa Fe for analysis, so if we're lucky, we should have some information in a few days."

"Jack, if the phone rang in her apartment, I would have woken up," Howie insisted stolidly.

"Would you? You slept through everything else real

good, bubba," Jack told him mildly. Howie was about to object, but Jack had no time for Howie's hurt feelings and didn't let him get started. "Howie, I'm sorry, but I've got to hang up now."

Howie sighed unhappily. "What about tomorrow?"

"Come by at eight-thirty unless I give you a call later. We'll plan our next move then."

Jack put down the receiver and searched on the bed for the cassette recorder. He was certain that somewhere in the confusion of details that Ed had told him, the truth was waiting to be found. He sat on the edge of his bed, made certain that there was a fresh tape in the machine, and began recording:

"Gilmer Good Day spent the night with Sherman Stone and Howie. Drove to Anna Montoya's apartment at approximately one-thirty a.m. Both Good Day and Howie state that going to Anna's was Sherman's idea. Anna Montoya worked as a maid in the house, and Stone had been having a sexual relationship with her for possibly as long as a year. Recently it seems that Stone and Anna had been quarreling. According to Good Day, Anna had begun to demand more from Stone than occasional sex. She wanted an emotional commitment, a future, etcetera. Stone, on the other hand, wished to keep things as they were—an occasional screw. There was bound to be conflict. According to Gilmer, Anna Montoya was asleep when they arrived and wasn't happy to be woken by a bunch of rowdy guys dropping over at such a late hour. She and Stone began quarreling immediately.

"Shortly before two a.m., Stone asked Good Day to go home and get a few bottles of champagne. Good Day lives just down the road, less than a quarter mile away, so this shouldn't have been a problem. However, complications ensued. As Gilmer was driving away from the Vandenberg Stone estate, he ran into Barbara Stone, Robin Vandenberg, Lionel Cordova, and Pooh Cordova, who were just coming up the driveway in Barbara Stone's Land Rover. Lionel was driving. Apparently, Barbara Stone had become upset after Sherman disappeared at the party, and she didn't want to be alone. So she insisted in her usual imperious way that everyone spend the night at her house rather than do any more driving late at night on Halloween when the roads were dangerous.

"When Barbara Stone saw Gilmer Good Day, she demanded to know where her husband was. They had a brief conversation, car to car in the driveway. After some initial hesitation, Good Day admitted that Sherman was with Anna Montoya upstairs above the garage. Good Day says he told the truth because he was tired, irritated at having agreed to fetch Sherman champagne, and he was sick of the whole situation. Good Day then drove to his own house, where he decided not to return to Anna's apartment with the champagne after all. The situation had become unpleasant with the return of Sherman's wife and family to the main house. He knew he was leaving Howie stranded, but believed that Howie could probably fend for himself. Incidentally, Good Day has a live-in servant, a local Hispanic man, Benny Rodarte, who has a small basement apartment in the house and corroborates Good Day's story. Rodarte states that he woke up at approximately two-fifteen a.m., hearing his boss come back into the house. This doesn't mean, however, that Gilmer couldn't have returned later to the Vandenberg Stone estate down the street.

"Meanwhile, Robin Vandenberg says that he was brushing his teeth when his mother knocked on the bathroom door and requested a favor. She wanted Robin to go next door to Anna's apartment and check on her husband—apparently, she was curious to know what sort of state Sherman was in, but she wasn't willing to lower herself by going to the maid's apartment herself. According to Robin, he was reluctant to carry out his mother's request but finally gave in. As close as he can estimate, it was two-thirty a.m. when he walked next door, went up the outside stairs, and found the door unlocked. He says Howie was asleep on the couch in the living room. He walked into the bedroom and found Sherman Stone and Anna Montoya asleep in bed, undressed, with the lights on. Robin says he turned out the lights, left the apartment, and returned to the main house to report to his mother. According to Robin, his mother seemed more resigned than angry when he told her what he had seen. Robin claims he left his mother in the living room and went upstairs—he was using the bedroom he used to have as a child. He was exhausted, it was late, and he went to sleep immediately."

Jack put the cassette player on pause. He sat on the edge of his bed thinking, trying to remember everything that Ed Gomez had told him. After a few moments he began recording again:

"Questioning Lionel and Pooh Cordova confirms all aspects of the conversation with Gilmer Good Day in the driveway. Lionel Cordova's statement also confirms Robin's impression about Barbara Stone's mood, that she listened to Gilmer's account with a kind of weary resignation rather than anger. But Pooh's statement contradicts this. She says that her mother, while remaining quiet on the surface, was clearly boiling mad underneath. Both Lionel and Pooh claim to have gone to bed immediately after they arrived at the house, using Pooh's old bedroom on the upper northeast corner of the house—the opposite side of the house from where the garage and apartment are located, quite some distance away. Nevertheless, there is a separate staircase on this side of the house and either Pooh or Lionel would have been able to walk downstairs, go out a side door, and make their way over to the garage if they had wished.

"Finally, Barbara Vandenberg Stone. When questioned, she admits to being upset at the news Gilmer Good Day had given her. She sent Robin over to the garage in order to see how things stood, and then she claims to have decided to let the entire matter drop until morning. She knew from experience that there was no way to have a constructive conversation with Sherman when he was drunk and high. In the morning she planned to have it out with him and threaten divorce if he didn't mend his ways. According to Gomez, Mrs. Stone seemed more angry about being ditched at the Art Association party than discovering that her husband was having an affair with the maid. Being left without an escort at the Art Association exposed her to public humiliation, and this seems to be her flash point, rather than sexual jealousy. Barbara Stone says that after Robin made his report to her, she poured herself a shot of bourbon and went to bed. Claims she heard nothing during the course of the night to indicate anything unusual happening next door. Robin Vandenberg, Lionel Cordova, and Pooh also claim to have heard nothing.

"In summary. . . ." The machine rolled for several seconds, then Jack sighed and put the player once again on pause. In summary, what? There was a time, not so many years ago, when Commander Wilder would have been able to summarize all these facts and witness accounts more easily than he could today. It was this slack semiretirement in New Mexico, he feared, that had caused his mind to lose its edge. "In summary," he continued, forcing himself to think, "either Barbara Stone, Robin Vandenberg, Lionel Cordova, Pooh Cordova, or Gilmer Good Day could easily have left their respective beds and made their way upstairs above the garage at some time in the night to smother Sherman with the pillow. Everyone except Gilmer Good Day has a strong motive. For Barbara, jealousy and anger. Robin, because he was being blackmailed by Sherman. Lionel and Pooh to keep Babs from conceivably leaving a large portion of her fortune to Sherman rather than to them. This doesn't leave Gilmer Good Day free of suspicion, though we have found no motive yet. He could have walked from his house to the garage in a little over seven minutes, and no one would have been the wiser.

"Another interesting possibility, of course, is that Anna Montoya smothered Sherman—they were quarreling, after all. Possibly, she put the pillow over his head in anger but did not realize she had actually killed him until she woke up the next morning. Then she panicked, ran down the stairs, and drove away too quickly, causing her own death on the dangerous switchback from the mesa. According to Gomez, there may have been ice on that road early in the morning, making it particularly treacherous for someone who wasn't paying attention. So we may be talking about one murder and one accidental death. Or two murders. Or just about anything at all. . . ."

Jack exhaled a long breath and listened to the tape turning. Life was like that, he thought bleakly. A tape slowly running itself out. He continued: "We must wait optimistically for the pathology report. Another question, of course, is whether the deaths of Sherman Stone and Anna Montoya are related to the shooting last Thursday of Manny Lucero and the still-missing canvas, *Red Moon.*"

Jack shut off the record button, rewound the tape, and punched PLAY. He sat and listened to his own impromptu rendering of the facts twice through, hoping for some thunderbolt of understanding.

"Jack!" Emma called from downstairs. "We're getting hungry, darling!"

"Just a few more minutes!" Jack called back. "Have yourselves another cocktail, and I'll be right down."

Jack played his tape one more time. At the end of the third listen, he believed he knew who had murdered Manny Lucero, Sherman Stone, and possibly even Anna Montoya.

Nineteen

Monday was the Day of the Dead, *El Día de los Muertos,* the Spanish Halloween—as Claire Knightsbridge thought of it, inaccurately. In the year she had spent in New Mexico, Claire had done her best to understand local customs, but it wasn't easy for her. At heart, she was too Midwestern to be completely comfortable in this strange, ancient valley. The land itself overwhelmed her with its huge expanse of desert, mountain, and sky. Sometimes she found herself wishing for the more limited horizons of her childhood, the gentle green hills and rivers of Iowa.

Claire had given Sunday over entirely to her personal life: Howie, the children, and the police who wanted to ask her questions about Sherman Stone. But on Monday morning, she did her best to get back into a work mode. She had a hundred things to do at the Art Association that could not be put off: thank-you letters to write, checks to deposit, arrangements to be made for cleaning the PAC, even a financial report to be sent to the board of directors detailing how much money they had taken in on Saturday night. (Close to $38,000, Claire estimated, which was good but still far short of the $60,000 balloon payment that needed to be made to the bank on January 1.)

Claire sat at her desk in her small office trying to concentrate on the tasks at hand. But her mind wandered. The very office reminded her of Sherman Stone and all the terrible things that had happened. It was incredible, really. Two people she knew had been murdered!—first the poor, sad Rainbow Man, and now a man she had disliked intensely, but who had been a human being nevertheless. Shortly before ten o'clock, Claire felt so stressed that she locked her door and stretched out on her office floor. She breathed deeply, slowly, trying to relax. Breathe in, breath out . . . life was such a melodrama, sometimes you just had to let it slip away. Lying on her back, Claire performed the Lamaze breathing that she had learned years ago in a childbirth class—it had helped her through the contractions of giving birth, and surely it would calm her now.

After five minutes, Claire felt better. She exhaled in a long, luxurious sigh and was about to get up from the office floor when she noticed a small brass object that had fallen between the bookshelf and the wall. It was a key on a loop of string. A visitor had probably dropped it, then some stray foot had kicked it beneath the bookshelf. Claire crawled on her hands and knees to retrieve the key. There was engraving on one side: USPS DO NOT DUPLICATE 01655. It was a post office box key; she had a similar one herself, as did many people in the rural reaches of San Geronimo County. Possibly the key had lain here for some time, undetected by the janitor who vacuumed her office rather cursorily once a week. She stood up from the floor and checked her bag for her own key; hers was on a key chain with all her other keys.

Claire couldn't imagine who might have lost a P.O. box key in her office, and frankly, didn't have the time to wonder—she needed to get to work. She turned on her computer and began writing a basic form letter to send to all the businesses and individuals who had donated to the silent auction on Saturday night; later she would individualize each letter with a sentence or two at the top or bottom. But as Claire worked, she glanced occasionally at the brass key on a string that she had set to one corner of her desk. It was a small mystery, but it intrigued her.

Around eleven, she stopped writing for a moment and frowned. Could Sherman have dropped the key on Saturday afternoon when they were wrestling? This was possible, though she did not think so. If the key belonged to Sherman, she imagined it would be on some hip and quirky key ring rather than a modest string.

But why, she wondered, would someone put a key on a piece of string? To wear it around their neck so it wouldn't get lost?

At eleven-thirty, Claire was writing to thank the McHardy family for a triple kindness to the Art Association—they had donated a painting for the silent auction, made a sizable financial gift of $1000, and had even provided two of their sons to haul away trash once the party was over. "Your three gifts to the SGAA are greatly. . . ." Claire stopped writing. *Three gifts?* The phrase stirred a memory. It was what the Rainbow Man had written on his blackboard when he came into her office last Wednesday, scaring her half to death when he had pulled out that horrible gun. Claire smiled slightly, remembering how she had frightened him in return, screaming so loudly that he had dropped the gun on the floor in confusion. . . .

Claire froze. *I have brought you three gifts.* Yes, that's what the Rainbow Man had written. It had seemed a small point at the time, just part of the general craziness of the encounter, and she had forgotten about it. But now she wondered. He had left her, in fact, only two "gifts": the sketchbook and the gun. So what was the third?

Claire stood up abruptly from her computer and turned her entire attention back to the key on her desk. A possible answer to the riddle had occurred to her. And if she was right, it wasn't such a small mystery after all.

Twenty

Howie picked up Jack and Katya at eight-thirty on Monday morning and took them to the office downtown. Jack had woken with a sense of unease. He was not particularly superstitious, but the fact that this was the Day of the Dead was not reassuring. There was a killer on the loose, after all. After some internal debate, Jack decided to wear his .38 Smith & Wesson Chief's Special in a shoulder holster concealed beneath a loose Eddie Bauer windbreaker. It was the first time he had worn a shoulder holster since his forced medical retirement from the San Francisco Police Department, and the weight of it against his breast gave him a satisfying sense of nostalgia. In fact, Jack had no permit to carry a concealed weapon in the state of New Mexico, and he was breaking the law.

Walking into the office, Howie pressed the play button on the telephone answering machine. There were two messages. The first was from Captain Gomez, whose voice on the tape was pleasantly rhythmic in a particular laid-back Hispanic way that seemed to Jack almost tropical:

"Oh, hey, you're going to like this, Jack! We ran Manny Lucero through the NCIC computer with some interesting results. Turns out your Rainbow Man wasn't such an angel after all. His full name is Manuel R. Lucero, and he has quite a jacket. Last year he got released from San Quentin after a twenty-year stretch for taking part in a California robbery where a 7-Eleven clerk got shot. Thought you'd be interested . . ."

The second message came from Robin Vandenberg. His voice was anxious, oddly hesitant, and not even slightly tropical: "Uh, this is Robin. It's, uh—Christ, what is it?—Sunday night. Look, there's something bothering me, and I just don't know what to do about it. On Monday I'm working at the Life Circle School, but I have a break between ten-thirty and eleven. So I was wondering if you could call then. Or just come by. It's . . . well, I really don't want to talk about it on the phone."

"So what's the plan, Stan?" Howie asked, settling in the rocking chair across from Jack's desk.

Jack smiled. "No need to be coy, Roy—the plan's simple. You go to Wind Horse Mountain and see what the hell's worrying Robin. I want to stay here and do some telephoning. As it happens, I have a few friends at San Quentin who should be able to give us the scoop on Manny Lucero. Maybe even the reason he came to San Geronimo to see his old friend Sherman."

Howie left the office at nine-thirty, leaving Jack on the phone to California. San Quentin was located in Marin County on the Bay just north of San Francisco, an exceptionally beautiful spot to build an ugly, maximum security prison. Jack knew a number of people here, both inmates and administrators. He decided to start with an assistant warden, Roger Schoenfeld, and see where that got him.

Roger was not in his office when Jack phoned, so he left a message with his secretary, waited half an hour, and then called again. This time Roger was in his office, but he was running out the door to an important meeting. He promised he would call back the moment he had a chance, but it was nearly eleven o'clock when he did. By then, Jack had placed a number of other calls to people in the California prison system who might be able to answer his questions, but none of them had returned his calls yet either. Apparently, getting back to a retired cop in New Mexico was not at the top of anybody's list of priorities for a busy Monday morning.

When Roger finally called, he was apologetic. "Jack, it's been one of those crazy mornings. How are you and Emma doing out there in New Mexico?"

Jack knew Roger Schoenfeld from the early eighties when they had both been assigned to the SFPD homicide squad. Roger never had quite the right personality to be a cop. He was reserved and mild—prissy, almost; he had never liked the bad jokes and rough camaraderie of a big-city police department and had dropped out in the mid-eighties to join the state prison system, a job more compatible with his urge for administrative order. Jack and Roger had never been close friends, but now with the passage of time, they pretended they were. It was obligatory for Roger to ask about Jack's life in New Mexico, and Jack in return got to hear about Roger's oldest son, Mark, who was just finishing up med school in Florida.

"So, Manuel R. Lucero," Jack managed to slip in at last. "I gather he's one of your graduates."

"Lucero? Oh, yes, I remember him well, as a matter of fact. Hold on, Jack, I'm at my computer . . . just bringing him up on the screen now . . . okay, he served twenty years for Murder One. A convenience store clerk got shot during a robbery in Oakland in 1976—Lucero didn't do the shooting himself, but he got a stiff sentence anyway. Became our guest here in San Quentin on May 13, 1978. Got out August 21, 1998. A very artistic person, I remember—crazy, but talented. He got religion in a big way about halfway through his sentence—this happens sometimes with some of our people who are serving a long term. Basically Lucero was a model prisoner, and he would have been paroled early except for the fact of his mental condition. The board thought it best to keep him as long as possible for his own good."

"What exactly do you mean, his mental condition?" Jack asked.

"One day in 1989, the guards found him standing naked in his cell with a huge smile on his face. He had seen the heavenly path, apparently, and he was brimming over with God's love. Our doctors diagnosed him as schizophrenic. He was hearing voices, the works, but at least they seemed to be benign voices as these thing go. In a sane society, he would have been put into a mental hospital, but the politicians find it a lot easier just to lock people like that up and forget about 'em. Eventually, we got Lucero to wear clothes again, but he never spoke another word. He had taken a vow of silence, it seems—it wasn't physical, at least, we were able to determine that. Since he seemed harmless, we kept an eye on him but left him alone. He just read his Bible and grinned and gurgled at everyone for the rest of his term. And he drew lots of pictures—of the guards and other inmates, everybody he saw. People liked him, and even some of the serious heavies tended to look out for his welfare. I know a number of guards who still have drawings Lucero did of them framed on their walls."

"Did he have visitors?"

"No one except his state-appointed lawyer. There was a sister in New Jersey who wrote him once a year at Christmas, and that was it."

"When he stopped talking, did he write messages?"

"Not at first. Finally, someone thought to give him a little blackboard and some chalk so he could communicate more easily. But he wasn't entirely cogent. He referred to himself in the third-person as the Rainbow Man. Almost all his scribbles were of a religious nature."

"Did he have any particular friends in prison?"

"Everybody liked him pretty much, as I've said. But the only real friend I recall was a black guy named Horace Markley. Horace is still with us, doing life. He killed his wife and her lover one day after he found them in bed together. Now he's a born-again Christian, very big on the Bible, so he had that in common with Lucero."

"Roger, I was wondering if you could do me a favor and have someone ask Horace a few questions?"

"Well, I think we could arrange that," Roger agreed without enthusiasm. "What do you want to know precisely?"

Jack wanted to know if Manny Lucero had ever mentioned a murder in Santa Fe in 1974, or a painting called *Red Moon,* or an old friend by the name of Sherman Stone. Jack also wanted these same questions asked to any other possible friends Lucero might have made inside the prison during his twenty-year stretch, either inmates and guards. This was a big request, so he spent some time giving Roger a rough outline of the three recent deaths in San Geronimo—for a possible triple homicide, Roger was willing to expend some energy.

"Just one more question," Jack said. "After Lucero left you, where did he go?"

"He went into a halfway house in Oakland. A place called Be Your Dream, Inc. I can give you the phone number if you'd like."

"I'd appreciate that. Also an address for the sister in New Jersey, if you have it."

Jack held his cassette recorder to the receiver as Roger

gave him the information he wanted. He put down the phone, wondering about Manny Lucero's religious conversion. It gave the case an odd spin, making it doubtful that Lucero had come to visit Sherman Stone for the more obvious purposes of blackmail or to retrieve his share of the Santa Fe burglary. But then, why had he come? Was it a spiritual journey in search of redemption of some kind? Of course, Lucero's insanity made the matter of motivation more complicated. One couldn't look for the usual logic. For all Jack knew, the Rainbow Man had been driven to New Mexico at the urging of invisible voices. Or it might have been a fleet of flying saucers that had chased him here.

Jack was picking up the phone to call Be Your Dream, Inc. when he heard footsteps coming up the stairs from the courtyard below. He wasn't expecting anybody. Katya ran to the door and made a funny sound in the back of her throat. Jack put down the phone with the number undialed and reached for his revolver.

The footsteps paused then resumed their journey more slowly than before, almost ponderously, up the stairs. Jack listened intently, feeling a prickly surge of fear. The footsteps moved across the landing, and in a moment there was a soft knock on the door. The hairs on Jack's neck stood up. He had an unreasonable urge to start firing at the door, emptying the gun; anything to protect himself from the terror of what he could not see. Then Katya began making little yelping noises of excitement, and Jack could hear her wagging tail slap against the door. He took a deep breath to steady his nerves. This was not good, allowing himself to be spooked so easily.

The knock came a second time.

"Who is it?" he called.

"It's Claire Knightsbridge."

Twenty-one

The Life Circle School on Wind Horse Mountain was a converted red barn on a sloping meadow that was golden with fall stubble, surrounded by aspen trees that were in the last phase of shedding their leaves. It was an idyllically pastoral setting for the parents who could afford to send their kids there for grades K through 4.

Life Circle had grown out of a parent collective, started by a group of parents who were home-schooling their children and had gathered together to share skills. Now there were more than thirty kids and several paid teachers, including Robin Vandenberg. Howie found Robin with a group of six young children outside by the edge of the meadow, where they had set up easels and jars of watercolors. The kids were busy splashing paint around, some of which actually ended up on their drawing pads.

Robin flashed Howie a harried look. He was dressed in paint-splattered overalls and a flannel shirt, his face pinched and sallow. He still wore his earring and ponytail, but he no longer looked so progressively hip to Howie as he once had. Today he just seemed tired and tense.

"You're early," he sighed. "We're about to clean up."

"I'll wait." Howie sat down on the dead meadow grass and watched Robin with the children. There were four little girls and two boys, all of them six or seven years old. They were shaggy and cute in a particular way that hippie children tended to be, like country kids from an earlier generation before shopping malls and TV. But Howie was uncomfortable watching Robin in their midst. He hoped Robin wasn't really a pedophile, but he couldn't be entirely sure.

A gong sounded from somewhere, indicating the end of the class, and the children rushed off with a great deal of noise. Howie stood up and walked closer to where Robin was folding the easels and stacking them against a tree.

"You're alone," Robin said. "Couldn't Jack come?"

"He's busy this morning. He sent me to see what's on your mind."

"What's on my mind?" Robin shook his head, as though what was on his mind was beyond human skill to tell. "So tell me, did you ever find out about that turquoise jewelry?"

"Not completely. It seems that your mother's insurance company reported it stolen, but then almost immediately, they canceled the alert. So either the jewelry was found, or your mother simply decided to call off the insurance company so that Sherman wouldn't get into trouble. Why do you ask?"

"Because that's what I hired you to find out about," Robin said sharply.

"Well, we've had a few distractions, Robin," Howie pointed out. "Like people getting killed. Not to mention the fact that you fired us."

"I *tried* to hire you again, if you'll remember. This wasn't supposed to end like this, and it wouldn't have if you'd done your job right. Now Sherman's a martyr."

"Is he? To whom?"

"To my *mother,* of course! Who else are we talking about? She informed Pooh and me last night that she's disinheriting the two of us. She's going to give her entire fortune to the Georgia O'Keeffe Museum in Santa Fe, so that they can build a Sherman Stone Wing. What do you think of that?"

Howie shrugged. Frankly, inherited wealth wasn't high on his list of societal concerns. "Did she give you a reason?"

"She said Pooh and I were always against her. That we never cared about Sherman like she did. And now that *she* didn't have Sherman, we were all going to be sorry, just like she's sorry."

"Well, it's her money. And she can do with it as she pleases."

Robin smiled unpleasantly. Despite his age, he looked to Howie momentarily like a bad little boy.

"I saw something on Saturday night," he said carefully.

"Something I haven't told anyone about. I know who killed Sherman—probably Anna as well."

"Who?"

Robin had been stacking easels. Now he stopped and turned to Howie. "We need to discuss this a little first. You can use my information, but I·don't want it known that it came from me. Do you think that could be arranged?"

"I'm not sure," Howie told him. "If it's evidence, the police will want to know."

"Yes, I understand that. But what if I'm a client—I *am* a client, aren't I? Then it's privileged information. You could go to the police and say you have something for them, but you can't reveal your source."

"I suppose that's possible," Howie agreed. "But I'd have to check with Jack."

"Well, check, then."

"Right now?"

"You bet right now. I want to get this settled. You have a cell phone, don't you? Give Jack a call."

Howie raised an eyebrow and walked back to the cab of the pickup truck where he had left his phone. He had the batteries charged now, but he wasn't optimistic about using the phone successfully. He turned the phone on, dialed the office number, but was not surprised when the display said NO SERVICE. He was out of range.

There was probably a phone inside the school that he could use. But Howie had a simpler idea. He walked back to where Robin was waiting in the meadow, seated on the ground in a loose lotus position. Howie joined him in a more comfortable Sioux squat.

"Well?" Robin asked. "Do we have a deal?"

"Jack says he can't promise you anything until he hears your information. But he's inclined to think that he can go along with client confidentiality if it's at all possible."

"That's no good. I want a guarantee."

"Robin, there have been two, more likely three murders in the past week. Guarantees just aren't possible when things get this hot."

Robin plucked a piece of straw from the ground and sucked on it thoughtfully. "Okay," he said. "Just do your best to keep me out of it. Do you promise me that?"

"I promise. Now, who killed Sherman?"

"It was my mother. I saw her do it."

"You *saw* her?"

"Well, I saw her go over to the apartment above the garage about three-thirty in the morning. That's fairly incriminating, wouldn't you say? Particularly since she lied about it to the police."

"Go on," Howie told him.

"Well, I couldn't sleep after the Halloween party. I was too wound up. I was staying in my old room, and it felt very strange. My mind kept churning over all the things that had happened, and what I'd do if Sherman told everybody that I was . . . well, you know, a child molester. It was a lie, but like I told you the other day, I couldn't see any way to defend myself against it. So I was thinking I'd go to South America and start all over again. Chile, maybe. I was down in Santiago years ago, and I like it there. Then about three-thirty I got up and went to the window to open it a crack—my old room was always the warmest in the house. That's when I saw my mother. She was outside on the path, walking toward the garage."

"You can see the garage from your bedroom window?"

"Perfectly. My bedroom's on the north side of the house. My mother must have gone out the side door. I watched her cross the path to the garage and walk up the outside stairs to Anna's apartment. Then I got back into bed."

Howie waited for more, but Robin sat with a self-satisfied smile and said nothing.

"That's it?" Howie asked.

"Isn't it enough?"

Howie didn't think so. He needed more.

"How was your mother dressed?"

"A nightgown with her big goose-down parka over it. I could see perfectly well in the moonlight."

"A *goose*-down parka. You're sure of that?"

"Of course. She's had it for years."

"What did you think she was going to do over the garage?"

"I thought she was going to have it out with Sherman. Which was about time. Maybe she would fire Anna as well, which didn't seem like a bad idea either."

"Tell me something, Robin—did you know that Anna and Sherman were having an affair?"

"Not until we ran into Gilmer in the driveway, and he told us where Sherman was. It didn't surprise me, though. Seducing the maid was right up Sherman's alley."

"All right. So you watched your mother go up the stairs to Anna's apartment. Did you hear her coming back into the main house?"

"No. Like I told you, I got back into bed and I fell asleep. I didn't wake up until morning.

"Why didn't you tell Captain Gomez about this?"

Robin's smile became more subtle. "Because she's my mother, and frankly I didn't blame her much for smothering that son of a bitch. But that was yesterday, and this is today. Today, I guess I'm a little angry, Moon Dear, finding myself suddenly forced to make my own way in the world. So I'm thinking that honesty is the best policy after all."

Howie stared at Robin Vandenberg, trying to figure him out. Obviously it hadn't been much fun for Robin to grow up a rich kid, ignored by his monstrously self-centered parents, feeling unloved. Then to top it off, his mother fixes him up with a stepfather from hell. There were probably good excuses for Robin becoming who he was, though Howie had trouble bending his sympathies too far.

"I'm not sure I understand exactly why you're doing this," Howie said after a moment. "If you're looking for revenge because your mother's giving all her money to a museum, why do you care if she knows who told on her?"

"Because once she finds herself the prime suspect, she's going to pay me for my silence. She doesn't know that yet, but believe me, she *is* going to give me something at last."

"You're going to blackmail your own mother?"

"It's not blackmail. My mom and I are simply going to come to an arrangement about things. I'm talking about justice here. Do you know what it's like, Moon Deer, to have a mother who's worth fifty million dollars and have to grub around at odd jobs for money? I make twelve hundred dollars a month at Life Circle, before taxes, and that's what I live on. I got the land where I built my tree house from my father's estate, otherwise I wouldn't even have that. Dad gave Pooh and I each a piece of land, but he left all *his* money to my mother—assuming, of course, that we would inherit eventually. So all I'm going to ask for is my part of my father's estate, about three-quarters of a million dollars, I estimate. I'll tell her I'll use it to start over again in Chile, and then she'll never hear from me again. And more importantly, from her point of view, Captain Gomez won't hear from me either."

"I still don't understand why you're telling me and Jack about what you saw."

"Because I wanted you to know who killed Sherman. You can't use my information directly—I'll deny it if you try. But I'm sure you'll find some other way to nail dear old Mom."

"You're walking a very tricky path here, Robin," Howie warned him. "You really think you can get your money and send your mother to prison at the same time?"

Robin stood up from his lotus position. "Yes, I think so," he said. "You know the old song, don't you?—'God bless the child that's got his own.' Well, I'm ready for my own, Moon Deer. And I've been ready for a long, long time."

Howie tried to phone Jack from the bottom of Wind Horse Mountain, but he was still in a cellular black hole. He tried again half an hour later when he was closer to town. This time the office phone rang, but to Howie's surprise, Jack was not there. Howie heard his own voice on the Wilder & Associate answering machine telling him to leave a message. He did, saying that he had important news and would call back.

Ten minutes later, Howie reached the main highway where he could choose to go south into town, or north to Valverde to confront Barbara Vandenberg Stone. He pulled over to the side of the road and tried Jack a third time. But Jack still wasn't answering. This was puzzling. Howie tried Jack's cell phone number, but it rang and rang without any answer at all. He glanced at his watch and saw that it was a few minutes past noon. Jack might have gone somewhere with Ed Gomez, but he was a stickler for staying in touch, and it was strange that he had not taken his cell phone along.

Howie sat thinking for a few moments in the cab, going nowhere. It all seemed very clear to him now, that although there were a good number of people who would have gladly smothered Sherman Stone, the list of suspects narrowed considerably if you tried to name someone who might have a reason to kill all three victims: Sherman, Anna, *and* Manny Lucero. Only Babs spanned the entire web of the drama. Babs, the collector of Georgia O'Keeffe. Babs, the betrayed wife of Sherman. Babs, who would not take gladly to an upstart maid in her household stealing her husband. Babs, with her huge ego, believing she had the right to do whatever she pleased. Howie did not pretend to understand exactly how it had all happened, but it seemed to him that Robin's three-thirty a.m. sighting only confirmed what he should have guessed earlier.

Normally, Howie would have preferred to consult with Jack before acting on his own in such an important matter. But he was impatient. This case had been up close and personal from the start, when the Rainbow Man had looked up into his eyes and died. Now the endgame was at hand, and Howie was anxious to have it over.

He found a screwdriver in the glove compartment and crawled under the truck to a specially installed panel near the rear fender. He removed four screws and reached inside for a small Walther P5 9mm automatic, fully loaded with a seven-round magazine. The hide-a-gun was Jack's idea. Howie had always ridiculed Jack's proclivity for hiding weapons in odd places. But not today.

Howie tried the office one last time, hoping to reach Jack, but there was still no answer. "The hell with it!" he said aloud. He stuffed the automatic into his coat pocket and drove as fast as he could to the Vandenberg Stone estate.

Twenty-two

After Claire Knightsbridge left, Jack rocked meditatively in his chair for some time, holding the key that she had left with him in the palm of his hand. He caressed the smooth flat surface and felt the jagged edge, hoping the key would fit into the tumbler of this puzzled affair. He ran his fingernail across the engraved indentation that Claire had helped him memorize: USPS DO NOT DUPLICATE 01655.

"Well, Katya," he said at last, bringing his chair to a halt, "I think we'd better call Gomez, don't you? If this really *does* belong to Claire's Rainbow Man, it's important evidence in a murder investigation."

Thump, thump, went Katya's tail.

"No, we *can't* just keep the key to ourselves," he told her firmly. "What if it was the other way around, if we were still in San Francisco and some blind private eye withheld a piece of crucial evidence? We'd be mad, wouldn't we? Goddamn furious, as a matter of fact. To put it bluntly, we'd make certain that particular P.I. never worked again."

Katya scratched at a flea with her hind leg.

"Well, let's get it over with," he said listlessly, picking up the phone and punching the number for the substation. But Captain Gomez was not there. The operator, Rose, told him that the captain had gone to a Department of Public Safety meeting in Santa Fe for the afternoon. "It's a budget meeting," Rose confided in a dramatic whisper, for Jack had cultivated her friendship over the past several years. The captain could be beeped, but only in case of an emergency. Jack told her it wasn't an emergency; he left a message asking for Ed to call him when he had a chance.

Jack smiled. He had done his duty, now he could do as he pleased. He reached for the receiver again. This time he dialed Howie's cell phone. There was no answer after six rings, and he hung up. He opened the crystal on his braille wristwatch to check the time. It was 11:36. Howie must still be on Wind Horse Mountain, out of range. Howie had always insisted that cell phones were more of a nuisance than a help, and Jack was starting to agree—at least in the wilds of northern New Mexico.

He sat at his desk and continued to think. He knew he should wait either for Howie to call in or for Captain Gomez to get back to him. In the old days, Commander Wilder had been known for his patience and restraint; it was one of the qualities that had helped him avoid serious mistakes and climb up the bureaucratic ladder to the upper reaches of police officialdom. But these were not the old days, and Jack was restless. He had an idea how he might find out which post office box Claire's mysterious key opened, and he was not in a mood to sit around helplessly waiting for seeing eyes.

He came to a decision and stood up so abruptly that Katya wasn't able to get her tail out in time from beneath the sudden backward rock of his chair. She yelped in pain. "You gotta stay on your toes, Katya," Jack lectured. "A person must always expect the unexpected."

He found her leather harness and fitted it around her body. "Stop wiggling!" he commanded. "Time for you to earn your keep, my friend."

Jack held onto the rigid handle of Katya's harness with his left hand as they walked together down the sidewalk. All his senses were tuned to the darkness around him, trying to understand the chaos of sounds and smells through which he and Katya moved: cars, voices, the bass thud of car stereos, distant laughter, exhaust fumes, the pungent aroma of coffee as he passed near the New Wave Café, Howie's favorite haunt. A blind man walking down a busy street had to be a good detective: constantly seeking clues, signs, and omens, then putting the evidence together, and coming up with a true picture of the world and its dangers. Fortunately, Jack had a $25,000 German shepherd to help him. Katya had been taught to avoid danger to herself, to stop at curbs and look for traffic, and not proceed until it was safe. She had been trained for this task since early puppyhood, spending the first two years of her life with a special family in Sacramento and then entering a six-month program at San Rafael Guide Dogs for the Blind, a school north of San Francisco. Finally, she had been paired with Jack in an intensive two-month program, where dog and man had learned to work together. None of this had been easy for Jack; after six years, he was still not entirely comfortable with blind navigation.

Katya led them along the narrow sidewalk through a crowd of tourists who hurried out of their way. She stopped at each intersection, allowing Jack to feel for the curb with his right foot. Katya had been trained specifically for "intelligent disobedience," to ignore Jack's commands if it would lead them both into danger. Not long after leaving the office, Katya pushed back sharply on the rigid harness, and Jack nearly fell backward onto his ass. He was starting to bawl her out when he heard a car rush by very close to where he had been standing. "Good girl," he managed sheepishly.

He was headed to the main post office, a fifteen-minute walk from Wilder & Associate. He had done this particular walk with Howie a number of times, since he and Emma received their residential mail at a box there. But he had never gone with only Katya to guide him. He could visualize the way: a right turn up Sangre de Christo to Dolores, then left three blocks—or was it four?—to Sanchez. From here, he only had to walk straight on Sanchez, though he wasn't certain precisely how many blocks he would need to cross several busy intersections.

Blind navigation required strict concentration. But Jack was distracted today as he pondered the interconnections between *Red Moon*, Manuel Lucero, Sherman Stone, and Anna Montoya. He was thinking hard about Anna, wondering how exactly she fit into the puzzle, when he realized he had not been paying attention to how many blocks he had traveled. He had forgotten to count! He felt a momentary swell of panic, certain that he was lost. The world around him seemed suddenly huge and unknowable, with cars and people racing about in mad chaos.

He forced himself to stop, wait, listen, breathe, and get a grip on himself. He wasn't really lost, it had only felt that way; he was somewhere on a sidewalk in San Geronimo with people nearby. He patted his parka for the reassuring bulge of his cell phone, thinking he could always dial 911 and wait for help if he got really desperate. But here he had a bad surprise. His pocket was empty; he had left his phone back at the office, absorbed as he was by other thoughts. This was bad. A blind man could not afford to become distracted. Now, among other things, Howie would not be able to reach him when he came back into telephone range from Wind Horse Mountain.

Jack was standing on the sidewalk, wondering if he should go back for his telephone or onward to the post office, when a woman nearby asked if he needed help. She seemed very kind—a young woman, from the timbre of her voice. "What an awesome dog!" she said, scratching Katya's head. Jack hated the word awesome; it represented to him a slouchy, inarticulate, slacker generation that was so different from his own. But in this instant, he only smiled and agreed that yes, Katya was awesomeness incarnate. The young woman escorted them to the post office, which turned out to be only a block away, and she placed him in the line to wait for the next available clerk. Another person, a man, took him to the front of the line and helped him find the counter.

"What can I do for you today?" the clerk asked brightly. An Anglo, Jack guessed; his voice had a nasal twang of Oklahoma.

"I seem to be having trouble opening my box." Jack did his best to appear helpless and overwhelmed as he pulled the key and string from his pocket and placed it on the counter. "You know what I've done? I think I've picked up my friend Manny Lucero's key by mistake. He came over for coffee this morning and somehow I got all turned around."

"Well, let's see what we can do," the clerk said patiently. "What's your box number?"

"Fourteen-fourteen," Jack said.

"And you want your mail, I suppose?"

"Yes, I'd appreciate that. But most of all, I'm hoping you can tell me if this is my key or Manny's. These things are awfully difficult when you can't see. Perhaps you could check the number of the key with your computer. . . ."

Jack waited as the clerk took the key and stepped into a back room. A few minutes later he returned.

"Here's your mail, Mr. Wilder. I checked the number on the key, and you're right, it isn't yours. But it doesn't belong to your friend Manny Lucero either."

"Really? Can you tell me whose it is?"

"I'm sorry. Postal regulations, you know."

Jack had an inspiration. "I bet it's Claire's!" he said, adding wildly: "That's my daughter-in-law. Claire Knightsbridge."

"Well, I'm not really supposed to say. But I suppose under the circumstances . . . you're right, it's your daughter-in-law's. The box was rented to her just two weeks ago."

Jack nodded. "She and my son moved here from South Dakota recently. I'm going to see them later, so if it's okay, I'll take her mail too."

"Oh, I'm terribly sorry, but I can't do that. Besides, her box is in Valverde, Mr. Wilder."

Valverde! Unless Claire had a secret life, he presumed that Manny Lucero had rented the box in her name. Jack fixed the clerk with his dark glasses. There was nothing like a blind stare to give a seeing-eyed person the heebie-jeebies.

"Of course, I remember now. There's a small post office at Valverde in the general store. Claire told me all about it." Jack took off his dark glasses to scratch the old scars and give the clerk a glimpse of dead eyes. "Box two-four-nine, isn't it?"

"Box thirty-seven," the clerk said hurriedly, deeply unnerved.

"Thanks so much," Jack told him, setting his glasses in place. "Is there a pay phone here?"

"In the lobby."

Jack and Katya moved from the counter into the post office lobby, where another helpful stranger guided them to a pay phone on a wall. Jack oriented himself on the unfamiliar telephone, feeling for the four rows of plastic buttons. Then he used his memorized phone card number to give Howie another try. But there was still no answer. Next he called the office and left a message for Howie on the machine, should Howie return.

Jack stood thinking, the phone in hand, his mind racing.

Should he, should he not . . . that was the question. He went back and forth and then decided to take a chance. It was a big gamble, but he believed he knew what he was doing. If he was right, he could wrap up this case in a few hours.

Jack phoned information and got the number for Barbara Vandenberg Stone. A few moments later he reached the matriarch herself.

"Mrs. Stone," he said. "This is Jack Wilder. We've never met, but I believe I know the whereabouts of a Georgia O'Keeffe painting by the name of *Red Moon* . . . yes, that's right, I've found it . . . yes, I'm sure it's a *very* important canvas. Look, I wonder if I could prevail upon you to give me just a small helping hand in order to retrieve it. I know this is a difficult time for you, of course. What I need you to do is simply to make a phone call for me. . . ."

Jack spoke for some time, then put down the receiver with a thin smile on his lips.

Twenty-three

Howie drove up the long, stately driveway to the Vandenberg Stone house shortly before twelve-thirty. The driveway was lined on both sides with poplar trees, their branches bare, like dead soldiers standing at attention. The big unhappy house at the end of the avenue stood unnaturally still in the midday silence, it's rose-colored facade staring emptily at a pale autumn sky.

Howie was surprised to find Gilmer Good Day's red Jaguar convertible parked near the front door. It was certainly an automobile to drool over; Howie had to admit, he'd enjoyed driving it the other night. But now in the shadowless light of midday, it struck him as all wrong for an Indian, even an Indian from Malibu. It was like Gilmer was trying too hard to show off what a nouveau native he was, a glitzy guy who was not your grandfather's aborigine.

Gilmer came out from the front door just as Howie turned off the ignition of the truck. Gilmer was dressed in a plaid cowboy shirt, jeans, and dusty white sneakers, his long gray-black hair tied in a braid. You could almost mistake him for a guy from the rez, but not quite. He was so preoccupied that he didn't see Howie in the driveway. He turned and gazed back at the house as though something were puzzling him.

"Hey, Gilmer," Howie said aloud.

Gilmer literally jumped.

"Jesus, Moon Deer!" he cried, turning to the driveway. "You scared the shit out of me! What are you doing here?"

"I thought I'd pay Mrs. Stone a visit," Howie told him, stepping from the cab of the truck. "How about you, Gilmer?"

"That's what I just did. I was curious to see how a woman gets along after she's just killed the man she loved."

Howie studied Gilmer's face, not certain he was serious.

"And how *is* she doing?"

Gilmer shrugged. "About like I would have expected. She's wandering through that big old house like some kind of ghost, lugging around a bottle of vodka with her. Not many people have come by to see how the old bitch is doing. A few showed up yesterday, but she told me that I was the first one to drop by today. Most people in this town hate Babs, despite all her damn money. So you see there *is* justice in this world, after all. People get what they deserve, Moon Deer. And what Babs is going to get is a very lonely ending."

"Or the rest of her life in prison," Howie remarked. "Do you really think she killed Sherman? Did she confess to you?"

"No. And she's not going to confess either. Or apologize, or explain. It's not her style. But who else could have done it?"

"A number of people," Howie mentioned, for the sake of discussion. "Robin, for instance. Or Pooh."

Gilmer shook his head. "No, they wouldn't have the balls. It's Babs, all right."

"But she loved Sherman," Howie objected. "You said so yourself."

Gilmer smiled at Howie's earnestness. "You're still kind of wet behind the ears, aren't you, Moon Deer? People kill the things they love all the time. It's why there are old people with regrets. And people like Babs who need a bottle of vodka to sleep at night."

Howie glanced up at a second-story window sensing movement there. Was she watching? But the glass was dark and empty. When he turned back, Gilmer was walking toward his car.

"So what are you going to do now?" Howie asked, following after him.

"Me? I'm going to do what I always do—paint. The world is full of melodrama. Full of shit, if you want to know the truth. But an artist keeps on working, regardless. That's just the way it is. The good news, Moon Deer, is that you and I are Indians. So what the hell does it mater to us what these white people do?"

"I thought Sherman was your friend."

"Sure he was my friend," Gilmer agreed, shaking his head bitterly. "A long, long time ago . . . look, Moon Deer, I have a proposition for you. When I finish my airport mural, I'm thinking of taking off to live in France for a while. Maybe a year or two. With Sherman dead, it's going to be depressing around here, and frankly, I'm ready for a change. How'd you like to come along and be my assistant?"

"You're offering me a job?" Howie asked in surprise.

"Well, sure. I'm going to need someone to help me set up a studio in Paris. Someone to help me run the practical side of day-to-day life over there. You speak French, and we get along pretty good together, I think. Sometimes I look at you, and I get a feeling that I'm seeing myself as a young man. So think about it. I'll pay you whatever you want."

A job in Paris was attractive, but Howie wasn't certain he liked the idea of reminding Gilmer of himself as a young man.

"I'll think about it," he agreed.

"Do that. If you want, you can bring along your woman and her kids, so don't let that be a barrier. I have lots of money, Moon Deer. More than I need. And the way I look at it, the dispossessed of the world should stick together."

"You think I'm dispossessed?"

Gilmer smiled. "It takes one to know one, doesn't it? Just look at your life."

Howie was starting to find this a disturbing conversation. "My life's pretty good," he objected.

"Sure it is," Gilmer agreed. "An Ivy League Indian who can't go home again because his own people would find him about as alien as some guy dropping in from another planet. Yeah, you're doing great. Living with a pretty Iowa girl who's as totally out of place in New Mexico as you are. Add a few stepkids who've been snatched from their real father—they probably hate the schools here and everything else about San Geronimo. Am I right?"

"Gilmer, you're an interesting guy, but I'm not sure I'm in the mood to discuss all this."

"Hey, I dig it!" Gilmer said quickly, raising the palms of his hands from the steering wheel. "And I'm not saying that being rootless is the end of the world. I've learned to live with it, and so can you. When all is said and done, our traditional brethren are stuck on the reservation. It's the lost natives like you and me, bro, who find ourselves with interesting opportunities for adventure from time to time."

Howie watched as Gilmer Good Day put the key in the ignition and started up his engine. The Jaguar purred like an expensively spoiled pussycat.

"So think about Paris," Gilmer said as he was pulling away. "Believe me, Paris has always been the answer for Americans who can't make it at home. *Au revoir*, Moon Deer."

Howie rang the doorbell and waited, but no one answered. There came no sound from inside the house, nothing to disturb the stillness. He tried the doorknob and found it was unlocked. The heavy Spanish door creaked opened.

"Mrs. Stone?" he called into the quiet house. "It's Howard Moon Deer. I was wondering if I could speak with you."

Howie stepped into the foyer, leaving the front door open behind him.

"Mrs. Stone?" he called again. The house was dark and stuffy and quiet as a tomb. He peered into the huge living room and saw that the curtains were closed against the day, letting in only a few thin shafts of dusty light. There were dirty glasses on a coffee table, a half-finished bottle of wine, and an ashtray with several butts.

Howie wondered what he should do next. He put his hand on the gun in his pocket for support, but a gun wasn't much use against the heavy aura of despair that seemed to lay in every dark corner of the house. After some hesitation, he turned from the living room back toward the foyer and forced himself up the stairs to the second floor.

"Mrs. Stone? It's Howard Moon Deer!"

At the top of the landing, he came to a narrow window that was framed by dark, heavy drapes. The window looked out onto the rear of the estate, and Howie stopped for a reassuring glimpse of natural daylight. He was surprised to see an old woman on the grounds below. She was dressed in a bathrobe, walking erratically down the path toward Sherman's Quonset hut art studio, holding a bottle loosely by the neck with one hand. Howie recognized her as Barbara Vandenberg Stone, the town's richest woman, only by logical deduction: the bottle, the drunken weave, and her destination. She must have left the house by a rear door while he had been talking with Gilmer.

Howie jogged back down the stairs and out through the open door, glad to escape the oppressive atmosphere of the house. He ran along a path that took him between the house and the garage. Yellow police tape blocked the entrance to the stairs leading up to the second-floor garage apartment, but otherwise there was no sign that anything unusual had occurred here. As Howie ran, he tried to imagine what Babs was up to. Perhaps she was only wandering aimlessly, revisiting Sherman's haunts.

He slowed to a walk as he approached the Quonset hut, his right hand jammed down onto the butt of the gun in the pocket of his coat. The studio door was open, and a single bare lightbulb overhead illuminated the chaos of half-completed metal sculptures and materials inside. At first Howie saw no sign of Barbara Stone. Then he spotted her at the far end of the room. She had placed the bottle on the floor—Absolut, he noticed—and was standing on a stepladder, reaching up to a storage loft overhead.

"Don't just stand there. Give me a hand," she commanded unexpectedly.

Howie glanced behind him to see if there was anyone else she could be speaking to.

"You, young man," she ordered imperiously. "Come here."

Howie walked across the studio to the foot of the ladder, where he had a better view than he wanted of varicose veins on the old woman's legs, which protruded from the end of her dressing gown.

"Here, take this," she said. For one crazy instant he thought she was going to hand him the missing painting, *Red Moon*. But she passed down only a cardboard shoe box. She accepted Howie's help getting down the ladder.

"Give that to me," she said when she was back on the floor, taking the box from him. "Who are you anyway?"

"Howard Moon Deer. Don't you remember. . . ."

"I'm too old for remembering," she told him curtly. "There's a light switch by the stereo. Make yourself useful and turn it on."

Howie did as she told him, filling the cavernous interior of the studio with a harsh flood of florescent light from long tubes overhead. Meanwhile, Babs knelt on the floor by Sherman's arrangement of cannibalized car seats that he had set up into a kind of sitting room area. She spilled out the contents of the box onto the floor. Howie saw that they were all old photographs of Sherman Stone. A bit of memorabilia, apparently.

"Mrs. Stone, I'm sorry to bust in on you like this. But I need to ask you a few questions."

"Later," she told him.

"Mrs. Stone. . . ."

"Kindly shut up and let me concentrate . . . what did you say your name was again?"

"Howard Moon Deer," he told her again wearily, doubting she would remember. He watched her go through the photographs on the floor. As Gilmer had warned, she looked terrible. Her face was ravaged and lined. Her gray-white hair was hanging wild, and the dressing gown she wore was stained with food and other things Howie didn't want to imagine. It was hard to believe that this witchlike creature was the same bejeweled woman he had seen on Saturday dressed as Marie Antoinette at the Halloween ball.

"Yes, this is what I want," she said distractedly, pulling a 3 x 5 color print from the pile. The color looked old and faded, but Howie couldn't' see any more of it than that. She put the picture in her dressing gown pocket, reached for the bottle of vodka on the floor, and stood up with difficulty. With an exhausted sigh, she sat down again almost immediately on one of the disembodied car seats.

She took a long drink from the bottle and studied Howie with displeasure.

"Do you have any children?" she asked.

"I have stepchildren."

"Then you know."

"Know what, Mrs. Stone?"

"How you give and give and get nothing in return. My son molests children and my daughter's an idiot. I did everything I could for them. But they've disappointed me greatly."

"I'm sorry to hear that."

"Not as sorry as they're going to be. They all wanted Sherman dead. They were jealous of my happiness. They said he only married me for my money. Why else would a person like that marry a bulldog-faced old lady like me? But he loved me intensely, young man. He wasn't always faithful, but we loved each other in our own unique way. I will *never* get over this terrible loss," she said, lowering her voice self-dramatically.

She took another swig on the bottle and belched, which did not strike Howie as a particularly ladylike thing to do. Nor did her next statement.

"We had great sex," she announced, almost belligerently.

"I'm sorry?"

"*Sex!* Sherman's penis was ten-inches long. What do you think of *that*, young man?"

"You, er, measured it?"

"Naturally I measured it. Why shouldn't I?"

"I, uh . . . well, I always supposed that for women it wasn't the meat as much as the motion," he managed.

"It's the meat," she assured him curtly. "My first husband had a very small penis, so I know these things. I'm convinced it's the reason my children came out so disappointingly. They're constricted, you see. They have no largesse."

My God, she was nuts! Totally whacko! Howie supposed that when you had that much money, there was no anchor to keep you in reality. He gripped the comforting butt of the gun in his pocket and decided to remain standing.

"Mrs. Stone, let me get to the point. On Saturday night, after you got back from the party, you were seen leaving your house at about three-thirty in the morning and walking over to Anna Montoya's apartment above the garage. I think you'll feel better if you tell me about it."

"You think *I* did it?" she asked with a harsh laugh. "You think *I* killed my husband?"

Howie did his best to give her his most knowing Jacklook, one eyebrow slightly raised. Jack always managed this perfectly, causing people to squirm and talk compulsively. But Howie's imitation had no such effect on Mrs. Stone.

"Who saw me walk over there on Saturday night?" she challenged. "It was Robin, wasn't it? I thought I caught a glimpse of that little shit lurking by his window."

"If you want to know, it was me," Howie said dutifully, protecting his source. "I wasn't really asleep when you came in."

"Weren't you, now? You certainly gave a good impression of it!"

"Tell me about it. Please."

"Why should I?" she began querulously. But then she leaned back in the car seat and seemed to change her mind. "Well, I couldn't sleep, that's all. And I wasn't certain I believed Robin. He would say things just to make me unhappy. So I had to see for myself if it was true."

"Did you know that Sherman was having an affair with Anna?"

Babs glared at Howie. "Of course not!" she snapped. "I would never have tolerated such behavior in my house! Naturally I knew that Sherman had his little adventures. I'm much older than he was, of course, and I'm no fool. All I asked was for him to be just a little discreet. I assumed he would have better taste than to go for the maid and soil the home nest. We had an understanding, you see. But there were certain rules."

"So you walked over to Anna's apartment to see if he had broken the rules?"

"The lights were on upstairs," she continued. "And the door wasn't locked. I saw you asleep on the couch in the sitting room. Then I walked into the bedroom. Sherman and Anna were passed out under the covers. I was glad to see them, frankly. Imagination makes these things worse, you know. But the truth of it was shabby and rather predictable, so I decided I wouldn't be jealous after all. Why should I lower myself to such a common level?"

"You can simply decide not to be jealous?"

"Of course. Jealousy is an indulgence, especially at my age. You can turn it on and off like a switch."

"Okay. You turned off your switch. Then what did you do?"

"*Then* what? I turned around and came back home and slept like a lamb."

"After you smothered Sherman with a pillow, of course."

"Oh, come, come! Don't be daft!" she said loudly. "You think I'm some stupid schoolgirl? Listen to me, whatever your name is—if I couldn't tolerate Sherman's behavior, I'd simply throw him out. I assure you, I'm *much* too selfish to risk my own discomfort in prison by committing some senseless crime."

This last statement had a ring of truth to it, leaving Howie momentarily stymied. "You're telling me that Sherman was alive when you left the bedroom?"

"That's *exactly* what I'm telling you. I didn't take his pulse, naturally. But he was snoring with a good deal of gusto, which I interpret as a sign of life. And now, young man, I'll thank you to get the hell out of here . . . what did you say your name was again?"

"Howard Moon Deer," he told her for the third time. "Would you like me to write it down?"

"There's no need to be sarcastic. You work for that private detective, don't you? Jack Wilder."

"That's right. I'm Jack's assistant."

"Good. Then you can do me a favor and give him this."

To Howie's surprise, she took the photograph from her dressing gown pocket and handed it to him. The photo had serrated edges, and the color was faded, like looking back through a tunnel in time. In the picture three long-haired young men stood with their arms around each other's shoulders in front of the old St. Francis cathedral near the Santa Fe plaza, grinning at the camera. Their wardrobe was as dated as their haircuts: collarless shirts that looked as if they had been made from bedspreads, headbands, patched blue jeans. You could almost smell the distant whiff of marijuana and patchouli oil.

Three young men, the best of friends. In Santa Fe a quarter of a century ago.

"Damn!" Howie cried as he recognized the faces, rearranging their features in his mind with different hair and adding the burden of years.

"Yes, damnation, indeed!" said Babs dryly, watching his expression. "You don't know everything after all, do you, Howard Moon Deer?"

"I've got to go," he told her.

"Yes, you do," she agreed. "Quickly."

Twenty-four

"I keep losing you," Jack Wilder told Howie on the telephone. "Say that again . . . Howie, for chrissake, you're going to have to tell me this again. Slowly, please. . . ."

Jack sat at his desk in a pool of afternoon sunlight, trying to understand what Howie was telling him. The window behind him was cracked open to let in a cool undercurrent of autumn breeze and cooking smells from a touristy Mexican restaurant two doors away. Someone was making up green chile stew, and the aroma reminded Jack that he had missed lunch today. But right now he had more urgent problems than the growl of an empty stomach. Howie had finally managed to get through on his cell phone, but the call kept breaking up into static. It was like a bad connection to the moon.

Then, while Jack was struggling to hear, Katya began barking, and there was a knock on the office door.

"I've got to go . . . *shut up, Katya*! . . . no, not you, Howie. Where are you?"

"Just down . . . erde by the . . . along. . . ."

The knock came again.

"Goddamn it, I can't understand a thing you're saying! If you can hear *me*, come back to the office, Howie. Get here as fast as you can!" Jack put down the receiver, took a deep breath, and checked the time. It was 1:23 according to his braille watch. He adjusted his jacket so that the zipper was attached only at the very bottom, allowing easier access to his .38.

"Come in," he called to the door.

"It's Gilmer Good Day," came a voice from the doorway.

"Gilmer," said Jack, rising to his feet. He managed a stressful smile. "This is a surprise."

Gilmer settled himself across the desk from Jack in the same rocking chair Robin Vandenberg had chosen the week before.

"Sorry not to call first," he said, launching the old chair back and forth in squeaky motion, "but I was in the area, and I thought I'd just drop by. I left Moon Deer a little while ago, and frankly, I've been going back and forth about whether I should come see you. You know, Jack, among the Cheyenne the blind are often revered as holy men. We like to think that if a person can't look outward, his vision is more acute for searching inward to the core of things."

"Did you learn this bit of Indian lore growing up in Malibu?"

Gilmer laughed. "I see Moon Deer's been telling you my checkered past. Look, the reason I'm here is that I was hoping you could give me some advice. But I need to be sure our talk can remain confidential."

"Absolutely," Jack assured him. Then added with a smile, "Unless you've killed someone, of course. Then I'd have to turn you in."

Gilmer laughed. "Oh, no, it's not like that! I haven't committed any crime at all myself. But I *am* in a bit of a jam. The problem is, I've been less than honest with the police, and I'm starting to worry about my legal position. You see, I *know* about a crime that involved two of my friends, and I've kept quiet about it. It happened a long time ago."

"In 1974," Jack agreed with a nod.

"That's right. I told Howie part of this the other night at Pinky's. I met Sherman in seventy-three when I was bumming around Europe. I was just a poor art student back then, and Sherman . . . well, Sherman was quite the revolutionary, a real bohemian thumbing his nose at conventions. I flew back to Los Angeles after that summer was over, and Sherman returned to art school in New York. The following spring—the spring of seventy-four—he called me about three o'clock in the morning one day and said that he and his buddy Manny Lucero had just decided art school was a bunch of bullshit, so they were going to drop out and hitch to Santa Fe. Sherman made everything sound idyllic—how an artist could live cheaply in New Mexico and do as he pleased. And if I joined them, we could all rent a house together, each of us would have a space to paint, and it would be a kind of art commune. He said Manny was the most talented American artist since Jackson Pollock, and I'd love him. Nothing was really happening for me in L.A. at the time, so I let myself get seduced by Sherman's enthusiasm—I took him up on his offer."

Gilmer's chair hesitated, then continued it's back-and-forth motion with less energy than before. A more tentative rock, Jack noted.

"Go on," Jack said.

Gilmer exhaled a long sigh. "Well, it turned out to be the biggest mistake of my life. I drove my old VW van to Santa Fe, and we rented a house together, the three of us. A lot of what happened next is hard to understand unless you remember what it was like in the early seventies, what with the Weathermen and Patty Hearst, and a lot of crazy ideas in the air—not to mention all the dope we were smoking. God, we were so young! Manny Lucero was an anarchist, you see. A maniac, really. Frankly, he scared the shit out of me, even back then. It's ironic that he took a vow of silence later, because that summer you couldn't get him to shut up. He'd talk for hours about the revolution and art and the new society we were building. We would have these bull sessions that went on all night long. Sherman was totally under his spell."

"But you weren't?"

"Well, yes and no. Manny impressed me, but like I say—he worried me a lot too. The guy was obviously brilliant, but he didn't have any limits. Me, I guess I've always had a more practical streak than either Manny *or* Sherman. All I wanted was to become a good artist, and maybe make some money at it too. So after a while, it got to be a classic there's-a-crowd situation. Manny and Sherman were tight as they could be, and I was the odd man out. Particularly when they started stealing."

Jacked raised an eyebrow. "Stealing how?"

"Robbing houses when the owners were away. They even held up a gas station once—they did it with toy guns, but it was a holdup nevertheless."

"And you participated in these robberies?"

"Oh, Christ, no! I didn't want any part of it! It was all Manny's idea, of course—it was supposed to be very avant-garde, or something. Don't ask me how. Sherman and Manny managed to convince themselves that every true anarchist revolutionary artist positively *had* to be an outlaw as a matter of principal."

"But you didn't turn them in either, did you?"

"Well, no, of course not. They were my friends, after all. I just tried to ignore what was happening. I started painting like crazy—thirteen, fourteen hours a day. Trying to pretend to myself that these guys I shared a house with weren't really criminals. It got hard to ignore, believe me. Particularly when the living room was stacked up to the ceiling with stolen TVs and stereos. Then late one night, Sherman and Manny came home, and even they were freaked out—they had just killed someone. They told me it was an accident, that they hadn't meant to do it. They were robbing a big old house in a quiet neighborhood near the Old Santa Fe Trail when the owner came home unexpectedly."

"Juan Antonio Mendez," Jack supplied.

"Yeah," Gilmer agreed unhappily. "Apparently, he was an art collector. Sherman was upstairs looking at some of the art, and Manny was downstairs in the living room when Mendez came home. Mendez must have sensed something wrong immediately, because he got his gun out and found Manny in the living room with a burlap sack full of stuff he was stealing. The way I understand it, Manny started talking a blue streak—telling Mendez that he was only an art student trying to make the rent, etcetera, etcetera. And if Mendez would give him a break just this one time, he'd never rob again, honest. He'd even give the guy one of his paintings as a kind of memento of the night. Incredible bullshit, but apparently Mendez was starting to buy it. Meanwhile, Sherman began sneaking down the stairs, trying his best not to make any noise. Manny saw what Sherman was doing and started talking louder. Sherman was able to creep up on Mendez from behind, then they both jumped him. They were both frightened, and their adrenaline was up, so I guess they jumped him a little too hard. One of them got hold of the guy's gun arm, and I guess he was shooting bullets into the ceiling—it must have been a crazy scene. Then one of them knocked Mendez over the head with the base of a floor lamp. Neither Manny nor Sherman ever told me which of them killed the guy, but I always suspected it was Manny. Neither of them *meant* to kill him, of course. They only wanted to get the hell out of there."

"Yet that didn't stop them from taking a half-million-dollar Georgia O'Keeffe on their way out the door," Jack remarked.

Gilmer paused once again with his rocking. Jack almost felt he should take Gilmer aside to warn him that if he ever found himself again involved in a murder investigation, he really needed to learn how to rock and think at the same time.

"It was Sherman who took the painting," Gilmer continued. "He told me later he didn't know it was an O'Keeffe—he just took it on a whim. Manny grabbed the burlap bag full of the stuff he had been collecting before Mendez showed up—mostly booze and electronics. As he was leaving, he picked up Mendez's gun from the floor as well, a 9mm pistol. Then they got the hell out of that house as fast as their legs could carry them. I was asleep when they came home, but they woke me up and told me the whole story. Sherman was so upset, he was crying. And I was freaked out too, of course. Christ, I sure as hell didn't want to be an accomplice to murder!"

"Then, why didn't you go to the police?"

"Are you serious?" Gilmer cried in astonishment. "Well, I *thought* of it, I must confess. But Manny and Sherman were my friends—my God, I couldn't turn them in! And, besides, I wasn't certain about my own position. I mean, I'd been living in a house full of stolen loot all summer, and I wasn't sure the cops wouldn't arrest me too. You have to remember, I was young, I had long hair, I was an Indian—cops didn't exactly smile benevolently at people like me. All in all, it seemed best to keep quiet and hope for a lucky break. A few days after the killing, we all decided to split up. Believe me, we were ready to take a very long vacation from one another. So I drove my van back to L.A., and Manny got on a Greyhound to New York. I heard later that Sherman stayed in Santa Fe for a while, which was fairly nervy of him. He got arrested later that fall for selling a bag of pot to an undercover cop, and it took him a few months to get out from under his legal problems. Then he went to New York, I understand. And after that, Europe. We all lost touch with each other for a whole bunch of years. I never saw Manny again from that summer until the time he showed up in San Geronimo last week."

"Tell me, how did you divide up the loot from the burglary?"

"Well, we argued about that," Gilmer said. "I told Manny and Sherman they were insane to even consider keeping anything—my God, it would tie them to the murder if they got found with it! The day after the killing, I convinced them to use my van and dump everything in a landfill north of Santa Fe. But at the last minute, Manny decided he wanted to keep the pistol. He'd gotten attached to the gun by then, maybe thinking it made him a *real* revolutionary. Manny was starting to flip out, I can see that now. He was always a little strange—*more* than strange, actually. But the killing took him over the edge."

"And *Red Moon*?"

"After Manny said he was keeping the gun, Sherman insisted he wanted the painting. He said it spoke to him, or some nonsense—he refused to throw it into the landfill."

"Maybe he knew it was a Georgia O'Keeffe and worth a fortune?"

"No, I don't think so. In seventy-four, we weren't exactly O'Keeffe fans. She wasn't hip then, you know. Not our idea of the sort of stuff people liked in New York at that time. None of us even knew her work very well."

"Still, this division seems a little unfair," Jack remarked. "Manny got a three-hundred-dollar handgun out of the burglary, and Sherman a half-million-dollar painting."

"Jack, there was nothing fair or rational about the whole damn business, start to finish! Manny wanted the gun, Sherman wanted the painting—to be honest, I think we all assumed the gun was the more valuable of the two items. It certainly would have been easier to sell. Personally, like I told you, I was trying to convince them to get rid of *everything*, but they wouldn't listen to me."

"You drove them to the landfill, I assume?"

Gilmer exhaled another long sigh. "Yes, yes," he said wearily. "I suppose that makes me an accessory to the crime. But all I wanted was to get the whole ugly mess over with so I could go on living my life. After that, twenty-five years went by, and I didn't hear anything more about *Red Moon* or the gun. Jack, you have to understand, I thought this whole incident was dead and buried forever. Just a little bit of youthful insanity that I was lucky to escape."

"When you became neighbors with Sherman years later, it must have come up between you in conversation?" Jack suggested.

"No, never. Sherman seemed as anxious to forget that summer as I was. Honestly, after twenty-five years we almost convinced ourselves that it was just a bad dream. Until Manny showed up."

"He came to see you?"

"No, he went to Sherman. And then Sherman came to me. I only heard about this secondhand."

"What exactly did Manny want?"

"Forgiveness for his sins," Gilmer said wryly. "Redemption. Peace with God. Believe it or not, he *walked* here all the way from California, pushing his shopping cart down the highway. Apparently, Manny had gotten himself a major case of religion while he was in prison for some other crime. He wanted Sherman and him to go together to the cops and confess to how they had killed Juan Antonio

Mendez back in their days of sin and hedonism. According to Manny, it was the only way they could make amends for what they had done. And they *both* had to do it together, you see, or it wouldn't count—apparently, Manny had personal conversations with God, and God told him this. Sherman said no, naturally. *He* sure as hell didn't want to spend the rest of his life in prison! He thought he could talk Manny out of the whole thing. But a guy who had walked all the way from California wasn't going to be talked out of anything."

"When did this conversation take place?"

"About ten days ago, I gather. Again, I got all this secondhand from Sherman, so I can't swear to its accuracy. The way I understand it, Manny came to Sherman's studio, and they had it out—Manny wrote everything on a little blackboard he kept around his neck. When Sherman said no, Manny came back the next night and stole *Red Moon* from where Sherman had it hidden in his studio. He had never gotten rid of that damn painting, you see, like he should have. He still had it."

"But how did Manny know where the painting was?"

"I don't know. Maybe God told him. Or maybe Manny just got lucky, or Sherman was so stoned that he was careless. All I know for certain is that Manny went through that damn Quonset hut and somehow found the thing. Once he had the painting, he used it for leverage. I'm sure he thought it was the only way to get Sherman and him to go to the cops together and make a nice clean confession, so that God would forgive them and they could both go to heaven and sing with the angels. Manny disappeared for a few days, and that's when *I* heard about all this—Sherman came to me, and he was frantic. It seemed a pretty bad joke to him that his old dope-smoking buddy from the seventies had become a Christian fundamentalist! Then Manny showed up again at Sherman's last Wednesday. This time Manny wasn't *asking* Sherman to go confess with him, he was *insisting*. He said he had the O'Keeffe hidden away in a safe place, and if Sherman didn't go along with his plan, Manny was simply going to take the canvas to the police and implicate him anyway. Sherman pretended he needed to think, but Manny said no more thinking—too much time had passed already, and God was impatient. Sherman saw there just wasn't more use arguing, so he got his .22 rabbit rifle from the house. Manny tried to make a run for it, but Sherman chased after him and shot him in the fields down below from the mesa."

"Yes, I'm curious how that happened exactly," Jack admitted.

"I don't know the details, thank God. Sherman started to tell me, but I shut him up. I told him, for chrissake, man—I don't want to know!"

Jack leaned back in his chair and put his hands behind his neck. "Well, well, this is interesting," he said. "So Sherman shot the Rainbow Man. But I wonder who smothered Sherman? Was it Babs?"

"Possibly. But my guess is that Anna did it in a fit of anger. And then the next morning she woke up and couldn't live with herself. So she drove too fast down that switchback, deliberately."

"Well, well," Jack said again, deep in thought.

"So you can see the bind I'm in," Gilmer concluded. "My only crime was to share a house with the wrong two guys back in seventy-four. But I know it would be hard as hell to prove I'm innocent. The last couple of days, I've been wandering about like a crazy man wondering what to do. I can't sleep, I can't work. Finally, after talking with Howie just now, I decided, hell—I have to tell somebody about this and get some professional advice. So that's why I'm here, Jack. I'm hoping you can show me the way out of the mess I'm in."

"My advice is that you should go to Captain Gomez and tell him what you just told me."

"But I've lied to him. I pretended I didn't know Manny or anything about *Red Moon*. Won't he be suspicious if I come to him now with a whole new story?"

"Sure he'll be suspicious," Jack agreed. "Cops are always suspicious. That's why they're cops."

Gilmer's rocking stopped completely. "Look," he said, "I've thought of a possible way out of this. But I'm not sure what you'll think."

"Try me," Jack suggested.

"Well, let's say I hired you to find *Red Moon*. That painting must be somewhere close by. I'd pay you a lot of money if you'd find it for me. Let's say $10,000."

"And then what?"

"I'd do what should have been done years ago. I'd destroy the damn thing, that's all. Then there would be nothing to link this whole present mess with what happened twenty-five years ago. I could just go on living my life. The problem is, if the painting's found, it's going to open up some very serious digging into the past. Someone for sure is going to find out that I was living in the same house with Sherman and Manny back when Juan Antonio Mendez was killed, and then you can imagine how hard it's going to be for me to defend myself."

Jack shook his head. "You're asking me to commit a felony, Gilmer. Destroying evidence in a homicide investigation is a serious crime. Anyway, *Red Moon* isn't the only link to 1974. There's the 9mm Beretta that Manny dropped in Claire Knightsbridge's office. It's the gun Manny took from Mendez."

"I know," Gilmer agreed. "But a gun's not going to cause the same kind of stir as a lost Georgia O'Keeffe. Look, Jack—to be honest, I think maybe my fingerprints might be on the painting. I mean, I *touched* it back in seventy-four. And I read somewhere that fingerprints last forever, that they never go away."

Jack shrugged. "Well, prints don't disappear on their own—not in a vacuum, anyway. But in the real world, Gilmer, a lot of things can happen. Sherman might have cleaned the painting, for instance, during the course of twenty-five years."

"Sherman never cleaned anything. He was a slob, Jack. And I'm not going to wait around being a nervous wreck wondering when the cops are going to knock on my door. Look, I tell you what—I'll raise the ante to $20,000. I know what I'm asking you to do is illegal, but you're smart enough to figure out a way to get away with it. The way I see it, morally speaking, you won't be committing a crime, because I'm innocent. And twenty grand would be worth it to me, just to put this whole thing behind me once and for all."

Jack nodded thoughtfully and remained silent for several moments. "You know, there's just one part of this that confuses me," he said finally. "Anna Montoya, the maid. I still can't help thinking she had some greater role. Tell me,

Gilmer, you had a close relationship with Anna. Perhaps she confided in you?"

"No, she only modeled for me, Jack. I realize that people who aren't artists might find this a little risqué, a young woman allowing someone to paint her in the nude. But, I assure you, it's very mundane, no big deal."

"How did she happen to become your model?"

"I had seen Anna at Babs and Sherman's quite a number of times. I'd always wanted to paint her. I'd look at her, and it's like I was seeing all Indian women from the dawn of time. Do you know what I'm saying? She had an archetypal power, a beauty, the hardness of native life in her eyes, but also the deep connection with the earth. So when I got the commission to do the airport mural, I decided to ask Sherman to approach her for me."

"Then, you knew that she and Sherman were having an affair?"

"Oh, yeah. Sherman liked to kiss and tell. To be honest, he was starting to find Anna a little too clingy. He just wanted sex, you know. *She* was the one who wanted a relationship. So he thought that posing nude for me would . . . well, open her up a little. He even suggested that I would be doing him a favor if I seduced her."

"And did you?"

"No, I don't sleep with my models. I did that once or twice when I was young, and found it to be more trouble then it's worth. Anyway, Sherman approached her and got her to more a less agree. Indian girls from the rez tend to be a little body shy, particularly here in New Mexico where they have Catholicism to deal with as well. So it took some convincing. Finally, it was the money that did the trick. It turned out that Anna was ambitious to better her lot in life."

"How much did you pay her?"

Gilmer hesitated. "Well, it was a lot."

"Look, Gilmer—the state cops are going over every aspect of her life with a fine-tooth comb, starting with her bank account. So you may as well tell me."

"Okay. I gave her $35,000. I know that probably seems like a lot of money, but it was meant to cover however long I needed her to pose. Anna told me she had plans to open up a boutique in town with the money. Frankly, it pleased me to think I was helping a girl from the rez get a start in life."

"That was very charitable of you."

"It *wasn't* charity, Jack. There are six Indian women in my mural, and they all have either Anna's face or Anna's body, to one degree or another. She was essential to the project. . . . you know, I'm sorry about what happened to Anna, both professionally and personally. But what do you say about my offer? I'll raise the amount to $35,000 if you can get me *Red Moon*. Just what I paid Anna."

Jack smiled. "That's a handsome offer. Of course, I'm afraid neither Howie nor I will take off our clothes. That would be extra."

Gilmer forced a laugh. "All right, $35,000 it is. How long do you think it will take you to find the painting?"

"Oh, not long. But did I agree to $35,000? I meant to add a zero." Jack leaned forward ruthlessly across his desk. "Three *hundred* and fifty thousand dollars," he said dramatically. "How about that?"

Gilmer said nothing.

"Oops. The price goes up with silence," Jack said. "How about one million dollars, Gilmer? Would you pay that? One million bucks for *Red Moon*. We'll even throw in a few extras, like some creative reconstruction of the past. For one million bucks, maybe I can make this come out like you want it—that you were only a reluctant roommate back in Santa Fe in seventy-four. And that Sherman killed Manny Lucero, and either Babs or Anna killed Sherman—take your choice. And poor Anna just drove off the road. That ice, as you know, is really treacherous."

Gilmer exhaled the breath that he had been holding. "Would one million dollars really get me out of this jam?"

Jack shook his head. "Not really. To be honest, Gilmer, you may be a very good artist, but you're lousy at crime. You should have stuck with what you know."

"Shit!" Gilmer said softly. But his voice had moved from the rocking chair to the side of the desk. Jack hadn't heard him get up.

"I think you've told me the truth, pretty much," Jack said calmly, turning to where he could hear Gilmer's labored breathing. "Except for one small detail. It was you and Manny who robbed that big house in Santa Fe, wasn't it? *You* were the one who stole that painting and kept it all these years. Not Sherman at all."

Gilmer's ragged breathing sounded like a wounded animal, but he said nothing.

"You know how I see it, Gilmer?" Jack went on. "I think Sherman was the sort of guy who was all talk, but no action. He didn't have the nerve to be either a great artist *or* a thief. Oh, I bet he loved to bullshit about how the three of you were wonderful outlaw artists, just like Robin Hood. But when it actually came to breaking into people's houses, he was chicken and stayed home and probably rolled himself a big joint instead. Isn't that the way it was? It was you and Manny who killed Mendez."

"Jack, why don't you just let this drop."

"Oh, no, we can't let it drop, Gilmer. Sherman knew too much, didn't he? He knew everything. So after you killed Manny, you had to kill Sherman as well. You couldn't trust him."

Gilmer sighed, but still remained silent.

"Come on, Gilmer. Give this up," Jack urged him. "This business has followed you around like a shadow your entire miserable adult life—you made just one stupid mistake when you were young, but it won't leave you alone, will it? You and Manny killed Mendez. Then you killed Manny and Sherman, trying to make the past disappear."

Gilmer laughed strangely. He was silent for a moment, then began to speak in a voice that was different, low and fast, his words running together: "That night at Pinky's, Sherman was going to tell Moon Deer everything. I was sure of it. Anyway, I was sick of how he was always hitting me up for money. Ordering me about. It was like he was playing some game, taunting me . . . *'oh, Gilmer, run home and get me a couple of bottles of champagne!'* . . . man, that was the last straw!"

"Sit down," Jack told him in a soothing voice. "You can relax now, Gilmer. It's all over."

"No, I can't relax. This thing never ends, it just goes on and on. I tried to warn you—you should have left this alone, Jack. Now we have ourselves a problem."

Jack decided it was time to play his last card. With a swift motion, he pulled out the .38 revolver from his shoulder holster and pointed it at Gilmer's invisible breathing bulk.

"Sit down and don't be silly," Jack ordered. "And believe me, I can hear better than most people can see, so don't try anything foolish."

It sounded good. Jack was impressed by his own calm. But suddenly something heavy came down on his gun arm—a chair?—knocking the weapon from his hand. A fist exploded into the side of his head, and he fell backward, crashing out of the rocking chair onto the floor. A second later Gilmer was on top of him, jamming the barrel of the gun up his right nostril. Jack could hear Katya's agitated whining from across the room, but she did nothing to help. Apparently her expensive education did not include this type of personal protection.

"Okay, are you satisfied?" Gilmer cried. "Now, tell me where the hell that painting is! I'll kill you if you don't give it to me!"

"I don't know where it is."

"Don't lie! Babs phoned me an hour ago and said you *knew* where the painting was. She said you would have it by the end of the day—okay? So no more talk. I want it now!"

Jack grunted in pain as Gilmer shoved the gun barrel farther up his nostril. His dark glasses tumbled onto the floor. As it happened, Babs had phoned Gilmer because Jack had asked her to, setting his little trap. Unfortunately, Jack was the one who had gotten caught.

"All right!" he said. "I'll tell you!"

Gilmer was weaving out of control. "*Red Moon* is mine! I have to have it back, do you hear me? Where is it?" he cried.

Jack tasted blood flowing from his nose into his mouth. He was close to fainting from the pain. "It's at my house," he lied.

Twenty-five

The traffic in the old part of town was its usual snarl. Get here fast as you can, Jack had told Howie. But that was easier said than done. Four blocks from the office, Howie found himself paralyzed on a narrow street, sandwiched in between a bus full of Japanese tourists with camcorders and an oversized RV. Traffic in San Geronimo had moved more quickly seventy-five years ago than it did today. Wasn't progress wonderful! Howie thought sourly.

He had finally reached Jack on his cell phone shortly after leaving Valverde. But since the call kept breaking up into static, he wasn't certain how much Jack had been able to understand. Jack for his part had rung off abruptly, giving no information in return, only that Howie should get back to the office quickly. Howie tried to gain time by taking a detour through a back street, but several thousand other locals seemed to know about the shortcut as well. It was nearly two-fifteen by the time he pulled into one of the two reserved parking places at the rear of their small office complex.

As Howie was locking the truck, he heard Katya bark from the office above. It was an unhappy bark, more of a high, coyotelike wail. Howie ran through the courtyard and up the steps to the second landing. Katya jumped up on him the moment he opened the door. She was whining and upset, and Jack was nowhere to be seen.

"Jack!" Howie called.

Everything felt wrong. The rocking chair behind Jack's desk had fallen over on its side. Even worse, Jack's dark glasses lay on the floor a few feet from the chair. There was a chance, Howie supposed, that Jack might have gone out without Katya, but he would never have left the office without his glasses. Not voluntarily.

Katya kept barking, making excited sounds in the back of her throat. Howie had never heard her like this.

Unfortunately, dog language was a bitch to understand. Howie didn't have a clue what had happened here. He set the rocking chair upright and sat at Jack's desk hoping to find a note, some answer to this riddle. As his eyes scanned the room, he saw Jack's white cane propped up against the kiva fireplace at the far end of the room. The feeling of wrongness just kept getting worse and worse; if Jack had left the office without Katya, he would certainly have taken his cane. Howie picked up the phone and dialed 911. It took a moment to explain the situation to the operator, but even then, she did not sound as worried as Howie was.

He put down the phone, not encouraged. A 911 call in San Geronimo meant that someone would probably respond within the next forty-five minutes or so, as long as there was a patrol car available with gas in the tank and they could actually find your address. But you shouldn't bet the farm on it. For Howie at the moment, this wasn't good enough.

"Come on, Katya," he said at last, standing up abruptly from the desk. "Let's find Jack."

Jack was woozy and disorientated. Worse, he felt a fool in thinking he could handle Gilmer himself, no problem. What conceit and arrogance! It had been years since anyone had knocked him around the way Gilmer had done. The bleeding had stopped, but his nose hurt and his heart was beating alarmingly fast. He was imprisoned in the luxury of the Jaguar's bucket seat, restrained by the shoulder harness and seat belt. The windows were shut and the convertible top was raised, enclosing him in what felt like an expensive tomb.

"How did you guess it was me?" Gilmer was asking nervously.

"Maybe I'll just keep that my professional secret," Jack told him coldly.

"You don't have any secrets anymore. Not from me. I want to know."

Jack shrugged. "For a while, I kept going back and forth between you or Babs. Eeeny, meany, miney, moe. But then after Sherman was killed, I decided it had to be you. You know why? There were plenty of other suspects, and as it happened they were all sleeping at the Vandenberg Stone house that night. But none of them would have seriously believed they could have gotten away with killing Sherman—not *that* night, anyway. They all had too much of an apparent motive for wishing him dead, and they weren't entirely stupid. So unless they were suicidal, they would have waited for a better opportunity. You were the only one without any apparent motive. Ergo, I figured it *had* to be you. None of the others would have risked it."

"That's kind of twisted logic, isn't it?"

"No, not really," Jack told him. "There were other things too, of course. You were the only person on Halloween night who could have possibly known that Sherman was going to talk to Howie about the past. You couldn't allow that conversation to take place. No, it had to be you. I was almost sure of it."

"*Almost* sure?"

Jack smiled very slightly. "Well, I'm pretty sure now, aren't I?

"Not that it's going to do you any good," Gilmer said with a harsh laugh.

As they drove, Gilmer began to talk. His words were not strictly linear but rambled forward and backward in time. He spoke of Sherman, about how he almost got them caught the first time he and Manny and Gilmer had tried to pull one of their avant-garde burglaries back in '74. Sherman had dropped a case of wine they were trying to steal from a restaurant after-hours, making so much noise that the neighbors called the police and they escaped just in time.

"It was crazy!" Gilmer said, thinking back. "For Sherman it was all a big joke, even then. He was stoned all the time, of course. Finally it got so we had to leave him at home. Then it was just Manny and me. Breaking into houses every night, our little ritual . . . and, man, it was a thrill, if you had the nerve for it! Like skiing down a very steep slope. You know what I mean, Jack? You know that breathless feeling? Manny and me, we'd get in and out of these tight places together and it was like we became blood brothers. I mean, we really *shared* something . . . and that's what hurts, you know. That's what really goddamn *hurts*. . . ."

It worried Jack the way Gilmer was going on, speaking like a dam burst loose. After all these years of keeping his secret, it seemed now desperately important to him that someone finally know and understand. He made burglary sound like the most fun thing ever. Until the night came when everything went wrong.

Imagine robbing a house, Gilmer said, standing upstairs with all your senses heightened and having your flashlight beam shine upon the most wonderful painting you had ever seen up close and personal. "Man, I *loved* that canvas . . . it was so astonishingly simple: only a tree, a desert at night, and a harvest moon overhead. . . . I mean, there I was robbing a goddamn house, and suddenly I had this huge moment of perception. . . . Up to then, Jack, all my art was total bullshit. I had been trying to paint in this borrowed Abstract Expressionist style that wasn't me at all. And then I looked at *Red Moon* and it was like my brain exploded with understanding. I saw the way I had to paint from then on—a kind of magical naturalism. *Red Moon* taught me how to do it. And from that moment I've been a huge success. It's like everything came together in my mind."

"Well, that's just swell," Jack remarked. "But it's a pity Juan Antonio Mendez had to die in the process."

"Yes, it's a pity," Gilmer agreed solemnly. "I feel he sacrificed his life for me, so that I could find my true path."

Jack laughed unpleasantly. "And Manny and Sherman and Anna—I supposed they sacrificed themselves for you as well?"

"*Anna*! Man, that wasn't *me*!" he cried. Despite his many crimes, Gilmer seemed outraged to be the victim of a single false accusation. "That stupid chick, she just freaked out and drove too fast on the goddamn ice! Anyway, forget Anna—I'm trying to tell you about *Red Moon*. . . ."

As Jack listened, he tried to keep track of where they were, block by block, turn by turn, in case he had any opportunity for escape. It didn't seem likely. As discreetly as possible, he allowed the fingers of his right hand to explore the door panel, feeling for the handle and the lock.

But cars were more complicated than they used to be; he couldn't find anything that resembled a simple door handle.

"You can stop feeling around with your hand," Gilmer told him, interrupting his story. "I can control your lock on my side. And I have your gun right here in my lap. So behave yourself, Jack . . . do you want to hear this? Or is it wasted on you?"

"No I want to hear," Jack assured him. "Tell me, where have you been keeping this precious painting all these years?"

"It was insane—I had *Red Moon* in a storage shed in Albuquerque for nearly a decade!" he said with a rueful sigh, as though amazed at his own strange saga. "I knew it was dangerous to keep, but I couldn't stay away from the thing. My blood's on it, you see. Literally! I was making a new frame for it when I cut my hand and bled all over the back. . . God help me, if anyone ever did a DNA test, it would come home right to me. So you can see why I've got to get it back. . . . Finally, I made a lot of money, and I built my house here in San Geronimo, and I made a special room without any windows where I could hang *Red Moon*. Nobody knew about the room except for me and Sherman."

"How did Sherman know?"

"Well, I showed him. About three years ago one night when we were both drunk. Up till that time, he thought I'd gotten rid of that canvas decades ago. But, you see, when you own something so beautiful, it makes you lonely to keep it all to yourself. I thought I could trust Sherman. I thought I could share it with him. But, man, was that ever a mistake! Forever afterward, whenever he wanted money, or a ride somewhere to score dope—anything at all—I had to do it for him."

"You must have showed the painting to Manny as well," Jack mentioned. "Why did you do that?"

"No, I didn't show it to Manny. I wasn't *that* foolish."

"But if Manny took it, how did he know where it was?"

Gilmer drove in silence for a few moments. "Sherman told him," he said finally. "I don't know why, really. Maybe it was just on a lark. Sherman hated me, I think. He was jealous that I was so successful as an artist and he wasn't. I know it was Sherman because the painting disappeared one night when I was down at a gallery opening in Santa Fe. It was a night Benny Rodarte, the man who works for me, had off—he's usually downstairs. So I realized later that Sherman must have helped Manny plan everything. No one else knew about where the painting was, or what my schedule was."

"And once Manny had the painting, he blackmailed you with it?"

"Yep. He figured I wasn't going to go along with his idea of redemption without a big push, and of course, he was right. Last Thursday morning he showed up at the studio again while I was painting Anna, and he threatened to give the O'Keeffe to the police if I didn't come confess with him. You can see what a bind I was in. I offered him money. I said I would take care of him for the rest of his life. But Manny had become a fanatic."

"Anna helped you kill him, didn't she?"

Gilmer paused. "Yes," he said after a moment. "That was the real reason for the $35,000, of course. It wasn't modeling. When you told me in the office that the police would go over her bank account . . . well, I was trying to think of something to explain so much money."

Gilmer's voice became mean and cunning. "Anna was a lot more than ambitious, frankly—she was a greedy bitch, and this was her big chance. I told her to keep Manny busy while I went back to the main house to get the rifle I keep in my den. I pretended I was just going to change clothes, and we'd go to the police together, but Manny must have sensed what I was up to. When I came out of the house with the gun, he was already running away across my front yard. He was too far off for a shot, so I started chasing after him. The snow made it hard going for both of us, but Manny just wouldn't stop. He took off like a rabbit down an old trail at the edge of my property. By the time I got there, he had already made it down off the mesa to a field below. I was terrified that he was going to get away. So I rushed back to the studio to get Anna."

"So *she* was the one on the snowmobile?"

"That's right. I drove her back to her apartment and dropped her off. We used her truck because there was so much snow, and she had four-wheel drive—I have a Jeep, but it was parked in the garage and it would have taken too much time to get it out. She fired up the snowmobile while I continued down to the highway to a pull-off by the river. I parked and began walking back alongside the bank to where I thought Manny would come out. I was hoping that between Anna and me, we could move in on Manny from opposite directions and get him into a trap. I was hiding in the trees when I saw him on the meadow. I had a clear shot, and I winged him. But he just kept going. I was about to follow after him and finish up the job when I saw Howie Moon Deer skiing along with his stepson behind him. It complicated matters, as you can imagine. I saw Manny limp into the trees, and I crept back along the river to see what was happening. Manny looked like he was in bad shape. Moon Deer was bending over him on the ground, and Manny seemed to by trying to say something. I snuck up from behind and walloped Howie with a fallen limb from a tree. While Howie was out, I searched through Manny's pockets trying to find some hint of what he'd done with *Red Moon*. But there wasn't anything."

"But why did you think that Howie or I had the painting?" Jack asked. "That was *you* in Howie's bathroom that night, wasn't it?"

Gilmer sighed. "I thought I'd just get *Red Moon* back, then I wouldn't have to kill him. This sure turned into a farce, sneaking around bathrooms at night! Later, I broke into your house too, Jack. It was Sherman who told me about Manny's fixation on Howie's girlfriend, Claire—this was a few days before Manny came back the final time. Sherman had seen some of the drawings Manny did of her—he thought it was funny as hell the way Manny had idealized her into some kind of angel. So when the painting was stolen, I tried to think from Manny's point of view, what he might have done with it. I was desperate, you see."

Indeed, Gilmer sounded desperate. "Man, I thought and I thought, and every way I looked at it, it seemed to me that Manny was too damn shrewd to keep *Red Moon* himself. He was homeless, for one, which would make it difficult to take care of a valuable painting. And he would want some protection in case he—" Gilmer laughed self-consciously "—in case he met a sudden end. That's when I thought of you. I became convinced that if Manny had been stalking Claire, he would have found out about Wilder &

Associate and figured you would be good insurance if I proved difficult to deal with. When I saw Howie appear out of the blue just as Manny was dying, I was sure this was what he had done. It just seemed too coincidental that two private detectives would be involved in the whole drama otherwise."

Jack wondered if there was some truth to this, that Manny Lucero had deliberately lured them into his plan of forced redemption for Gilmer Good Day. It would explain why Manny had left the Beretta 9mm pistol in Claire's office, a direct lead to the 1974 murder. Was Claire meant to give the gun to Howie? Were Howie and Jack supposed to trace the gun's history and discover the murder of Juan Antonio Mendez and the theft of *Red Moon*? If so, the silent Manny Lucero had found an indirect but most eloquent manner of speech.

Meanwhile, Jack knew from the speed of the car and the curves of the road that they had left the downtown district and were not far from Calle Santa Margarita. In a few minutes time, they would arrive at Jack's house, where he would be faced with a delicate problem: how to stay alive. There was no doubt in his mind that Gilmer Good Day was going to be a seriously unhappy camper when he discovered Jack had lied to him, that *Red Moon* was not at his house. The most obvious option, of course, was to confess the truth and give Gilmer the key to Post Office Box 37 in Valverde, which he assumed contained some message from Manny Lucero that would lead to the painting. But he preferred not to do this. Not only would Gilmer get the painting, but Jack suspected that Gilmer could not afford to leave him alive once he had what he wanted.

Jack felt the Jaguar leave the paved road and cross the familiar crunchy gravel of his driveway. Time had just run out. Jack had a glimmer of an idea how he might save himself, but it was a thin hope, and it would need to be done while the car was still in motion.

"Gilmer, listen to me," he said. "You've been running all these years, and I know you've suffered. Why don't you come with me to Ed Gomez and tell him what you've just told me. Manny had the right idea, you know. You're not going to rest easy until you make your peace with the past."

"No, it's too late for that, Jack," Gilmer told him, his

voice suddenly weary. "I wouldn't do well in prison. I'm too old and used to my comforts."

"But think what the publicity would do for the price of your paintings. They'd go sky-high, Gilmer."

Gilmer laughed. He seemed to think that was funny. And while he was laughing, Jack made his move. He slammed his left foot down onto the top of Gilmer's right foot, pushing the gas pedal to the floor. The Jaguar jumped forward like a startled beast. Jack knew his driveway well. Either they would crash into the trunk of a huge old cottonwood tree or they would fly off into an irrigation ditch, depending on the angle of the front wheels.

It was the cottonwood tree.

Twenty-six

Gilmer screamed at the impact. Jack felt himself jerked forward then yanked back, restrained by his seat harness and an air bag that exploded in his face. The air bag came as a surprise, leaving Jack momentarily stunned. But he forced himself to keep moving, groping Gilmer's lap for the gun. Gilmer swore and violently pushed Jack's hand away.

"Goddamn!" Gilmer cried. He seemed to be entangled in his air bag, almost as disorientated as Jack and certainly more surprised. But he wouldn't let go of the .38.

Jack's door had swung open in the collision. He undid his seat belt and slid out from behind the air bag, tumbling onto the ground with a hard thump. The fall made his nose start bleeding again. He scrambled off in a spider's crawl on his hands and feet, not certain his legs would carry him. Behind him, he could hear Gilmer swearing and struggling with his air bag. Jack was gathering momentum when suddenly he tripped and fell headfirst into his irrigation ditch.

He cried out in pain. *I'm too old for this*, he thought dismally. Then a shot rang out behind him. The bullet zinged over his head and thudded into the trunk of a tree. Jack decided he wasn't too old after all. He picked himself up and crawled forward as fast as he could. Beyond the irrigation ditch was a stand of piñon that would offer some protection if he could only reach it. Further still there was a clearing, and if he could cross that he would come to his back porch. *If* his navigation was correct—and if Gilmer didn't shoot him first.

Jack stood upright to run, and ran directly into a piñon. The limbs bent and threw him backward onto the ground. *"Ah-ah!"* he cried. It knocked the breath out of him and left the taste of pine sap and blood in his mouth. Then another shot exploded behind him. He got to his feet and kept going, running with his arms swiping the air in front of him for obstacles. He wasn't certain any longer that he was going in the right direction, but any direction was better than standing still.

Whack! He ran into another tree. This time he gashed his forehead, and he found it harder to get back on his feet. But the tree was an aspen not a piñon, and this gave Jack a navigational clue. Now he only had to run across a twenty-foot clearing, and he would arrive, theoretically, at his back door.

"Jack, don't be silly!" Gilmer shouted. "All I want is *Red Moon*, and then you can go."

"Right," Jack called back. "Just like you let Manny, Sherman, and Anna go!"

From Gilmer's voice, Jack judged he was twenty, perhaps thirty feet away. Gilmer sounded shaky and out of breath; it was possible that he was hurt from the crash, which gave Jack a small surge of hope. He paused long enough to feel the direction of the afternoon sun on his bloody face. He was almost certain he had himself oriented again. With a burst of adrenaline, he ran in an erratic zigzag trajectory across the clearing, trying to make himself a more difficult target.

Boom! Another concussive gunshot took him by surprise, and his right leg collapsed beneath him. He fell to the ground and rolled into a wooden planter: one of Emma's wild roses, in hibernation this time of year. He was shot, though he couldn't tell how seriously. The pain was just starting to spread upward from his leg to his brain. Maybe he could outrun it.

The house couldn't be far. There was nothing to do but pick himself up and stagger forward, putting most of his weight on his left leg, hopping like a maniac. Just as he was getting up some speed, he tripped and fell hard against the steps to his back porch, banging his good leg and getting a handful of splinters as he reached wildly for the railing. Pain threatened to overwhelm him. But he couldn't stop now. He clawed at the steps, dragging his body bump by bump to the door.

He turned the doorknob, but there was a new obstacle: the door was locked. He hadn't thought of this, preoccupied as he was with more urgent concerns. A simple matter, but it was going to defeat him. He could hear footsteps on the path behind him. The sound was syncopated. *Ka-thump . . . ka-thump . . . ka-thump.* Gilmer was limping, favoring one leg. He *had* been hurt in the crash; it was slowing him down, but not enough. He was going to limp over and shoot him dead. Stubbornly, Jack reached into his pocket for his house keys. It was hopeless, but he wanted to be doing something when the shot came, not just lying there waiting.

While he was struggling forward, Jack heard the crunching sound of a car coming up his driveway. He recognized the engine. A second later Katya barked.

"Howie, for chrissake! Damn you, get out of here!" Gilmer shouted wildly.

"Don't move. I've got a gun," Howie shouted back.

Jack didn't wait. He took advantage of the diversion to pull himself up onto his good leg, using the wood railing for support. His hand was so shaky it took him three attempts to fit the key into the lock.

The door opened, and Jack tumbled inside onto the floor of his back pantry. The pain was excruciating, head to foot. Behind him, more shots rang out, but it was a different gun. It was Howie shooting what sounded like the Walther P5 9mm from the truck. Gilmer's .38 answered, louder than the Walther. Jack wondered how many bullets Gilmer had fired. It occurred to him that the revolver must be nearly empty. But his mind was too frantic to do anything as simple as count.

Ka-thump . . . ka-thump . . . ka-thump. Gilmer was limping his way in a fast syncopated rhythm, trying to get to the house to find cover from Howie's fire. In another moment he would step up into the back pantry and kill Jack. If he had any bullets left.

For Jack, everything hurt everywhere. His right leg was on fire, slimy with blood. He dragged himself like a human snail sluggishly across the floor to the fifty-gallon bin full of beans near the back door. Pinto beans. Enough beans, Howie had once joked, to keep all of San Geronimo farting for years. The beans were smooth and always odd to the touch as Jack reached down through them to the plastic Ziploc bag below. The Ruger Mark II .22 automatic was still inside. Had he left the gun loaded? He prayed so.

And now, dear God in heaven, Gilmer Good day was limping up the back steps. *Choo-shaw . . . choo-shaw . . . choo-shaw:* the sound had changed, but the intent remained the same.

Fortunately, time had almost stopped; it was moving microsecond by microsecond, frame by frame. Jack had all the time in the world. He opened the Ziploc bag and took out the pistol. A .22 was no match for a .38, so he had to make the first shot count. If only his damn hand would stop trembling.

"Game's up, Jack," Gilmer said nearby, almost cheerfully. "I hate to do this, you know."

Jack hated to do it too, but that wasn't going to stop him. He waited until he heard Gilmer in the doorway. Then he swung around and raised the .22 and fired blind. Not aiming. Only feeling. Guiding the bullet from his solar plexus. *Surprise, surprise, Gilmer! Thought I was helpless, didn't you?*

He heard Gilmer stumble backward down the steps. Jack crawled after him, pulling his slimy leg to the door. He kept firing until the gun was empty. Then he struggled to his knees. With no more bullets left, he threw the gun at the place on the ground where he imagined Gilmer Good Day to be.

"Jack, relax, he's down! You got him!" Howie was calling from across the driveway, running his way. Katya was coming too, barking excitedly, bounding over the earth. Wonderful sound, a dog and a strong young man running. Like Beethoven's Ninth, and then some.

"You got him with the first shot," Howie said.

"God in heaven!" Jack cried in triumph. He lay back in the open doorway, unable to move any longer. It felt to Jack as if his life was ebbing away, a great exhausting vagueness overtaking him. "I can still shoot, can't I?" he managed to say.

His words came so soft and dreamy they seemed to float into the sky. But Howie answered.

"Yes, you sure can, Jack," Howie agreed.

Twenty-seven

It was dark by the time Captain Ed Gomez, just back from Santa Fe, led a four-car convoy of vehicles to the tiny post office at Valverde. It was little more than a window and a few dozen boxes located at the rear of the Valverde General Store, a musty adobe built in 1857.

The post office closed at four-thirty, but the postmaster had been summoned to the scene, in case help was needed. Also on hand were three state troopers, two sheriff's deputies, a representative of the Department of Public Safety, and Carol Wardman, the assistant curator from the Georgia O'Keeffe Museum in Santa Fe. The media had arrived separately: three vans from different Albuquerque television stations, as well as reporters from several newspapers. The press had only just become interested in the story. Homicide was so common in New Mexico that it took something special to attract media attention—Albuquerque generally had a double or triple-murder every few months, and there was currently a sensational rape-torture-murder case in the town of Truth or Consequences. With so much competition, a few killings in San Geronimo would have had little entertainment value except for the fact that there was a ton of money involved in recovering a long-missing Georgia

O'Keeffe masterpiece, and Gilmer Good Day was a celebrity.

Howie sat by himself at a picnic table outside the old general store/post office watching the media circus and various self-important officials as they came and went. It all seemed sad and ridiculous to him. The table was sticky from microwaved burritos and spilled soft drinks consumed by passing tourists. A state police car had been sent to fetch Claire Knightsbridge, for the Valverde postmaster had insisted that P.O. Box 37, rented in Claire's name, could not be opened without her presence or a court order. As a result, four carloads of law enforcement officials had little to do at the moment but gather in small groups and talk football.

Howie watched with a jaundiced eye as a dozen feet away, a TV reporter with a deeply masculine voice gave a live update in front of a camera and lights, telling his audience about the series of murders that had "rocked" the northern town of San Geronimo, as he put it—a community where "one out of every ten residents is an artist." That was scary, all right! Art and violence. Beauty and blood. Howie thought of Gilmer Good Day's unfinished mural at the Albuquerque airport, his pictorial history of New Mexico, and Gilmer's joke about putting a mushroom cloud at the center of the painting. This was the basic paradox of New Mexico: land of enchantment, a place of breathtaking scenery, yet also the birthplace of the atomic bomb. It seemed to Howie that the two things must be somehow interconnected—violence and beauty—but he was too dispirited at the moment to figure out exactly how.

As Howie sat in the middle of his thoughts, he saw Claire arrive in a sleek black state police cruiser. The TV floodlights snapped on immediately, turning the night magnesium bright; three separate crews began videotaping as she stepped from the car. Claire looked beautiful tonight, long and lanky and blond, like a movie star arriving at the premiere of her latest film. A crowd of police gathered around her, contributing to the illusion of celebrity. As Howie watched her grand arrival, Claire seemed lost to him, out of reach. He just couldn't imagine someone that beautiful living in a tipi with an obscure Indian graduate student who had a part-time job as a P.I. Howie had just decided that he was what was known in the love business as a "passing phase," when Claire saw him sitting glumly by himself in the dark.

"Howie!" she called. "Excuse me, I've got to speak to Howie for a minute," she insisted to the group of cops and reporters, wedging her way through their midst.

"What are you doing just sitting here in the cold?" she scolded. Then, before he could answer: "How's Jack?"

"He's going to be okay. They're keeping him in the hospital, but it's only a flesh wound in his upper thigh. He lost some blood and got banged up a lot running into trees. But Jack's one tough customer. I spent most of the afternoon at the hospital, and he's already complaining about the lousy food."

Howie forked his middle finger at the TV cameras that had just panned their way—very adolescent, he knew, but he wasn't in an obliging mood.

"Put *that* on family TV, you mothers!" he said gleefully.

"Howie!" Claire took him by the arm and led him behind a trash Dumpster at the side of the store, where it would be difficult for the cameras to follow. "And what about Gilmer?" she asked.

"Well, Gilmer's a different story. They've helicoptered him to Albuquerque. He's in critical condition with a collapsed lung, but they're saying he's going to live."

"Oh, Howie!" she cried, "I don't know about any of this!"

Claire fell into his arms, and she felt so good that Howie supposed he must be wrong, that he wasn't a passing phase after all. He was suddenly, inappropriately, very horny. He had a wild urge to lean her against the Dumpster and give in to primal lust, and get down and dirty in the trash. He reached up under her sweater to touch one of Claire's perfect breasts. Sex was real, sex was fine, sex was understandable; this was the best thing that had happened to Howard Moon Deer all day.

But it was brief.

"Mmm, ahem," said Captain Ed Gomez, appearing around the edge of the Dumpster, clearing his throat. "Sorry to interrupt, but we're waiting for you, Claire."

Claire blushed, and Howie sighed. He followed her into

the general store to discover whatever it was that was waiting for them in P.O. Box 37.

The inside of the Valverde General Store was dark and crowded, an historical remnant of a pre-Anglo Yuppie past. The post office occupied a back corner, past shelves of potato chips, candy bars, spongy white bread, and coolers full of bologna and American beer. Howie stood near the marshmallows and hot dog buns as he watched Claire insert the key into Box 37. The media, to their regret, had not been allowed entry to this ceremony, but their camera lights bathed the outside of the building, casting harsh shadows inside.

"A million and a half bucks for a painting!" Howie heard someone say. It was one of the uniformed cops guarding the door. "If I had that kind of money, shit, I'd move to California!"

Claire pulled a white envelope from the box, and once again, Howie had visions of Hollywood and some crazy award ceremony. Inside the envelope was a brief handwritten letter, which Claire tried to read to herself, but Captain Gomez took it gently from her hand and read it aloud:

> My Angel Claire,
>   You are the last person I believe in. There is a *morada* behind his building. I ask you to return the contents inside to the proper owners. Stealing is a sin, but with your intercedence, God may yet find mercy upon my tired soul.
> Yours with love,
> The Rainbow Man

Claire took the piece of paper from the police captain's hand, her eyebrows knit together in concentration as she reread the note. No one else seemed to have any further interest in Manny Lucero's posthumous message.

"Morada?" said Captain Gomez. "I didn't know there was a *morada* in Valverde."

"It's just a ruin on the east side of the village," the postmaster told him. "It doesn't have a roof. There's not much more than a few crumbling walls. I don't think it's been used for a hundred years."

Moradas were what the *penitentes,* northern New Mexico's secretive religious sect, called their primitive adobe churches.

"Well, you'd better show us where it is," Ed said to the postmaster.

Claire was still holding and rereading her letter from the Rainbow Man. A deputy sheriff tried to take the piece of paper from her hand, but she pulled away violently.

"This is *mine!*" she declared, shooting the deputy such a look of pure savagery that he stumbled backward into the Hostess Twinkies.

The ruins of the old church were nestled against the side of the hill a few hundred yards behind the general store. Holding hands, Howie and Claire followed the group of officials as they walked together from the post office past a few Russian olive trees up a sloping field to where the jagged adobe walls stood, a ghostly presence in the moonlight.

Inside the roofless building, a half-dozen flashlight beams crisscrossed upon a single object among the weeds and old beer cans: a glitzy chrome and red plastic Lucky's Supermarket shopping cart that was packed full of bulging black plastic garbage bags.

"Don't touch anything!" Ed cautioned.

Another half hour went by while a two-person crime-scene unit was summoned from town. The experts photographed the shopping cart from a dozen different angles and then, wearing latex gloves, carefully inventoried the items inside. There were two blankets, an extra pair of rainbow trousers, a few drawing supplies, a Bible, a plastic jug of water, a cup, a knife, fork, spoon, a can opener, and three cans of baked beans in tomato sauce.

And that was it. There was no Georgia O'Keeffe painting, *Red Moon.*

Claire giggled unexpectedly. A dozen unhappy eyes turned her way.

"Sorry," she told them, "but isn't this a little ridiculous?"

"The picture must be here somewhere," the assistant curator said grumpily to Captain Gomez. "In the letter, Claire was supposed to return something stolen to its proper owners. What else could he have meant except the painting?"

"He meant the shopping cart, of course," Claire pointed

out, doing her best to stifle a new surge of giggles. "He probably stole it from a parking lot in California."

"Shopping carts are, er, actually quite expensive," added the man from the Department of Public Safety pompously.

Claire's giggle turned into an outright laugh, which drew some stern and disapproving looks.

"Are you okay?" Howie asked her.

"I'm perfectly fine. Personally, I think this is a riot, everybody standing around this dumb shopping cart with such solemn faces!"

Claire was obviously overwrought, not her normal, calm Iowa self; Howie asked Captain Gomez if he could take her home. As they passed the TV vans in the village, they overhead an impossibly square-jawed reporter giving his viewers a live update for the Ten O'Clock News. He announced regretfully that the O'Keeffe painting, *Red Moon*, whose value he described as "possibly as much as two million dollars," had not been found.

"It'll be three million dollars by tomorrow!" Claire said loudly, causing the TV man to turn her way with a worried expression. "What bullshit! This is *not* what art is supposed to be about! . . . you know, Howie, I think the Rainbow Man is the only honest person in any of this."

"Well, he liked you, Claire."

"And I liked him," she replied fiercely. "Maybe he did some bad things a long time ago. But a person can suffer so much that they change, don't you think? He was my guardian angel . . . *he* was the angel, not me. . . ."

"He was a little off in the head, actually," Howie suggested mildly.

Claire's eyes blazed. "Do you think if an angel appeared on earth, people would think he was *normal*?" she challenged.

She turned back toward the *morada* on the hill just as they were getting into the pickup. Howie had never seen her quite like this: angry and triumphant, on the verge of laughter and tears, all at the same time.

"My God!" she said with an astonished sigh. "I wonder what poor Georgia O'Keeffe would have thought of all this?"

Epilogue

Life settled down after a while. It astonished Claire how quickly everything became normal again. It seemed you could have murder at home and an atrocious war overseas—but you got used to it, and that was the terrible human truth. You said to yourself, well, that's the way the world goes.

They had a good Christmas that year. Howie was wonderful with the kids, which she appreciated greatly. He took Jonathan and Heidi downhill skiing, and he tried to teach Claire to ski as well. This was Claire's second season at San Geronimo Peak, and she still had not progressed beyond the basic snowplow. It was starting to be embarrassing. Howie was a terrific skier, of course, zooming down every hill in sight, and the kids skied like little maniacs too, entirely fearless. Claire was convinced she was the only person in all of the Rocky Mountain states who could not ski. Finally, she had to tell Howie, "Look, I hate speed, and I'm terrified of heights, so maybe this isn't my sport."

She saw Howie's face drop, because this was something he loved and wanted to share with her. But it was better for all of them when he took the kids up to San Geronimo Peak and left her in the house alone. She used the time to get in some serious eight-hour sessions on the cello.

During the week, Claire continued as the acting director of the San Geronimo Art Association. In January, there was a new crisis: the SGAA held a juried art show where the panel of judges decided that no single work was good enough to deserve first prize; as a result, only a second and third prize were given. The reaction was swift and furious. A dozen of the artists hired a lawyer and sued the Art Association for half a million dollars, intent on punishing the grievous and injurious harm that had been done to their collective egos. Claire did her best to laugh it off, but she received a serious reprimand from the board of directors. Claire fired back that it was the jury that had refused to give a first prize, not her. But since Claire had chosen the jury, she was a convenient scapegoat. It was terribly frustrating and difficult for her.

In early February, Claire received another letter from her friend from music school, Erin Yaeger, who was founding the Chicago Chick Quartet. Even in classical music you seemed to need a gimmick these days, and this particular gimmick—the all-woman chamber ensemble with a spicy name—was already making a splash, even in its planning stage. Erin wrote to say that they had a number of gigs lined up for the summer, as well as a possible recording contract with Sony. But they still didn't have a cellist they liked. So wouldn't Claire reconsider? If she could come to Chicago by mid-April, they would have the spring to rehearse for their first concert, scheduled for June 13 and 14, a two-night gala where they were going to perform the entire cycle of Beethoven's late string quartets. They hoped to show the world that Chicago Chicks weren't only pretty faces, they could kick ass as well—musically speaking.

Claire had to admit that she was even more tempted by the offer than she had been last fall. But among other considerations, she was broke; she really couldn't afford the move to Chicago, putting her kids in school there, and all the expenses the relocation would entail. Then she read the postscript. Because of its commercial potential, the new group had already received serious financial backing. Erin was offering Claire a starting salary that was more than eight times what she was making at the Art Association.

Late Beethoven *and* plenty of money! There was no denying that this was a tremendous opportunity. Claire didn't tell Howie about Erin's letter. She simply couldn't force herself to speak to him about it. How could she leave him? For several days she cried a lot, she practiced her cello with fiendish energy far into the night, and she had sex with Howie as often as possible, usually bursting into tears simultaneously with her orgasm. Howie was skiing almost every day at this point of the winter and was often distracted, speaking wildly about steep chutes and fabulous snow conditions—but even he eventually noticed that something wasn't right.

"Claire! You've got to tell me—what could be wrong?"

But she could only shake her head and cry and have sex and play the cello.

On a Tuesday afternoon in mid-February, Claire returned to her office from a meeting with her board of directors to find a freight delivery had been made to her at the Art Association: a flat square crate nearly three feet long and three feet wide. The shipping papers listed a woman she did not know as the sender and a Trenton, New Jersey, return address. Claire was mystified. She assumed it was a painting because of its shape, but she could not imagine why this particular shipment had come directly to her. She found a hammer and crowbar from the utility closet next door at the Performing Arts Center and spent the next half hour dismantling the wooden crate, gradually revealing the painting inside. At last she stopped and stared in astonishment.

Claire locked her office door and did not answer her phone when it rang. She propped the canvas against the far wall and studied it for a long time. To Claire, it looked as if a child had painted it, or a genius, or a madman: someone who had absolute certainty about what they were doing, and had put that certainty into every brush stroke.

She recognized the painting, of course, for she had seen the reproduction that Howie had shown her. It was a simple landscape: a gnarly old piñon tree, dark green, almost blue. The desert was a swirl of Impressionistic color—brown, red, yellow, gold. The night sky overhead was purple and blue, filled with stars and childlike wonder, immense. And the strange red moon that gave the painting its name, a moon that was in no way natural—not like any moon Claire had ever seen—but that somehow struck deep into the dreaming soul of night.

She had seen paintings in museums that were surely as good—Renoir, Breughal, Picasso, van Gogh. But it was quite a different experience to have a work like this simply propped up against her wall in her tiny office. Claire was deeply, profoundly moved.

There was an envelope inside the crate with a letter inside:

Dear Claire Knightsbridge,
   Last November I received this wooden crate from my brother, Manuel Lucero, with instructions to send it to you in December in time for Christmas. I'm sorry, but I put it down in my basement and didn't get to it until just now. Please forgive me, but Manny sometimes asks me to do some pretty odd things, and to tell the truth, it gets a little tiresome. I suppose this is one of his paintings that he wanted you to have, I hate to be petty, but I'd appreciate it if you would send me a check for $119.93 to cover the shipping cost. If you see Manny, please tell that crazy brother of mine to give me a call one of these days. I hope he's staying out of jail. He has a lot of talent if only he would settle down.
Sincerely yours,
Christina Lucero Dorfman

The woman obviously did not know that her brother was dead, which was a pity. Claire would have to write her.

Claire sat on her floor and stared at the painting for nearly another hour. It was a luxury to have Georgia O'Keeffe all to herself. The painting filled her with successive waves of thought and impressions. It wasn't so much that it was "good," but rather that someone—a woman—had dared so completely and confidently to do it. That's what struck Claire the most. She knew that she wasn't a genius herself, far from it. And yet, who could say what she might achieve if she, too, had the courage and faith to truly try? *Red Moon* seemed to whisper in her ear: *Just look what you can do if only you have the courage to let go of your fears and risk living your dreams!*

By the time Claire phoned Howie to say guess what I've got in my office, she had made a major decision about her life.

On a spring morning in early April, Howie drove Claire, Jonathan, and Heidi to the train station in Lamy, a tiny village twenty minutes from Santa Fe. There was nothing but a single track, a platform, and an old building in the middle of nowhere. It was hard to believe a train traveling daily between Los Angeles and Chicago would actually stop at such a lonely spot.

Howie had gone through several stages of torment and acceptance since Claire had told him of her decision to join the string quartet. He would visit her in Chicago in June, and then again in the fall; no matter what happened, they would be connected, he and Claire, for the rest of their lives. He tried to look on the bright side. It was great that he could help Claire find her destiny; or at least not stand in the way. He had always known that she was much too passionate a musician to hide from the world forever in a small New Mexico town. So who was he to keep such a talented person all to himself? When he looked at it in this way, it seemed almost petty and selfish to dwell on his low animal urges, and the cold empty spot she was going to leave behind in his bed, and in his heart.

At the station, Howie helped Claire and the kids with their luggage, and then they stood together on the platform by the empty tracks.

"This is a first. I've never lost a woman to Beethoven before," he told her as they were waiting on the platform.

"You are *not* losing me, Howie. You know that."

"Look, Claire—are your really sure about this? It's not going to be so easy making it as a single mother in a big city."

"I'm going to be fine. Really, I am. Or maybe I *won't* be fine," she admitted. "Maybe I'll give my first concert, and everybody will boo. But I have to try. I have to know that I've given it my best shot."

Jonathan and Heidi ran down to the far end of the platform, leaving Howie and Claire momentarily alone. There was a subject that Howie, being a discreet sort of Sioux, had not brought up until now. But he thought he'd better give it a whirl.

"Look, Claire, I'll understand if there are guys in Chicago. I just want us to be honest. . . ."

"*You're* my guy," she told him fervently. "Anyway, no one's going to look twice at a beanpole like me."

"Oh, yes, they will," he assured her. "You're beautiful."

"You just think I'm beautiful because you love me."

There was so much more that Howie wanted to say, but

Heidi was running back now, chased by Jonathan into her mother's arms,

"Howie, I certainly don't expect you to survive forever with just the old hand," Claire said quickly. But not quickly enough.

"What do you mean, the old hand?" Heidi demanded.

"Never mind," they told her together.

Howie sighed. "Claire, I don't want anyone else."

"Shh," she told him. "Let's leave an element of surprise. For all I know, maybe I'll be back here on the next train west."

"Well, *I'm* coming back to San Geronimo to ski next winter," Jonathan said determinedly.

"You bet you are," Howie told him. They had already worked this out. Jonathan hadn't wanted to come to New Mexico, but now he didn't want to leave.

"Here's the train!" Heidi shouted. She was too young to fully understand how her life was changing, but meanwhile the brilliant white eye of the train was coming down the track from a long rumbling distance, and she thought it was wonderful. Howie kissed the children, then he kissed Claire, and helped her with the big cello case and all the luggage that wasn't being checked.

"I love you," she said from her compartment window as he stood on the platform.

Howie waved and blew kisses and fought against the great chasm of loneliness that threatened to engulf him. He had a stake in Claire's future. He was glad for her; he was sending her forth into a world of music and hope. In the end, it was a joy to set her free.

"Hell, I feel almost noble," he told her.

"My noble savage," she said, then turned away to hide the tears that were running down her cheeks.

The train only stayed five minutes in Lamy and then with a groan of wheels, the engine chugged and pulled and gathered speed. In a moment the cars disappeared around a bend, leaving behind only a fading sound of thunder.

Turn the page for a preview

of the next

Howard Moon Deer Mystery,

Ancient Enemy

Coming soon from Signet . . . .

A cat crossed the alley, moving in a slow, predatory crawl toward the trash Dumpster at the rear door of the Shanghai Cafe. Howard Moon Deer raised his infrared binoculars to get a better look. It was a fat cat, a long-haired Siamese, obviously someone's pet. The binoculars gave the cat, the Dumpster, and the back door of the Chinese restaurant a red-orange psychedelic glow, as though they were radioactive. The color was slightly sickening, reminding Howie of the sweet and sour pork he had eaten here a month ago.

"They're eating pussy at the Shanghai Cafe," was how his boss, Jack Wilder, had put it, chuckling at his own crude joke. Jack had a truly awful sense of humor. "Your assignment, Howie—should you accept it—is to catch them in the act of putting pussy in the pot!"

Howie lowered the binoculars and the night returned to its usual color, illuminated by a harsh blue-white street lamp shining down on the alley. He was parked at the rear of a strip mall on the north end of town. As strip malls went, this was decidedly low-rent, even for New Mexico. Along with the Chinese restaurant, there was Suzie's Sewing Shop, Anita's Wash-O-Matic, a small pet store with one lonely parakeet in the window, and an accountant's office—Timmy's Tax Returns. It was said in town that Timmy was the sort of accountant to see if you wished to keep two sets of books for your business, official and unofficial. The only halfway upscale business in the entire complex was the San Geronimo Pharmacy, which in the past few years had been waging a heroic but losing battle to compete with the new Wal-Mart.

It was the second week of June, but the nights were still cold in northern New Mexico this time of year. Howie was bundled up in a ski parka and a wool cap, with a thermos of hot coffee propped up on the passenger seat alongside him. The coffee was a special Kona blend of organic beans, since Howie was a coffee snob—a fact that Jack teased him about mercilessly. Jack always insisted that caffeine from 7-Eleven was an essential part of the triumvirate of the detective experience: angst, boredom, and indigestion. Last night Howie had staked out the restaurant in the Wilder & Associate pickup truck, but tonight he was using his own car, a battered old MGB with a convertible top that was held together with silver duct tape. He pulled off his gloves to log a note in his journal:

"Eleven-fourteen p.m. Plump long-haired Siamese visits Dumpster. Color probably white . . ." He debated adding a small twist to the old joke, that all cats were gray in the dark—except when you looked at them through infrared binoculars. Then they were orange. But Jack was an ex-cop and took paperwork seriously. So Howie finished his entry with a simple, "Can't determine if animal is wearing a collar."

He raised the binoculars once again and watched the cat languish on the Dumpster. After a few minutes, something frightened the animal and it dashed off down the alley, out of sight. Lucky puss, so plump and juicy. Add a little MSG and some gloppy bright orange-red sauce . . . Howie gagged at the memory of the sweet and sour mystery meat he had eaten at the Shanghai Cafe a month earlier, his first and final visit to the restaurant as a customer. He had been on a date with a self-serious young woman who kept asking him all sorts of anthropological questions about his faraway people, the Lakota Sioux. Between the questions and the terrible food, it was no wonder that the romance had never gotten off the ground that night.

This was Howie's third night on the stakeout and he was nearly catatonic with boredom. The first night he had spent reviewing his life like a drowning man—Part One, from his childhood on a desperately poor South Dakota reservation to his fancy scholarship education at Dartmouth and Princeton. The second night, he relived Part Two, a year in Paris, some romance and heartbreak, and the various reasons he had put his Ph.D. dissertation on hold. Tonight he had been pondering Part Three, wondering what in the world had ever possessed him to move to the small

New Mexico town of San Geronimo and take a job as a seeing-eye assistant to a blind ex-police commander from California.

As cases went, keeping watch on the rear door of the Shanghai Cafe was the bottom of the food chain. Still, they had an actual paying client, which was always something of a miracle. An elderly lady, Mrs. Eudora Harrington, who lived near the strip mall, had lost two of her seven cats during the past month and was certain the Chinese restaurant was responsible, abducting her dear pussys for nefarious culinary purposes. Mrs. Harrington was a mild lady, sweet as she could be, but in this instance her anger had been roused. She wanted Wilder & Associate to "nail the bastard perps"—she obviously watched a good deal of TV—and hinted furthermore that if there happened to be a shoot-out and the entire management and staff got blasted off the face of the planet, she wouldn't be a bit displeased.

Howie found it all very discouraging. "Remember, there are no small cases, only small detectives," Jack liked to say. Still, after three nights of tedium, Howie could not help but sigh and wish he was somewhere else. He was starting to catalog past girlfriends—grading them from one to ten for their sense of humor, which was the number-one quality he sought in a woman these days, now that he was thirty years old and past the mere allure of flesh—when the rear door of the restaurant opened. It was Yang Li, in food-splattered kitchen whites, putting out the garbage for the night. Howie raised the night-vision binoculars to his eyes hoping this would be a crucial moment. Yang Li had recently arrived from Beijing, a cousin of the Wei family who owned the Shanghai Cafe. He was a short, stocky man, in his late thirties, a hint of Mongolia in his wide cheekbones. He could almost pass for Navajo, Howie thought, focusing the lenses more sharply. For the next ten minutes, Howie watched as Yang Li pulled out first a number of plastic garbage bags, then a small flotilla of cardboard boxes from inside the back door, crushing them flat with brutal resolve and carrying them to the Dumpster. As a spectator event, it was not very fascinating. Fortunately, the Beijing cousin did not bother to glance down the alley to where Howie was lurking in his car a hundred feet away. He was probably too tired to notice much at all.

"You should recycle that cardboard, Yang, my friend," Howie murmured with a yawn. But with the exception of this lapse in environmental correctness, he witnessed no crime. No wandering pussycats shanghaied into the back door of the restaurant for tomorrow's All-You-Can-Eat Buffet, $4.99 for lunch, $6.99 for dinner. Eventually, Yang Li returned inside and shut the back door securely behind him. A few minutes later, all the lights inside the restaurant went off.

It was nearly twelve-thirty, a long day. Now the entire family began to file wearily out the rear door of the restaurant. Besides Yang Li, there were Connie and Cherry, the two teenage daughters, very pretty and Americanized. Then came Rose, the shrewish mother. Albert Wei was the last to leave and he carefully locked the door behind him with two separate keys. Finally, without exchanging a word among themselves, the group walked toward the south end of the alley, in the opposite direction from where Howie was parked, to the family's ten-year-old Dodge van. After a fourteen-hour day, their steps were heavy; they would get only a short rest before rising in the morning to begin once again the endless cycle of lunch and dinner. Howie was impressed and strangely moved; it seemed to him vaguely heroic to work so hard in the service of truly terrible Chinese food.

"Good night, Shanghai Cafe!" Howie said aloud, shaking his head at the folly of it all. He had a few notes to make in his log before he could go home as well. He turned on a flashlight, since secrecy was no longer required, and did his best to chronicle the past hours of nothingness that he had just witnessed in a way that might conceivably justify the salary he was receiving from Jack for this particular assignment. Twenty-five dollars per hour was a small fortune in New Mexico.

Howie was still writing when he heard a car drive into the alley from the direction of the San Geronimo Pharmacy at the far end of the strip of buildings, its headlights shining brightly in his eyes. There was something about the vehicle that made Howie immediately wary; the engine was too loud, and it was driving too fast down the alley, weaving erratically. With the glare in his eyes, he couldn't be sure if it was a pickup or a car.

"Slow down!" Howie breathed, half aloud. As if the driver heard, there was a squeal of brakes and the headlights came to an abrupt stop alongside the trash Dumpster behind the restaurant. Howie could just make out a figure stepping from the vehicle and carrying something to the Dumpster. Most likely, he was getting rid of his empty booze bottles in case the cops stopped him. If so, this was a particularly tidy drunk. Usually the late-night rowdies of San Geronimo just threw their empties out the car window. After a moment, the figure got back into his vehicle and mashed his foot on the gas, revving the engine and making the tires spin before they grabbed hold of the asphalt. The pickup—it *was* a truck, Howie decided—lurched forward, gathering speed, bearing down directly on where he was parked.

"Goddamn!" It was incredible, but the drunken fool was going to run him down! Howie managed to start his own engine, but there was no time to get out of the way. The white glare of the headlights seemed to explode in his face.

Then he was hit. The noise was sickening, an ear-splitting screech of metal against metal. The front of the oncoming pickup smashed against his rear fender, spinning him around violently in nearly a complete rotation. Howie felt as though he had been seized by a cyclone before he jerked to a stop against a telephone pole at the rear entrance to Anita's Wash-O-Matic. He sat for a moment catching his breath, making certain his body parts were still attached in their prescribed manner.

"*Asshole!*" he shouted, full of impotent rage. He stepped from his car in time to see a pair of glowing red taillights disappear onto the four-lane road that led toward the center of town. Howie was okay, only shaken, but the left rear fender of his MG looked as if it had been hit by a freight train. The metal was smashed against the tire and Howie saw that he wasn't going to be doing any more driving tonight.

"Dysfunctional idiot!" he cried. He let loose every four-letter word he could think of, and some five-, six-, and seven-letter words as well. They helped a little, but not much. As it happened, Howie was particularly fond of his old MG convertible, which he felt made him a very chi-chi Sioux, and highly desirable to the opposite sex.

Finally he sighed, shook his head, and walked around to the pay phone at the front of the laundromat to call 911 and Triple-A. Now he would have a wait; the way things went in San Geronimo, he expected it would be at least fifteen minutes until the cops arrived, and an hour before Triple-A managed to send him a tow truck.

With time to kill, Howie walked down the alley to the trash Dumpster, curious to see what kind of empty bottles the mother of all maniacs had left behind. Tequila, he imagined, probably a quart—for the collision had been too violent and senseless to be inspired by a mere twelve-pack of beer. He opened the green metal top of the Dumpster, feeling the start of a headache coming on.

Then he froze.

For an instant he wasn't certain he was seeing correctly. There was a human face peering out at Howie from on top of the flattened cardboard boxes. The face had two ears, a nose, and a mouth half open in horror. But the face was blackened and shriveled, as though it had been cooked over a fire. And worse still, the face had no body.

Howie stared at the decapitated head in grisly fascination, unable to tear himself away. Then something brushed against his leg and he screamed. It was a cat, the same plump Siamese he had seen earlier through his night-vision binoculars. The cat had something in his mouth, a late-night snack.

Howie bent over and vomited on the animal's magnificently furry back. The Siamese let loose an outraged yeowl, then gathered its dignity and pranced off into the night, clearly not impressed by the graceless ways of man.